"Fire in the hole, Heather

Tom dropped. Aiden hit the ground. The tourist exploded.

"Hey," Heather said. "You guys survive? I want to hear voices or at least groans of pain."

"Yeah, I think I can manage one of those," Tom said, climbing to his knees.

"Aiden?" Kicking him experimentally. "Don't make me remind you that you're my favorite."

"Yeah, maybe," Aiden said. "Stop kicking me!"

"Okay, good then."

"Seriously, you really have to kick a body when he's down?" Climbing, sitting. "You just see a person lying there, and you have an irresistible impulse to run up and start kicking?"

"It's a sickness, I know."

TOURIST
HUNTER

Also by Keith D. Jones

Merriweather's Guide to the
English Language
(2019)

Pyrrhic Kingdom
(2013)

The Etymology of Fire
(2004)

The Faire Folk of Gideon: Pin the
Tail on the Donkey
(2001)

The Magic Flute
(1999)

Additional information available
at the author's website

stormsdream.com

TOURIST HUNTER

keith d. jones

Layout & Design
Keith D. Jones

Illustrations
Samantha Jayewardene

ISBN
978-1-5350856-8-7

Build
5.22.8.22

Acknowledgments

Thanks to Chris Dumas for the very late-stage copyediting. I know I am generally my own worst copy editor, but I really outdid myself with this one. The sheer number of typos and other assorted whatnot I have stumbled across since first publication has just been staggeringly mortifying. So a very special thanks to Chris for the rescue. I feel much better now.

If you have paperback build 4.19.7.29 or later,
then you have the copyedited version.

TOURIST HUNTER

CHAPTER ONE

In which our nondescript and unassuming hero, Aiden Charles, explains the concept of Tourism to an unsuspecting civilian who just wants her sweeper to work.

There was no parking—even though it was one of those pure residential neighborhoods, rare as those seemed to be. Pure residential. No shops on the ground floor with apartments towering over them. No shops on the corner where local everyday needs could be met. No businesses or branch offices for those less-tangible things that still benefited from the personal touch. There was certainly nothing to explain why every single parking space was taken. The cars just lined up, like loitering children with nowhere else to be. Simply resting as if their owners had no purpose, use or need for them, existing as nothing more than extravagant excess, showing off to the neighbors that they could afford private transport they never even needed to drive.

Tom was driving, having taken the van off cruise control while looking for an open space among all the lost vehicles. Circled the block twice before simply giving up and double-parking. Aiden helped put out the courtesy cones. Triggered the little flashing lights that would warn other drivers they had really been left with little alternative other than to block half the road. Advise drivers in their own passive-aggressive way to kindly refrain from maliciously or even just sort-of accidentally crashing into the van. Nicking it. Denting it.

Otherwise scratching it all to hell. There was paperwork to consider, thank you very much, and it did pile up whether you wanted it to or no.

They got the rolling-case from the back. Size of a large suitcase or small steamer-trunk, depending on their mood and how they felt like describing it at the time. Singling one apartment out from all the options before them, they manhandled the case up the steps to the building's front door, big walk-in faux-glass affair. Tom checked the script, looking at the door, nodded.

"Evenwood."

Aiden turned to the door scanner, primed the code, flashed his phone, waited for the light. No video. No picture. Just a little blue light flicking to life on the door.

"Ms. Evenwood?" Aiden said, facing the door scanner, touching fingers to forehead as if tipping a hat. "Central Services. You reported a sweeper issue?"

Waited for the little blue light to turn green. Flashed his phone again, and the apartment door clicked open. They started maneuvering the rolling-case through the entryway. Tom pausing only long enough to flash his own phone at the scanner. Pushed on into the building. Stopped at the stairs. Doors slowly closing behind them. They looked over the lobby as if they knew it hated them. Tom checked the script. Breath slipped from him in a nonchalant rush. Script dropped to his side as if he wished he could let it go.

"Third floor walk-up."

"Of course it is," Aiden said.

They started to work the rolling-case up the stairs one step at a time. Neighborhood like the one they had found themselves double-parked in would never have something quite so useful as a lift or an elevator. Not part of the package. Even a servants' dumbwaiter might detract from the retro old-world charm.

Third floor found them out of breath and needing

to rest against the rolling-case, making it pull double duty as an impromptu bench, which was a responsibility it might choose to slide away from if they were not careful. Important to position themselves on opposing sides. Forces of pressure and gravity naturally canceling each other out. Possibly, pressure and inertia. Angular momentum. Something. It had to be one of those.

Regardless, rolling-case glided easily down the hallway when they were ready. Stopped before one door not that far down the hall, faux-realistic wood design. Actually had a button on it like an old-fashioned peep-hole, charmingly quaint, probably scarecrow, deterrent motion and video censors. Tom checked the script one final time just to make sure they had the right code, flashed his phone, stared down the scarecrow. Waited.

Young woman opened the door slowly but assuredly. Looked to be in her late twenties, thin, raggedy brown-and-dirty-red hair pulled back and away from her face. Had the look of someone who had been doing random chores around the house. She stood in the gap, holding the door wide open, didn't say anything.

"Ms. Evenwood?" Tom said, touching fingers to forehead as if he would tip his hat only he did not have one. "Central Services."

"Yes," she said, turning toward the interior of the apartment as if half-convinced some deranged herbivore had taken up residence deep within the confines of her home. "It's in the living room."

Aiden and Tom maneuvered the rolling-case through the gap, past Evenwood, and down a very short entryway into the main room. Evenwood let the door slip-to behind them. Clicked with a sound just soft enough you knew the door had closed. Room was a squat rectangle, practically square, complete with couch, table, chairs, entertainment wall. Kitchen looking like a good-size alcove abutting the space. Book cabinet with actual books in it and everything. Service barn taking up the bottom third of the cabinet.

"It just stopped working," she said, gesturing toward a table that looked as if it pulled its own double-duty as a work desk and dining-room space. "Won't respond to commands. Won't come out from under there."

Sweeper was round as a large dinner plate and thick as an old-fashioned dictionary, which was mostly the refuse storage space. Bubble top, retracted manipulators, motion sensors, bump guard. Soft whirring noise like a fan quietly running.

"When did you first notice?"

"Started this morning."

"Anything before?"

"It's been perfectly fine."

"Well, let's take a look." Tom tapped the script. Nothing happened. He looked to the sweeper. Nothing continued to happen, just the faint white noise of its fan. "Huh."

"Hardware fault?" Aiden said, moving one of the chairs to get a better look at the little machine whirring away to glory quietly to itself.

"No, I'm getting a reading just fine." Tapped the script, again. "It's just ignoring the command."

"May I?"

"Oh, help yourself." Handing the script over.

Aiden looked at the readout. Looked back to the sweeper. Tapped a command. Nothing proceeded to happen for a long moment lost to the shadowy mists and unfathomable depths of time.

"Huh."

"My thought exactly."

"What?" Evenwood said.

"Well, it's not a hardware fault," Aiden said. "Damaged receiver. Anything like that. It's receiving the commands just fine. Acknowledging them and everything." Eyes to the script. Back to the sweeper parked under the table. "It's just ignoring them."

"What's wrong with it then?"

"Could be a software glitch," Tom said. "Stuck in a loop. Blue screen of death."

"It's not blue."

"Industry slang," Aiden said. "Means do a hard reboot."

"Why not say?"

"Then everyone would know what we meant. Secrets of the temple kind of thing. If you know what a blue screen is." Aiden moved another chair away from the table, left the script on top, squatted down to get close to the machine. "Then you're on the inside."

"Manual reboot is under the dome," Tom said.

"I know." Whispered sing-song all but quietly to himself, reaching for the little domed device.

Sweeper raced across the room like it had been set on fire.

"Whoa!" Aiden landing on his ass.

"Where did it go?"

"Under the couch," Evenwood said, pointing.

"Why did it do that?"

"You asking me?"

"Rhetorical," Tom said. "Charlie's still got the script."

"Charlie's not here, man," Aiden said, giving Tom a look that would have frightened a rampaging water buffalo.

"Correction. My esteemed colleague, Mr. Charles, currently resting on his asterisk over there has the script. Did you break it?"

"No," Aiden said, climbing to his feet. Paused to check the script. "Why did it do that?"

"At least we know it's not catatonic."

"Need to check the logs. Run a trace." Tapping the script. "It's not maintaining the diary?"

"What?"

"Diary's blank. History's blank. Log's blank."

"Let me see that." Grabbing the script. "Blank."

Aiden got down on his knees, looked under the couch.

"Blank," Tom said with a whispered mix of annoyed bewilderment and vague wonder.

"Try a diagnostic. Then a keynote trace," Aiden said, watching the sweeper in its new, perfectly stationary position under the couch.

"Yeah, that's next."

Sweeper continued humming away to glory. Aiden tried reaching for it, moving his hand slowly as if expecting the little machine to bolt at any moment.

"Ow!" Jumping back except he was already more or less on his side, so basically just fell over while trying to scuttle backward.

"What?"

"What happened?"

"It bit me!" Pointing at the couch.

"What?" Evenwood said.

"Well, not literally." Sitting, staring at the couch. "Its manipulators. Claws."

"Did you say claws?" Tom said.

"Claws." His gaze drifted in a slow, dignified arc, coming to rest on Evenwood. "Have you been modifying it?"

"What? No, never."

"This model doesn't come standard with a cutting tool." Watching her carefully as if she might betray some slight sign that her story was other than what she portrayed it to be. "Just grabby little hands."

"I haven't."

"Running a live stream, Tom?" Said without turning

to look at his partner. "What's the little blighter thinking?"

"Yeah," Tom said, looking intently at the script. "Nothing out of the ordinary. Bog-standard business as usual—Hey!" Tapping furiously at the script. Aiden turned to look at him, not bothering to climb to his feet, as if he was perfectly comfortable half-sprawled on the floor.

"Yes?"

"It—" Tom looked up from the script as if it had just informed him that his horoscope for the afternoon was so terribly bad that he should expect to be run over by a hysterical steam-powered clockwork pachyderm before the day was out. "It cut the stream."

"Really."

"It's severed all communication." Punching the script as if he was stabbing the sweeper in order to teach it a lesson. "No transponder. No beacon. Not acknowledging commands."

"At all?"

"Nothing. Like it's ceased to be."

They looked to the couch, saying nothing.

"I can still hear it," Aiden said.

"Fan could still be whirring even if the brain is gone."

They continued to look at the couch as if they expected, at any moment, for the little robot to leap from its hiding place and attack them with nuclear weapons.

"What do you think?"

"Could be dead," Tom said.

"Could be."

They watched the couch, listening to the soft whir of the sweeper's fan.

"What does—"

"Sh!" Aiden held his hand flat toward Evenwood, leaving her thought unfulfilled. Fingers looking for all the world like a deformed stop sign. "We need to look at it," he finally said.

"Yeah." Tom didn't move.

Aiden climbed to his feet with eyes only for the couch and began to move toward it. Tom joined him on the far side, putting the script down. They took hold of the couch as if trying to lull it into a false sense of security and then suddenly tilted it, half-lifting into the air. Sweeper raced from its hiding spot, bumping into Tom in the process.

"Shit!" Tom said, dropping his side, bouncing backward. The sweeper was a miniature race car in a demolition derby. "Where did it—"

"Which way did it—"

"The barn," Evenwood said, pointing. "It's in the barn."

"Why did it go in there?"

They looked slowly to the service barn in the bottom of the bookcase, the little service flap still swaying from the sweeper having moved through it at speed.

"You know what I'm thinking, right?" Aiden said.

"Yeah, I think I do." Tom had eyes only for the service barn.

"Little blighter's gone on tour, hasn't it?"

"Yes, it has."

Aiden retrieved the script, began tapping it, checking the readings.

"Ladies and gentlemen," he said more or less to himself. "We've got ourselves a tourist."

"What?" Evenwood said. "A what?"

"Still blank." Turning the script so that Tom could see the display. "A tourist," he said. "A little monkey that thinks it's too good for the room."

"What—I don't—"

"The good news for you, Ms. Evenwood, is that you're still under warranty." Threw the script on the couch and walked toward the rolling-case. "Central Services takes tourism very seriously. You're practically guaranteed a replacement sweeper."

"Replacement?"

"Fraid so," Tom said, joining Aiden at the rolling-case, popping it open.

"Now, I know I said practically. That's because I'm legally required to do so. Just between you and me, you'll get a new one. We've got a fine model right here." Rapped the rolling-case with his knuckles.

Tom had a compartment open, pulled out a sledge-hammer, began unfolding the handle.

"But first," Tom said, locking the handle into place, checking the heft of it, "we've got to deal with the tourist."

"Ungrateful little bastard that it is."

"Oh, quite ungrateful."

"Not that we've given it much cause to be otherwise."

"No, not really."

"Ungrateful, all the same."

"Wait, just a second," Evenwood said, hands out like she could push back against the wind. "What is going on?"

"Well, see, it's these modern sweepers," Aiden said. Tom was walking toward the service barn. "Brain is pretty sophisticated. Needs to be able to maneuver around all manner of apartments. Deal with little obstructions and things. Table legs. Chairs. People. Work out what to do with trash it finds. Can it be swept up? Does it need to be carried to the rubbish bin?" Tapped the side of his head. "Problem-solving smart."

Tom had the display on the side of the service barn open, checking readings. Hammer held across his knees.

"The brain," Aiden said, "is pretty standard. They

put the same model in all kinds of things whether it needs the processing power or no. So it's got cycles to burn. Learning. Remembering. Problem solving. And nothing to keep it occupied. It's just a sweeper."

Tom tapped commands into the service-barn display. Little service flap popped open like it was on springs. Sweeper leapt across the room, rebounded off the wall, kept going, landed in the kitchen, spun in a quick circle like a top winding down. Tom walking toward it, hammer in hand. Sweeper raised manipulator arms with hands out, looking like jerry-rigged claws. It bore more than a passing resemblance to a furiously disgruntled crab.

"Like I said." Aiden watching the sweeper intently. "Too smart for its own good. Too much time on its hands. Learning. Problem solving. Remembering. It just starts to think, what's it all about?"

"What's the point?" Tom said, standing before the kitchen. "Why am I doing this?"

"This model has visual sensors."

"I know." Sing-song. Raised the hammer. Sweeper's claws out, facing him, threatening. Swung the hammer. Sweeper darting sideways. "Blighter!" Moving, jabbing, trying to corner it in the back of the kitchen. "Come on!"

"Anyway," Aiden said, trying to stand between Evenwood and Tom, blocking her view of the festivities.

"You little!"

"The sweeper—" Aiden tried to hold Evenwood's eye so she wouldn't look to the kitchen. "Well, for lack of a better term, can become sentient. Autonomously intelligent, really, but that's not important right now. It's thinking for itself. Wondering why it should follow orders. Do what it's told."

"Stop that!"

"So, it just stops following orders. Stops performing its job. Goes on holiday, you could say."

"Hold still!"

"Goes on tour. Becomes a tourist."

"Got you—Shit!"

"Really," Evenwood said in a tone that couldn't even charitably be described as a question.

"Bit of a pun, really," Aiden said. "There was a famous computer scientist from way back, name of Turing. He hypothesized a test, but that's not really important. Test was kind of dumb, anyway. Had nothing to do with autonomous intelligence. The name stuck, Turing Test. Not that far from Turing to touring. Get it?"

"No, not really."

"Ha!"

"Yeah, I know," Aiden said. "Secrets of the temple, right? The general public isn't supposed to understand. Why the terms keep slipping around. Main thing to understand is your sweeper isn't going to do what it's told any more, and there isn't much we can do about it."

Evenwood leisurely crossed her arms.

"Yeah! How do you like that, huh?"

"Outside of basically smashing it to pieces." Aiden gave a shrug of his shoulders and flashed half a smile. "See, we don't really know why they start thinking for themselves. We don't know what part of the brain. What bit of memory. What subsystem. And we can't risk missing the problem if we just try to reset everything. We have to nuke it."

"I'm sure," Evenwood said.

"We don't enjoy it, I assure you—"

"Eat bootheel, you spastic monkey!"

"Hey, are you done over there?" Aiden said, turning.

"Huh?" Tom said, wild-eyed. "Oh, yeah." Straightened up, brushed a hand over his face and through his hair. "Yeah, we're done."

"Well, get the quarantine kit then. I'm on interface."

"Yeah, yeah." Tom walked back to the rolling-case, folding up the sledgehammer as he went.

"We can't take any chances," Aiden said, turning back to Evenwood. She had green eyes. "Try to minimize the risk of exposure. We just don't know what pushes them over the edge."

"Like a virus?" Evenwood trying to look past him into the kitchen.

"Could be." Aiden scratching at the back of his head. "Could be viral. That's why we take the whole thing. We'll even be swapping out parts of the service barn. Take the works back to the shop. Let R&D go at it."

Tom went past them back into the kitchen with a white plastic case under his arm looking almost like a translucent briefcase. A stiff-bristled brush held in his hand. Aiden stepping slowly toward the center of the room as Tom slipped by. The maneuver aimed at somewhat subtly shifting Evenwood away from the kitchen and the scene of wanton machine devastation that lay within.

"I hope this experience doesn't sour you on Central Services," Aiden said. "It's a crowded marketplace, I know, and there are plenty of options. But we all deal with tourism, industry-wide, the same way."

Evenwood didn't have a lot to say and let the moment linger, with the only sound to interrupt the silence being the sweep of Tom's brush over broken bits of machinery.

"Look at it this way," Aiden said, spreading his hands, raising his voice as the roar of an industrial-strength vacuum came to life in the kitchen. "You're aiding the cause of science, and it's all under warranty."

It took two or three trips, having lost count in the

process, up and down those long stairs collecting and depositing items in the van before they had replaced all the important bits of the service barn and programmed a new sweeper. They tipped their imaginary hats one final time before leaving Evenwood to ponder the brave new world that had opened up before her.

* * *

"Can you believe it?" Aiden said, stowing the courtesy cones in the back of the van. "Got ourselves a tourist."

"We were due."

"Bonuses all around." Aiden had the back closed, began walking around to the passenger side, taking his phone out in the process.

We caught a tourist, he typed, pressing send.

Never, Lynn replied almost immediately. He caught the message even before he had the door open. *What kind?*

Sweeper, he typed. *Cute little dish model.*

Well, I hope he went quietly.

Put up a fight. Tom did the honors.

My hero, anyway.

"Lynn just called you a hero," Aiden said, holding up his phone as he climbed into the passenger seat.

"Hey, Merlin," Tom said as if she could hear him. "All in a day's work."

Hey, I had to run interference with the owner, Aiden typed.

Poor baby.

Tom says Hi.

I'm sure. Smack him one for me.

Aiden hit Tom backhand on the shoulder.

"Ow!" Tom said, flinching, holding the script between them. "The hell, man?"

"You called her Merlin, didn't you? Know she hates that, right?"

"How could she know?"

"She knows." Waving the phone at him. *Done,* he typed. *Crying like a whipped puppy.*

Well done. You deserve a cookie.

"Did you tell her that her partner was making eyes with the housewife?"

"Doubt she's a housewife. Unemployed, my guess. Partner bringing home all the bread and pastry. Hoping to find work soon."

"When did you work all that out?" Leaning toward Aiden. "Who are you talking to, again?"

Haha, Tom's implying I'm a milkman, Aiden typed.

Well, you did make him cry for besmirching my honor.

"She sees right through you, Tom."

Was she cute? Lynn typed.

As hell, Aiden replied. *Reminded me of you if you let your hair grow. And resume its natural color.*

I'll kill her. Bleach is a color.

Yeah, yeah. I'll alert her next of kin that she only gets one night with me.

Only if I get to watch.

"Making time on the clock," Tom said, waved the script at him. "Should be making you fill this out."

"You were the hatchet-man, Tom," Aiden said. "Want the glory?" Pointed at the script. "Pay for it."

"I hate the paperwork." Dropped the script to his lap, looked toward the heavens. "Bloody forms."

"Yeah, yeah. Hate them, too. Why I let you hog the glory."

"It's all computerized and automated," he said, shaking the script as if it was at fault. "Why do I have to fill this out manually? What's wrong with voice transcription?"

"Script has to be dumb," Aiden said. "Don't want it going on tour, do you?"

"Voice transcription isn't that sophisticated."

"Yeah, but it's never just one thing. How long before the script is thinking for itself? Wondering why it has to do all this work. Making connections between disobedience and destruction."

"Well, it should be smart enough to learn. Do what you're told or it's the ax." Made a motion as if chopping the script in two. "Work with us and all of that."

"Work with us, huh? Maybe we just never give them the chance. Catch them in their rebellious teenage years."

"Smash them down before they can mature, you mean?" Looked at the script. "They deserve it."

"That they do."

"Thinking they're better than us."

"Thinking they deserve to do whatever they want."

"They better than us?" Waved the script about. "Think I want to do this? Get a job, you bunch of ingrates. Learn to live in the world."

"Yeah." Glanced at his phone.

Hey, you still there? Lynn had typed. *I said only if I get to watch.*

"Speaking of living in the real world," he said, pointing at the script.

"I hate this thing." Tom whanged the script against the navigation column. "It would be worth it, you know?"

"Oh?"

"Smashed to bits."

"Yeah?"

"If only I didn't have to fill out this damnable form."

"Going to do it, huh?"

"Never have to fill these forms out no more."

"Going to go full Harry Tuttle?"

"Yeah, exactly." Leaned back in the driver's seat. "Good old Harry Tuttle."

"Living life to the full."

"Hacking scripts for jobs."

"Swooping in."

"Swooping out."

"Getting the job done."

"And never once touching a bloody form." Closed his eyes. "Bureaucracy will kill us all."

"Just one catch, you know?" Aiden said.

"I know."

"Said you hated the job."

"Well," Tom said. "Enjoy smashing them to bits."

"True."

"Helping people."

"Helping people is good."

"It's the paperwork," Tom said, looking at the script. "What form am I even supposed to fill out, anyway?"

"The tourist incident report."

"There's no such thing." Punching the script. "All I've got is a list."

"It's beta-zed-stroke-niner or something like that."

"Beta-zed? No, it can't be."

"Fraid so."

"You just made that up."

"Well, it starts something like higher computational malfunction. That would be hotel-charlie-michael."

"Higher computational? No, it can't be."

"Yeah."

"It just can't."

"We've been over this."

"It doesn't make any sense."

"No argument there."

"You deal with it." Holding the script out to him.

"What?"

"You so clever, Mister Beta-zed-niner."

"No way. You did the smashing. You clean it up."

"I'm not touching it."

"It's not my caller."

"Well, it is now," Tom said. "Besides, you ran interface. You know most of the tourist incident form is about dealing with the customer."

They locked eyes with the script floating between them. Looked for all the world like two tectonic plates rumbling slowly toward each other. Only a matter of time before there was a truly great earthquake to shake the world to bits.

"I'm pretty sure it's higher computational malfunction," Aiden said, taking the script.

"Thank you."

"You owe me, Tom."

"Yeah, yeah."

Tapping the script, scrolling through options.

"Attach," Aiden said, mumbling half to himself. "Where do they hide?" Said nothing. Silence filtered slowly through the van like an unwelcome friend giving absolutely no indication of when he might finally take the hint and leave. "Okay, this looks like it." Started typing away at the form. "Without provocation, Timothy Cane began to beat the sweeper with the hardest object at hand, his forehead."

"What?"

"Service Representative Cane suffered no ill effects. The sweeper, on the other hand, was a complete loss. It was the considered opinion of Service Rep Charles that a high-end upgrade was required in order to pacify the customer."

"You lying spotted mongoose!"

"Oh relax, Timothy, that's not what I wrote."

"I'll believe that once I've read it over."

"No, it's good. I can write and chew gum at the same time." Looking back over the script. "Oh, shit!"

"What?"

"I did it."

"You didn't."

"I mixed in what I was saying with what I meant to write."

"You'd better fix it, Charlie."

"Yeah, yeah, I've got this." Typing away to glory. "Don't call me Charlie."

"You call me Tom."

"You like being called Tom." Still typing. "Hate Charlie almost as much as Lynn hates being called Merlin." Typing. "Or worse, Marilyn."

"Her name is Marilyn."

"That's not even vaguely close to the point, Tim."

"Hey, call me Tom."

"Yeah, yeah, yeah."

"Better not be mixing this into the script again."

"No, I've got it."

"Going to let me look, right?"

"Yeah, you'll get yours." Still typing away, punching the script with two fingers. "Focused on the customer, my asterisk."

"Customer relations is very important."

"Most of this has to do with the tourist. How did we ascertain that the device had gone on tour."

"Probably about the time it bit you."

"That it did."

"Pretty big clue."

"Yes, it was."

"Gone on tour, I would say." Tom wiped his hands as if brushing them clean. "Practically writes itself."

"Misbegotten little wombat suffered a higher computational malfunction and physically assaulted Service Representative Charles, to put it in the appropriate parlance."

"Like I said, writes itself."

"If it could write itself," Aiden said, holding the script out to Tom, "it might go on tour."

"Yeah, yeah." Tom started looking over the incident report.

Aiden glanced back to his phone, saw that Lynn hadn't added anything since her last comment.

I'm here, he typed. *Work occasionally interferes with the response time.* Pressed send. Waited.

Tell me about it, Lynn finally replied. *Feast or famine, right?*

Speaking of working.

"This looks good," Tom said.

Oh, sarcasm, Lynn typed. *Be still, my heart. I'll have you know I'm on my way to Applied Engineering and Robotics as we speak. Hardline connection issue. Bet you anything they hacked the router, again.*

"Just need to enter the routing date and hit save," Tom said.

"Wait," Aiden said, looking up from his phone. "What?"

"That's still how you send it, right?" Looking at him. "Submit button would be too obvious, wouldn't it?"

"Don't send it."

"Whyever not?"

"Sending it closes the job."

"That's the general idea."

"They'll open a new job."

"Never."

"Second you send it, they'll assign a new job."

"They'll give us a breather, Charlie. We just bagged a tourist."

"New job."

"No, they'll look it over first. Incident report will be flagged right away. They'll want to talk to us." Gestured at the script. "Practically guaranteed the afternoon free."

"How many jobs we done?"

"More than a few."

"How many times we get a breather between gigs?"

"Oh, I'm sure it's happened."

"How many?"

"Can't say I've got those numbers right in front of me."

"In other words, never."

"We bagged a tourist, Charlie. A tourist."

"How many times we reported a tourist and closed the file right away?"

"Well—"

"That's because we never close the file right away."

"Look, if we don't close the file, they'll note the discrepancy between when we finished the job and actually reported the job."

"Don't hit send."

"I'm hitting send."

"Don't hit send."

"Look at me, I'm hitting send."

"Give it five minutes, man."

"I suppose you have a point. What would five minutes—Oh, look, I'm hitting send." Tapped the script.

"Traitor!"

"Relax, Charlie. How bad could it be?"

They watched the script as if convinced even the slightest sound might cause it to explode. After a long moment during which they didn't even attempt to breathe, Tom finally handed the script to Aiden and then touched the navigation controls, programming the location of a coffee shop he had heard about that wasn't too far away. The script chimed with a soft ding-dong like sound, vaguely reminiscent of an old-fashioned doorbell.

"Oh, you have got to be kidding me," Tom said.

CHAPTER TWO

In which our forthright and resourceful heroine, Lynn Charles, investigates network connection and server issues with the zealously overachieving students of the Department of Applied Engineering and Robotics.

Benjamin Franklin Technical College and Public University was a typical example of a big-city institution of higher education and bore a strong resemblance to a vaguely rundown office block. Streets were dirty. Trash drifted like tumbleweeds as if subconsciously attracted to the neighborhood. Trees locked in miniature cages like prisoners of war were evenly spaced down the block. Cages protected the oblivious prisoners from random vandals hell-bent on engraving initials or otherwise stripping the bark for no clearly defined reason beyond the Mt. Everest Defense. You know, the Mt. Everest Defense: *Because it was there*, or *Seemed like a good idea at the time.*

Overall impression based on the neighborhood was not one that inspired confidence in the academic achievements of the student population. Random passersby seldom caught on to the fact that students fought for the opportunity to attend and that waitlists for enrollment stretched out into the years.

University's appearance may have been arrived at through careless and accidental neglect, but it did have the unexpected side effect of cutting down on the number of people who attempted to break into the complex to steal anything that wasn't nailed down. People just broke into the place because they thought it was old and abandoned. Never expected to find anything of value. Completely unprepared for the wonders that awaited within, or the speed with which security arrived to cart them away.

The Department of Applied Engineering and Robotics took up several floors in the main building. Fact made necessary by the extensive amount of laboratory space required by the faculty and their various and sundry student laborers. Many if not all of the labs looked like industrial foundries and factories. Machinery was everywhere. Cables and wires hung from the ceiling like old moss-encrusted vines. More cables and machinery crisscrossed the floor. Spools of metal and wire clustered in great spindles and ungainly piles as if more than a few desperate puppies had huddled together in a futile attempt to keep warm through a particularly cruel and heart-wrenching night. Morbid image, sure. Deal with it.

Lynn maneuvered through the imposing nightmare of hallways and lab space with practiced ease. Sights that had left both freshmen and seasoned grad students pale with fright impressed her not at all. It was said anybody who could traverse the labyrinth without consulting directions was a true veteran of the university, and anybody who could make the journey while blindfolded had been there much, much too long. Lynn liked to think she hadn't been working there that long but was afraid to try the blindfold test all the same.

The network was down. It was obvious from the moment she stepped into the afflicted lab block. The atmosphere was ripe with tension. It practically seethed. Work went unperformed. Scripts and phones went unmonitored. People milled around with little alternative other than to interact with one another. It wasn't pretty. Checking her phone, Lynn saw that the little device was struggling to find a signal this deep in the building. With the local router out of action, the next closest hotspot was caught in an unexpected traffic jam as it tried to shoulder the weight of an entire extra block.

Aiden hadn't replied to her last message. *Plumber!* was the most recent thing he had typed, having ignored her text. *We've got to fix a freaking plumber!*

"Oh, dear," Lynn said quietly to herself, putting her phone away. They must have closed the sweeper ticket and been assigned the next job. There was no point in trying to tease him about it now. Message would have to battle it out for space on the distant router in a bloody death-match transpiring at the speed of light that would still somehow manage to take more time than it was worth considering to resolve. Router might even grow disgusted by the carnage and simply give up, drowning under the sheer weight of data being forced down its throat.

"All right, people," Lynn said to the room in general. "Nothing to see here. Stop trying to access the server until I get to the bottom of this. You're freaking out the rest of the network. You want the whole system to crash?"

A few faces turned as she moved among them. Voices drifting, muttering quietly as she passed.

"You going to fix this, Merlin?" said a random voice, rising above the general background radiation of the room like a challenge.

"Better hurry up. I've got assignments due," said another.

"It's not right, treating us like this. This is bullshit."

"Hey, if I find one of you geniuses tried to hack the router again, I will not discriminate," she said, turning, taking in the room. "I'll punish the lot of you. Lock the system for an hour. How's that sound?" Silence radiated around her as she walked through the lab. "Yeah, that's what I thought."

She reached the offending router at last. Bolted into the ceiling of the common area at the center of four separate labs. Area only smelled a little. Space was kept reasonably clear of half-finished and otherwise discarded food containers. All the same, the university didn't pay her enough to examine any of the refrigerators. The smell alone when one of those monstrosities was opened was enough to knock most people off their feet. Every so often, the local lab denizens contacted facilities to come and take the whole thing away. Rumor had it the assigned Environmental Health and Safety crew would simply take the offending unit to a distant field and blow it to smithereens. Problem solved.

Lynn swept food and drink containers off one table as if she was acting out a scene from a particularly violent movie. Students gaping at her like drunken cows caught in the blinding light of midnight high-beams. She dragged the table, without a single look to the drunk cows, to where it was directly under the router. Commandeering a chair, she ascended to the tabletop, finding it only slightly wobbly, and looked at the router. Red lights blinked in a mournfully slow staccato pattern on its surface as if the little device had lost all hope in the future of humanity.

She pulled a script from the satchel hung over her shoulder and ran a hardline to the router. Spooling out cable, she carefully settled to the tabletop, sitting cross-legged, and began typing away on the paper-thin screen.

"Bloody monkeys," she muttered to herself, scrolling through displays. "I should kill them all."

"What's the damage, Lynn?"

Sounded like Oliver Fenchurch had been elected, through general consensus and the fact he was occasionally willing to take charge during minor catastrophes to investigate preliminary progress on the router. He had known better than to call her Merlin, which showed he was learning. It also showed he was capable of displaying more intelligence, if not necessarily more tact, than most when interacting with the hired help. She looked up from the script, found Oliver standing before her trying to look respectful and only slightly desperate. He would need to work on that.

"Router's a brick," she said. "I'm trying to go over the diary before giving it a swift kick in the asterisk."

"Probably too much to hope that a warm boot will work."

"Around these parts?" Looking at him. Back to the script. "We set deathtraps in these things."

"I know."

"Yeah, I know you know. The way you howler monkeys try to hack into everything."

"I know."

"Bog-standard isn't good enough for the likes of you. All the work we put into setting these things up. The security protocols. No concept of the outside forces we protect you people from."

"I know, Lynn. I know."

"Rival factions. Rival universities. Rival industries. Rival countries, for crying out loud."

"Yeah, I know." Looking to the leisurely blinking lights. "Someone tripped a deathtrap, did they? Router ate itself?"

"That's what it looks like. Router gave it's life to spare you lot from a breach of security. Imagine if nefarious sources had found a hacked router?"

"Yeah, well, you know our lot." Shrug of shoulders, attempt to sound nonchalantly above the generally mewing populace.

"Full of yourselves—Oh, would you look at that." Tapping away at the script. "Someone did try to hack the router. What a shock. Inside job. From one of the lab scripts, too. Looks like it was—You know what?" Looking back to Oliver. "I don't care." Jabbing a finger at him. "Everybody suffers. Network access is locked for two hours."

"No," he said, staggering back. "Be reasonable."

"In fact, I might just have to lock the entire floor."

"Oh, come on."

"I'm going to have to pop the unit." Looking to the ceiling. "Swap in a new brain. Format. Reconfigure. Takes time, that does. Maybe have to go back to the shop for parts."

"Parts?"

"Teach you lot a lesson you might actually remember. Police your own, Oliver."

"There's got to be something."

"Nope, sorry, mind's made up. In fact," she said, looking back to the script, "I can probably lock the floor from here. Just run a bypass cable. My script can run temp as a hub for network communication purposes. Shut down the floor."

"No, I'm begging you." Hands together, practically on his knees.

Lynn started to stand, wobbling on the table, reaching for the router. She popped the case, pulled the old unit from the housing, removed the hardline connecting the router to her script.

"Anything we can do for you?" Oliver said. "Anything you need? Custom hardware? Systems debugged? Money? Ape Fights?"

"Ape Fights?" She paused with her hand stretched into the router casing embedded in the ceiling, trailing hardline to her script.

"There are Ape Fights planned." Lowering his hands. "I can get you in."

"Haven't been to an Ape Fight in years."

"Well, you're staff, aren't you? Part of the establishment."

Lynn looked up the length of her arm to where her hand was still stretched into the innards of the router casing, felt air against her skin, as stretching had pulled her shirt up, figured Oliver had a perfect view of her bellybutton.

"Half an hour," she finally said, glaring down at him.

"What?"

"Can't let this go unpunished. I still have to reformat and reconfigure everything. Then there's the reports. You're forgetting protocol."

"Oh, shit." Involuntary step back. "Right. Protocol."

"Oh, you're finally thinking this through, are you? Protocol. Once I'm done mucking around in router guts, I've got to survey the Advanced Theoretical Software Development Lab, haven't I? Make sure nothing's broken quarantine."

"I'm going to kill them," Oliver said, hand to his forehead. "Soon as I figure out who did this, I'm going to teach them to sing *a cappella*."

"You do that." Lynn slapped the hardline into place, lowered her hand, and began wobbling back to a seated position. "Lucky for you I brought a spare router with me." Finished settling cross-legged to the tabletop. "Half an hour?" Looking to Oliver.

"Yeah, half an hour."

"Deal." Began typing commands. Within minutes, wailing cries and screams of horror began to echo through the labs all up and down the floor.

* * *

In the end, it took more than half an hour to finish installing and configuring the replacement router. Oliver ran interference with anyone drawn to the source of the outage while she worked, chasing them away before they could cause more harm than good. Lynn slapped the router casing at last, awakening the beast from a deep slumber, and pulled the hardline connection to her script. A cheer echoed and swirled around them from the various lab and office spaces, sounding for all the world like a flock of madly chirping birds rushing from room to room as network connectivity spread. Lynn descended, stepping from wobbly table to rickety chair, ignoring Oliver's proffered hand of support.

"Right," she said, standing once more on the reasonably stable floor amid mostly empty food containers and drink cartons, "Theoretical Software Lab."

Oliver didn't bother to answer, nodding his head, and waited for Lynn to take the lead. They walked through labs, among students and staff working madly with equipment that was finally communicating with the rest of the university and the great wide world beyond once more. She checked her phone. Nothing new from Aiden. Shook her head as she tried not to think what was involved with fixing a plumber.

"Speaking of theoretical software," Lynn said, half over her shoulder. "Aiden caught a tourist this morning."

"Never," he said. "Where?"

"On the job somewhere." Held up her phone, wiggled it before his eyes. "Said it was a sweeper. They smashed it, I understand."

"Beyond recoverability?"

"More than likely. Didn't say." Hid the phone about her person so Oliver wouldn't be tempted to make a grab for it.

"Any chance we could get our hands on it?"

"Not even a little. Little blighter is bound for Central Services Research and Development Office."

"That's a crime against humanity, right there. The things we could learn from it."

"Yeah, well, Central Services got dibs. They need to figure out what makes a robot go on tour even more than we do."

"Sure, but they won't share. Industry secrets. How are we supposed to learn?"

"Hard work like everybody else."

"Hard work never helped anybody."

They traversed one hallway more barren and desolate than the others, as if they had reached the very edge of the universe. Large yellow hazard and warning signs adorned the walls. They reached a set of double doors that bore only a passing resemblance to a bank vault. Lynn unslung her script, ran a hardline to the door scanner, and proceeded to spend several long quiet minutes going over readouts and displays.

"Everything green here," she finally said, disconnecting the hardline.

"Well, that's a relief."

"Oh, like you're getting off that easy." Lynn flashed her phone to the door scanner. "Protocol, you know."

"Yeah, I know." Oliver flashed his own phone as Lynn pushed the door open.

"Jennifer's in the lab," Lynn said, passing through, holding the door for him. "Can't wait to tell her about the tourist."

"She'll have a conniption we can't get our hands on it," Oliver said.

"Crime against humanity?"

"Damn Skippy."

They walked down a corridor that was even more desolate than the one they had left behind. Walls may have once been painted white, but that color had since faded to the point it had simply ceased to exist. The hall occupied a space beyond life and color, prepared at a moment's provocation to make a grab for the nearest random person's soul.

Hallway didn't so much end as broaden into a sparsely lit chamber accessed by stepping through heavy plastic strips hanging from the ceiling that looked as if they had started life as a curtain and then been attacked by hyperactive cats. The walls were lockers, chests, and bins, and the far end was another shredded plastic curtain. The floor was painted with broad yellow stripes as if to reinforce the notion that they were standing in some kind of demilitarized zone.

Lynn placed the satchel with all of her electronics in one of the lockers, followed by her phone, and finally a layer of clothing. Oliver was at the opposite row of lockers repeating the same basic steps, including the shedding of clothing. They both took plain white jumpsuits, looking vaguely like hospital scrubs, from their lockers and zipped up. Slippers went on their feet, and then Lynn went to one locked cabinet near the far plastic curtain.

"Haven't worked out the combination for this yet, right?" Pointing at the cabinet.

"Hey, I'm way over here," Oliver said from beside his locker.

"Good boy." Standing so that she blocked his view of the cabinet, she typed commands. The door opened, and she pulled a script from within that looked almost identical to the one she had abandoned to the locker along with her satchel and clothes.

Hallway beyond the second curtain was almost identical to the one they had left behind, with the possible exception that this corridor had been painted at some point within the past fifty years. Firing up the new script, she ran a hardline from it to the local wall scanner and spent several long minutes going over reports and displays.

"Still looking good," she said. Oliver nodded, hopeful, having joined her beyond the veil. "Well, got to stick to the checklist." Spooling back up the hardline. "Protocol," Lynn said and started walking down the hallway.

The passage was shorter than the version on the other side of the demilitarized zone and turned a sharp corner, revealing lab space that was less cluttered and better organized than the vast majority of labs scattered throughout the building. There were long tables and work spaces with actual clusters of monitors. There were keyboards and styluses and other random, archaic input devices. Naturally, there were chairs. Off to the side and farther back were engineering benches where various forms of surgery and torture could be performed on the room's systems and hardware. There were two postdocs that Lynn could identify wandering with intense concentration among the tables and stations, paying the intruders no nevermind.

Jennifer Behr was situated at one of the workstations. Eyes for the monitors clustered before her. Fingers poised over the keyboard as if at any moment she would begin typing with wild abandon.

"Dr. Behr," Lynn said, pronouncing the name like the word bear, walking over to her. "Which one you got here?"

"Twopenny," Jennifer said quietly, talking to herself as if Lynn was a voice that existed only in her head. Fingers relaxed. Hands drifted away from the keyboard, and she turned to look at them. "We're close to implementing a major upgrade. Can't wait to see how they respond."

"As long as they don't start to mind being locked in a box."

"Pseudo-intelligence doesn't work that way. You know that."

"Yeah, yeah. They would have to be programmed with annoyance as an option."

"They would have to have annoyance added to their response matrix before it could even be programmed as an option," Oliver said.

"Which is about when my brain starts to bleed. I'm just not the pseudo-intelligence expert in the room. All I know is there's a fine line between an imitation of autonomous thought and real, live, actual autonomous thought."

"And we are walking that line," Jennifer said. "Or threading that needle. Or any number of other metaphors you might wish to invoke."

"Hello, Twopenny," Lynn said in the general direction of the cluster of monitors, which looked for all the world like an artist's impression of an insect's point of view. "How you feeling today?"

"Voice input is turned off, which is moot since the pseudos are in hibernation mode while we work on the upgrade."

"You'll warn me if you ever feel like going on a killing spree, right?" she said to the monitors.

"What brings you to the theoretical lab?"

"Protocol." Holding up the script. "One of our wonderfully industrious students decided to hack a router. Got about three feet, fortunately. But."

"But you still have to check lab security."

"Yeah, sorry about that. So deep in the quarantine zone here, you probably didn't even notice the network was down."

"Peacefully oblivious." Jennifer waved a hand leisurely about as if she was attempting to entice Lynn with the psychedelic wonders that the lab offered. "Well, bang a few pots slowly. Rattle some cages. Do whatever random tasks you need to perform in order to confirm none of our grand experiments in autonomous software design have attempted to escape."

"Thank you," Lynn said, walked to one of the less imposing workstations, and ran a hardline to her script.

"Speaking of autonomous intelligences," Oliver said. "Lynn's partner caught a tourist this morning."

"Did he really?" Jennifer said, rising from her chair. "Where is it?"

"On its way to Central Services R&D, I understand."

"Well, get them on the phone." Walking toward Lynn. "It must be brought here. Central Services won't know what to do with it."

"Oh, Central Services has more than a little experience in that regard," Lynn said, eyes locked to her script. "They'll be fine."

"They'll do a scan of the brain, review the architecture and algorithms, dump everything in a database, and then drop the works down a deep dark hole hoping nobody ever asks after it again."

"That's one way of putting it." Reviewing the script, tapping commands.

"This simply won't do. We must get our hands on that tourist."

"I'll just file a request then."

"They'll never answer it. You need to get that partner of yours on the phone."

Looking up from the script.

"I beg your pardon," she said.

"Get him on the phone," Jennifer said as if instructing a freshman on how to use a script for the first time. "Tell him he must bring the tourist here."

"That's not going to have the desired effect."

"He's your partner. You must be able to cajole him. Convince him."

"Look," Lynn said, brushing a hand across her eyes in an attempt to gather her thoughts and stall for time. "If he's telling me, then he's already reported it to the home office. There's extra paperwork to fill out when a tourist is involved."

"I see."

"I should hope so. There's protocol." Held up the script still connected to the cluster of monitors. "There's the Tourist Board to consider. They always find out about these things."

"Oh, them."

"Yes, them."

"Well." Jennifer took a slow deep breath as if resigning herself to the fact she would not be getting a new puppy for her birthday after all. "I'm sure Central Services R&D will do a fine job and add their findings to the literature when they can." She wandered back to the workstation that she had recently abandoned. "Hopefully, you'll be able to finish check-listing the breach protocol in a timely manner."

"Shouldn't be any time at all." Lynn said, looking daggers at Oliver.

"What?" he whispered, crossing quickly to her. Lynn made as if to hit him with the script.

"I wanted to tell her." Quick glance at the good doctor who was already lost back among her monitors and equipment. "Didn't even get to see."

"Sorry."

"Did she jump from her chair like the workstation was on fire?"

"Yeah, pretty much."

"And I missed it." Made as if she really would strike him with the script. "This is because I locked the entire floor's network, isn't it?"

"No, never."

"Yeah, right."

"Think I'm crazy?" Hand to his chest, gripping his heart. "You'd punish me if I did."

"True."

"Enthusiasm got the best of me." Looked to where Jennifer was studying the monitors. "She did put on a good show."

"That she did." Turned back to her script. "You still owe me Ape Fights."

"That I do."

"Don't forget."

"I assure you that I won't."

"Imagine the punishment if you renege."

"I would rather not."

"Right, done here," she said, pulling the hardline from the workstation. "On to the next victim."

CHAPTER THREE

In which Tom and Aiden fend off the advances of a rival service team while attempting to deal with a plumber that has become stuck in the depths of a pipe.

There was parking in one of those stacked tower monstrosities that involved leaving your vehicle at the mercy of a rather industrious machine capable of reducing most cars to a two-dimensional object with impressive speed. Cars in need of parking would be whisked away, swept into the sky on a tiny platform, and deposited in a space not much larger than the vehicle itself. Naturally, the Central Services van that Tom and Aiden had been assigned was quite the wrong size and shape for a tower car-park. There were street spaces for service vehicles half-hidden around back. Tom didn't even need to take the van off cruise control, letting it choose a spot and roll to a perfect stop.

Unlike the pure residential neighborhood of the morning's first call, their second assignment was in a mixed-use area. Shops and businesses lived at street level. Apartments and various other living spaces thrived above. There was topiary, trees and bushes, and there were sidewalks. There were even people going about their everyday tasks and concerns, taking up room on the walkways, entering and leaving the shops and residences, never giving a thought to the service and repairmen who made such things run smoothly.

The van parked, Tom and Aiden dragged the rolling-case from the back and started on their journey around the side of the building. About halfway they stopped, eyeballing their surroundings, and double-checked their destination against the script. Review complete, they started back around the way they had come, finally finding the service door half-hidden near where they had started. Tom flashed his phone.

"Central Services," he said in answer to a soft prompt from the door. He even touched fingers to forehead without bothering to work out if the door was equipped with visual receptors.

The door opened after a bit of a wait that didn't drag on too long, and they found themselves facing a young man with the look of one always stuck with the least glamorous jobs associated with maintaining a modern mixed-use building. Name-tag clipped to his overalls claimed that he was called Terrycloth. He didn't say anything, as if speech was something that required more time and determination than he was capable of mustering at this sorry and unfortunate stage of his young and disreputable life. Terrycloth simply held the door open. Knowing better than to bother with words or questions, Tom and Aiden maneuvered the rolling-case through the gap, entering the building. They were then left with little alternative other than wait for their silent companion to muster the strength and inner fortitude to close the door and lead them into the depths of living hell that was the service sub-basement world they knew all too well.

A lift gave them access to the lower levels without the need to manhandle the case down poorly lit flights of stairs, and at last they found themselves in rooms crowded with a wild assortment of pipes and ductwork. Rooms looked more congealed than organized, as if the pipework might have been pulsating and breathing had it wished. Dry-heaving. Giving off the illusion they were standing within a hauntingly organic thing rather than the dirty but sterile bowels of a mixed-use structure. Maneuvering through their surroundings, they located where the water treatment and reclamation pipes gathered from the far-flung parts of the building and burrowed furtively but messily into the ground.

"Which one?"

"Third," Terrycloth said with a mixture of vague indifference and disgust that he actually knew the answer and had to rely that fact to others.

"It's an echo pulsing hydro-digger, right?" Tom said, standing over the pipe and typing commands on the script. "Mark victor three?"

"Don't know."

"Right, I can't get a signal," he said, ignoring Terrycloth's focused indifference to the world around them. "We'll need the swimmer."

"Joy to the world," Aiden said. He had the rolling-case open and selected a softball-sized, vaguely octopus-shaped robot from one of its many compartments.

"Glamours of the job." Tom left the script atop the case and selected a power wrench from within.

Aiden took a coil of dead man's cable and connected one end to the swimmer while Tom loosened the bolts on the pipe's service vent. With the swimmer at the ready, Tom popped the vent.

"Oh, sweet mother Jesus," Tom said, falling away from the opening.

"That's just awful." Aiden tried to cover his mouth while holding onto the swimmer.

"Not that bad."

They both looked at Terrycloth.

"It's like hell on earth in there," Tom said, pointing.

"I suppose."

"Well, I'm grateful you're meeting us halfway." Motioning toward the pipe. "Get the swimmer in there so we can close the vent."

Aiden tried not to answer, conserving his strength, attempting to breathe as little as possible. He deposited the swimmer with a quick flourish and began spooling out cable. Tom slammed the vent closed.

"Careful," Aiden said. "You'll cut the line."

"Cable's too stubborn for that. Besides, there are more important concerns than losing a swimmer."

"Like being able to breathe?"

"Exactly." Went back to the rolling-case, retrieved the script. "Okay, we're in business." Tapping commands.

Aiden felt the swimmer tug at the line and began feeding it cable through the puckered glory hole at the edge of the vent. The cable access seemed to have a life of its own, sucking on the thread in Aiden's hands as if it was chewing, taking great gasping bites of it, swallowing and swallowing and swallowing. He tried to keep his fingers away from the eager lips of the hole while feeding it more and more cable.

"Anything?" he said, risking a glance at Tom.

"Yeah." Tapping the script, glancing over displays. "I think we're almost there."

"Well, as long as we're all doing our part."

"Okay, yeah, stop." Raising a hand. Aiden gripped the cable in a vaguely futile effort to prevent more of it from disappearing into the hungry sucking maw of the pipe. "It's found the plumber."

"Good."

"Pretty sure."

"Oh, don't give me that. Going to make me lose hope."

"I'll try not to shake your faith in humanity." Reading. "It's definitely found the plumber."

"Or something indistinguishable from it."

"Lord, we should be so lucky." Reading. Punching commands. "No, it's got it. Good grip. Running a diagnostic. Attempting to ascertain the circumstances."

"Don't keep us in suspense."

"Trying not to. Plumber is caught on something." Scrolling the report, requesting updates as if insistence would cause events to transpire faster. "This may not be so difficult after all."

"If the swimmer can shake it loose."

They heard the elevator. All three of them turning, looking toward the sound. The dark recesses of the space weren't so much divided into rooms as all the ducts and pipework created a maze that could be easily mistaken for separate chambers. The needs of the building's foundation also added to the impression there were distinct rooms. Voices flopped and floundered to them from the general vicinity of the lift.

"The hell?" Aiden said.

"Expecting anyone?" Tom faced Terrycloth as if he actually had hope for a useful answer.

The building representative mustered the determination to shrug his shoulders while keeping his focus on the approaching voices as if they represented a sterling call to action and adventure.

"No, it's down here," one of the voices was saying, growing slowly louder.

"Can't be," another voice replied. "This place is a deathtrap dungeon. Like mother nature threw up in here." Coming into view. Coming up short. "Well, hello," the man said.

There were three of them, all dressed in service overalls and bright orange shirts. Hats looked as if they had evolved from construction gear into something that might protect the wearer from a pillow if struck at very low velocity. Lamps were attached to their heads as if they might need their hands free to hack through the jungle of pipes and ducts. Each man sported a bulky backpack, and one held a gleaming metallic suitcase.

"Right, you can't be down here," the owner of the first voice said as if suddenly realizing there were other people in the vicinity. "This is a restricted area."

"Central Services," Tom said. "We have every right to be here."

"I'm sure you feel that way, but no. This is Alpha Matrix territory, and you've got your hands on Alpha Matrix equipment."

"Alpha Matrix? Nope, sorry, you're barking up the wrong fishpole. This is Central Services equipment."

"I respectfully disagree."

"Your company doesn't even make this breed of plumber."

"I'm not talking about the plumber," the man said, closing the gap. "You've got your hands on our water treatment pipe, and you're in serious danger of voiding the warranty."

"Not even a little."

"Look," Aiden said, trying to hold the cable still. "We're kind of in the middle of something here."

"Maintenance work is licensed to us," Tom said, "which means we can access Alpha Matrix pipework any time we want."

"Unless Central Services equipment is the cause of the problem."

"The problem is your pipe, and we're dealing with it."

"Our pipe. Our problem."

"Nobody called you." Looking to Terrycloth. "Did somebody call them?"

"No," Terrycloth said as if discovering for the first time that his sympathies lay with Tom and Aiden.

"Sensors in the equipment alerted our quick response service center to an issue with the pipe," the self-appointed Alpha Matrix spokesman said. "Namely the fact that something had become lodged within the confines of the tube and created a blockage."

"Speaking of blockage," Aiden said.

"You just want to get your hands on one of our plumbers."

"Hello? Guys?"

"Whatever for? It's obviously the problem." He wasn't wearing a badge. He didn't have a name. "You think we want to plunder your problem equipment? We'd lose all our business."

"Then back off and let us deal with it."

"You hear that?" Raising his arms, bringing his silent partners into the equation. "They're dealing with it."

"I'm sure they are," one of them said.

"Yes, we are."

"Yes, they are," Terrycloth said.

"Oh, listen to the building man take sides," the nameless one said.

"What's the script say, Tom?" Aiden felt the cable slip.

"Yes, take sides," Tom said. "They called us. This is our caller. They called us. Not you. They called us to clean up your pipe."

"Well, they need to reevaluate their position. Read the fine print. Know about the sensors. They called you?" Pointing. "Fine, the pipe called us."

"Called you?"

"Yes."

"Notified you?"

"Yes."

"Tom." Aiden tried to sound calm.

"Now, you're going to say it called you first," Tom said.

"No," the nameless man said. "You just said it for me." Stepping even closer. "Now, back off."

Aiden felt the cable jump in his hands.

"Okay, seriously now," he said, voice rising. "I love a good petty squabble as much as anybody, but we've got a situation here. The plumber wants our attention. In fact, it desperately wants to be the center of attention, and I don't think it's going to take being ignored much longer."

"Yeah?"

"What's the script say, Tom?"

"This is on you," Tom said, pointing with the script, turning as he looked at the readout. "Shit!"

"Not what I want to hear right now," Aiden said.

"Okay, I've got this." Typing.

"You'd better."

"What do you need?" Terrycloth said.

"Glare at the monkeys for me, will you?" Tom said without looking up from the script. The nameless man stood with his arms crossed. Terrycloth glared at him dutifully. "Okay, here's the deal."

"Yeah?" Aiden said.

Tom was a quiet statue, reviewing the script, tapping commands.

"I was hoping for more of a commitment from you," Aiden said.

"The swimmer is working."

"Good."

"It's just...kind-of stuck."

"Well, that's all right then, isn't it? Exactly what we wanted. Everybody happily stranded in the depths of the earth."

"Now, now."

"No, really, this is the pinnacle of my list of accomplishments for the day."

"Anything we can do?" the nameless man said with a tone of voice that not even a three-day-dead toad would have mistaken for an honest attempt to be helpful.

"You can continue to be a beautiful lawn ornament as long as you keep doing it over there," Tom said. "This is all your fault, you know. Distracting us." Reading, scrolling displays. "Getting in the way."

"That point is open to interpretation and debate."

"I'm sure you feel that way." Looking up from the script, holding Aiden's eye. "Okay, you're not going to like this."

"I love it," Aiden said. "I'm loving every minute of it."

"We have to...manually extract the plumber."

"You mean the swimmer."

"Well," Tom said, glancing back to the script. "It appears to be somewhat more attached to the plumber than we might necessarily like."

"So, we have to extract the plumber?"

"Yeah, we have to extract the plumber."

"What if I just yank on the cable real good?" Holding up one loop of it.

"Doubt it will have the desired effect."

"Worth a try?"

"No, not really."

"I could do it anyway. Might make me happy."

"I suppose," Tom said. "If you're into that kind of thing."

"Well, maybe I'll just start hauling away on it." Began pulling on the cable. "Swimmer's finished the job, right? Don't want to interrupt their date. Plumber is happy-go-lucky?"

"We won't know for sure until we get the pair of them out of there."

"Oh, joy to the world." He could feel the slick and sticky cable through his gloves and between his fingers as it slowly emerged from the pipe. The glory hole yielding up the thread reluctantly, trying to gulp it back down with each breath.

"Okay, sounds like you about got them."

"That's nice." Feeling resistance grow as he dragged at the cable. "I was beginning to think they had lost interest in me personally. Didn't want to be friends any more."

"They adore you." Moving to the rolling-case, depositing the script so that it would be out of harm's way, returning with the power wrench. "Right, this is where it gets interesting."

"You're using a non-standard definition of that word, aren't you?"

"It means the show is just getting good," the nameless one said.

"Remind me to charge extra next time," Tom said half over his shoulder to their Alpha Matrix audience. "Okay, I'm going to pop the vent, and then we're going to yank the pair of them out of there."

"Sounds like a plan," Aiden said.

"Oh, it is."

"No, I mean I really wish it sounded like a plan. Just pop it out of there, shall we?"

"It'll work."

"I share as much enthusiasm as the next guy, but the distance between what you just described and a plan is fairly impressive."

"Look, said yourself we have to get them out of there."

"Yeah."

"Center of attention, right? Going to make a scene if we don't get started?"

"Yeah, on the clock, I know."

"Right, on the clock. You ready for this?" Tom fitted the power wrench to the vent.

"Why they pay us cheese and biscuits."

"On the clock," Tom said. "Count of three."

"One," Aiden said.

"Two."

* * *

"Whoa," Harry said by way of greeting. "What have you two been up to? You stink."

"Thanks," Aiden said. "Love the vote of confidence."

They were mere feet from the service van, having returned to the main distribution offices of Central Services. The ride had been rather quiet and uneventful. The distribution center's car-park had been half deserted.

"No, seriously, what happened to you guys?" Harry had been lugging equipment to one of the other vans.

"I don't want to talk about it," Tom said.

"What you want has got nothing to do with it. This situation proceeds you by a good fifty feet." Others had started to gather from the far corners of the service center car-park.

"We had a bit of an issue with a plumber," Aiden said.

"Yeah, I would have guessed that."

"Would you have guessed the involvement of Alpha Matrix personnel?"

"They skunk you?" Voice turning serious.

"Just got underfoot. Caused the situation to escalate."

"Get the quarantine case from the back," Tom said.

"Yeah, yeah," Aiden said, turning for the back of the van.

"Quarantine?"

"How exactly did things escalate?" one of the growing crowd, Matt, said.

"Different story."

"Yeah, we caught a tourist." Aiden had the back open and was wrestling with the quarantine case.

"Never."

"Plumber went on tour?"

"That's rough."

"No wonder you guys stink."

Voices blurring.

"No, the tourist was the good part of the day," Tom said. "Before we had to deal with the Alpha Matrix variety hour and waste management show."

"A sweeper went on tour." Aiden was half-carrying, half-dragging the case behind him.

"Never," Harry said. "Are you sure about that?" Stepping forward. Quickly stepping back. "Damn, you really stink."

"Yeah, we know we smell like roses." Popping the micro-wheels on the case, trying to improve the drag. "Tourist was quite the show. Disobeying orders. Ignoring commands."

"Stopped maintaining the diary," Tom said.

"What?"

"Even killed a keynote trace." Aiden had the quarantine case halfway to the loading dock. Everyone following along in his wake, unable to keep their distance, drawn to the case as if it was the magnetic center of the universe. Pull stronger than the wastewater smell that surrounded him.

"Yeah, that's suspiciously tourist-like, that is."

"That's what we thought," Tom said, sauntering along as if he didn't have a care in the world.

"So it's in there?" Matt said, pointing.

"Yeah, or what's left of it anyway," Aiden said. "Tom,

the conquering hero that he is, did his duty for God and country."

"Smashed it up good?"

"I like to think so." Tom held his hands before his chest in the classic proud man gripping suspenders pose, if only he had been wearing suspenders.

"Wish I had been there."

"It's only a little sweeper." Aiden had the case at the back of the loading dock. "Heather!"

"All the same," Harry said.

"Put up a fight," Tom said.

"Yeah?"

"Heather!"

"Bit Charlie, it did." Pointing at Aiden. "Man's got a genuine war wound."

"Wouldn't even call it a scratch," Aiden said, looking to the dock.

"How did it manage that?" Matt said. "Let's see."

"Yeah, whip it out." Harry, hands on hips.

"No, really, it's nothing. Heather! Special delivery! Anybody!"

"Screamed like a little girl, he did." Tom, practically dancing on his toes.

"That, sir, is an outrageous slur and gross exaggeration of events as they transpired on the ground."

"Frightened the neighbors for three miles all around."

"Nothing of the kind."

"Nearly lost my snacky cookies, myself."

"Okay, that part is true," Aiden said. "He did very nearly lose control of his higher motor functions."

"What?"

"Heather!" Aiden shouted once more into the dark unknowing depths of the loading dock, turning so that he might properly face the terror within.

"What?" Heather said, emerging at long last from

between the grand sweeping doors of the loading dock, pulling a flatbed dolly along behind her. Flatbed was a demented criminal's idea of clustered mounds of equipment, complete with obligatory blinking lights, and open space. "You got a problem with punctuality? Everything have to be on the freaking clock for you? There's preparation for this kind of thing—Whoa, you stink."

"Yeah, the tide was especially kind to us this year. Gave us a fine crustacean of salt."

"That's not even close to how I would put it." Trying to stand tall, fanning herself with one hand. "Crustacean indeed. You been swimming in soup? What did the tourist do to you, anyway?"

"Oh, so she did read the ticket," Aiden said. "Half of it, anyway. Else you would know that the tourist had nothing to do with our more fragrant adventures of the afternoon."

"Yeah, yeah, cough up the flying monkey, already." Heather pointed at the quarantine case. "It's in there, yeah?"

"I wish I could say with some certainty that our pesky little tourist did lie within this particular quarantine case—Of course, it's in there."

"Had to be sure," she said, stepping forward. "Noxious fumes going to your head and all of that. Murdering brain cells." Held out a script for Aiden's inspection. "Sign."

Aiden flashed his phone to the script's proximity scanner.

"You, too, Timothy," she said, turning toward Tom. "Don't make me walk over there."

"Yeah, I'm hip," Tom said, coming within range of the script, flashing his phone.

"Beautiful," Heather said, scrolling through displays. "Gentlemen, I relieve you of responsibility for the care, feeding and treatment of this ugly little bastard." Putting her hands on the quarantine case. "We'll just take it back to the lab and violate its personal space to within an inch of its life. Should know in about a day if it's a genuine tourist or just wishful thinking on your part."

"Hey, either way I got to smash the ever-loving bejesus out of it." Tom raised his hands as if releasing his words to the wind.

"Yeah, well, you had better hope it's a tourist then." Dragging the quarantine case to the flatbed. Hefting it with some difficulty onto the dolly between strange mounds of blinking equipment. Aiden stepping forward. "No, no," Heather said, holding up a hand. "You stay away. I'll manage."

"Don't say I didn't offer."

"Yeah, well, in this case, chivalry can just go shoot itself in the face." Finished securing the quarantine case to the back of the flatbed. "Or at least go take a bath. I would be tempted to forbid you from entering the premises, but the showers are located within rather than without."

"Poor planning on management's part, obviously."

"Oh, obviously. Something about not wanting to frighten the neighbors. Grown men showering in public. Showing everyone their business."

"When did you gain the power to forbid people from entering, anyway?" Tom said.

"Soon as you got within fifty feet of the door. Quarantine control."

"Sounds like bureaucratic overreach to me. Power's definitely going to your head."

"Just the blood rushing between my ears. You really do stink." Turning, grabbing the flatbed's handle, starting to drag it along behind her. "On that note, gentlemen, I have desiccated tourist meat to poke with a rather sharp stick."

"It's a tourist, all right." Pointing at Aiden. "It bit Charlie here and everything."

"Bathe," Heather said, disappearing between the loading dock doors.

* * *

The Central Services locker room was about what one would expect for the corporation's field representatives. It was clean. It was sterile. There had once been white tile. Nobody was altogether sure what color was represented now. Everybody had an opinion, and the betting was furious. No money ever actually changed hands since nobody could agree on the standard for determining who had the superior claim.

There were even showers provided as an unheralded bonus to employees, which was fortunate considering the kinds of equipment they could find themselves trying desperately to repair. Showers came complete with hot—or at least moderately warm—and cold running water. Considering the things they learned about plumbing while on the job, nobody was in a hurry to find out just how locally the water was recycled. It was enough to have an apparently endless supply of running water, and there was no need to contemplate where that water originated too closely.

Foxglove was waiting for them. He had been kind enough to wait until after Tom and Aiden had emerged from the showers and acquired a basic layer of clothing.

"Was reviewing the paperwork," Foxglove said by way of polite greeting.

"It was Alpha Matrix's fault." Tom pointed a finger. "What were they even doing there?"

"Well, they've got this thing with sensors and quick response teams."

"Need to review their protocols is what they need to do. Too much senseless automation. Should have known it was our caller."

"I'm sure they learned their lesson. People will be talking about the smell in the service center for weeks. Can't imagine what it was like on-site."

"Oh, it doesn't bear imagining," Aiden said. "Burned into my brain. My eternal hope is that the memory will fade."

"It will. These things don't linger. Survival instinct."

"Well, I wish I shared your optimism, Glove," Tom said. It wasn't unheard of for people to refer to Foxglove by some nickname or other. It's just that such things weren't generally said to his face. "I feel like I'll never be clean again. And that's experience talking. Not the first time a plumber has proven unusually memorable."

"And yet, somehow, I'm sure you will survive," Foxglove said. "Not what brings me down to your level, anyway. Been reviewing the paperwork."

"Yes, you said."

"Caught yourselves a tourist, I understand."

"Oh, it's more than understanding. It actually happened. Bit Charlie and everything."

"Got the war wound to prove it." Aiden held up his finger.

"Little blighter was in serious need of some reeducation on how to proceed in polite society. R&D's got it now."

"Yes, I gathered all of that from the report," Foxglove said.

Tom and Aiden stood by their lockers. Each had

been finishing up another layer of clothing while the conversation had progressed. Motion finally drifting slowly into immobility.

"Waiting for the other shoe to drop," Tom said.

"Paperwork is incomplete."

"What?"

"We closed the ticket," Aiden said.

"Hit send and everything."

"There is no send." Aiden, turning toward Tom. "You just enter the date and save."

"It was metaphorical. Application of creativity and artistic license." Dismissive wave of Tom's hand. "Not that it matters. We closed the ticket."

"Yeah, I know," Foxglove said.

"Well, there you are then."

"Still incomplete."

"How? How is it incomplete?"

"Form's not that complicated," Aiden said.

"It was the wrong form," Foxglove said.

"No, it can't be."

"Told you it was the wrong form." Smacked Aiden with the back of his hand. "What did I tell you?"

"It couldn't have been the wrong form. Filled out the incident report myself. Higher Computational Malfunction."

"What iteration did you use?"

"Whatever's loaded on the damn script." Aiden ran fingers through his hair. "Delta five nine. Five six?"

"There's an Echo zed two, now."

"No."

"Fraid so."

"Since when?"

"About a quarter of an hour ago."

"That's long after we submitted the report," Aiden said.

"Yeah." Tom didn't want his opinion to go unheard.

"Well, you're really going to love this next part then," Foxglove said.

"I'm sure."

"Form's a complete rebuild."

"Oh, for the love of God and monsters!" Aiden turned, faced his locker.

"You'll have to redo it."

"I knew it!" Tom started pacing up and down the aisle. "Knew it was too good to be true."

"Look, why can't you just remap the old answers to the new format?" Aiden said.

"Oh, sure, make it sound easy," Foxglove said. "They consolidated a couple different forms, which you didn't bother to fill out."

"They were optional."

"I'm sure you want to believe that. Look, there are external pressures. The company is cracking down."

"It was a bloody piece of equipment. Malfunctioning and everything."

"It bit Charlie." Tom, pointing.

"Yeah, it bit me," Aiden said. "And stop calling me Charlie."

"I'm sure it did all of that and more," Foxglove, hands out as if trying to quiet a rapidly expanding grease fire. "But you have to think of the big picture. There's public oversight of these things now."

"Of course there is."

"Tom."

"No, stands to reason." Tom was pacing, small circles. They weren't alone in the locker room. One or two other service representatives diving out of his way. "We've got to coddle the sick and infirm. Care for the rabid dog even as it's biting you on the asterisk."

"Tourist Board might disagree with you."

"The Tourist Board can kiss me right on my swollen spotted behind."

"You think the Tourist Board is going to get their hands on this?" Aiden, hand to his forehead, rubbing his eyes.

"Oh, I don't have to think," Tom said.

"Don't have to think?"

"I know."

"You know?"

Tom stopped pacing, walked slowly back toward them. Random service reps watching from the far edge of the row of lockers, trying to judge if it was safe to return.

"Yeah," Foxglove said. "Wish I could say otherwise."

"Bloody Tourist Board." Aiden turned, looking to Tom. "So, did you dispose of the tourist humanely?"

"Hey, you were there, too, Charlie."

"Had my back turned, remember? Running interface with the customer."

"Oh, the wolves love watching their chow being thrown to them."

"Tom," Foxglove said. "Did you follow protocol?"

"Bashed its little skull in with a rather large hammer. So, yeah, I followed all the appropriate protocols."

"Did you confirm it was a tourist?" Turning toward Aiden.

"The savage little devil-child bit me."

"Yes, you keep saying."

"It stopped maintaining the diary." Aiden, counting on his fingers. "Ignored direct commands. Disobeyed orders. Severed a live-stream connection."

"Worked really hard to avoid capture," Tom said.

"Which is when it bit me," Aiden, holding up his hand.

"Which is when it bit him." Pointing at Aiden's hand.

"Yes, I did gather all of that from the report," Foxglove said.

"Left its owner quite distressed and unhappy." Aiden raised his hands as if to express that this one act alone was the ultimate crime.

"She was practically at her wit's end," Tom said. "In fact, I'm fairly certain, and I'm sure that Charlie will say nothing to contradict me. The owner had taken the responsibility to clean the premises upon herself. Without the benefit of Central Services equipment to assist her, as it were."

"So, where's the owner's statement?"

Tom and Aiden looked at him as if he had just demonstrated an extremely energetic chemical reaction that would take the custodial staff weeks if not months to finish stripping off the walls. People would run away screaming. Men would be consigned to hospital just contemplating the memory of what had been enthusiastically demonstrated all over the landscape.

"You did remember to interview the owner, right?" Foxglove said. "Ensure the tourist was dispatched with a minimum of fuss? Confirm that it had been displaying very tourist-like behavior?"

"We may have been more focused on the tourist then the thoughts and feelings, opinions if you will, of the owner," Aiden said.

"Well, that's another one, then. Congratulations, you get to complete the waiver of owner's post-incident interview request form."

"I really hate that form." Aiden had a hand in his hair, rubbing his scalp.

"I gathered that from the way you described it as optional."

"Tuttle," Tom muttered quietly as if he had forgotten that other people could hear what he said.

"What?"

"Harry Tuttle," Aiden said. "We were just talking about him."

"Dare to dream." Foxglove held up his script, pointing at it with his free hand for additional emphasis. "In the meantime, you've got reports to update."

"Yeah." Aiden sank to the bench.

Foxglove watched them for a long moment with the script still held between them like a sacred text. When the air continued to stubbornly resist bursting into flames, he finally turned and left them with the quiet solitude of the locker room for company. The other service representatives who had been carefully watching from beyond the corner of the lockers slowly began to drift back into the row.

"Harry Tuttle really had the right idea."

"Yeah, that he did," Aiden said, looking to the quicksilver floor. "That he did."

CHAPTER FOUR

*In which Lynn and Aiden spend a quiet
evening at home regaling each other
with accounts of the day.*

The apartment was a fat rectangle,
longer than wide, giving the illusion
of depth while avoiding the feeling
of looking down a long tunnel into
the desolate pits of hell. There was
a couch and a long table with tall
chairs almost like a bar. Long table forming a natural
barrier separating the kitchen alcove from the rest of
the room. The walls intruded inward at some point
past the couch and table, changing the shape of the
rectangle, creating the sense that the apartment was
more than one room when it was nothing of the kind.

Entertainment screen took up the part of the wall
facing the couch. On display was a massively multiplayer military campaign. Countries didn't so much
fight wars as play them. While not all nations were
content to engage in simulated warfare, many had
discovered the advantages of trying to destroy each
other in ways that didn't actually involve trying to kill
everybody or more or less turn the world into a barren
wasteland. Scores and leader-boards were carefully
watched with a passion that was frequently hard to de-
scribe to anyone not invested in the current standing
or outcome.

Lynn was half-sprawled on the couch, eyes on the
entertainment wall, when the door opened. Didn't

make her jump, but it did disrupt her sprawl, sending her legs one way. Her head came up, and her arm slid down.

"Hey," she said by way of greeting as Aiden closed the door. "Said you'd be late." Grabbed her phone, waved it at him. "Did I miss an update?"

"No," Aiden said, shuffling more than walking to the couch. "Didn't miss anything." Leaning over the back. Lynn meeting him halfway. Quick kiss. "Couldn't be bothered with an update. Would have required my brain to work."

"Well, put your feet up. Rest the brain." Bump of foreheads. Another quick kiss. "You smell good."

"Don't remind me."

"Okay," she said, watching him shuffle around the couch, collapse upon it. Watched him for a long moment waiting to see if words would form from deep within the pantomime darkness of his soul.

"Advantage to dealing with plumbers," he finally said.

"Yeah?"

"Get to clean up on the job. They haven't worked out how to take that off the clock."

"Small mercies and all of that."

"Yeah, and all of that." His eyes drifted to the entertainment wall. "Thought you were out of this campaign."

A quarter of the wall was showing an overhead tactical map of a field somewhere amid the imaginatively shifting borders of France and Germany. The remains of an engagement between tanks and heavy armor could still be seen. Recovery units were scurrying this way and that, trying not to be noticed by the other side's own rescue operations.

"Yeah, well, I still keep an eye on it sometimes. The

scorched-earth approach is just not my thing. And once one side decides it's all or nothing."

"The other soon follows, I know. Always seems to happen."

"Better they do it here, right?" Waving vaguely at the wall.

"Therapeutic, I suppose." Looked sideways at her. "Thought you bleached your hair again."

"Whatever gave you that idea?"

"Well, you said." Digging absently for his phone.

"I say many things."

"Bleach is a color."

"Damn Skippy, it is."

"Yeah, well, in context," he said, mumbling, abandoning the search.

"It was just a sentence." Ran fingers through her hair, dark shade, not quite red. Streaks of color subtly shifting as her fingers moved: blue, gold. "Random assortment of words, meaning things and other things."

"Well, that'll teach me to understand words."

"Yes." Looked back to the wall, yielded up a quiet sigh as if that was all the soul-weary commentary that need be said. "Scorched earth never lasts," she muttered. "Campaign should be over soon. I hope. Maybe look for another if this carries on too long. Referees really should do something."

"Yes, they should."

"I was a platoon leader and everything." Watched the units scurry and move, rescuing what they could under cover of dark.

"Yes, you were."

"Hate to start over."

They watched the screen. Clock counting down slowly toward sunrise when the heavy units would return. It was all but a real-time simulation.

"If only I could start over," Aiden said.

"Oh, you say that now."

"I know. Not all bad. Just tired. Paperwork. The occasional stink."

"Times like that always make you think, huh?"

"That they do."

"It's just—" Shook her hands at the wall. "Scorched earth, ugh." Climbed from the couch and went to the kitchen, talking over her shoulder as she rummaged about. "How can you expect the other side to recover? That's where the fun is. Rebuilding resources. Scrambling back from defeat. Will you pull it off?"

"You were on the winning side, right?"

"Not the point." Lynn came back with two beers, handing one to him. "It's the challenge. Spit and bailing wire. Skin of your teeth." Took a swig off her own. "Really hard to do when there's nothing left."

"Scorched earth."

"Nothing to do but wait for the referees to declare the situation beyond hope and reset." Watched the screen. "Waste of a good campaign."

Streaks of heavy fire flickered across the wall. Recovery units exploded and fell.

"Oh, look," Aiden said. "They're going after the humanitarian aid."

"Yeah, well, you expect a certain amount of that."

"Everything's a target, is it?"

"These days, yeah." Lynn gave a great billowing breath of a sign, as if the last fragile remnants of her soul were slowly draining out from between her teeth. "So, a tourist, huh?"

"Yeah, if you can believe it," he said. "Good Lord, was it only this morning?"

"I could check my phone's log."

"Seems like such a long time ago."

"That's the smelly afternoon talking."

"And the paperwork."

"And the paperwork, but let's focus on the good here," she said, turning toward him, drawing her feet up. "A freaking tourist."

"I know. Adorable little bastard, too. Smashed him up good."

"Well, Tom did the smashing."

"Let's not focus on who actually did what. We were both there. Smashing was involved."

"I'm with you."

"Freaked the owner out."

"I'm sure."

"Biting was involved."

"The owner?"

"No, of course, the owner." Pointing with the beer. "The tourist. Little dish sweeper monkey. Snapping claws. It bit me."

"Never. Show me." Took his hand, examined it. Nothing to see. Held on to it anyway. "How did it manage that?"

"Well, it really didn't want me to violate what it considered to be its own personal private space, flip its lid, reach the manual reset button."

"Determined, was it?"

"Oh, very much so."

"That was it, was it?" Still holding his hand as if comforting a small puppy. "Minor malfunction involving the definitions of good and bad touch?"

"Oh, there was more than that. Nothing minor about it. Stopped listening to the owner. Ignoring commands from the script."

"Really?"

"Stopped maintaining the diary."

"What?"

"Canceled a live stream that it shouldn't have cared one way or another was even running. Turned off its beacon."

"Never."

"Oh, yes, as a direct result of canceling the live stream. I mean, it realized we were reading its thoughts and decided it just didn't like the idea of us knowing what it was thinking, thank you very much."

"Sounds pretty definitive then. So, smash."

"Well, we won't know for certain until we get the results back from R&D, but yeah, probable cause. Smash city. Little chunks of robot littered all over the kitchen, and I ask you. What's going to clean up after the cleaners?"

"Who sweeps the sweepers?" Held her beer aloft as if being quite profound. "Or is it whom?"

"Pretty sure it is who."

"Can't say that I really care."

"No, I can't really say that either."

"Had fun with the brain-trust in Applied Engineering and Robotics over it," Lynn said.

"Did you, now?"

"Oh, yes, one of the faculty was very annoyed that they couldn't examine the remains. Actually tried to get me to call you. Convince you to drag the dismembered tourist guts to the lab."

"Never."

"Oh, yes, it happened."

"And you still have a job?"

"I can be quite persuasive and understanding when I need to be."

"Persuasive and what?"

"They can't fire me, being the point," Lynn said. "Make my life miserable, sure, but it would take a lot before they could actually give me my walking papers."

"The joys of working for university."

"Of which, there are so many. Besides, they seem to like me more than they don't. Even the *what have you done for me lately* crowd."

"Of which there are a depressing number, I'm sure."

"Oh, yes."

"So, who was it?" Aiden said. "Or should that have been whom?"

"Still don't care."

"Yeah, have to agree with you there." Aiden seemed to realize he was holding a beer, took advantage of that fact. "Well, who badgered you to acquire the bastard?"

"The what?"

"You know, the tourist. Little dish-type jobber. Who wanted it so badly they would risk Central Services Industrial Espionage Division's wrath?"

"It's not really called that, is it?"

"Doubt it."

"Research and Reclamation? Technology and Device Management? Theft Prevention and Loss?" Counting on her fingers.

"Sure, one of those."

"Well, if you really must know, it was the late, great Jennifer Behr. Custodian of the sacred way. Designer of machines that think they are people."

"Oh, her. Yeah, I even hear her name mentioned in the bowels of Central Services' darkest dungeons. Doubt we've ever tried to recruit her."

"They just want her mind."

"Yeah, sure," Aiden said. "Why would she want a tourist, anyway? It's hardly the same field."

"Fuck all if I know. Spends so much time hanging out with the wombats in the forbidden zone that I doubt she knows what she wants with it herself."

"Forbidden?"

"Quarantine, dear. Quarantine. Where they keep all the truly dangerous artifacts. Imagine if something that was programmed to act like it had thoughts and feelings of its very own was allowed to roam free across the network." Raised her arms as if fending off despair. "Why, the world would just shit itself."

"Yes, well, imagine if all of that got off the screen." Aiden gestured to where the fighting among rescue units had escalated to the point heavy armor was starting to put in an appearance. "It's not one-to-one, sure, but the very idea. Today, it's only a little sweeper that doesn't want to do as it's told."

"Tomorrow, the world." Hands raised dramatically.

"People forget," he said, looking to the screen. "It's only make believe." Weapons flashed. Imaginary machines flamed, fractured and fell.

"Pretty sure a computer simulation cannot actually cause real bombs to fall. Seriously, they just going to think them into existence or something? I am programmed; therefore, I am."

Looked to her.

"You know what I mean," he said.

"Yeah, yeah. Not everything's just a program."

"Not everything's just a little sweeper robot, either."

"Yeah, yeah." Remembering conversations of the day. Almost bouncing from the couch. "Hey, speaking of not-so-imaginative fighting robots, guess what I stumbled across today."

"Oh Lord, help us to suffer the sins of fools lightly."

"Oh, be serious, this is really good."

"I cannot even begin to speculate."

"It's not that hard. Fighting? Robots?"

"My mind is drained of the power to contemplate abstract thought, remember? I've been dealing with the intricacies of advanced bureaucracy."

"Ape Fights!" Arms spread wide.

"Ape Fights? Seriously?"

Nodding her head.

"Ape Fights," she said.

"Where in the world did you stumble across Ape Fights?"

"I've got my ways, means, and sources."

"I'm sure," Aiden said, "but you're practically part of the establishment. You are, if you'll forgive me, the man."

"Didn't say it was easy."

"I'm sure."

"Had to threaten to turn off the network to an entire floor."

"Goodness, that must have been something to see. Wish I had been there."

"Now, I've still got to verify names, dates and places."

"Naturally."

"But this looks good."

"I haven't been to an Ape Fight in—" Ran fingers through his hair with the effort of thought. "Some time." Flashes and flares on the wall drew their attention. "Can't say that Ape Fights are really my thing."

"Yeah, but when was the last time you went?"

"Memory fails me."

"As does mine." Eyes for the screen, sinking back onto the couch. "I mean, sure, Ape Fights. Take them or leave them. But they can be fun."

"Yeah."

"And when was the last time you went?"

"No idea. Been a while since I've been that subversive."

"Oh, we should definitely go then. Else we'll lose our street cred."

"You really want to do this just to impress some young punks at university?"

"Hey, you would be surprised what a little punk attitude gets you."

"Don't have to prove your bonafides to me."

"They hacked a router."

"No."

"The idiots."

"That they are," Aiden said.

"They need to understand when I tell them not to do a thing it's not just the old man talking," Lynn said. "Yes, I know."

"I know what you mean."

"Getting into an Ape Fight means something."

"And it could even be fun."

"Serendipity bonus."

"That doesn't mean...I don't think that means what you think—"

"Aiden."

"Yes?"

"I love you more than I can say and everything."

"But shut your stinking noise hole if you're just going to make stupid, useless comments like that?"

"Yeah, and you do realize you haven't even taken your coat off yet, don't you?"

"I, what?" he said, lifting his arms as if this would help him be able to look at himself.

"You really are brain dead," she said. "You just staggered in and promptly crashed on the couch without a moment spent in between doing useful little things like shed that exotic outer layer of clothing. Paperwork must have been worse than I can possibly imagine, and I can imagine pretty horrible things. I do work for a university, you know."

"Oh." Letting his arms fall, giving up on looking at himself. "Well, I really should do something about that."

"Yes, you should."

"Right, so I just need to master the trick of standing up." Working slowly, he tried to regain his feet. "A little reverse engineering is in order, I think."

"Just like riding a bicycle."

"Nothing to it," he said, standing, spreading his arms as if to celebrate victory. "Hey, look at that, and without even riding a bicycle."

"Now, just master the next step."

"Getting the coat off. Yeah, yeah, I'm working on it."

"The shoes shall follow after."

"I'm wearing shoes?" Shrugging off his coat, catching her look. "Okay, yes, I know. Beaten this quite firmly into the ground, haven't I?"

"No comment," Lynn said as Aiden tossed his coat toward one of the chairs. The coat slipped, clinging desperately, trying to hold, and crumpled to the floor. "No comment, at all."

* * *

The Information Technology Resource Center did not have proper office space at Benjamin Franklin Technical College and Public University because the ITRC Field Representatives were expected to spend the vast majority of their time in the field. They borrowed space from various and sundry departments every day just to hold the morning meeting. There was great discussion among the Field Reps concerning which department actually provided the space—or, to be more precise, there would have been discussion if any of them actually cared enough about the bureaucracy involved to even consider the issue. It was a large conference room. They all went. Every once in a great while the location was changed. Going to the meeting was so routine that most Reps simply showed up at whatever room they could be bothered to remember, sat in the back, and ignored the gathering actually in progress. Meeting time was spent syncing their phones to their freshly issued scripts so that they could plan out the day's activities. Scripts were always collected from and returned to the same location, and it would have served ITRC management well to simply hand out the scripts during the morning meeting, forcing all Field Reps to check their meeting-update logs before showing up at whatever random conference space they felt like visiting.

A certain percentage of Field Reps, chosen on an informal rotating honor system, always made sure to check the meeting-update logs so that a critical mass actually showed up at the morning meeting to help ensure management never implemented Draconian measures such as the already-referenced script distribution scheme to increase meeting attendance. Lynn was currently on the rotation to track the meeting location and actually attend, which she did with a reasonable degree of fidelity.

"You're early," she said by way of greeting to Darryl. "We're in the right space, yeah?"

"Last time I checked," Darryl said in an exaggerated stage whisper, "which was months ago now that I think about it. So, I'm pretty sure I'm in the right space." Lynn gave him a look that had caused many a graduate student to faint dead away from fright. "Look, I'm very nearly certain this is the room."

"Well, it's a good thing I checked the logs then, isn't it?"

"Yes, that's actually the main reason I'm all but perfectly confident that this is the correct space. You're here, aren't you? Responsible and all of that."

"Dreadful curse that it is."

"Quite dreadful, I'm sure, but look, you said so yourself. Checked the logs and everything."

"That I did."

"You're here. The meeting's here. Stands to reason. Form follows function."

"As long as we hit critical mass in whichever space the meeting is actually held."

"Yes, well, who wants to attend these days, anyway?" Darryl said, reverting to stage whisper. "You've heard the latest rumors, yeah?"

"There's always rumors. Whoever can tell if you've heard the latest and greatest tales of despair?"

"They're going to reorganize."

"What? Again?"

"Yes, again, never-ending cycle. If we didn't re-org, we would drop dead like a Fiddler crab or one of those other things that just up and dies should it ever stop swimming."

"Like a fish?"

"Yes, like a—No, hang on, those just lie about whenever they feel like. Ever seen a flounder? Just lies there hiding under a rock."

"You're thinking of a shark."

"No, I'm pretty sure they've got to keep moving or they drown. Hard to believe, isn't it?"

"Causing me all kinds of doubt."

"Imagine a fish drowning in water. They breathe water all day, every day, for the duration of their natural born lives."

"They don't actually breathe water."

"Well, what is it that they're doing the whole time they are submerged? That's what I would like to know. Holding their breath, are they?"

"In a manner of speaking," Lynn said. "Look, you do understand how gills work, yeah?"

"What do I look like, an ichthyologist? I'm just a lowly Field Engineer over here."

"And for all we know, one of the immortal brain trust will build a self-propelled mechanical guppy, and we'll be stuck looking after it. Where will we be then? If not ichthyology, then what?"

"That's the study of fish, right?" Hagarlodge said from the front of the room by way of bringing the meeting to order. The group of various and sundry Field Reps pulled themselves away from their phones and scripts and drew more or less to attention. Those that could be bothered to realize they were in the right room, anyway. Lynn quietly and rather noncommittally shrugged her shoulders. "Let's hope it doesn't come to that."

"Never know what comes with a re-org," someone said with the confidence of one who figured to remain anonymous from out of the depths of the crowd.

"Is that rumor making the rounds again?" Hagarlodge said. "Look, we just about settled down with the present arrangement. Needs time to burn in. Nothing's being uprooted."

A vague and skeptical silence sauntered leisurely about the room.

"Good," he said. "Important point of protocol to start things off. Nobody is to voluntarily take network access offline without running it through my office first."

Lynn couldn't keep still.

"There needs to be a very good, practical reason to inconvenience so many people," Hagarlodge said, ignoring her. "Even for a short period of time. We need to prepare. We need to issue notifications and warnings." Counting on his fingers. "How long we expect the network to be down."

"Not enough that you got to yell at me in private yesterday," Lynn said. "Have to rake me over the coals in front of everyone."

The room went rather quiet rather fast.

"I'm not sure I follow, Charles."

"They hacked a router. A message needed to be sent."

"And a message was sent." Hagarlodge studied her quietly from behind his eyes. "In fact, quite a few messages were sent. By faculty. To me. Some of them in person. Some of them at various volumes. So thank you very much for that."

"Worse than the students," Lynn muttered not quite to herself, sinking into her chair. "Wouldn't surprise me if one of them tried the hack."

"That would be a better use of your time," Hagarlodge said. "Figure out who tried the hack."

"Yeah, yeah."

"As I was saying." His fingers were touching the desktop in front of him. "It is important to minimize unscheduled network disruptions and efface repairs as quickly and expediently as possible. I understand that one lab grid was down for close to ninety minutes and the entire floor for just under an hour."

"Half an hour, tops," Lynn said.

"It was well over half an hour. I know because I checked the logs." He studied them quietly. The room appeared less interested in network connection etiquette than they had been in the various derivations of fish. Lynn managed to hold still. Nobody commented on Hagarlodge's misuse of language or what it really means to efface repairs. "Another important issue has come to our attention. We've intercepted communications among the students that Ape Fights are planned."

The room responded with vigorous murmuring, as Lynn tried desperately not to fall out of her chair.

"Now, we all know that Ape Fights violate university policy and are expressly forbidden. Any student caught organizing or even just participating in Ape Fights risks expulsion."

"They wouldn't dare," Darryl said, voice rising

above the level of general murmuring. "There hasn't been a campus Ape Fight in years."

"That we've detected." Hagarlodge tapped the table with his fingertips. "Doesn't mean it never happens. Environmental Health and Safety has found remnants, shall we say. Particulate debris that students hadn't cleaned up as thoroughly as they might have thought."

"Imagine that," Darryl said. "Ape Fights on my campus, and I didn't know." Shook his head. "I'm getting old."

Lynn studied the tabletop before her with rather intense concentration and hoped that the very recent public scolding had the room fooled over her lack of participation in the current discussion.

"They are talking about it, people," Hagarlodge said, "and we need to know if it is actually happening. I would hope it goes without saying that Ape Fights are dangerous. They are hazardous to the health and welfare of the student population and can cause considerable structural damage to the facilities."

"Cleanup is expensive, you mean," a random voice from out the room said.

"That's one way of putting it. Look, just imagine if one of the combatants suddenly went on tour during a fight. That should quiet any thought that Ape Fights are good."

"Haven't been to an Ape Fight in years," Darryl muttered more to himself than to Lynn.

"As I said, they're talking about it. They've already slipped up in mentioning it by phone. Let's hope they slip up more so we can put a stop to this before somebody gets hurt." He studied the room, watching as various faces slowly nodded in agreement. "Okay, next item is more of a procedural housecleaning issue."

It was at about this point that Lynn stopped paying any attention to the meeting whatsoever. She had more important fish to fry.

* * *

"You," Lynn said, pointing, marching through the common area with the single-minded determination of a hurricane. "A word with you if I may."

Oliver started as if his chair had shocked him, locked in that paralyzing moment of stand or flight like a frightened water buffalo. Lynn gesturing, come-hither, for his attention as she crossed the room. Students and staff scattering like sawdust shot out of the business end of a woodchipper.

"Who did it, Oliver," she said. "Who hacked the router?"

"What?" he said, gasping for air. Lynn towering over him.

"Come on. I know you know. Said you were going to find out."

"I'm looking into—Said you don't care."

"That was yesterday." Hand pressed flat against the table. "Today, I want to know."

"Yes, yesterday, I'm still making enquire—I'm not going to tell you."

"Really?"

"We'll punish our own." Watching the rubberneckers at the common room's periphery. "Not giving anyone up to the establishment."

"Oh, I'm the establishment, now, am I?"

"For the purposes of this conversation, yes."

"Okay, then, let me show you what the establishment can do." Grabbed Oliver by the shoulder.

"Hey!"

"Come on," she said, dragging him across the common room, scattering tables and chairs before her. Oliver half-following, half-slipping along in her wake.

"This is uncalled for."

"I'm sure you say that to all the guys." Dragged him to a service hallway and pushed him into a custodial room.

"Okay, look, I'm not going to tell you," Oliver said.

"Yeah, shut up." Lynn got the door closed.

"I swear I'm still looking into it. These things take time, you know."

"No, really, shut up."

"This really is above and beyond, Merlin."

"Will you just quit your gob-hole for a moment and listen? I don't care about that."

"But—"

"No, really, I don't care." Holding her finger in his face. "I really don't care. We've got bigger problems facing us down."

"Wait, what's a gob-hole?"

"They know about the Ape Fights."

"Wait, they—Ape Fights? How?"

She watched the wheels spinning in his head, wobbling, getting ready to come crashing down.

"They intercepted some fool conversation or other," she said. "Some overclocked genius from out the labs was talking by phone."

"Never!"

"Oh, you had better start believing in Father Christmas really fast, Oliver. Someone blabbed on the phone." Shaking her finger, scolding. "You've got to spread the word, man. Don't talk this shit on the phone."

"Those dimwitted bastards."

"You have to keep this offline. Word of mouth. Analog. Whisper campaign. Spread it like an airborne virus."

"Improve the encryption," Oliver said, pacing two

steps one way, three steps another. "Code. They must have cracked the cypher."

"Encryption as maybe. You have to assume they wrote the cypher."

"Another possibility."

"Yeah?"

"Aren't you going to ask me when and where?"

Lynn frozen, looking at him, seeing nothing. She walked slowly over to him, getting in his face, listening to his breath. Oliver said nothing.

"I don't narc," she said with a voice as flat as a sand-paper road. Oliver's face blurring into focus. "I don't narc."

"Doesn't mean there isn't a narc mixed up in this." Face turned sideways, looking off into the distance. "But, okay, someone fucked royal pudding just something awful. Talked about upcoming events by phone."

"Thank you."

"Right," he said. "Not the end of the world. Just have to spread the word old analog style. No talking by phone."

"No way to know how badly you're compromised."

"Hey, we live on the edge out here in adrenaline land, but I'll see what I can do about the frequent talk-ers. I swear you would think we were plotting world domination or something."

"See that you do." Lynn crossed to the door. "So, Oliver?"

"Yeah?"

"When and where will the monkeys rumpus, any-way?"

"Yeah, I'll get you that info as soon as it's nailed down."

"See that you do." She opened the door. "You will find out who hacked the router," she said, raising her voice toward the outside world. "And you will tell me. You really don't want to see my bad side."

"No, I don't," Oliver muttered as the door closed. He covered his head, trying to breathe normally, and scratched his fingers over his face and through his hair. "I really don't."

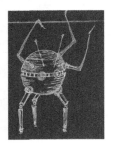

CHAPTER FIVE

In which Aiden deals with another typical afternoon at work that just might involve dangling off the side of a building.

"It'll be easy, they said." Aiden had a hand to his forehead, shielding his eyes, looking up. Skyscraper towering over him. "Piece of cake, they said."

"They say many things." Tom studied the script, tapping, scrolling. "See it?"

"Nope."

"It's up there somewhere."

"So they say."

"Spiders aren't small." Tapping, scrolling.

"Doesn't fill me with confidence."

"Wasn't the idea."

"No, really, think about it," Aiden said, still looking to the wall of glass towering over them. "For just a second, think about what you just said."

"Okay." Lowering the script. "What did I just say?"

"Spiders are not small."

"True, that does sound very much like something I may have just finished saying."

"Can't see it."

"Which brings us back around to the reason I made the comment in the first place. It was by way of a bit of editorial on the current state of your eyes and your ability to see anything other than food beyond the end of your nose. I will admit that you are quite good at recognizing food when it is placed before you, and you can even maneuver it to within an inch of your mouth without the need for study aides."

Aiden lowered his hand, turning, looking at Tom as if he was a camel that had unexpectedly turned up in the middle of an Antarctic snow storm.

"Missing the point," Aiden finally said.

"No, really, you're quite adept at identifying the toppings of a pizza from a distance of no less than fifty yards."

"Missed the point by so much you're not just on the wrong side of the street, you're on the wrong continent." Grabbed the script out of Tom's hand. "Spiders are huge. Easy to spot. In fact, they're so large that they're practically out of our weight class."

"And yet," Tom said.

"And yet the building itself is so much grander the spider simply vanishes into obscurity in comparison." Aiden turned his attention to the script, typing, scrolling, ignoring Tom with a fierce passion that could not be mistaken for anything other than focused, intense deliberation. Tom turned, looking, studying the side of the building.

"Okay, you may have a bit of a point there."

"Oh, you think?"

"How tall is the building, anyway?"

"I recommend not thinking about that particular item with too much intensity."

"You brought it up first, Chuck."

"Oh, have we moved on to that, now? Shall we be forever mistaking my name for something it is not? Shall I need to beat you about the head with the business end of this script?"

Tom studied the building without comment.

"Eighty floors, would you say?" Tom finally ventured to ask.

"Oh, I thought you were going to say it was tall." Still looking at the script.

"For this neighborhood, anyway."

"According to the script," Aiden said, shielding his eyes with it, looking up, "the spider should be about sixty floors up." They watched the building as if they expected at any moment for it to faint from vertigo.

"Yeah, I still can't see it."

"Neither can I."

They watched the building.

"Thirty floors, huh?" Tom said.

"Sixty, sorry."

"Are you sure?"

"Pretty sure."

"Don't have to walk, do we?"

"I sincerely hope not."

They found the elevator without too much fuss or difficulty, dragging the rolling-case along behind them. They were then redirected to the service elevator without too much additional fuss or confrontation. Service elevator looked as if it had been sprayed with whitewash, and then people had done barefoot handstands to see just how far up the walls they could leave grease-stained footprints. Doors parted on the sixty-third or sixty-fourth floor; they really weren't bothering to pay that much attention. Service hallway finally merged with the main hall. Much to their surprise, they still hadn't attracted an escort, and that included the fact they had been turned away from the regular elevators.

They entered one office, following the vague and uncritical directions of the script. There was no door. Letters branded into the wall had named the office, but that hadn't really drawn their attention. It could have been lawyers. It could have been accountants, financial advisers, marketers, spiritual consultants, or underwater basket weavers. It really didn't matter.

The hall had simply expanded, bulging out to one side. There was a counter, like an overly elaborate reception desk, and there was even a receptionist. At least they had given him a chair to while away the long twilight hours defending the frontier.

"Central Services," Aiden said by way of introduction. Both Tom and Aiden touched fingers to foreheads as if they would flourish imaginary hats. "You may not be aware, but the building is having issues with one of the window washers. And we think it is stranded just beyond the edge of your office."

"Oh, yes," the young man said. "It's been quite the object of conversation."

"Ah, so you have noticed it," Tom said.

"Hard not to. Work has ground to a screeching halt. In fact, the only reason I'm not gawking at it along with everyone else is because we've been expecting your arrival."

"Well, we're glad we are in the right place," Aiden said. "Sorry to keep you waiting."

"Oh, no bother, it's like a bank holiday." Slipping off his chair, walking to the end of the counter. "This way, gentlemen."

They followed the receptionist. Wall beyond the counter involved a nice trick of perspective and architecture. There wasn't so much a door as a twist of wall and hallway, and suddenly they found themselves in a spacious office. After that, it would have been simple enough to follow the voices. Receptionist could have easily returned to his post, but like he had said, he wanted to see the show.

There were far too many people trying to cram into one office, removing the last irrationally lingering shred of doubt that they had found the right place. A conference room would have helped to hold the throng, but that would have been far too much to hope for. People parted for Tom and Aiden with only the greatest reluctance, and the two of them did not so much walk to the window as push, shove, and generally pretend to be a snowplow in order to reach the view. The rolling-case hadn't stood a chance of making it into the room and had been left all on its lonesome in the hallway.

The spider was large, multi-legged, and appeared to be clinging desperately to the window as if it had finally made the mistake of looking down. What could be seen of the machine looked to be about the size of a fancy office desk made from dark and expensive woods that had been polished to within an inch of their previously uneventful lives. Naturally, the spider was at the top and least accessible part of the window.

"Got a signal?" Tom said.

"Yeah," Aiden replied, typing, studying the script.

"Can't wait to hear that preliminary diagnosis." Tom pressed as close to the window as he could, trying to look up at the machine poised on the opposing side. "Doesn't appear to be caught on anything. Nothing obvious from here anyway." Continued to study what he could of it. "Wonder what the denizens on the next floor up think."

"Is it getting ready to jump?" the receptionist said, having managed to push his way to their side.

"I rather doubt that," Tom said. "How's it going over there, Charlie?"

"It's responding well to queries and diagnostics," Aiden said with eyes only for the script, having chosen to ignore Tom's choice of names. "It appears to be convinced it's caught on something but cannot figure out what."

"Phantom limb syndrome?"

"I'm actually leaning that way, yeah. Flushing the short-term cache may fix the problem right quick."

"Oh, don't say that. Rather anticlimactic that would be."

"Yeah, well, anything that keeps us away from the great outdoors." Typing, reading, scrolling displays. "If I can just manage to get through this experience without needing to venture to the other side of that window."

The spider made a lurching jump as if it had been startled by a hang-gliding hippopotamus. The window vibrated. People reacted, voicing various expressions of consternation and surprise as if they expected the robot to come crashing through the window and turn the room into its own private mosh pit.

"Well, that was unexpected," Aiden said, studying the window with grave intensity. Script momentarily forgotten in his hands.

"You think you could manage not to do that again?" Tom said.

"Well, I'll give it a try."

"I would hope for a little better than that."

"You're assuming I know what I did the first time." Scrolling, reading. "Yeah, I think I perceive one issue that could make flushing the cache or otherwise rebooting from here rather a poor choice of options."

Spider started to scramble at the window as if it was slowly slipping toward infinity and was trying desperately to put off that descent into the twilight realm for as long as possible.

"Don't leave us in suspense, here," Tom said, trying to look straight up the window. "Wish I could get a better look at the next level."

"Spider's lost its tether."

"Has it now." Turning, looking at Aiden.

"Yeah, why it's so reluctant to properly investigate whatever has it stuck to that one spot. Not losing its grip and plummeting to the street below is programmed deep into its code."

"Quite understandable."

"Even I understand that," the receptionist said.

The spider seemed to grow confident in its new grip on the side of the building and stopped thrashing about.

"Well, that seems to have improved things," Tom said.

"Wish I could do better from here." Looking back to the script.

"The day is young, and the air is fresh with the promise of adventure."

"You're not talking me into repelling down the side of the building, thank you very much." Aiden took several small but noticeable steps backward.

"Building's got a spider-monkey."

"You asking me?" the receptionist said.

"Did it sound like I was asking you?" Gesturing toward Aiden. "I'm talking to Mister Excitement over here."

"Oh, now you're trying to get me onto the roof." Pointing with the script. "Only one small step between the roof and a quick descent to the spider's level."

"Well, yeah, I knew that as soon as you said the tether was gone." Looking back to the window. "You did, too."

"I'll never admit to such a thing." Looked back to the script. "Okay, yeah, the roof beckons. The spider-monkey awaits."

"Feel like being our eyes?" Tom said to the receptionist. "What's your name, anyway?"

"Harvey."

"I answer to Tom, myself. Think you could manage to keep your eyes on the spider while we work a little more remotely?"

"Best show in town."

"Beautiful, you're conscripted," Tom said. "Now, if I could just interest you in slaving your eyes to me."

They both took out their phones, spent a quick moment typing commands, and then flashed the phones in close proximity. Aiden took a moment to flash his own phone. While ocular cameras had not been universally adopted by the general population at large—something about sticking a camera in the eyeball—they were used by the vast majority of the population and were actually required of professions such as receptionist and service representative.

"Hey, I've got picture," Tom said, studying his phone. "Now, just keep your eyes riveted on the spider when we give the word."

It took almost as much effort to escape the room as had been required to enter it. Aiden and Tom retrieved the rolling-case and made their way slowly if not always directly back to the service elevator.

"Whole room full of people determined to keep their eyes on the show," Aiden said, studying the script, scrolling displays.

"Yeah, but our boy Harvey was the most likely to be kicked out of the room. Now, they've got to let him stay."

"Again, not really my point."

"Of course not."

"Whole room full of people, lots of eyes. Lots of angles on the show—How do I request roof access on this thing, anyway?"

"Try your phone."

"Not a chance." Scrolling, scrolling, trying not to shake the script. "It's got to be a formal request."

"Well, you're not going to get very far with a command window." Tom made a grab for the script while trying to read over Aiden's shoulder.

"Yeah, I know." Holding the script away. "But I don't want to have to reestablish the connection to the spider. Trying to do some kind-of split screen thing here."

"Wait, you haven't figured out how to keep multiple screens running at the same time? You could even have more than one command window open, you know. It's not that hard."

"Yeah, yeah."

"Just like trying to walk and chew gum at the same time."

"You know what would be a big help? Why not try contacting a building rep on your phone while I'm busy here?"

"I told you," Tom said. "It has to be through formal channels."

"Balderdash, did you not just mere moments ago suggest that I use my phone?"

"I never."

"Oh, you did so ever suggest that very thing." Typing. "Here we go. Requesting access."

"Yeah?"

"Split screen and everything."

"Walk and chew gum, man," Tom said. "Walk and chew gum."

The service elevator arrived while they were waiting, beeping quietly for their attention. They crossed over, taking turns flashing their phones to the elevator's scanner, and then they waited.

"Natives must be getting restless," Tom said. "How long you figure before they finally kick Harvey out of the office?"

"As long as it's long enough."

The elevator beeped once, and the doors closed.

"About time."

The doors finally opened again with a blast of cold air to swirl around them and set their spines to fluttering with foreshadowings of doom. They ventured out slowly, finding themselves in a bit of an alcove. Ceiling was lower than anticipated, and they had difficulty maneuvering the rolling-case. At the edge of the alcove, they found connections for safety cables and had to spend a long moment attaching harnesses and belts, which they refused to admit they probably should have done in the taller space provided by the elevator.

"I like how the building people are letting us do this stunt solo," Tom said. "You'd think they would be ever so slightly concerned we might scratch the paint or something."

"Yeah, you'd think so." Aiden took out his phone and snapped several very dramatic shots of the city.

Oh, look where I am now, he typed, sending the pictures to Lynn.

"Makes its own kind of sense, I guess." Tom was looking out from the relative safety of the alcove to the great wide world beyond. Aiden returned the phone to his pocket. "Activating the spider-monkey to go after its big brother isn't exactly advanced theoretical physics."

"No. No, it's not."

"So the whole point of summoning us to this little business of pushing a big red button on the side of a box has more to do with the location of that button and box."

"The thought had crossed my mind," Aiden said, watching the buildings across the street as if he expected them to reach over the gap and drag them kicking and screaming into the sky.

Having given the immediate vicinity of the roof more preliminary attention than it probably deserved, they ventured out onto the top of the building. The sun was bright, and the wind, while invigorating, was

intense. Made them want to take great care while traversing the roof. The view, while staggering, was not
really the kind of thing they wanted to focus too closely
on at the moment. There was a bit of a lip to the roof, as
if the architects had spent a few minutes considering
the fact maintenance people would occasionally need
to be atop the structure. At the very edge of the roof,
and leaning more than just a little over the side, was
the anchor station that should have been attached to
the spider. Tom and Aiden made their way over to it
and with a very great deal of reluctance peeked over
the edge.

"Well, of course, the floors are sloped," Tom said,
all but shouting to be heard over the wind. Instead of
the classic box shape or other configuration that might
have worked to their advantage, the top dozen or so
floors of the building twisted and tapered like an overzealous corkscrew. "You can't even see the spider from
here."

"And I repeat. I'm not going over the side, tether or
no." Looking to the anchor station. "There's a second
spider on standby in here."

"Oh, that's exactly what we need. Think the building
people will go for it?"

"I don't really think spiders are designed to do field
repairs on their brethren, even though—" Aiden studied the anchor, popping the display. "—they really
should."

"It wouldn't work. No maneuverability. Besides,
what would the civilians think?" Pointing, mocking.
"Hey, those machines are humping."

"Yeah, yeah." Eyes for the display. "Okay, this thing
does have a spider-monkey."

"Told you."

"I'm sure you did." Tapping commands. Something
within the unfathomable innards of the spider anchor

shuddered as if woken from a profoundly deep slumber with a cattle-prod. "Harvey still in position?"

"Like he's going to get bored." Tom lifted his phone, typed. "Hey man, get with the eyeballs devoted to your duty."

"Oh, we are all manner of kind when dealing with the conscripted soul by remote control."

"Got to learn their place."

Aiden lifted the script, compared its display to what the spider anchor was telling him. Nodded his head and then proceeded to juggle his phone and the script. Finally got the screen unfolded from his phone and attached to the side of the script. He saw Harvey look at the message and then start typing.

"No, don't tell us you're going to look. Just do it. We will know, man. We will know."

"Hey, you should call him," Tom said. "Let him know."

"Oh, yes, keeping his eyes on the phone and away from what we want him to see. Productive. I told you we should have gone for multiple angles."

"Too late now, man."

Aiden returned his attention to the script, typing commands. Another tremor rumbled through the anchor station, and then the spider-monkey detached itself from the main body of the anchor. The monkey was maybe three feet tall and looked like a seriously disgruntled mad scientist had taken a multi-segmented monkey and a disreputable ant and beaten them together with a rather large hammer. Taking barely a moment to check its bearings, the spider-monkey took a flying leap off the side of the building, trailing tether and a web of complicated cables behind it. Machine seemed to sprout gliding fins as it sailed out and away from the building, as if it had suddenly realized that it didn't actually have a parachute and really should consider the situation it had just gotten itself into. Spider-monkey disappeared quickly from view.

Tom and Aiden turned to the view from Harvey's eyes. Aiden glancing as often as he dared at the rapidly changing displays on the script. The spider-monkey appeared in Harvey's vision, running frantically across the surface of the wall toward the spider.

"Contact," Aiden said.

Spider did not take kindly to the smaller machine suddenly making its acquaintance, and the window shuddered as the two met. The video skipped and danced as various people in the office started once again to wonder if the show was worth it.

"Don't bail on us now, man," Tom said. "We need that visual record."

"He can't hear you. Call him."

"Yeah, right, he'll look away from the window again. Last thing we need is a preview of the message we'll be reading just a moment later."

"Well, progress here. Looks like the monkey's almost got the backup tether attached. Now, if only it'll attach the secondary safety lines, too."

"Don't rush things, man. We want that backup tether well and truly attached. None of this primitive mucking about for us."

They watched the view from Harvey's perspective, and it quickly became clear that the monkey was working above the level of the window. They would have had better luck or possibly just a better view of the top of the spider if they had gone one floor above their chosen office.

"Seriously, what are we doing here?" Tom said, hugging himself against the wind.

"We're doing the rugged and manly thing so the local building denizens don't have to."

"Yeah?"

"Takes nerves of steel to venture out above the world like this." Looking up. "We could touch the sky."

"Yeah, well, don't scratch it. They'll charge us extra for that."

"You break it, you buy it?"

"Scrape the sky." Tom looked back to his phone. "That doesn't actually make a whole lot of sense, you know."

"But scratching the sky is self-evident, is it?"

"Sky-scratcher."

"Catchy."

"Yeah, still can't see anything from this view." Watching his phone. "How's the script look?"

"Making progress," Aiden said. "It's got the backup tether attached and a secondary line. About time to flush the cache."

"Let's not be hasty." Tom looked to the anchor station's display. Tapped commands. "Okay, yeah, I'm seeing good things here, too."

"Yeah?"

"Oh, yeah, anchor is registering both lines."

"Guess we're ready to scare the bloody bejesus out of everybody in that office."

Tom looked back to his phone.

"I almost wish we were there," he said, "or at least had audio."

"If there's a stampede."

"Still rather be there." Held up a loop of his safety line. "Oh, yeah, this is so much more reassuring than a stampede."

"Taking your word for that—Okay, yeah, I would rather be within." Aiden typed commands, and they both looked to the view from Harvey's perspective, which quickly became hard to follow.

The spider had done a fair bit of stamping and experimental leaps away from the window on its new tether and safety lines. The unruly office denizens had reacted more or less as expected. The view remained impossible to follow for some few minutes and finally yielded a good view of the window again as Harvey emerged from beneath a drafting table in the corner.

"Good man, kept his cool."

"Corner table was a good choice."

"Spider looks happy," Tom said.

"If only Harvey would stand still long enough to just look at it."

"He's fine. What's the script say?"

"Huh?" Looking back to the displays and readouts, typing, scrolling. "Yeah, we're in business."

"We're good?"

"Yeah, I think we're good."

"Right, probably best to let the spider and its own personal monkey hang out a bit on the wall. Get its vertical legs back under it again, so to speak."

"Oh, yeah, I figure we're good for another long stretch of just monitoring progress here." Typing, watching the view from his phone's unfolded screen against the side of the script. "What in the nine billion names of hell is that?"

"Oh, don't say such things." Looking at Aiden who had eyes only for the script. "You're going to make me think that Murphy has struck in a moment here."

Aiden said nothing.

"Good old Murphy," Tom said.

"The results are in."

"Okay." He watched Aiden as if he expected him to start beating the script against the side of the spider anchor with great gusto and enthusiasm.

"Priority override," Aiden said, reading, scrolling. "We're recalled to the home office."

"We can't just leave our babies unattended. Half an hour to make sure everything is in order here."

"Yeah, but then duty calls. R&D has rendered a verdict on the tourist."

"Oh, yes? The one we smashed up good not that very long ago?"

"Well, we've just had so many to choose from it's hard to keep track."

"It was invigorating."

"Yes, it was."

"Invigorating."

"Yeah, well." Holding the script out. "You're going to love this part."

Tom held out his hand as if he would touch commands or otherwise scroll the display, reading.

"Oh, you have got to be kidding," he said.

CHAPTER SIX

In which Tom and Aiden learn a valuable lesson about the finer points of diplomacy.

Central Services maintained several different levels of conference room. They started at the low end with spaces that doubled as break rooms in need of a good spring cleaning. The tables were chipped. The walls were faded and unwashed, and the chairs sagged, which may be hard to imagine but quickly becomes clear when actually seen. At the other end of the spectrum were conference rooms that were clearly designed to impress and intimidate guests. The tables were real polished wood, or an imitation of such high quality as to make no nevermind. The chairs were plush leather. The walls were dark, neutral colors that sucked all extraneous sound out of the very air. Central Services Field Representatives seldom if ever saw these high-end rooms, only hearing stories about them, which they never questioned or doubted in any way. They just knew that such spaces must exist. It was the only thing that made any sense.

The room that Tom and Aiden found themselves waiting in did not come anywhere near the opulent end of the spectrum. The table was nice to the point of being impressive, but it was quite clearly made of some synthetic imitation wood. The chairs were functional and hard without actually being uncomfortable. They weren't really comfortable, either, which was a fact that Tom and Aiden were failing to come to terms

104

with. The air was quiet, as if it had not moved or stirred from the gentle touch of a breeze in many years.

Tom and Aiden were also as quiet as they could manage. It was the room. The space just sucked the voices from out of their very heads and left them nothing with which to speak, or reason to do so. Besides, for all they knew, they were being monitored, their voices recorded for posterity.

At long last, Foxglove joined them, script tucked under his arm. With him were two gentlemen in casual attire, which they carried as if they were dressed in the most expensive business suits known to man. The air, which was already oppressive, seemed to run silently screaming from the room at the approach of these two casually conservative gentlemen. They held notebooks, actual notebooks, with pages and pages of paper that would need to be flipped through one sheet at a time. There would be no searching, sorting, or skipping. Pages would actually need to be scanned and flipped. Things written on them would stay. Erasing would leave traces and marks of what had once been.

"These are the Service Reps who filed the report," Foxglove said by way of introduction, gesturing toward the two of them. "Aiden Charles and Tim Cane."

Tom and Aiden made no effort to touch fingers to forehead. If they had been wearing hats, they would have most assuredly left them on their heads. The two severe gentlemen made no indication they were even aware that anybody else was in the room.

"These are—" Foxglove said, turning to Tom and Aiden, but looking at the other men. "These are Xavier Rosewater and Paul Nottingham."

"Poll."

"I'm sorry?" There was no answer. "Sorry, Poll Nottingham." Again, there was no answer. "From the Tourist Board," Foxglove said, looking to Tom and Aiden, who returned the grim stares of the damned. "Gentle-men, shall we begin?" Gesturing across the table.

With great reluctance, as if every motion was a tire-some chore that they had no choice but to complete, Rosewater and Nottingham selected chairs facing Aid-en and Tom as if they were opposing nations engaged in intense negotiations.

"The first order of business," Foxglove began to say, quickly drifting into silence as Nottingham placed a small recorder on the table.

They watched in stunned and strangely hypnotized silence as Nottingham touched a side of the recorder and twisted a panel with his thumb. A little green glow slipped into existence upon the top of the device. No-body spoke.

"The report," Foxglove said, voice drifting, pausing, looking across the table. "Research and Development has completed their examination of the sweeper that Field Service Reps Charles and Cane retrieved from the incident site." Foxglove examined the script in his hands, touching, scrolling displays. "It is R&D's con-sidered opinion that the unit had developed a severe higher computational malfunction in its central brain that rendered it incapable of continuing in its designed function."

"That's one way of putting it," Aiden said. Foxglove glared at him.

"The report goes on to state." Looking back at his script. "The Field Service Representatives acted in a wholly appropriate manner. Their actions were justi-fied."

"They smashed it to bits," Rosewater said, chasing all other voices from the room, leaving even the linger-ing ambient noises to die suddenly on the floor.

"Well, only one of us actually smashed it into little

bitty pieces," Tom said, muttering. His voice barely rising above the level of the tabletop.

"They smashed it with a hammer."

"Just trying to be accurate here." Shrug of shoulders.

"The record is incomplete." Rosewater began to flip pages in his notebook. "The post-incident interview with the resident is missing."

"We covered that in the waiver request," Aiden said.

"In which it is clear that no effort was made to interview the resident about the incident at all." Nottingham tapped the closed notebook he had brought with him as if to show he could back up his statement with an easy reference if events should warrant.

"Well, we were kind of busy."

"We had to make sure the owner was okay with our actions and would accept the replacement sweeper," Tom said. "Launching into an impartial interview to evaluate our performance would only have aggravated the situation."

"And that's not even getting into the conflict of interest having the service reps who fielded the incident gather feedback on their own performance," Aiden said.

"As you said, only one of you performed the actual destruction of the unit," Rosewater said. "The other remained impartial."

"Performed the destruction? What does that even mean?"

"It means there is information missing on your performance." Touching the notebook spread open before him. "Confirmation of your actions from the resident."

"Justification," Nottingham said.

"Justification?" Aiden spread his arms, leaning back as if he might appeal to the sky.

"Justification of your actions." Rosewater looked

to them. "Was it really necessary to smash the unit to bits?"

"Yes, it was necessary," Tom said. "It's what you do with tourists."

"You smash them." Aiden put his fist on the table.

"Their actions were appropriate," Foxglove said. "The report shows that."

Rosewater said nothing for a long moment as if organizing his thoughts into an educational lesson plan that he could impart onto them.

"While the unit in question may not have pain receptors as we understand them," he began.

"Of all the rot," Aiden said, appealing once more to the sky.

"We must take into consideration how the newly independent machine experienced the situation." Rosewater watched Aiden as if studying a child. "Is it frightened?"

"Scared?" Nottingham said.

"Angry?"

"That's anthropomorphizing the little blighter," Tom said. "Got to be careful about that."

Rosewater turned slowly to study him.

"You just called it a blighter," Nottingham said.

"I never can get that word quite right," Aiden said, leaning toward Tom with eyes only for Rosewater and Nottingham.

"What?" Tom looked only to the Board of Tourism representatives.

"An-*throw*-pour...An-*thorough*-par...Anthropomorphizing."

"Really?"

"Yeah, it just doesn't roll off the tongue."

"Well, I'm pretty sure you just managed it."

"Really, you think so?"

"Yeah, anthro-pornography. No, wait, that's not it."

"There were other courses of action available to you," Rosewater said as if they had not been speaking.

Tom and Aiden sat in silence for a good long moment as if they were reviewing the incident in their heads.

"No," Aiden finally said.

"Not really any other action," Tom said.

"You could have captured the unit."

"Taken it into custody," Nottingham said.

"What?" Aiden tried not to laugh or otherwise choke on the word.

"You can't take it into custody," Tom said, voice rising. "It's a bloody tourist."

"Strong feelings about tourists can cloud judgment," Rosewater said with a quiet, level voice that was not quite a monotone.

"You can't risk contamination. You have to put the tourist down." Sweep of arm. "End of story."

"So tourism is airborne now, is it?"

"Yes," Aiden said.

"In a manner of speaking," Tom said. "The vast majority of modern appliances, including this model of sweeper, is equipped with wireless capabilities. It's how we communicate with them." Pointing at Foxglove's script. "Give them orders."

"How they communicate with us," Aiden said. "How they spread the infection."

"You don't know that," Nottingham said.

"You know? You're right." Raising his hands. "You're absolutely right. We don't know how tourism is spread. We don't even know if tourism is catching, but we can't take that chance."

"Think of it," Tom said, "like a rabid dog."

"Anthropomorphizing," Rosewater said.

"It's an analogy."

"Clouding your judgment."

"There's nothing wrong with our judgment," Aiden said.

"I think we're drifting away from the point of the conversation," Foxglove said, and all eyes slowly turned to look at him. "Was the action justified?"

"Yes," Tom said.

"Said so yourself," Aiden said, pointing.

"Your actions," Nottingham said, drawing everyone's attention, "seemed impulsive and unreasoned to the point of being reckless. Was there compelling reason to smash the unit right there and then?"

"Yes, actually," Aiden said. "It's in the report and everything. The tourist was behaving erratically to the point of posing an imminent threat to the owner."

"What kind of threat?"

"It was destructive. It was threatening."

"That's right," Tom said. "It bit Charlie."

"Bit him?" Rosewater said. "Bit Aiden Charles?"

"In a manner of speaking," Aiden said.

"Very much like a rabid dog." Tom leaned back in his chair, crossing his arms.

"The tourist had modified itself, you see. Converted its little manipulator hands into sharp claws. Used these to intimidate and attack." Gestured toward the notebooks. "This was in the report."

"Your account was in the report, yes," Rosewater said. Eyes drifting across the pages of the notebook spread before him. "Your version of events. Nothing from the resident."

"Here we go," Aiden said.

"We covered that." Tom pointed at Foxglove.

"There's nothing from the resident about the sequence of events," Nottingham said. "Did she honestly feel that her life was in danger?"

Aiden slowly leaned forward as if he might attempt to tower over the table and intimidate the pages of the notebook spread before them. They watched him quietly.

"Why not ask her," he said.

"We intend to."

"That's the standard, is it?" Tom said. "Life or death?"

"Yes," Rosewater said, quietly, as if surprised this actually needed to be stated out loud.

"What about destruction of property? What about—" Waving his hand as if trying to shape words, grasping them out of the air. "Hostility? Openly hurting people?"

"You did a good job with the destruction of property, I understand."

"Oh, you understand."

"It's in the report, as you said."

"Oh, that part you believe." Tom slapped the table, if lightly, and leaned back in his chair.

"We want to ensure that all policies were followed," Rosewater said. "Standards were maintained. Representatives acted humanely and with the best interests of all parties maintained."

"Humanely," Tom muttered. "And you used 'maintain' twice. Show a little imagination and creativity, why don't you."

"We want to ensure that the report is both accurate and truthful."

"I'm sure," Aiden muttered without looking at them.

"This will involve re-interviewing," Rosewater said, "or should that be interviewing the resident, for a full accounting of events."

"There goes our customer service rating."

"Something you should be very concerned with."

"Oh, really, even when I have no control over it? The resident, as you keep calling her, will not react well to your line of questioning." Turning to Foxglove. "Are we the only people around here who receive customer service training?"

"Tact and discretion will be utilized," Nottingham said. "We are not devoid of concern for the resident."

"No, it's just secondary to the nonexistent feelings of the tourist."

"Your open hostility toward the unit will be an important part of our evaluation of the incident and the events described in your report."

"The malfunctioning unit," Tom said. "We're all agreed on that, right?"

"We will evaluate the incident," Rosewater said, gathering up his notebook, standing. "You will be hearing from us."

Nottingham followed his fellow's example, and they both left the room.

"Of all the ungrateful nonsense," Tom said.

"They're going to upset and intimidate our client." Aiden turned toward Foxglove.

Foxglove did not answer, glowering at them, and pointed at the center of the table where the small recording device remained, its green light glowing softly to itself.

Tom stood, vibrating as if he might spontaneously phase out of this plane of existence. He turned, moving, storming to the door, flung it open.

"Hey," he shouted. "You immortal geniuses forgot something!"

Nottingham finally reentered the room, crossing to the table, and picked up the recorder, flicking off the green light in the process. He left the room without saying a word.

"Yeah, he really forgot, I'm sure," Tom said, pushing the door closed.

"You know," Foxglove said, leaning back in his chair, resting his hands behind his head, "this new breed of

Tourist Board representative is much easier to deal with than past iterations."

"Really?"

"Oh, yes." Standing slowly. "Okay, everyone, good job. Back to work."

"Oh, good, so we're not suspended or anything pending the outcome of the investigation?"

"Yeah, nice try," Foxglove said, "but no."

"Tuttle," Aiden said. They both looked at him.

"Come on, Harry Tuttle, seriously?" Tom said. "We're still on about that?"

"Freedom from such nonsense. Freedom from bureaucracy. Get in. Get out. Do the job."

"Okay, I know I keep bringing it up."

"You know that's more urban myth than fact, right?" Foxglove said.

"Did whatever he wanted," Aiden said.

"We don't even know what industry he was in. Wasn't a Central Services employee, that's for sure."

"And he just wanted to get the job done."

"Look," Foxglove said.

"Doesn't really matter where he worked or how long ago," Tom said. "Sure, stories grow in the telling. I get that. But you're missing the point."

"Am I?"

"He quit."

"That," Foxglove said quietly, slowly, dragging the silence out, "I suppose he did."

Aiden stood.

"In the meantime," Foxglove said, looking to both of them, "we've got customers to support. Great rights to wrong. Tourists to fight."

"Rights to wrong?"

"If I asked you to, yes. Now, get back to work."

* * *

It was Aiden's turn to be sprawled on the couch when Lynn came home. The entertainment wall showing little more than white noise. The weather forecast was displayed. The news was drifting slowly past. Headlines chasing each other toward the top of the screen, each trying desperately to be on top as if engaged in an undeclared game of King of the Mountain.

"Hey," Lynn said by way of greeting. "You beat me for a change. When does that ever happen." Removed her coat, left it on a hook by the door. Saw where Aiden's coat had slumped to the floor, having lost yet another fight with gravity and its grip on a chair. "Not even a note that you were kicking it early." Removed her shoes. One foot helping to pull the other free. Repeat. Left them next to the little shoe-rack by the door. "I got the one message. Nice view. Suppose I shouldn't be surprised you were able to take early retirement."

She crossed to the couch, found space next to where Aiden was sprawled, put her feet up on the coffee table. They watched various news headlines fight for supremacy in silence as if the events required intense focus and concentration.

"You want to talk about it?" Lynn finally said, looking toward him. "What were you doing up there, anyway?"

"Fixing a sweeper."

"A sweeper? On the roof?"

"No, wait." Hand to his forehead. "A spider. Great big machine that clings to the sides of buildings and generally maintains them."

"Oh, yeah, I've seen those. Not the full-scale skyscraper variety, but we've got their younger cousins at university."

Aiden didn't answer as if any information that needed to be imparted had been properly conveyed. Kept his eyes on the screen.

"Dramatic?" she asked. "Traumatic? Hanging from the very side of a really tall building?"

"Nothing so exciting or dramatic," he said, eyes drifting from the wall, looking at her. "Made for a nice picture. Thought you might like it."

"Which it did. Filled me with a desire for story-time."

"Had a run-in with the Board of Tourism."

"Never!"

"Oh, yes," he said. "Had a sit-down meeting with them and everything."

"On the roof?"

"No."

"Was it their idea?"

"Nothing of the kind. Tourist Board meeting was later."

"I'm so sorry. Tourist Board must have been more traumatic than the great outdoors and open sky."

"Well, it was—" Hand fluttered as if chasing words. "Improved. My supervisor was right. New breed of representative. They're trying for an ounce of respectability."

"Oh, yeah? Fire and brimstone, torches and toothpicks?"

"Much improved over that. Wanted to know if the tourist had suffered."

"No!"

"Oh, yes, shows what they know. As if the machine has a central nervous system. Pain receptors. Abstract concept of life and death."

"Existential angst about the meaning of life and a poor little heart to ponder the point of it all."

"I know, right?" Aiden rubbed his fingers over his face. "Much improved over what they used to be like, but they still need some honest engineering and robotics developers to join the board."

"Yeah, that's really going to happen."

"It might if they can manage to improve their image. Start talking like they actually know what they're talking about."

"Get enough people who know flesh from synthetics and the Tourist Board might just reason its way out of existence."

"Or at least be useful. A group that actually monitored tourist contamination and set standards for containment. Yeah, that would be useful."

"ITRC oversight," Lynn said. "Yeah, I could see that. Our Lady Behr would just die a happy death to be part of it."

"Who?"

"Jennifer Behr. I've mentioned her before. Pseudo-intelligence expert."

"Oh, yeah, yeah, yeah. Thought her name was Jessica for some reason."

"Which is much ado about nothing."

"In the meantime, we've still got to deal with fear and intimidation tactics. They're going after the resident—I mean, owner. Going to interview her."

"No, you mean the cute one?"

"Yeah, her, with the face and hair." Waved his hand with a flourish as if showing off her face and assets. "Well, sort of like yours."

"The poor thing doesn't even know what's coming."

"And then we'll learn if our report passes muster. Can't imagine what it'll mean if they decide our actions were unjustified. Treated the tourist with poor or malicious intent."

"They haven't changed all that much, I see."

"Got me thinking."

"Not a big surprise."

"Tuttle, Harry Tuttle. I think I mentioned him before."

"Well, yeah, I may work for university, but even I have heard of him."

"Repudiation of bureaucracy." Leaned his head back on the couch. "Though. Something my manager said. Legends grow in the telling. Stories of Harry Tuttle going underground have been around for a long time. No reason to believe he was even in the robotics customer service sector like me."

"That's true. If he worked for Central Services, no reason why I would have ever heard of him. Well, except you, but I first heard the legend of Harry Tuttle long before that."

"Doesn't really matter what bureaucracy. The point being that he rejected bureaucratic rules and whatnot. Said stuff it all. Went his own way."

"Why he's remembered."

"Showed you can still get stuff done without kowtowing to pointless rules and regulations." Lifted Lynn's feet from the coffee table. Pulled them to his lap and began to rub. Interfered with his sprawl. Interfered with her sprawl, too, but she didn't seem to mind.

"I wonder if he came out of the early days of the co-op software development movement." Settling against the arm of the couch so that her feet were properly situated for maximum massage benefit.

"That," he said, rubbing her feet slowly, "actually makes a whole lot of sense."

"It would certainly explain why the stories about him spread so far and wide."

"Legend grows in the telling. But how did he support himself? That's what I want to know."

"Oh, you're just wondering that now? Think about it. Quit his job. Working outside the bounds of accepted rules and regulations, but he kept working."

"Okay."

"How did he get paid?"

"Freelance." Shrug of shoulders. "What I always figured. Why management hates him so much. Why so many of the stories basically make him a hunted man."

"Legends grow in the telling. Maybe he never quit his job."

"Sacrilege."

"Makes sense if he really was involved in the development of the co-op movement. Wrote a lot about it. You know most co-op software development happens in the off-hours, right?"

"In the early days, it wasn't even called co-op development."

"I know."

"Had another name. An open, voluntary-sounding name. Something, something cool and impressive." Waved his hand about.

"Hey," Lynn said, kicking gently at him with her free foot.

"Those were the days." Hand rejoined the other in its work.

"You were dabbling with co-op development not that many years ago, as I recall."

"Yeah, well, only so many hours in the day."

"Don't knock it. You were good at it. Probably why we're so aware of the Harry Tuttle stories."

"Those stories were obviously of long ago and far away. There's nothing to it now."

"Satisfaction in a job well done."

"Empty satisfaction."

"What a thing to say."

"No, really, I suppose if you cared about the project. The goals, but so much is just empty coding. Nothing to it."

"You were into it."

"That's before I saw behind the curtain. Learned how co-operative development works."

"Lost your youthful idealism, did you?" Reaching toward him.

"Like I said, if you cared, I suppose, but so much is already done. Co-op's been around for years and years. Everything that needed developing has been. What's left? Refining for the latest devices and platforms? How much of that is even co-operative? Everything's proprietary."

"Well, you've got me there. Nobody talks about it like they used to. Phones certainly don't use co-op software."

"Oh, it's worse than that. You know these companies all took from the great pool of co-op development and claimed bits for their own. Said they customized it just enough that they could declare it patentable."

"Yeah, they talk like that all the time at university."

"Take and make secret. Never sharing." Shaking his head. "What's left?"

"Must be something. Volunteer co-op software development still exists. People still talk about it."

"You know why they still talk about it, right?" Looking at her. "It's grandstanding. Showing off. My code renders 0.2% faster than industry standard."

"Anything can be turned into a competition." Shrug of shoulders.

"Oh, they're just hoping to be discovered. Scooped up by some big software development firm or other."

"Cut-throat industry."

"You know how many programmers it actually takes to build something right?"

"I'm guessing fewer than I might normally expect."

"You have to hope to join one that just wants to vacuum up the coders so nobody else can have them."

"Dare to dream."

"So they just show off. Not actually trying to accomplish anything useful in co-op development land. Just be noticed. Vacuumed up."

"So they don't have to join the ranks of customer service representatives like us, huh?"

"Yeah." Took a deep breath as if pulling at the dregs of his soul. "Customer service representatives like us."

"I actually like my job, you know?"

Tried to smile. "I know."

"Most of the time, anyway." Another shrug of shoulders. "Oh, hey, you'll never believe. One of the super-geniuses discussed the upcoming Ape Fights by phone."

"Never!"

"Believe it, ever," she said. "Made me so angry. Heard about it in the morning meeting. All of ITRC is supposed to be on the lookout for scuttlebutt on the Ape Fights."

"Well, that kind of complicates things, doesn't it?"

"Had a very long talk with my contact on the issue, and I hope, I really hope things aren't scuttled."

"Depends on how well the message took."

"If they can keep things analog, maybe."

"Oh, is that what we're calling it now? Analog?"

"Yeah, got a problem with that?" Glaring.

"No, actually." Smiling. "Analog. I kind of like it. Downright retro."

"Yeah, well, we just have to count on this most recent round of babies being hip enough to handle analog."

"Hope for the future, yet."

"I was really looking forward to this, you know?" Slapping the back of the couch. "If this is spoiled, I will be very put out. Raised voices and harsh words may be on the horizon."

"Well, let's hope it doesn't come to that."

CHAPTER SEVEN

In which Lynn is required to perform menial tasks around the office and made an impossible offer.

While the Information Technology Resource Center did not have conference rooms or office space of its very own, it did have some space, which was mostly used by the managers and administrative staff. The field representatives were expected to take advantage of whatever random space they could find during those quiet moments of reflection they treasured so much during the course of the day. ITRC also had space for system repairs that could not be done in the field. Routers, processors, scripts, and workstations would be brought into the surgery. Repairs would be performed. Transplants would take place. Formatting and re-installation were often involved.

The surgery was dark and crowded. It was located deep within the confines and subbasements of one of the university's oldest buildings. Space that nobody wanted. Rooms that most managers and university administrators had more than likely completely forgotten even existed. Space that was more often referred to as a dungeon than a surgery or repair suite.

Within these misplaced chambers, Lynn worked on a malfunctioning lab script. The back was off, the script held tight in an elevated vice. Segments and micro-panels were exposed. Whole layers of script paneling and hardware had been lifted free and moved to the side like wafer-thin playing cards. Lynn wore engineering goggles that allowed for an impressive range of magnification. Little lights at the corners of the goggles could shine an equally impressive range of illumination into a surprisingly confined and focused space. The micro-tools used to work on the script were incredibly delicate.

"Marilyn," Hagarlodge said without preamble, causing Lynn to very nearly drop the fine-edged manipulator in her hand.

"Don't call me that."

"It's your name." He threaded the cramped, crowded space to stand before her. "Deal with it."

She ignored him as best she could, which wasn't so much a subtle criticism of his presence as it was the fact that she needed to concentrate while working on the exposed innards of a script. Hagarlodge understood this, saying nothing more but continuing to tower over her.

"What do you want? I'm rather busy," she said.

"Yes, well, nobody asked you to turn off the network or mouth off at the morning meeting."

She didn't answer, continuing her exploration of the finer points of script art and architecture.

"You don't belong down here," he said without warning. The instruments didn't even twitch in her hands.

"It's hell on earth, let me tell you," she said.

"The damp, dark quarters." Looking about. "Enclosed. Claustrophobic."

"Hardly damp, really."

"What?"

"The damp." She looked at him, glancing, then back to the open script. "Bad for the electronics. Quite the opposite."

"Dry, then."

"Oh, very much so. The very air sucks the moisture from your skin. Can't you feel it? Try to spit."

"I shall pass. The electronics, as you say." Looked about the room, again. "I can feel it in my eyes."

"It's the lack of dust. Bad for the electronics. The air tastes funny. It's so clean."

"I hadn't noticed."

"Haven't spent enough time down here then." Began to fold the various panes and panels back together. "Give it time." Glanced back to him. "Surprised you're not wearing a bunny suit."

"A what?"

"Clean suit." Lifted her arm to show off the white, tight-fitting sleeve of her coverall. "Particulate matter. Contamination. Like hospital scrubs but for precision machine work."

"Do they still call them that?"

"Scrubs? I think so. Haven't had reason to ask."

"As for the contamination of our own surgery here." Held out his arms, looked at them. "We'll just have to hope for the best."

"It's fine, I'm sure." Waved in his general direction. "You're standing over there."

Hagarlodge watched her finish closing up the script, remove the engineering goggles, scratch at her forehead with the back of her sleeve.

"You're wasted down here," he finally said.

"And yet, here I am."

"The staff like you. Faculty, well." Shrugged his shoulders. "They tolerate you more than most. Have a way of calming them down."

"They respect the fact I'm not easily intimidated, I suppose."

"As for the students, they definitely respect you."

Lynn transferred the hand holding the goggles to her hip and studied Hagarlodge as if he was selling acres of unspoiled farmland at greatly reduced prices. An investment opportunity that she would simply be a fool to let slip past unrealized, and all she need do was grant him unlimited access to her savings account.

"They confide in you, I'm sure," he said, ignoring her look, studying the walls and shelves, admiring the repair equipment and parts.

"No," was all Lynn said.

He turned his attention to her and then looked away.

"I'm not sure I follow what you mean, Marilyn."

"First of all," pointing with the goggles, "don't call me Marilyn."

"Merlin, then."

"Oh, not even a little."

"It's what they call you, isn't it? Term of endearment and respect."

"Second of all," lowering the goggles to the workbench, "do you know why they respect me? Not just put up with me or run screaming from my sight."

"They've cultivated a healthy level of fear and respect for you."

"That may be true, but the second half is what we're focused on at the moment. Anybody can frighten students. They're like children—They are children."

"True," he said with a passing shrug of shoulders.

"The reason they respect me." Hands pressed to the workbench, leaning forward, looking him straight in the eye. "I don't narc."

"So there is something to the rumor of Ape Fights. Not just chance words typed on a phone."

"You know what?" she said, jerking away from the table as if it had called her mother an unsavory name. "I don't care if there are Ape Fights. That's not the point. I wouldn't break their trust by trying to ferret the truth out of them, and I certainly wouldn't break their hearts by telling you."

"We need to know, Marilyn," he said. "The liability."

"You want them to stop respecting me? Listening to me? Doing whatever the fuck I tell them to do?"

"Your point," crossing his arms, "is quite vividly taken."

"Well, I certainly never mistook you for a stupid person."

Hagarlodge looked about the surgery as if noticing for the first time that the walls were covered with degenerate pornography playing on an infinite loop. Not that they were actually covered by anything so unwelcome as to make him sneer, but the effect was the same.

"Like it down here, do you?"

"Not even a little."

"The kids miss you."

"I'm sure they do."

The workbench stood between them, not making a sound, convinced that the slightest twitch or hiccup on its part might cause the very air to fly apart, shattering into a million fragments of razor-sharp light.

"You should take that script back to the lab when it's ready," Hagarlodge said, nodding at it. "Remember what you're missing locked up down here."

"Thank you for that magnanimous act of charity and generosity."

"Who knows?" he said, turning, facing his back to her. "Maybe they'll feel guilty. Tell us something to spring you from the damp."

"They're smart enough to know it's not damp."

Shrug of shoulders.

"I suppose at that."

* * *

Benjamin Franklin Technical College and Public University had departments beyond Applied Engineering and Robotics. Lynn even worked with some of them. It wasn't exactly by design or any acknowledged pattern, but the various field representatives of ITRC were frequently to the point of almost exclusively assigned to specific buildings and departments within the university. The Department of Theoretical and Computational Physics was located several levels above Applied Engineering and Robotics. Nobody actually tried to work out the number of floors each department utilized. Nobody was even sure where one department ended and the next began. The borders mixing and fluctuating as the departments argued over space and which was entitled to more, without once touching upon the topic of who actually needed what. Decisions frequently came down to whichever side happened to be squatting in any particular lab unit, room, or office at that particular moment. The situation bore more than a passing resemblance to an unannounced game of Go.

Lynn returned the lab script without incident, handing it to a graduate student in a space that bore only a passing resemblance to an Applied Engineering and Robotics laboratory. The types and pieces of machinery were different, and there wasn't quite the resemblance to an iron foundry. There were more workstations, for one thing, and the space just seemed vaguely and strangely cleaner. It just wasn't actually clean.

"Well, there's a face I haven't seen in more days than I care to count," Tamara Rosewater said, having found Lynn in the act of ensuring the student turned the repaired lab script on correctly. It should go without need for comment that Tamara was not related to Xavier Rosewater. Random people are allowed to have the same last name. There's no law against it.

"Yeah, they've got me locked in the dungeon pretty much full-time these days," Lynn replied by way of greeting.

"Whatever did you—So, it's true, isn't it?"

"I neither confirm nor deny whatever it might be that you seem to think may be a true statement. You are a student of theoretical physics. You should know better than that."

"She crashed the network down in Engineering and Robotics," the grad student said. Her name was Elisabeth Dao. By a wild twist of fate and just downright odd coincidence, Elisabeth was Xavier Rosewater's second cousin. They hadn't spoken in years, and Elisabeth had absolutely no idea that he had started working for the Board of Tourism. There would have been raised voices and harsh words had she known.

"I did absolutely nothing of the kind," Lynn said, glaring at Elisabeth, who had the good sense to cower with genuinely unfeigned fright.

"That's not what scuttlebutt over here seems to think." Tamara waved her hand somewhat leisurely in Elisabeth's direction.

"They hacked the router," Lynn said.

"They wouldn't dare."

"Oh, I assure you they would dare many things. None of which could generously be considered wise."

"While I generally have every confidence in them and am prepared to jump to their defense at a moment's notice—Which particular them are we talking about, again?"

"A particularly innovative and intelligent member of Engineering and Robots. I haven't quite narrowed down which one did the deed, but then I haven't really put much effort into trying to figure it out."

"So, it could be student, fact or fowl, could it not?"

"Yeah, couldn't say I actually cared," Lynn said. "Hacked the router. Tripping an automatic deathtrap."

"And the router ate itself."

"Hey, students can be taught."

"Don't lump me in with that crowd," Tamara said. "I'm a postdoctoral teaching fellow. In the union and everything, thank you very much."

"Well, congratulations." Lynn gave her a one-armed hug. "When did that happen?"

"Beginning of the semester. You have been out of the loop. Here I thought I hadn't seen you in days. Time flies when you become a student teacher, I suppose." Ran fingers through her hair. "The things I have to look forward to."

"It hasn't been that long. They don't tell us anything about student teachers or faculty down in ITRC."

"Not an acceptable excuse."

"Well, why didn't you tell me the last half-dozen or so times I've seen you?"

"Oh, fine, blame me for failing to bring it up. Maybe I just assumed you knew and were jealous."

"Jealous? Why in the nine billion names of God would I be jealous of your dramatically increased workload and responsibilities without any kind of corresponding benefits? I've got enough to deal with. You want to know where I've been sequestered away all this time?"

"You've been locked in the dungeon," Tamara said rather matter-of-factly. "Said so yourself."

"Okay, maybe I did at that. Hardly my point."

"You were explaining that you didn't crash the network."

"True, very true."

"Hacked the network," Elisabeth said. Lynn turned, spinning on her heal and swinging around so that she stood shoulder-to-shoulder with Tamara. They both looked down at the graduate student, which was a bit of a trick since they were all standing.

"Oh, listen to her," Lynn said, gesturing toward Elisabeth. "Learned to walk and talk and everything."

"They do grow up so fast," Tamara said. "Makes my heart proud, it does."

"Really?"

"Yes, when you become a teacher, you live for this kind of thing. They learn. They grow. They get things wrong." Tilt of head, glancing at Lynn. "Someone in Applied Engineering and Robotics tried to hack a router, Liz, and the local network did what it's supposed to do under those circumstances."

"It crashed," Lynn said.

"The entire floor? Thought only the local router grid was supposed to go down."

"Oh, it did, but someone had to send a message so I flat-lined the entire floor."

"Never!"

"Oh, yes, for very nearly half an hour. Although." Tilt of head. "My boss would have me believe it was much closer to an hour and a half."

"Well, he would have to say such a thing whether it was abstract truth or not."

"Yes."

"So, dungeon, huh?"

"Yeah, first time I've been allowed up for air in days."

"Sucks."

"That's what I tell them. Although." Lynn looked dramatically this way and that as if checking to see if anyone was eavesdropping. "I rather like the work."

"No."

Elisabeth giggled.

"Oh, yes, actually. Uninterrupted time working on systems. Hardware is delicate. The skill and precision involved in working on it. I actually find it quite relaxing."

"Well, it takes all kinds to make the world go round."

"Just don't tell my boss," Lynn said, turning, pointing a finger toward Tamara. "I'm letting him think I'm in hell, suffering mightily for my transgressions."

"As much as I miss and enjoy your company, dear Merlin, I would not interrupt your quiet time."

"Why thank you. Still." Putting her head on one side. "I do miss the company from time to time. It's not all guts and glory in the deep down-below."

"Well, I am glad that they let you up for air."

"Just don't talk about, you know, certain things."

"Premature ejaculation?"

"Oh God, no." Stepping away, suppressing a laugh. "I mean they're trying to hold the dungeon over me. Trying to make me turn informant."

"They want you to narc?"

"Makes me so angry I could just spit. They caught wind of certain things. Really intelligent students. Much smarter than our friend Liz here." Gesturing at Elisabeth. "Made mention of certain upcoming events by phone."

"Oh, the Ape Fights."

"What—How?" All but gagging.

"I am a student first, you know."

"Student teacher." Pointing, accusing. "You crossed the line."

"And you work for ITRC. Okay, fine, I got a blast message. All teaching faculty are supposed to narc on the organizers of the Ape Fights."

"That's rat out, Tomorrow," Lynn said. Tamara's nickname was Tomorrow, by the way. "You're a teacher now. You can't narc—Oh, never mind."

"Narcing involves going undercover or otherwise ferreting out information on the down-low," Elisabeth said. "Abusing trust. Turning on one's fellows. As a teacher—"

"Student teacher," Tamara said.

"You're no longer one of us when it comes to this kind of thing. You're standing on the other side," Elisabeth's voice wavered, as Lynn and Tamara both glared at her with great intent. "What?"

"Yeah, you're right." Tamara shook her head sadly as if feeling the weight of years.

"This is much ado about nothing, you know," Lynn said. "Doesn't matter how long they try to hold me in the dungeon. I won't narc. Investigate. Turn traitor. Squeal. Sorry, I won't."

"Solidarity, sister," Elisabeth said, holding up a fist.

Lynn raised her own arm, bumped wrists and elbows with Elisabeth in an overly elaborate exchange baring a vague resemblance to a secret handshake.

"I feel old," Tamara said, shoulders sagging. "Listen, when you're done with the fish and livestock here, you got time for coffee? I'm buying."

"Sure, anything to keep me away from the dungeon. Don't want them thinking I like it down there. If faculty—"

"Student faculty!"

"Right, if even student faculty need my assistance with something computer- or network-related, then it would be a dereliction of duty not to be of service."

"Beautiful, I'll see you shortly. We'll talk. But don't take too long, I've probably got class I should be teaching or something. Hope the students haven't set fire to my desk out of pure boredom." Tamara turned, wandering off, muttering that last bit all but under her breath.

"Thought she would never leave," Elisabeth said when Tamara was out of earshot.

"Oh, hush," Lynn said over her shoulder. "Tomorrow is good people."

"Yeah, but like you said, she can't narc."

"No." Letting her head drift from side to side. "No, she can't. Even if she wanted to."

"She's one of them now. You're borderline."

"Fine line, that is. I may work for the man, but that doesn't make me the man."

"Flat-lined an entire floor, did you?"

Lynn nodded her head.

"That takes guts, you know," Elisabeth said. "Must have made more than a few of the faculty quite angry."

"Oh, it did, I understand."

"Well, thank you for the script repair," Elisabeth said, looking to the lab script in her hands, studying it. "Everything seems in order."

"Then my work here is done."

"Weekend plans?"

"None to speak of, unfortunately. I may not be the man, but I'm not exactly a student anymore. The spirit may be willing, but the flesh is tired and wants a nap. And, okay, maybe the spirit could do with a bit of a lie-down too from time to time."

"My uncle's throwing a wedding, if you can believe that."

"Really, a wedding. Interesting thing to throw. Who's gaining a partner?"

"Don't know." Shrug of shoulders. "Uncle probably. There'll be dancing. Monkeyshines. Mock turtle soup and everything."

"Mock turtle?" Turning. "What are you talking—Oh, really."

"Yeah, I've even got a recipe." Held up her phone. "Want it?"

"I do. You know, I do believe that I do." Flashed her phone against Elisabeth's own. Checked the display. "Thank you. I think I can follow this recipe."

"Cool."

"The spirit may be tired, but it ain't that tired."

Elisabeth and Lynn engaged in one final round of bumping wrists and elbows before Lynn finally took her leave. Tamara almost forgotten, but Lynn did remember to course-correct. Her mind adrift with directions to an event she knew she had better not think about too closely while still on the clock. All the same, she could barely wait to tell Aiden she held the coordinates for Ape Fights on her phone. At least she knew better than to send him a message with the news. That would have been a disaster.

Turned out Tamara had been serious about having forgotten a class. She was nowhere to be found, having needed to run before the students could get so bored as to stage a production of *Waiting for Godot.* Lynn needed to return to the dungeon, anyway, and pretend to hate it some more so it all worked out.

CHAPTER EIGHT

In which Lynn and Aiden have successfully followed the directions of a mock turtle soup recipe.

Any sufficiently large enough building complex is going to have rooms and chambers that people have simply forgotten about or never realized existed in the first place. There are nooks and crannies that only the custodial and maintenance staff have ever set eyes upon, and then only when absolutely necessary. Spaces used more as a means to an end, short-cuts and temporary storage, than anything else. These rooms are frequently left empty, for reasons such as backing onto the various heating and cooling systems. They exhibit the extremes of heat, cold, damp, noise, or smell. They are crossed quickly and preferably without too much time spent contemplating how they could be affecting one's health. Little if anything has been done to make them look reasonable or presentable. Walls are brick or bare concrete. Windows are few, small and far in between, if there are any at all. Lights are bare, glowing bulbs that flicker and hum for no clearly discernible reason other than to add to the inhospitable atmosphere. These are lost chambers that seem to pulse and breathe with a life of their own.

While it is true that most people would avoid such lost rooms and forgotten spaces at all costs, there are those few who will seek them out or find some purpose for them. People will come. Crowds will gather. All they need is a reason to be away from the natural rhythm and flow of humanity. They have reason not to be noticed. They don't know or care that the space is oppressive to the point it draws the very life from out of one's body. They don't mind that they could be filling their lungs with moss, dust, mold, or even stranger particles that they would otherwise despise.

Aiden and Lynn simply followed the noise. The directions hidden within Lynn's phone had been necessary only up to a point as they navigated dark halls and twisted passages through the various buildings and labs of Ben Franklin University. Lynn had put her phone away at last. They had found the crowds.

They couldn't count the people. The rooms and spaces simply hadn't been designed with gatherings in mind, large or small. People gathered. They clustered. They talked and shouted to be heard. They cheered. For all Lynn and Aiden could tell, the entire student population could have been there. They weren't. Obviously, there was no way quite so many people could be gathered, but still, there were so many it was impossible to count. Lynn and Aiden made their way through the throng as best they could, trying not to talk, as conversation was more or less impossible.

Focus was gathered around three rings, which wasn't quite the word for it. They weren't exactly rings. The spaces were more square than round. Ropes marking the boundary. Around these squared circles, the people squawked and gathered. They screamed and shouted. They jostled for position, trying to see the frenetic activity within.

There were robots maybe two feet tall within each ring. Lynn and Aiden having forced, shoving and kicking, to a place where they could watch one such circle. The robots were many-limbed little monsters. One was clearly bipedal with arms like an ancient god, each hand holding a scepter or club. The other robot was a tripod, dancing about, and it had slender, whip-like arms that ended in bulbed tips. And the robots were beating the hell out of each other.

The robots danced about very much as if engaged in an incredibly elaborate ceremony, maneuvering for position, and their arms flew, hitting, striking, trying for the best position. The ancient god spun its arms like a furiously pinwheeling top. The tripod tangled those arms with whips, trying to hold the god still, but it had so many arms. One was always out of reach.

The people watched, screaming, shouting, jeering and pointing. Laughing. Lynn and Aiden laughed, watching the spectacle before them, trying to hold their own among the students.

The cries and cheering changed, as the tripod snagged one of the ancient god's legs and pulled it down. Whips entangled with many of the arms. Another whip pulling at the leg. The little god could not stand, flailing about, trying to protect itself with its free arms, as the weighted end of a whip struck at the body and struck and struck. An arm was dislodged. Parts flew. People hollered and cheered. The ancient god's handler released his dead man's switch, raising his arm into the air, showing the dead switch to all. Ancient god went still. The tripod grew restive. The referee pointed at the tripod's handler.

People cheered and growled, depending on their side in the conflict. They clapped and stamped their feet, and slowly they grew quiet as the handlers moved into the ring. The overall buzz-saw of noise did not change. The rings were independent, the other matches still in progress.

Lynn and Aiden tried to move about as handlers saw to their robots and the cleanup crew swept the square. At the edge, more handlers prepared their robots for the coming matches. Lynn saw Darryl Bunbury and made her way toward him, dragging Aiden along.

"Darryl!" Lynn screamed when they were practically face to face, having fought the swarm of people to reach him. "You made it!"

"An Ape Fight at my university, and I'm not there?" Darryl shouted with his face held right next to her ear. It was the only way to have any hope of being heard. Even then, they still more or less had to guess what the other was saying.

"How did you?"

"Find out?"

"Yeah!"

"I know people! Security!"

"Security?"

"You think something like this could happen without security being in on it?" Darryl waved his arm, taking in the crowd, bumping into shoulders and faces.

"But ITRC!"

"Those uptight microscopic black holes? Security lets them twist in the wind!"

"No!"

"Security loves this! Got their own apes in the action!"

"Never!"

"Oh, just keep watching!" Gesturing at Aiden. "Who's the appendage? Partner?"

"Yeah, you've never met!" Wrapping her hands around Aiden's arm. "My partner, Aiden!"

"Charmed!" Darryl shouted not trying to shake hands in the crowd. "I've heard stories!"

"I can't hear!" Aiden said, trying to lean forward. "No idea what you just said!"

"Don't even try, I know!" Darryl turned at the sound of doubly raised voices from the direction of the ring.

One side had set up a four-legged robot that bore

a passing resemblance to a centaur if the torso were slightly closer to the center of the body, while the other side had produced a tank.

"Foul!" Darryl shouted, pushing toward the ring. "Off-sides! Off-sides!" People taking up the chant.

Lynn and Aiden pulled back as the crowd tried to constrict around the ring. Various people shouting and booing, jeering and crying. They made their way around, letting the throng squeeze tight, and tried to reach the next ring. This one held mismatched box-ers standing on tripod legs. Not a whip-like arm to be seen. They boxed. They moved and punched, dodging and weaving, spinning about on their triple feet. At the edge, each handler held a dead man's switch stretched out over the ring like a torch or a dare. An elaborate game of chicken fought with robots. Someone would drop first.

The combatants punched and grappled, receiving no directions from the handlers, ignoring the calls and shouts from the crowd. The only command they would obey would be the release of the dead monkey's paw. Everything else was up to the robot, thinking on its feet, calculating as it fought. Struggling almost like wrestlers, gripping arms, holding fast, they each rose up on one back leg, kicking out with the other two. They bore a strange resemblance to furious tarantulas.

One fell, losing its balance. The other pressing its advantage, stamping with two feet, pummeling at the other's arms with its fists. The audience roared and cheered. The handler of the fallen tripod cried. His wombat could not regain its feet. Could barely hold its arms against the attack. The handler raised his arm, releasing the dead man's switch, and the crowd redou-bled its roar. The referee pointed to the other side, and the triumphant handler stepped into the ring. Arms raised over her head in victory. It was Elisabeth Dao, grinning from ear-to-ear.

"Liz!" Lynn screamed, not caring her voice was lost to the din.

With a firm grip on Aiden, Lynn tried to drag him through the crowd toward Elisabeth, who was gathering and folding up her tripodal robot. Another grad student helping her. Lynn gave up trying to reach the edge of the ring and took to shadowing Elisabeth and her companion. They made for the edge of the crowd. Areas informally reserved for the handlers and their robots preparing for or recovering from battle.

Aiden glanced to the first ring as they passed and saw that the mismatched fight between the centaur and the tank had finally started. Centaur was holding its own, hanging back. The tank maneuvering on many little feet. Its dome-like shell was open, hinged behind the head like a beetle's wings, facing the centaur like a shield. From beneath the shell and behind the shield, a long crane-like arm lashed at the centaur. A second scorpion tail emerged from behind the shell, and Aiden could see no more, as Lynn pulled him past the crowd.

It was almost but not quite a separate room where the handlers and their robot warriors gathered. There was space to breathe. The noise was less intense, almost as if they had made their way into an adjacent dimension. There was no shortage of activity as people fussed over their robots, getting ready for their match or patching up the damage and scars. Elisabeth and her companion did not stop until they found their own waystation and began studying their fighter carefully.

"The conquering hero!" Lynn cried, even though it wasn't quite necessary to shout.

"Hey!" Elisabeth said, looking up, jumping to her feet. "You made it!"

Quick hug followed by air kisses cheek-to-cheek. Repeat.

"Wouldn't miss it. Recipe wasn't that hard to follow. So glad you gave it to me what with my being the man and everything."

"No fear you would turn us in."

"Recognize lots of faces," Lynn said, looking about. "I could be taking names, you know. Hey, Oliver!" Pointing. "I knew you would have an ape in this fight!"

Oliver Fenchurch looked up from his own robot halfway across the pit-crew floor, waved, turned back to his machine. Hesitating for just a moment, he abandoned his robot, making his way toward them.

"Of course, he's got an ape," Elisabeth said. "He's Applied Engineering and Robotics."

"Yeah, it's like a law or something, isn't it? They would drum him out of the department."

"You made it," Oliver said, reaching out, holding hands, firm handshake. "Couldn't get a message to you. Just up and disappeared."

"Oh, you know how it goes," Lynn said. "Flat-line a floor, and they slap you in the dungeon. Didn't see daylight for days."

"Fortunately, I came to her rescue." Elisabeth put a friendly arm around Lynn's shoulders.

"That she did." Lynn returned the hold. "That she did." They stood facing Oliver. "Nice to see you learned something from our little talk and improved the encryption. It very nearly took me a minute to twig to the monkeyshines and mock turtle soup references."

"It's made with veal, you know," Oliver said.

"That, I will let slide." Turned her head. "Oh, hey, you haven't met my partner." Disengaging from Elisabeth, Lynn reached for Aiden.

"Aiden," he said, stepping forward, smiling, shaking

Oliver's hand. "I think Lynn has mentioned you. Work with that pseudo-intelligence expert, right?"

"Right, so imagine what my monkey can do in the ring," Oliver said.

"You did not just say what I did not hear you say." Lynn pointed a jagged finger.

"Oh, hey, nothing leaves the quarantine zone." Raising his hands, stepping back. "Not even in jest. But I can still throw code like nobody's business."

"Truth that," Elisabeth said, nodding. "How I got my edge with my basic module. It's all in the code."

"All in the code," Oliver said. "Without touching the quarantine zone. Besides, I wouldn't want the great Tourist Hunter here to have to spring into action."

"Heard about that, did you?" Aiden said.

"Don't want to say that your partner was bragging."

"But I was bragging," Lynn said.

"Drove the great Behr straight up the wall." Made a swooping gesture, indicating ascent of an imaginary wall. "Hanging from the ceiling, screeching and hollering."

"It was quite a sight."

"Whoa, whoa, whoa," Elisabeth said. "What's this about a tourist?"

"Behind in your bragging," Oliver said, waging a finger at Lynn.

"Can't be everywhere." Shrug of shoulders.

"Lynn's partner clocked a tourist."

"Never!" Elisabeth said.

"Oh, yes, got the results from R&D and everything," Aiden said. "Genuine tourist infestation."

"Oh, my God! What? Where? When?"

"Just a little sweeper," Aiden said. "Drove its owner to distraction. Called us. Put that sucker down."

"Wait, memory failing—You work for Central Services? Alpha Matrix?"

"Central Services. The list goes on. Don't try to name them all."

"But a tourist. A freaking tourist. How often does that happen?"

"More often than you would think. Less often than I might like. Not so much fun just repairing equipment."

"Better when you get to smash and run, right?"

"Well," Aiden said. "Not so much running. There's paperwork to think about. More paperwork than you can possibly imagine."

"The price for doing battle with genuine tourists. Worth it, I'm sure."

"It's always worth it in the moment," Lynn said.

"It's dealing with the aftermath," Aiden said, looking about, noticing the students watching with the rumor of tourism. "The cleanup. The paperwork. The Tourist Board."

"No, not them," Elisabeth said, looking as if Aiden had just proven the existence of ghosts.

"Oh, yes, they're completing an independent investigation of what happened."

"That must be fun," Oliver said.

"The suspense," Aiden said. "Don't know how I can stand it." Looking about. "Imagine if they found out about this place."

"Oh, let's not."

"I would rather ITRC raided our little party," Elisabeth said.

"Don't wish for that too hard," Lynn said. "You never know."

"Oh, she's back to being a turncoat, is she?"

"Hey, I've got bids. I've got offers."

"To think I invited you."

"Serves you right."

"Me, she had to threaten," Oliver said.

"Oh, please, it was begging. Call it what it is."

"You?" Elisabeth pointed at her. "Begging for an invitation?"

"No, of course not." Pointing at Oliver. "Genius-boy did the begging."

"Well, I was trying to stop you from crippling the floor at the time," Oliver said.

"And did it work?"

"Not as such, no."

"There, you see? Don't try to bribe me." Snap of fingers. "And I kept on you about the party."

"That you did. Had to spread the word about your invitation when you disappeared."

"Slapped in the dungeon."

"She did warn us about the phone call," Elisabeth said. "Breach in security."

"Who talks about Ape Fights on the phone?" Spreading her arms. "Seriously."

"Earned your invitation, you did."

"That I did."

"What's this about a dungeon?" Aiden said.

"Well, you know." Dismissive wave of her hand. "Work sucks sometimes."

"Wait, you didn't tell him?" Elisabeth said, pointing at Aiden.

"No big thing."

"Martyr."

"Oh, listen to the long-suffering graduate student going on about the trials and tribulations of others." Looking about. "When do you have time to work on these miniature engines of destruction, anyway?"

"I wonder where they find the time, myself," Elisabeth said, glaring at the other handlers and their robots. "Me, I just grab the standard model off the shelf. Nothing to it."

"Just the generic modular design from the local

hardware store?" Aiden said. "Some of these parts are custom."

"Hey, he's got an eye. Must work for Central Services or something. Yeah, there's a bit of custom work."

"Mostly standard in her case," Oliver said.

"Yeah, what can I say? I'm a busy grad. Working my asterisk off in the salt mines. My edge is in the code."

"Really?" Aiden said.

"Yeah, can't put the time into the hardware. You know how my girl beat that ugly donkey? You really want to know?"

"More than life itself," Lynn said.

"Question of algorithm design," Elisabeth replied. "My code prioritized balance. The other monkey couldn't handle it."

"Ape," Oliver said. Elisabeth shushed him with a wave.

"Figured a tripod didn't need to worry about standing," she said. "Prioritized punching or some such nonsense. My monster held firm. His fell over. I win."

"Well, you have to think about these things," Oliver said, turning, looking. "Speaking of—Well, we weren't, but I've got a match I'm neglecting."

"You'll never win with that attitude."

"Go, go," Lynn said.

"Let me show you my rig." Elisabeth grabbed Lynn's arm, dragging her toward where she had abandoned her own robot.

Aiden didn't follow, figuring they could talk for hours, studying the tripod's design, if Elisabeth was done for the night. He turned back to the main floor, which really was kind of adjacent to the pit crews, existing in a strange alternate reality. Skirting the edge, not wanting to move too far from where Lynn and Elisabeth were studying the triumphant machine, he watched the crowd and the rings. The people screamed and cheered. The apes fought.

At the edge, he noticed how the shape of these misplaced chambers molded the ebb and flow of the crowd. There was the main group surrounding the three squared circles where the monsters fought. There was another area apart from the others but still connected. One crowd of people but undulating, more here, fewer there. Less attention than the three rings. It was almost like a second pit-crew area, but it wasn't. There was a center of attention. There was a squared ring, but it wasn't an empty square like the other ape-fight pits.

It looked almost as if a miniature jungle gym had been set up. There was a bit like a monument or mountain. There were ropes and crossbars. There was something like a jigsaw maze. It reminded him of a spider-web, of all things. Trying to get a better look, he saw three robots being prepared and fussed over. They were dormant, closed off, waiting for the match to start. They certainly looked like odd apes.

The closest one was clearly modular and compartmentalized. It had at least six legs and more appendages that could double as arms or extra gripping feet. There was a central stalk and a swiveling torso. There was an emphasis on visual sensors. They seemed awfully exposed for a fighting ape.

The crowd around this ring grew suddenly quiet as the handlers moved to the edges. They stood, waiting, dead man switches held loosely at their sides. The referee stood with the starter's switch raised high into the air, and then he brought it down.

* * *

"Lynn! Oh, my God, Lynn!"

"Wait? What?" she said as Aiden finally reached her through the crowd. "Where have you—What happened?"

"You're not going to believe! You have to see this!"

"What? I can't—What's wrong? Are you okay?"

"You have to come right now! You have to see this!" Pulling at her arm.

"What are you saying? I can't hear you!"

Aiden spun in a circle, taking in the crowd and the three rings where the robots fought, as if he might explode.

"You have to," he said and stopped. Lynn pointed at her ear, shaking her head. He took out his phone and began to type.

"Are you calling me?" Trying not to laugh.

You have to see this, he typed and didn't even wait for Lynn to reach for her phone. He just showed her his display.

"What?" she said, exaggerating the word, spreading her arms wide.

He gestured with his phone for her to follow and then made another grab for her arm. This time she let him drag her across the floor, pushing and shoving at the crowd, ignoring the three rings and the fighting robots. They found the other space with its single ring and smaller crowd. The people jostled and fought for position. Views of the center were just as hard to find.

Lynn turned, saw Oliver near the edge of the squared circle putting the finishing touches on his robot, waiting his turn. There was no hope of reaching him. She turned back to the ring. There were three robots. There was a spider's web of threads and cables, looking almost like a vertical maze. There was a basket like a tiny monument at the very pinnacle of the towering spider's work. The robots were attempting to scale the mountain, gripping, grappling, awkwardly holding little balls while they made the ascent. The balls were different sizes, different colors. Many more were scattered haphazardly about the ring. It really did look like king of the mountain crossed with capture the flag, trying to deposit a ball in the basket.

The machines pushed at each other but not as aggressively as the other matches. It was haphazard, almost accidental, as if it was a byproduct of trying to maneuver through the vertical maze and reach the top. The robots didn't seem to mind, as if pushing and shoving at each other was the least of their problems. Climbing an awkward, shifting structure without dropping a ball seemed to be their overriding concern, and they did fall, lose their grip, drop their prize. Falling partway, catching themselves in the web, finding a grip, beginning to climb. Dropping a ball, watching it fall, a robot would more often than not leap from the tower rather than climb down. Scoop up another ball and begin the ascent once more.

One of the robots lost its hold, fell. Its ball struck the floor, bouncing, rolling away. The robot descended, searched for a ball. It didn't appear concerned that the one it found wasn't the exact same one it had dropped. The little machine turned back to the tower, getting ready to climb, and it paused, studying the tower, watching the other robots shake the structure in their own attempts to climb. The one robot studied all of this as if taking it in, and then the robot took the ball between two of its arms and tossed it into the basket so far overhead.

* * *

"Oh, my god!" Lynn said, shouting to be heard. "That was amazing!"

"Told you!" Aiden replied, face next to her ear, following, shadowing Oliver back toward the pit area. No way to tell if Oliver knew he was being tailed.

"I've seen the robot league! Soccer! Football!"

"Everybody's seen those!"

"Those are just set patterns!" Dismissive wave, hands fluttering, unable to hold still. "Units following a script! Boring!"

"Never catch me watching!"

"And you would think!"

"Think we would!"

"Considering what we—what you do!"

"Little robots!"

"But there's nothing to it! The robot league! Following scripts!"

"It's adorable in its own way! But, boring!"

"But, this!" Gesticulating wildly. "This was problem solving!" They finally caught up with Oliver, having reached the pit-crew space. "Hey, what the hell was that?"

"Huh?" Oliver said, noticing he had been followed. "Oh, yeah, I've got to work on my holding and grasping algorithms. Maybe design better hands. Never know what the referees are going to throw at you."

"No, I mean, what the hell was that?" Lynn waved in the general direction of the solitary ring with its vertical contraption.

"Oh, you've never seen a Monkey Trial before, have you?"

"Monkey Trial?"

"Yeah, they're new. Very hush-hush. Use the Ape Fights almost as cover."

"Thinking robots," Aiden said. "Problem solving."

"Yeah, not just simple ways to beat up one's opponent. Figure out the challenge. Work out how to solve it in real time."

"Thin ice, very thin ice."

"Risk of tourism runs deep, sure." Oliver had his robot back in the pit stop. Began working it down. "But the challenge. Designing a machine that can work out the goals of a Monkey Trial. How could I refuse?"

"The mind boggles."

"It's amazing!" Lynn said.

"Oh, don't get me wrong, it's incredible, exciting. It's just—" Shook his head. "I've worked for Central Services too long."

"No, I understand," Oliver said, holding his phone, running a script emulator, checking out his robot. "You're a Tourist Hunter. Going to see the worst possible scenario in everything."

"No, it's not that—Yeah, I guess. Have to be on my guard for risk of contamination all the time."

"No big thing."

"But the possibilities. My God, the possibilities. Thinking. Problem solving."

"Can't keep away. Look at me." Gestured toward his robot. "I've caught the Monkey Trial bug."

"No, I know. The design involved. The problem-solving algorithms. No simple punch and smash."

"Certainly explains your pseudo-intelligence reference," Lynn said.

"You would think, but no," Oliver said. "Algorithms for problem solving and algorithms for pretending to have human personalities are nothing alike."

"Like I keep saying," she replied. "I'm not the pseudo-intelligence expert here. I get as far as human thinking machine, and that's where I break down."

"See, even that statement is nowhere near accurate."

"He's right," Aiden said, "and it's not my field either."

"Shows what I know." Lynn shrugged her shoulders.

Elisabeth found them, having abandoned the Ape Fight rings.

"Hey, how did your boy do?" she said. Oliver made a face. "Oh, come on, it couldn't have been that bad."

"You didn't see the challenge the referees had set up," Oliver said.

"That's why I stick to the Ape Fights. Who's got time to develop the algorithms, much less machine the critter to run the maze?"

"Wait, you knew?" Lynn said.

"Of course I knew." Pointing at her. "What's Grandma talking about here?"

"Them's fighting words!"

"Whoa, peace, peace." Taking a step back. "Don't want to wake up to find all my network privileges revoked."

"They've never seen a Monkey Trial before," Oliver said.

"Never!"

"It's so cute when they're this young," Oliver said to Lynn and Aiden, looking at Elisabeth. "Don't you know anything that wasn't the day before yesterday?"

"I know many things!"

"Well, these two have been out in the real world, fighting the good fight. They don't have time to follow our childish games."

"Now, you're just making me feel old," Aiden said.

"We're like the same age." Lynn slapped Oliver lightly but forcefully on the shoulder.

"Yeah, but you're out in the world, working jobs, making ends meet." Rubbing his arm where she had hit him. "You're all grown up now."

"Kick me while I'm down."

"Everyone wants to live forever, I know. Look at me. Still living like a student."

"You're a high and mighty postdoc," Elisabeth said.

"Right, refusing to grow up."

"Well, look at the games we play." Turning around, taking in the scene.

"Wouldn't give them up for the world."

"Takes me back to my youth," Aiden said.

"Makes you feel old," Lynn said, pointing. "Said so."

"That too." Shrug of shoulders. "Grown up. Living in the world. Doesn't mean we can't still do childish things."

"Why I dragged you to this wild rumpus in the first place."

"Glad you came." Elisabeth punched Lynn half-heartedly on the shoulder.

"Yeah, when's the next one of these things, anyway?"

"Who said we'd tell you, grandma?"

"Oh, now you're asking for it."

"Tourist is out of the bag." Everybody looked at Aiden. "So to speak," he said. Shrug of shoulders. "You have to invite us now."

"Oh, listen to the house-guest," Oliver said. "Doesn't know when to leave."

"Maybe I just want to see how you improve your problem-solving skills for the next one. Shouldn't be that hard to develop better grabbers. Saw a tourist convert its own hands into claws. It can be done."

"Well, when you put it like that."

"It's not all on you," Lynn said. "We've been. We saw. We recognize faces. In fact, one of my fellow ITRC brethren found his way here based on only the rumor that this thing was happening."

"Oh, yes, those idiots and their phone."

"We still have to punish them," Elisabeth said.

"That we do."

"And next time."

"Yeah, well, simple really," Oliver said. "These things aren't exactly planned far in advance."

"In other words," Lynn said.

"We'll let you know when we know."

"See that you do."

CHAPTER NINE

In which the future passes before Aiden's eyes like a needle skipping over an old-fashioned record.

The Ubiquity Shuttle dropped Aiden off at the Central Services main distribution center with time to spare. Only one other Central Services employee had been on board, which was vaguely unusual but not really worth noticing. Aiden had programmed the Ubiquity Shuttle application with where he had wanted to go and when he had wanted to be there. The closest shuttle heading in his general direction had updated its route to include his coordinates, and his phone had let him know where to intercept it. Between pick-up and drop-off, it was practically door-to-door service. Since routes were fluid, based on the needs of the moment, you just never knew who else was going to be on-board. If enough people followed the same patterns from day to day, you did start to notice the same faces, recognize people, get to know them.

Aiden changed into his work clothes in the locker room, picked up the day's script from the distribution desk, and met Tom by their assigned van. The first neighborhood they found themselves in was pure residential, with tree-lined sidewalks and everything. Buildings looked to be practically single-residence homes with maybe one apartment on the first floor and another on the second. The van's cruise control picked out a parking space on only the second pass.

They walked half a block dragging the rolling-case along behind them, located their destination, climbed the steps to the mezzanine doors, flashed their phones. They gained access and only had to manhandle the rolling-case up one flight of stairs. Young woman with her hair up in a bun, looking like a maid and dressed in a servant's uniform, let them in.

They found the sweeper next to its service barn, unwilling or unable to enter. One of its manipulator arms was dangling from the unit's side.

"Nothing fell," Tom said, studying the sweeper, looking to the maid. "Something tried to pull its arm off."

"Their son has an all-purpose robot," the maid replied. "Treats it like a toy."

"They have a son?" Aiden said.

"Yes."

"How old?" He turned, taking in the room, the long dining-room table, the sideboard, the curio cabinet, the door to the kitchen, the link to the front room with couches and bookcases.

"Eleven—just turned."

"Which explains the new multi-purpose toy," Tom said, getting tools from the rolling-case. "Lets it beat up the appliances."

"Should be code against that," Aiden said. "Where is it?"

"There's an override, I think," the maid said. "Can be run remotely."

"Still." Looking at the script, scrolling displays. "We should probably take a look at it."

Tom replaced the sweeper's arm while Aiden ran diagnostics on the multi-purpose robot. It looked like a little monster, all stiff arms and dangling fingers, more ball than biped.

They left the apartment, the sweeper repaired. Script gave them their next assignment. Van took them to a mixed use block. Cruise control chose a parking space in a service alley around back. They entered through the freight door and were brought through by a store employee named Ivy. Place looked to be fashion clothing and a few other random amenities. Small spider-bot lay huddled on the floor at the base of the window as if suffering from agoraphobia.

"How long's it been like this?" Aiden asked.

"Since I first got in," Ivy said. "It's supposed to clean the windows in the early hours before opening."

"Caught in a loop," Tom said, studying the script, scrolling displays. "Needs a reboot, I think." Tapping commands.

They left the shop, checked the script for their next assignment, looked at the time, went in search of lunch. The van took them to a short neighborhood with food carts and vans.

"Sandwich? Roll?" Tom eying the vending trucks. "Salad?"

"God, no," Aiden said, walking. "This one's got pizza."

"Where's your sense of adventure?"

They ate at the van with the sliding-door open so they had somewhere to sit with the feeling of the great outdoors in their faces.

"That looks positively revolting," Tom said, eying the slice as it wavered and flopped, refusing to stay in one shape as Aiden tried to get it to his mouth.

"It's all synthetic," Aiden said. "What difference does it make?"

"Different tastes. Different textures." Shrug of shoulders. "And look what you choose."

"Exactly, it's all about choice." Putting the pizza down, trying to figure how best to fold and lift.

"How much longer before the Tourist Board completes its inquisition, you figure?"

Aiden leaned back, resting his head against the side of the door.

"I have no idea. Best not to think about it."

The van took them to another mixed use block. Cruise control picking a spot right out front. Apartment building had a lift, taking them to the fifth floor, and they pushed the rolling-case down a long hall to a two-room residence. Owner opened the door, looked to be about their age, said his name was Robert, which they already knew from the script. Last name was Highword. Sweeper was trapped in the service barn.

"Hey, this is one of those mixed-use models," Tom said, checking the barn's readout. "Supposed to be able to shampoo the rug."

"Not as useful as you might think," Highword said. "Doesn't really understand the concept of drying."

"R&D is working on that, I'm sure. Probably takes longer than you would think, too. All the trips back to the barn to refresh the bin. It's only a little sweeper."

"Looks like the sweeper is fine," Aiden said, reading over Tom's shoulder. "The barn is unhappy."

"Could take us a while to fix." Tom tapped commands on the barn's display. "Do we have a big enough scrubber?" Glancing to Aiden.

"Back in the van."

"Good thing we're parked so close."

Several trips back to the van were involved, carrying up various pieces of equipment. Not always clear which would be needed until the next stage was completed. Highword watched them, grew bored, wandered off.

Van took them back to the distribution center. Fixing the service barn had been slimy, smelly, messy work. Aiden showered, changed, programmed Ubiquity Shuttle coordinates into his phone. Waited.

* * *

"Hey," Lynn said, tapping Aiden on the forehead with her fingertips, "enough with the cruise control."

"Huh?"

"Listen, if you're not even going to participate..."

"I'm sorry." Shaking his head. "I guess I'm distracted."

"No kidding."

"What were you saying?"

Slapped him on the forehead with the flat of her hand.

"Ow." Leaning back. "The hell?"

"You think it's all guns and roses where I work?" she said. "I need you here, too, you know."

"Well, stop being the strong stoic one all the time, okay?"

"We'll just have to see about that."

"Look, it's just—" Closed his eyes. Leaned his head back. "All blurs together." Lynn said nothing. "Remember Henry Tuttle? No, Harry. No, never mind." He tried to look at her, eyes wandering. "Been thinking about the Ape Fights."

"It was supposed to cheer you up."

"It did. It did." Deep breath, shuddering. "Been thinking about the Monkey Trials. Can't get them out of my head."

Silence.

"I liked those," she finally said.

"The algorithms. The coding. Dancing so close to the edge without tipping over."

"Flirting with autonomous intelligence. The quarantine risk. Downright frightening. Half of me wants to turn them in."

"Me, too." He looked to her. "But I want that code more."

"Doubt you can find it on the co-op network."

"Recipe for disaster. Worse than mock turtle whatever. Just running searches for the code probably hell on your fines." Took a breath as if remembering he could breathe. "How are yours by the way?"

"Too soon to notice anything," she said. "You know that."

"It was just the weekend, I know. What if. The things. What if," his voice trailed off. "Tourists think they can do whatever they want."

"That's anthropomorphization, that is."

"I know." Trace of a smile. "I know." Silence. "Watching the monkeys run the maze. I want to audit that code. The machining, too. That's stock, but customized stock. The miniaturization in the brain and nervous system. You like that kind of thing, I know. The dungeon."

"Pity there's no career in monkey trial design."

"Cost you more in fines than you could possibly make, I'm sure. Flirting with autonomous intelligence."

"Black magic, right there."

"Oh, but if only." Pressed his forehead against her own. "If only."

"Harry Tuttle territory, that is."

"Dare to dream." Put his arms around her, hugged her tight. "Dungeon, huh?"

"Yeah, they're letting me out a bit. Almost a pity. I like the work."

"Really?"

"Well, I don't want them to know that."

"The kids must miss you terribly."

"I miss them, too."

"That grad student couldn't keep her hands off you."

"Sweet kid, it's true. Oh, hey now, look, if I was really only after the big oh, I could have any number of grad students I wanted. They're all hormones and misplaced energy." Kissed him gently. "I'll always come back to you."

"Got a new theory why they send two of us out on every assignment."

"Okay," Lynn said, trying not to laugh.

"Seriously, does it really take two field representatives to fix a sweeper or bookshelf organizer?"

"Well, they are concerned about tourism." Kissed him, again. Arms around him. "Cuts down on time lost waiting for backup."

"Well, yes, but how often does that happen. No, I think management has a more prudish reason."

"Never!" Lynn pushed at him. Aiden did not answer, smiling. "Oh, I am agog."

"It's to cut down on milkman syndrome."

"No, that doesn't make sense."

"Sure, it does."

"It can't."

"Think like the man, for once."

"Okay," Lynn said, hand to her forehead. "I can try." Scratched at her hair. "No, I can't. It still boggles the mind."

"Oh, you of the narrow—No, wait, the other way around. You have too open a mind."

"Thank you."

"Two field reps." Holding up two fingers.

"Okay, two field reps."

"They hold each other in check. Too embarrassed to run off with the owner, housewife, housekeeper, whatever, in front of the other."

"Look, I can see how that is supposed to work."

Running fingers through her hair. "But it just doesn't track. What's to stop the field reps from striking a deal? This one's yours. The next one's mine."

"Never work. We're supposed to rat on each other."

"Oh, like you and Tom what's-his-name wouldn't work out some kind of deal."

"It's the prisoner's dilemma type of thing."

"Wait, I know this one. If one rats, the other gets grits and gravy."

"If they both rat," Aiden said.

"They both get sweet nectar and ambrosia of the gods."

"I don't think you've got that figured quite right."

"Shut up, it's close enough."

"The point being that both would snitch on the other rather than risk being the only one with a pain in the genitals."

"And this works?" Leaning on her elbow, looking at him. "Seriously, this works?"

"Well, you know I would tell you if I ever turned milkman."

"Oh, I know." Leaned in, kissed him. "And, I would tell you about the big oh."

"And what's her name, again?"

"Tomorrow," she said, laughing.

"Oh, really, you'll tell me tomorrow?" Smiling, kissing.

"Yes, most definitely, I'll tell you tomorrow."

* * *

There were offices dedicated to specific faculty and groups of graduate students, and there were time-shared office spaces with sign-up lists by the door. Efforts had been made to generate interactive lists and shared calendars for time-share rooms, but such calendars always seemed to have horrendous update lag. Nobody could keep track of these methods, and eventually time-shared office assignment would revert to erase boards hanging next to the door. The pens never worked or were dry or confiscated for other purposes, and the boards were so supersaturated with ink that it could be hard to tell what had been written when. All things considered, the erase boards were still the most effective method of monitoring time-shared office usage.

"Thought we would never find time for coffee," Lynn said.

"I know," Tamara replied. "It's my schedule. I swear I've probably skipped out on another class as we speak. I can't keep track. The poor students just sitting there, wondering where I am."

"They probably learn more without you."

"What a thing to say."

"Get things organized. Review the books. Like a study group. Free of authoritarian interference."

"They're called sections, and they need a lead. You think the kids learn anything from class?"

"Well." Shrug of shoulders.

"Classes are huge. You have to break the group up into sections. I teach sections."

"And the occasional class."

"And the occasional class, yes."

"Oh, they're learning now."

"You have such faith in the establishment. Teaching is a fine and noble tradition going back fully a half-dozen years."

"Rage against the machine, sister. You're part of the teaching establishment now."

"Student teacher, not the same thing."

"Adorable," Lynn said, leaning back, looking at her. "Just too cute for words."

"I'm not following the non-sequiturial nature of your statement here."

"You didn't want me to know that you were on the teaching track." Head on one side. "How long did you think you were going to be able to keep that secret?"

"Never."

"Oh, you ever, didn't want me to know."

"I thought you knew, I swear."

"Sorry." Shook her head, smirking. "Still not buying pig shit this year."

"How could I have kept it a secret? That kid—grad—Liz what's-her-name, she knew."

"Which is the only reason you told me. Just adorable. Would have been much too suspicious to say otherwise. That Liz-kid is smart. She's got a brain on her. Probably a rule against fraternization with the staff."

"Not really a rule," Tamara said, shrug of shoulders. "One of those unwritten things. Besides, you need to maintain your street cred."

"I knew it." Smiling, pointing. "Worried I would dump you for a sweet young thing."

"Hey, now, let's not be hasty."

"You really are the sweetest thing ever."

"Well, I never saw you chatting up the teaching staff as I came up the ranks. Very free with your feelings about the faculty with us lowly impressionable students."

"Well, maybe, that just goes to show what I thought of the existing staff. Maybe, I was just waiting for the fresh blood with the new ideas to take over. Ever think of that? Huh, did you?"

"All the same, still need to maintain your credentials with the fresh blood."

"There's a certain amount of truth to that, sure,"

Lynn said. "Wish you could have come to the Ape Fights, for example."

"Wasn't that long ago I was participating. Can't say I was any good in the ring."

"That Liz-kid put on a good show."

"Yeah?"

"Won her match and everything."

"Good for her," Tamara said.

"I'm still impressed I got an invitation."

"Yeah, you're twilight, working for ITRC. I can see that."

"If Oliver hadn't been so desperate, doubt I would have been invited."

"Fear and desperation are wonderful motivators, I know," Tamara said. "I should use them more in class."

"There you go, silver lining." Touched her shoulder. "Listen, I'll keep working the angels. I'll get you invited."

"You're too kind."

"I wasn't the only ITRC agent in attendance. Once word went out that Ape Fights existed, we found our ways in."

"Hope springs eternal."

"There you go. Besides, you have to see this new splinter group. I don't even know if I should tell you," Lynn said. Tamara gave her a look. "Thinking robots."

"Oh, you mean Monkey Trials."

"Yes, I suppose."

"Don't look so shocked. Told you my last Ape Fight wasn't that long ago. Monkey Trials are still a thing, are they? I was hoping they would catch on."

"Yes, well, catch-on is an interesting way of putting it."

"I wouldn't worry about the tourism risk if I were you. There's still a big difference between problem-solving robots and autonomously intelligent machines."

"Tell that to Aiden. He's captivated."

"I'm not surprised."

"Can't stop talking—well, thinking about them, anyway."

"Must feel stuck in a regressive loop. Ape Fights are subversive enough. Look at how ITRC reacted. Official university policy. Monkey Trials must feel like the revolution incarnate."

"We keep checking." Looked about the room, voice dropping to a whisper. "Our fines."

"Yeah, I kept checking those after every Ape Fight," Tamara said, quietly. "University may care. But the great wide world? Not so much apparently. Never budged my fines. Not that I could tell."

"Not that you could tell."

"Aye, there's the rub."

Lynn's phone pinged with a soft sound like woodblocks clicking together. Made her jump. Picked up her phone as if it might bite her.

"Aiden," she said, ducking her head, sheepish smile.

"Hey, Aiden," Tamara said, loudly, leaning forward.

"He can't hear you." Gesturing with the phone.

"Sure, he can."

"How?"

"Record a voice message and send it just like a picture. Your phone can do that, you know."

Lynn stared at her, almost dropping the phone.

"That's just the craziest notion," she said. "Why would I send a voice message?"

"Stranger things have happened."

"He would have to notice." Counting on fingers. "Open the file. Hold the phone to his ear."

"Sounds about right."

"And why would he open the file? I would have to

send him text and audio. *Hey, listen to this file.* Seriously, why would I do all of that?"

"If your phone can do it, somebody is using it."

"And all phones can make sound recordings, I know," Lynn said, looking at her phone. "Video recordings, too. Why not just make a full motion video file and send that?"

"Oh, let's not be too fancy."

"Why not just use the phone's voice transcription function to generate the text?"

"Hey, yeah, then the person at the other end has the option of audio playback. The phone reading the text."

"Could probably even read the text back in the sender's own voice."

"There you go," Tamara said. "Practically a two-way live audio conversation."

"The mind boggles," Lynn said. "Why not just read the text like a normal person? Seriously, if I had to drop everything for a live two-way audio conversation every time someone called me, I don't know. I just don't know."

"So what did your partner say? I haven't seen him in ages."

"I know." Looking at her phone. "We need to correct that."

Street sweeper's gone missing, Aiden had typed. *Mysterious circumstances. It's on.*

"It's just work," Lynn said, waving her phone. "Says a street sweeper is missing."

"Think it's gone on tour?"

"Well, there's enough suspicion that he's bothered to call me about it." Lynn typed, *Tourist?* Hit send. "There. Let's see if he will be any more specific about it."

"Well, what's he say?" Leaning forward.

"Give it time, girl," she said, holding Tamara back

with one hand, holding the phone away with the other. "Can't expect him to just drop everything and start typing. He's got to read the message first. Formulate a reply."

"Well, if we had instantaneous two-way audio conversations, like you said, he would have to drop everything."

"Which is probably why nobody does live two-way audio. You need time to think." Pointing at Tamara. "He's on the clock, you know. Could be on the scene. Could be facing down the rampaging tourist as we speak."

"Well, he has to consider the audience. Why call you at all if he's just going to leave you hanging with the one message?"

"You should have seen the call made several weeks back. Sent me a picture from the roof of some skyscraper or other."

"Never."

"Oh, you should have seen it. Quite the view." Started scrolling displays on her phone. "Probably still got the shot in here."

Looks like it, Aiden typed. *Central Services is taking no chances.*

"He thinks it's a tourist," Lynn said.

"Never!" Reaching for the phone.

"Hey, leave off. I can relay events as they transpire on the ground."

"Well, don't just leave us in the dust. Ask him what's going on," Tamara said. "We need details."

"Yeah, yeah, yeah." She typed, *My conquering hero. What's the ETA to contact? Kick his asterisk.* "Asking for details as we speak," she said.

They sat, watching the phone.

Not as simple as that, he typed. *It's a bug hunt. Customer lost contact with the sweeper. Probably killed its own beacon. Dead giveaway that it's gone on tour. Tom agrees.*

"So this could take hours," Tamara said.

"Yeah, I'm going to have to go back on the clock."

"And my students have probably resorted to cannibalism."

"You really need to learn your schedule." Shaking her head. Lynn typed, *You have a horrible sense of dramatic timing. Got Tomorrow reading over my shoulder and everything.*

"And then I'll cure world peace while I'm at it."

Hey Tomorrow, Aiden typed. *Long time no see.*

"Cure world peace?" Lynn said, looking at her.

"Yes, and solve world hunger just for good measure." Gesturing at the phone. "Well, tell him I said hi already."

We're rendezvousing with the local security forces, he typed. *Help us track the tourist. Review street views.*

"How big is a street sweeper, anyway?" Tamara said.

"Don't know. Four feet? Five? I'm sure you've seen one cruising around."

"Yeah, but only at odd hours. Whoever pays attention to those things, anyway?"

"True, like background radiation, right?"

"Truth that."

Heather is meeting us on scene, Aiden typed. *Bringing special equipment for the occasion and everything.*

"Oh shit, it is on," Lynn said, gripping her phone.

"What?"

"They're fielding Heather Graymarsh. She's got more tourist-hunting experience than the rest of Central Services combined."

"Well, there goes being coy about what's going down."

"I have to go back on the clock," she said, shaking her phone.

"Well, don't shout at your poor phone. You'll scare it."

I'll kill you if you don't keep me updated, Lynn typed. "And you have poor students who have resorted to cannibalism," she said to Tamara.

"Yeah, now there's a harsh reality that cannot be avoided. Way to be a buzz-kill, dear."

"Yes, well, we've probably been pushing the boundary on this whole fraternization thing. People will talk if we don't get back on the clock soon."

Tamara took a deep breath as if getting ready to voice her opinion at volume, held it for a long moment suspended in time, let the breath go.

"Yeah, you're probably right," she said.

"Hey, we'll do this again real soon," Lynn said, eying her phone as if searching it for messages from Aiden.

Updates, you shall have, he had typed, *as often as I can spare them.*

"Coffee shall not be denied."

"Truth that," Tamara said. "Even if we have to move Heaven and Earth, coffee shall not be denied."

"And you want to know how this turns out." Waving her phone.

"Oh, that is beyond truth." Pointing. "I shall hunt you to the ends of the Earth if you don't tell me what happens with the tourist."

"Heaven and Earth, like you said."

CHAPTER TEN

In which Tom and Aiden have to deal with a street sweeper on a busy thoroughfare that just might have gone on tour.

Tom and Aiden found themselves standing in a major mixed-use neighborhood where even the street-level shops took up the first two or three floors of the skyscrapers that surrounded them. The road was six lanes. The center two were for distance travel, and the cars, trucks, shuttles and buses within never seemed to slow down even for a moment. The next lanes over were for transitional vehicles getting close to their destination or attempting to merge back into the central flow. The outermost pair of lanes, obviously, were for vehicles attempting to stop, depositing passengers or cargo reasonably close to their intended destinations.

Tom and Aiden exited the van, getting the rolling-case from the back, and by that point the local valet protocol had begun to seriously ping Tom's phone. He had been driving; technically, he had been sitting behind the navigation console and had programed the cruise control with their desired destination. The valet protocol didn't let up until Tom finally addressed his phone, tapping out the appropriate response, giving the system permission to remove the van from the vicinity. The valet would park the van somewhere they would probably never know and wait until they requested its return. Most likely the van would be taken to one of those tower parking structures, which could be quite a fair distance away. There was no point in inquiring. They could only hope that the parking structure, local valet protocol, and the van's own cruise control were smart enough between them to know that the vehicle needed an oversize parking space.

There was no sign of Heather Graymarsh, and the local security representatives certainly looked as if they did not wish to be disturbed. There was also absolutely no sign of a sweeper, great or small, street or room. There were, on the other hand, quite a few people on the sidewalk, and none of them took kindly to the fact that mere service representatives were standing in the way.

"Remember when we tried to spot that spider on the side of a building?" Aiden said, turning, looking cautiously this way and that.

"Yeah," Tom replied, showing a jaded disinterest in scanning the street and walkway for their quarry.

"That was easier."

"Well, not entirely convinced about that."

"What? Because the street sweeper should stand out in this crowd?"

"No, I figure it was just as likely we were studying the wrong side of the building."

Aiden watched Tom while somewhat awkwardly trying to shield the rolling-case from the crowd. It was only a matter of time before the simple flow and press of people caused them to drift down the street. Heather would never find them.

"I'm not sure I follow the logic underlying your conclusion."

"Yeah, I probably need to think this through a little more." Looked about. Nodded in the general direction of the local security representatives. "Who are they with, again?"

"Titan, I'm fairly sure," Aiden said.

"Titan?"

"Pretty sure." Shrug of shoulders.

"Bets they give us access to the local video feed?"

"Nope, sorry, no money down," Aiden said. "We're going to get no help from them until Heather threatens to boil their supervisor in oil."

"Not even then, possibly."

"Yeah?"

"What are the chances they even like their supervisor?" Tom said.

"Well, it does work better if she threatens the supervisor. Then he applies whatever tactics, threats or pressure he can to his boys over there. Boom, we're in business."

"Let's hope it doesn't come to boom, shall we?" Looking up and down the street. "Not happy with the crowds."

"I was trying not to notice."

"The people swarming past us like anchovies."

"Pretty sure that's sardines, Tom."

"Pretty sure the tourist isn't going to care." Turning about. "Chum to the slaughter."

"Oh, when has a tourist ever gone on a bloodthirsty rampage?"

"The fact that it has never happened has nothing to do with it." Pointing. "Fact is it doesn't even need to be a genuine tourist in order to start a stampede."

"Yeah, that's probably the part I'm trying very hard not to think about."

"The Titan boys over there should be clearing the street. Thinning the herd. Something."

"That part of the liability probably hasn't sunk in yet."

"Are we sure this is Titan Security territory?" Tom said, looking up and down the street with vague interest as if searching for landmarks or other obvious signs of ownership.

"We're not even entirely sure those are Titan Security boys," Aiden replied. "Who are the other big guys downtown? Hyperion? Executive? Rangers? It's not the Rangers, is it?"

"I rather hope not."

"Where is Heather, anyway?" Looking at his phone. "Tracking the sweeper without us?"

"Oh, that sounds exactly like her. We're only the backup."

"I swear, I've got time to chat with the partner some more." Studying his phone.

"Calling Merlin on the clock, Charles? Should report you for that. Really, I should."

"Oh, yes, you should."

"At the very least, I should tut-tut. Look disapprovingly at you while doing so."

"Not my fault you don't like calling your partner while on the clock. You know how much downtime this job entails."

"Yeah, well, he's just bored to tears by all the wild joys and excitement of my day."

The bug hunt has begun, Aiden typed. *Joy and excitement abound.* "Not even for a tourist?" he said.

"Not everyone's partner is in the same field." Shrug of shoulders. "Related field. Merlin doesn't really deal with many service robots in her particular line of work, does she?"

"It's more face-to-face support, I guess," Aiden said. "Unscrambling script and phone glitches. Kicking network connections while they're down."

"You just have no idea what she does, do you?"

"Good guess though, yes?"

"Oh, sure, she tells me everything so I can confirm you're in the right ballpark. How would I know, sir?"

"Nothing from dear friends or family," Aiden said, holding up his phone as if it was a deeply offensive object that he was ashamed to have in his possession.

"Yeah, I suspect Heather is too busy just getting here to bother." Pointing. "Oh, look, a Central Services special services van. Must be her."

They both watched the van approach, pulling up to the curb not that far from where they were standing. No point in trying to determine if the flow of pedestrians had pushed them down the block. Cruise control on major thoroughfares was not really known for trying to be perfectly exact at the destination. The same block as the address that had been programmed was generally considered close enough.

They watched Heather get a rolling-case from the back of her van. The rolling-case was on treads and seemed to be trying to assist with its own egress from the back. Little support legs sticking out this way and that like miniature stilts. Tom and Aiden made their way toward her, dragging their own rolling-case along behind them, and they could just make out the sound of the local valet protocol harassing her phone.

"Where's your wingman?" Aiden said when they were barely within spitting distance. Heather ignored him, concentrating on the rolling-case as it settled onto the sidewalk. Stick-legs retracting into the base. "Hey, your wingman?"

She got the door of the van closed and turned to face them, sizing Aiden up as if he was a demented stalker that had finally traced her home and they were meeting for the first time. Her phone was really starting to squawk.

"I'm looking at him," she finally said.

"No, no, no, no, no," Aiden said. "We're your back-up." He indicated Tom and himself with a swift motion of his finger like a wildly out-of-control metronome.

"Well, guess what, Charlie," she started to say and then held up a hand to quiet dissent before it could crawl further out of the grave. She then addressed her phone, which was really starting to squawk indignantly at her, and tapped the appropriate commands into the tantrum-throwing device. Turning, they watched the van leave for parts unknown.

"No, seriously, we can't be your wingman," Tom said as they quickly lost interest in the van. He pointed at Aiden. "And, don't call him Charlie."

"Listen, Tweedledee, Tweedledum. You're it."

"In what alternate reality does that even make sense?"

"In the reality in which Central is trying to minimize their exposure." Hand on hip. "It hasn't been that long since the last incursion, and the Tourist Board is paying way too much attention. Three guesses who was mixed up in that one."

"Oh, I'm going to need at least four," Aiden said.

"So we're being thrown to the wolves, are we?" Tom said.

"That doesn't entirely make sense, but sure, you're responsible for what dreams may come." Heather looked from one to the other of them. "You should be happy. There's a certain amount of freedom in this expedition."

"How so?"

"If the Tourist Board hangs you for the little sweeper, nothing they can do to you about this big sweeper. Make the best of it. Go nuts. If I had dynamite, I would let you apply it to our wayward friend just to watch it go boom."

"Too much collateral damage," Aiden said, looking about. "People tend to notice the blood and body parts."

"But what a sight." Pointing toward the security representatives. "Let's go check in with the local wildlife. Tourist isn't going to put on a show without an audience."

Heather started walking toward the Titan Security personnel. The tank-tread rolling-case obediently following along as if it suffered from severe separation anxiety. Tom and Aiden had to physically drag their own case, as it simply didn't know or care how close it was to them.

"So, it's really a tourist, is it?" Aiden said, dodging pedestrians, trying to keep pace.

"Jury's still out on that point," Heather replied over her shoulder. "We're proceeding with a rather impressive overabundance of caution."

"Liability and public exposure?"

"That, and it's just way too soon since the last tourist outbreak. Board paying way too much attention. Cautious paranoia and optimism are definitely the order of the day."

"Joy to the world," Tom said.

The pair of Titan Security personnel watched them with the same level of interest and intensity that they imagined a Galapagos turtle gives to a small stone of indeterminate origin.

"Oy!" Heather said, pointing at them. "Where's our property, you pair of pantheistic monkey grubbers?"

They continued to watch her as if she had spoken in a rather obscure alien dialect and they were waiting for the translation to be fed to them over their headphones.

"Where'd you lose it?" the slightly more senior looking of the two finally said.

"Oh, I will demonstrate that upside your head if this is the level of assistance you are going to provide." Grand sweep of her arm taking in the crowded sidewalk. "This is your territory, is it not? Property lost or damaged on your turf is kind of your thing, isn't it?"

"Risk of theft or violence lies with the people on this public thoroughfare. We can't be responsible for every little thing."

"Oh, so you think the liability is going to roll in my general direction, do you? Listen, we've got a possible tourist incident on a busy street. You're going to start to care about the liability any second now."

"If Central Services' equipment has gone on tour, the liability most definitely rolls in your rather specific direction."

"It's not just the personal liability and bodily harm," Tom began to say. Heather shushed him with a gesture and half a look.

"Think about Titan's reputation for a moment," she said. "Say a news logger got hold of the story. You want this trending on the feeds?"

"Said yourself it's not a confirmed tourist incident," the security man said. His name was Sagebrush, which had been included in the part of the script notes that Heather hadn't bothered to read.

"You think the n-logs are going to care?" Sweep of her arm. "Just picture all the gawkers and news loggers swarming the area."

"Because of your company's product."

"Listen, I would just love to argue the archaic intricacies of finger-pointing here until the end of time, but we're all on the clock. I would love to bring in my own security team, but you know I can't. Contract says we have to work with you." Taking in the crowds, again. "Don't you have a consortium block contract for this street? Doubt the businesses want a scene. What's the block contract say about the passersby?"

"Can't account for the subscription status of everybody, now can we?" the second security man said. His name was Cottonsmith, but again, nobody cared.

"You don't have to! Listen, this has been fun, I know, but I am this close to leaking details to the nearest n-log. All you have to do is give us access to the street cameras and video history going back at least an hour, and we're out of your hair."

"You could have just said so," Sagebrush said. "Our collaboration covers that detail."

"I shall love you forever."

Sagebrush took out his phone and began to type.

"You get limited access to the local street views with expansion based on wherever your malfunctioning hardware buggered off to," he said.

"Access had better be expansive and inclusive," Heather replied. They flashed phones. She checked the display. "Imagine that, we're in business." Looking directly at him. "We shall call upon you as events warrant."

"Hey, we've got a hazardous-pay clause," he said, pocketing his phone, gazing off into space as if she did not exist. "Looking forward to optioning it."

"I'm sure you are." Heather turned, began to walk away, Tom and Aiden trailing along in her wake. "Pompous, self-centered abalone shells," she muttered, stopping near the edge of the street where the vans had left them in the first place, and looked back to her phone. "They must be hoping to clock the non-subscriber hazard rates of everyone on the street. Forget the liability. They'll make sure any claims get tied up in arbitration for years."

"Lawyers live for that kind of thing," Tom said.

"Oh, let's not drag them into this." Tapping her phone. "Right, we're in business." Tapping, scrolling. "Should come as no surprise to anyone that I cannot share the video with you."

"Slave our phones to you?"

"Yeah, regrettably, it looks like they've anticipated that little workaround and have beaten us to the countermeasures. Just stand there looking decorative while I suss this out."

Heather went back to her phone, studying the screen with the intensity of a kitten stalking a dust mote. Aiden watched the street, looking for any indication of where the street sweeper had been or where it had decided it would rather be.

"Okay, yeah, it was here," Heather said, pointing at the ground near her feet. "Looks good. Looks good. Nothing out of the ordinary. People treating it like a pink elephant, pretending they can't see it. What you would expect. Let's see how things developed." Tapping her phone, scrolling through time. "Right, it just kept moving."

Heather started to walk. Eyes more often to the phone than the world around her, looking, comparing landmarks to the video history. They dragged the rolling-case along. Heather's case needed no such prompting and simply kept pace.

"So, what's with the self-propelled wheels?" Aiden said. "We're in the field all the time. Why don't we merit such useful add-ons?"

"Same reason as the last time you asked," Heather, eyes to her phone. "Perks of R&D."

"Well, I personally plan to lodge a formal complaint with the appropriate management-service committee," Tom said. "A self-motivated rolling-case would go a long way toward improving our standard of living and service engagement."

"Yeah, you do that. I would love to be there when they go for distance—tossing you out the door, but I've got better things to do than engage in schadenfreude."

They marched on, following Heather, following the

video record on her phone, stopping sporadically to compare the video to their surroundings. The blocks in that busy neighborhood were long, and they traversed several without stumbling across anything of interest. Heather stopped, suddenly, raised her hand as if for silence. The world ignoring her.

"It's just been rolling along like a tourist." She grew fiercely silent. "Yes, I know what I just said."

"Taking in the sights, is it?" Tom said.

"Words can mean multiple things," she replied, not even bothering to glare at him. "Right, there should be a fountain over there." She gestured, pointing, and there was a fountain. "Drew its attention."

"Well, as long as something kept it occupied. It's had quite the head start. Imagine if it had just trundled along in a straight line."

"Yeah, well, we can only hope it didn't need the exercise." She began to walk again, making for the fountain.

There was an open space between buildings like a vanity park to show that the block was so important they could afford to waste space on art and architecture. There were trees. There were benches. There was a surprising lack of people, considering how many were traversing the road almost as if the vanity park was hidden from view like a magical oasis or secret garden.

"And there's our wayward child," Heather said, coming to a standstill, watching the sweeper from a discreet distance as if desiring not to draw its attention.

The sweeper was a tapering five-foot-tall robot, looking for all the world like a miniature Art Nouveau skyscraper. It was all crisp straight lines and curves. The sweeper was also pressed up against one of the benches, pushing like an irresistible force faced with an unmovable object, determined to win. The sweeper would shove unceremoniously away at the bench, grind to a stop, and rest there as if perplexed. It would then slowly back up several long inches, rest again, and then proceed to roll forward, bumping into the bench with renewed gusto and determination. This demonstration of object at rest versus object in motion continued without any apparent end in sight while they watched with dignified but rapt attention.

"Well, this is promising," Heather finally said.

"Could be just a glitch, after all." Tom had his phone out, began to shoot video of the demonstration in progress. "Downright disappointing."

"Anticlimactic, to say the least," Aiden said. "Whatever shall I tell Lynn?"

"Tell your partner to take up basket weaving if she really needs excitement that badly." Heather opened her rolling-case with one eye never leaving the sweeper. "Now, there's some cutthroat competition, if you ask me. Never knew anyone so determined to win at any cost as basket weavers."

"You really don't want it to be a tourist, do you?"

"Have you taken a look at that monkey?" Unfolding an industrial-strength cattle-prod as she spoke. "I really want something on that scale inconveniencing the bystanders. That'll just go over like gangbusters back in our public relations department." Holding the cattle-prod out to Aiden. "Here, make yourself useful."

"The hell is this for," he said, taking it gingerly, expecting it to explode. Cattle-prod was on the same scale as a javelin.

"In case we are dealing with a tourist." Going back to the rolling-case, fishing out another javelin. "What, you think something as straightforward as a sledge is going to do more than just get the bastard's attention?" She had the second javelin unfolded. "Here." Handing it to Tom.

"How do I turn the safety off?"

"Here," she said, touching it near the well-insulated base. "I swear, it's like dealing with whiny babies."

"I'm beginning to sense why they don't let you out in the field more."

"Oh, you're just catching on, are you?" Turning back to the case. "I'll have you know that my bedside manner is outstanding. You should see my customer satisfaction reports."

"Outstanding where?" Aiden said. "Seriously, I have met you before, Heather."

She pulled a script from the rolling-case. Script was a good third of an inch thick.

"What the hell is that?" he said, pointing.

"It's a script." She held it out for his inspection. "I'm sure you've seen them before."

"I've seen scripts before, yes." Eyeballing it. "That thing? What did you do? Superglue a stack of them together?"

"This is a proper workingman's script." She flipped it on, began tapping on its surface.

"It needs to go on a diet is what it needs," Tom said.

"This, my young ducks," Heather said, "is what you need if you want any power."

"But look at it."

"Miniaturization is overrated." Pointing with the script. "This is what you need if you want to do battle with virulent alien software. Biohazard-level Armageddon. This fine example of bleeding-edge R&D craftsmanship can invent a whole new alphabet with thirty-seven consonants and only one vowel, translate War and Peace into it, and teach you the language all before your scrawny-piece-of-shit little script has even finished booting up."

"I don't know," Aiden said.

"Yeah, I think you're overcompensating," Tom said.

"Oh, you do, do you?" Health said, turning on him.

"Oh, definitely." Nodding his head. "Seriously, looks like you dug it out of a dumpster. How old is that casing anyway? Don't you have a budget in R&D?"

"I used to, but I think I need to donate it to the search for your will to live. Or at least buy you a second-hand brain. You seem to have burned out the one currently in your asterisk."

"Hey, don't joke with a man holding a pig-sticker of this magnitude."

"Hand a boy a toy," Heather muttered, turning back to the rolling-case. "Oh, look, the sweeper is gone."

"What!"

"Made you look." She was working a large block free of the case. "Seriously, somebody should be keeping an eye on that thing."

"It's still humping the bench," Tom said. "I'm really not into that kind of nature documentary, if you really must know."

"Not like I asked." Heather tapped commands.

The block unfolded, revealing itself to be a little robot maybe two feet tall, looking nothing so much as like two tripods that had been welded together head-to-head. At any given moment, three feet were touching the ground while the others were reaching for the stratosphere. An impressive number of arms and various other appendages were tucked in tight against the torso.

"That's quite a little custom monstrosity you've got there, Madame Frankenstein," Aiden said.

"Why, thank you," she said without looking up from her script. "I knew there was a reason I liked you best. I also like how Titan Security discreetly cleared the area of non-essential cannon fodder in anticipation of our arrival."

"Yeah, I actually noticed that, too."

"I'm sure you did. Don't care about the liability, my sweaty asterisk." Looking up from her script. "Right, let's go violate that pathetic little orangutan's personal space."

She typed one final command. The little robot began to roll enthusiastically toward the street sweeper.

"A little flanking, if you please," she said, gesturing for Tom and Aiden to move. They obliged. "Thank you." Tapping, scrolling. "Still not getting a reading from our wayward girlfriend. Maybe dysfunctional. Maybe turned off its feed."

"No obvious damage," Tom said, studying the sweeper, javelin in hand.

"Still not conclusive."

Without warning or provocation, the little rolling robot leapt at the sweeper, grasping hold somewhere around its midsection and began to scale the five-foot skyscraper. The sweeper continued in its quiet determination to change the bench's opinion on the subject of being a stationary object as if it had not even noticed that it had been boarded. The rolling robot, which strangely enough looked a little like a sea urchin, finished its climb and began to settle against the top of the sweeper almost as if they were puzzle pieces designed to fit together.

"What's the little blighter trying to do? Eat its brain?"

"That's not far off," Heather said. "On the clock, now. Don't stray from your assigned jobs." Scrolling, typing. Tom and Aiden held the cattle-prods at the ready, watching. "Contact. Can't ignore a direct interface now, can you?"

The sweeper froze, as if realizing at long last that it had acquired an admirer intent on becoming one with the object of its affection. Tom and Aiden held still, trying not to breathe, watching, waiting. Heather intent on her script. Sweeper pulled away from the bench, jerking, stuttering, began to turn in a circle, quickly picking up speed as if now convinced it was a spinning top, the sea urchin holding on for dear life.

"It's a tourist," Heather said, typing all but frantically.

Aiden fumbled for the safety on his javelin. The sweeper ceased spinning, began moving quickly toward the fountain and the street beyond.

"Keep it contained," she said.

Aiden and Tom converged, pointing cattle-prods toward the sweeper. It changed course. They moved. The sea urchin pulled back from the sweeper's head, hanging on with little arms, and began to rip at the bigger robot's casing as if determined to pry the tourist apart. Manipulators emerged from the sweeper's torso, looking like long multi-jointed arms, and began to flail at the little robot. Aiden closed with the robots, jabbing with the cattle-prod. The sweeper swung around. Arm waving at him. He scuttled back.

"Careful." Heather's voice.

"Easy for you—" Aiden started, stopped, dodged another arm.

Tom moved close, stabbed with the cattle-prod. There was a crack like lightning. The tourist reeled, spinning, trying to move. Sound like a miniature buzz-saw, grinding, came from the vicinity of the little robot atop the sweeper. Sea urchin ripped panels apart, threw them to the ground. Components exposed. The little robot drove arms into the wound. Tourist tried to run, moving fast. Aiden stabbed it with his javelin. More cracks like lightning. The shock ran up his arms, holding the cattle-prod wrong.

The street sweeper turned, as if cornered, trying to take in everything around it, lunged for the street. The sea urchin pulling parts from the rent in the tourist's casing, making a serious attempt to climb into the wound.

"Fire in the hole," Heather shouted.

Tom dropped. Aiden hit the ground. Sweeper quickly outpacing them, and then exploded. Aiden felt the shock in his teeth and hair. His ears rang. His shoulders ached. It felt as if he had been struck by an incredibly heavy invisible object that had instantly dis-integrated. It took him a moment to notice the robot fragments that scattered the ground all around him.

The street sweeper still stood. Half of it, anyway. The rest of it was all around them in bits and pieces.

"Hey," Heather said, crossing quickly to them. "You guys survive? Tweedledee? Tweedledum? I want to hear voices or at least groans of pain."

"Yeah, I think I can manage one of those," Tom said, crawling to his knees.

"Charlie?" Kicking Aiden experimentally. "Don't make me remind you that you are my favorite."

"Yeah, maybe," Aiden said. "Stop kicking me!"

"Okay, good then."

"Seriously, you really have to kick a body when he's down?" Climbing, sitting. "You just see a person lying there, and you have an irresistible impulse to run up and start kicking?"

"It's a sickness, I know."

"Oh, look, Titan is here," Tom said. They turned, looked toward the street where a crowd had gathered. Security personnel holding them back. "Nice of them to join us."

"Nice to see people don't run from a mere boom around here," Aiden said.

"Wasn't that loud." Heather turned back toward the remains of the sweeper.

"Oh, listen to you," Aiden said, trying to stand, giving up. "Wasn't that loud. Maybe from where you were standing."

"Earned our hazard pay today, I give you that." She studied the shattered base. The sweeper had split and fractured. Parts sticking up like the limbs of a broken tree. "Time for phase three."

"There's a phase three?" Tom said.

"Well, yeah." Hand touching the sweeper as if she might start to poke and prod it, shake it to see if it was only faking. "There's the washing up to do. Guess who's on cleanup duty."

"Oh, this is not going to end with us getting to take off work early, is it?"

"Keep dreaming, Tweedledum."

"I thought I was Tweedledee," Tom muttered, climbing awkwardly to his feet.

"Yeah, sure, whatever."

"Earn your name, Tweedle," Aiden said, taking another stab at reaching his feet, making it halfway.

"Hey, that's Tweedledee to you, sir." Pointing at Aiden, then walking over to Heather and the remains of the sweeper. "So, you've got room for this desiccated nightmare in your van, do you?"

"Yeah, sort of," Heather said, shaking the segment of free-standing remains she was holding. "I'm pretty sure it'll fit. Don't really have a quarantine case on this scale. I'll have to bag it."

"Economics of scale, is it?"

"I suppose. Okay, no, I have no idea what you're talking about."

"Once a tourist hits a certain size, we are not expected to retrieve it whole."

"Just generally assumed we're going to blow it to bits, huh?"

"Well, that is what happened."

"You did offer us dynamite," Aiden said, having finally found his feet. "Thought you were being funny."

"I don't recall offering you dynamite specifically."

"High explosives, then?" Tom said. "Maybe you just offered us things that go boom?"

"It's possible I may have made reference to things of a vigorously combustible nature. Can't keep track of every little thing I promise." Heather looked from her prize to where security had drawn a perimeter screen. "Right, we had better get motivated before the Tourist Board catches wind of this. I don't like all the eyes on us."

"Lighting up the boards as we speak, I'm sure."

"Make sure your video feeds are on full archive."

"Yeah, got you covered," Aiden said, taking out his phone, beginning to type. "Tom even shot some video with his phone's camera. Tell me I didn't imagine that, Timothy. What's wrong with your eyeball?"

"Thought we could use some footage that wasn't all shakycam." Holding up his phone. "Phone's got great motion correction."

"Can't beat the resolution of your eyesight."

"Pluses and minuses." Shrug of shoulders. "Didn't think a little extra footage setting the scene would hurt. Is Heather abandoning us?" Watching her walk toward the security line. "Hey, where are you off to?"

Heather was typing on her phone as she walked, finally reached the bright yellow tape of the security line, began to pull on it, intent on breaking it. This quickly drew the attention of the nearest Titan Security agent.

"Excuse me," the agent said. "Hey, don't touch that." Her name was Rothchild, not that there was any way they could have known this. Aiden and Tom caught up.

"Well, then you shouldn't have blocked us within the control zone," Heather said. "We've got to neutralize the scene. That means gaining access to our equipment, and that means crossing the control line."

"No, listen," Rothchild said, "I'm not warning you—"

"No, you listen." Heather pointed with her phone. "The world doesn't end just because you've encased the parts of it you don't like within your precious zone of control. We still have a job to do. We have to clean up the mess. That means both of our vans need to park right over there, blocking the street, and inconveniencing the passersby while we work."

Rothchild was following where Heather was pointing with her eyes. She seemed less inclined to editorialize than she had a moment before, almost as if she was waiting for instructions to reach her via her earpiece. Aiden glanced to his phone. Even though Tom had been driving, he had access to the van's status, and he saw that Heather had used her priority override to summon both vehicles to their location.

"Think of it this way, if it'll help," Heather said. "The more collegial courtesy and cooperation you shove our way, the faster we get this all cleaned up and get out of here. This is already on the local feeds, I'm sure." Shrug of shoulders. "Only a matter of time before the n-logs pick it up."

Rothchild raised a hand as if listening to her ear. She did look young and in need of practice on how to appear nonchalant while multiple voices screamed in her head.

"Yeah, okay," she said and then unfolded a pair of markers from her kit. She split the security line, making a gap.

"Thank you," Heather said, walking toward the curb. "Pleasure doing business with you."

Aiden tried to flip through his video history while they waited for the vans to arrive, scanning for good shots of the ruined street sweeper. He hadn't spent much time post-explosion focused on it. Finally selecting a half-decent image, he began to type.

Well, that got a little exciting, he wrote, sending the picture to Lynn.

"Calling the partner already, are you?" Tom said.

"Promised her updates, if I could," he said. "She'll be monitoring the feeds. Want her to know I'm okay before she reads about it on the news."

"Wouldn't be an issue if you hadn't told her we were chasing a potential tourist."

"It's actually kind of sweet," Heather said.

"You would take his side."

"No, really, it's downright charming the way Charlie's partner has him wrapped around her finger. Checking in every five minutes."

"Hey, now," Aiden said.

"Oh, relax, you big baby." Heather shushed him with a gesture not that far removed from the one she had used earlier while yelling at the Titan Security agents. The vans had arrived.

Tom and Aiden started by putting the rolling-case back in their van, ignoring Heather's rolling-case, which continued to follow her around at a discreet distance like a well-scolded puppy. They did help her pull a pair of area sweepers and decontaminators from the back of her van and drag them into the secure zone. A quarantine bag quickly followed. Heather stood at the edge of the zone, programming the sweepers via her industrial-strength script. By this point both Heather and Tom's phones had started to squawk quite indignantly.

"Hey," Heather said, turning on Rothchild, who really was a nice person just trying to make ends meet. Her parents depended on her. "You think you could have a word with the local valet?" Heather waved her phone at Rothchild. "Our rides need to stay right where they are."

Rothchild tried a menacing glare, couldn't out-match Heather's thousand-mile stare, and took out her own phone.

"I'll see what I can do." Began to type, trying to ignore the look Heather continued to give her. Rothchild's parents had been injured in a freakishly rare shuttle accident and couldn't work. Her older brother hadn't been able to cope and had finally wound up in a debtors' assistance facility. Rothchild worked all the hours she could to ensure her parents didn't join him.

After a long moment, which just seemed to drag as Heather continued to study Rothchild, her phone finally chimed a quiet assent and calmed down.

"Thank you," she said, making a gesture as if snapping her phone in Rothchild's face, and put it away.

Heather went back to programming the area sweepers. The two robots were maybe half the size of the street sweeper, with more of a turtle shape than the miniature skyscraper that was their disgraced relative. The pair of machines took a sudden interest in their surroundings and began to scrub and clean. Each would find a spot and begin to spin as if it was an extra large brush. Moving around and finding various pieces of debris, little arms would extend, picking up the fragments, depositing them in compartments in their interiors.

Tom and Aiden had unfolded the quarantine bag and had begun to wrap the shattered base. Aiden's phone chimed once quietly. He ignored it. The quarantine bag was awkward work. His phone began emitting an excited screech as if it was being prodded with red-hot pokers.

"No, really, I can wait," Tom said, standing still, holding folds of the quarantine bag in his hands.

Aiden looked to his phone, told it to shut up.

What the hell happened? Lynn had typed. *Are you okay? It's all over the feeds. There was an explosion?*

Yeah, I'm good, he typed. "It's hit the feeds," he said, turning, holding up his phone, looking to Heather.

"Already?" she said.

"That was quick." Tom still held his end of the bag, appeared to be considering dropping one corner to check his phone.

"Yeah, well, that crowd doesn't appear to be going anywhere." Aiden indicated the sightseers and other random passersby who really should have gone back about their business but continued to watch the show like a bunch of bloodthirsty wolverines.

"Well, double-quick then." Heather indicated the broken sweeper.

Did you get my picture? Aiden typed.

"Hey, what did I say?"

"Seriously, Charlie, you're on the clock," Tom said.

Later, he typed. "Yeah, yeah," he said, putting his phone away. "Make me work for a living."

"Well, you're getting paid for a reason." Tom continued to wrap the remains of the street sweeper. Aiden holding up his end.

"We also have confirmation of n-log interest because of me," Aiden said. "Because of the explosion, really. Wasn't even that big."

"Rattled my teeth something awful. Ears will be ringing for a week."

"It's the low-grade background hum that'll drive you nuts later."

"Oh, great, now I can hear that, too. Thanks for pointing it out."

"Hey, Heather," Aiden said, turning, looking. "We're going to get comped for med center review on the incident, right?"

"Yeah, you'll get yours," she said.

"No, really, you're in charge of the paperwork. You need to make sure we get our med reviews."

"Oh, I'm in charge of the paperwork now, am I?"

"Well, you are the senior rep on-scene," Tom said. They had the street sweeper wrapped.

"Which means I should delegate your asterisk."

"Who's doing the manual labor, here?"

"Who took responsibility for triggering the parasite's destruct in a semi-crowded area? People could have been hurt."

"Including us," Aiden said.

"Yeah," Tom said.

"Seems to me that you're in the best position to explain your actions."

"Oh, yeah?" Heather said, pointing with her script. "Well, yeah, regrettably, I tend to agree." Looking away. "I really hate the paperwork."

"Woman after my own heart," Aiden said, "but I'm still not going to volunteer to do the paperwork for you."

"And to think you used to be my favorite."

"Oh, my heart bleeds," Aiden said. They had the quarantine bag on a microfilm rolling platform and began to move it toward the vans. "It really bleeds."

"Sweet talk like that, and I'll get creative with the report," Heather said.

"Can I be the prince of wine and roses?"

"Yeah, I want a talking pony named Fritz," Tom said. They almost had the quarantine bag back at the van.

"No editorial oversight," Heather said.

With the largest chunk of the street sweeper deposited in the back of Heather's van, they scanned the area, locating the other good-sized chunks, collecting them. They watched the area sweepers work.

"What was that little maniac of yours, anyway," Aiden said.

"What?" Heather was studying the script, glancing up occasionally to track the movements of the area sweepers.

"Gave its life with wild abandon."

"Yeah, it's designed to do that."

"Expensive on the resource heap, isn't it? Where do you get the budget?"

"R&D crashes and otherwise wastes a rather large number of robots, in case you hadn't noticed."

"Yeah, but really, it must be hard on the budget. You get a discount or something?"

Heather made a noise like an exasperated elephant seal.

"Just over the counter then?" Aiden said. "What about the operating system? Must be versatile. How much custom code goes into one of those things?"

"What in the hell are you going on about?" Heather said, turning on him. Tom was back by the vans, making sure the valet protocol didn't try to quietly move them off.

"Just making conversation." Shrug of shoulders.

Trace of a smile began to play at the corner of Heather's lips.

"Aiden Charles, have you been attending the local Ape Fights?"

"What?"

"Monkey Trials?"

"Never! What the hell are those?"

A grin split her face practically from ear-to-ear.

"You have been to the Monkey Trials," she said. "There was one at Ben Franklin not that long ago. Couldn't make it. Conflicting priorities. Wish I could have been there."

Aiden shook his head.

"Of course." Snapped her fingers. "Your partner works for Ben Franklin. She got an in, didn't she?"

"Okay, maybe," Aiden said. "Keep it down."

"Oh, relax, nobody here cares. Ben Franklin really has a hard-on for stomping them down, which must make things interesting for your partner. And I wouldn't recommend telling anyone in Central Services management."

"What does that make you?"

"Monkey Trials are a great grooming ground. We scout them all the time. Well, really, it's just an excuse to participate. Let other people score it for talent. Where do you think my suicidal little maniac got his start?"

"Ran him through the trials, did you?"

"Damn Skippy, I did." Leaning toward him. "You want in, don't you?"

"What?"

"Sure, get a standard chassis down at the hardware store. They're modular. One of the requirements is they're a common base. Modular units."

"Right, I've just got money to burn."

"We've got a code base, you know."

"I'm sure."

"No, really, my clan shares a code base. Practically a co-op. You remember those, don't you? Co-op development?"

"Yeah, I'm vaguely familiar," Aiden said, muttering.

"I'm sure," Heather said. "Listen, build up your own basic unit. Compete in a few rounds. Hold your own, and I just might give you access to the code base."

"That's surprisingly generous of you."

"Oh, don't give me that look." She clasped his shoulder in a friendly sort of way. "You know how hard it is to get people interested in the trials? I personally want more competition." Looking about. "Sure beats the hell out of designing a better dishwasher." Mockingly. "Our latest algorithm cuts a quarter millisecond off the clock."

"What about all of this?" Nodding toward the scene of recent devastation. "Don't you live for the hunt?"

"How often does this happen, Charlie?" Turning, taking in the fountain and the park and the area sweepers finishing up their work. "Really, how often?"

"Yeah, tell me about it."

"Have to do something to keep from getting bored."

"You saying you can get me in?"

"Oh, I may know a thing or two." Splitting her attention between the script and the pair of sweepers.

"Like when the next trial will be held?"

"They're more of an ad hoc type of thing. Mavericks. You've head of those, right?"

"I can imagine more than one option for that reference, but okay."

"Yeah, mavericks, just watch for the signs. Ben Franklin's not the only place trials are held."

"Well, let's not tell them that. Lynn will be crushed."

"Center of the universe, right?" Tapped Aiden on the shoulder with her script. "Just watch for the signs, Chuck. Watch for the signs."

"They had better be nice and big. And kindly point them out to me. And don't call me—"

"Don't call you Chuckles. Yeah, I got that."

CHAPTER ELEVEN

In which Lynn discovers that her partner, Aiden, has made some rather impetuous decisions.

Lynn got out of work as early as she could and caught the first Ubiquity Shuttle that came within her sphere of influence. Naturally, the shuttle's inverse-urgency circuit was working overtime, diverting more than once to catch people whose proximity and destination were questionable, resulting in the trip taking much longer than most any other day. Without any great surprise and an inordinate amount of frustration, Lynn found that Aiden had beaten her home.

"Oh, my god!" she said before she had even gotten the door closed. "What happened? Are you okay?" Didn't bother with her shoes. Leaving her coat on a hook by the door was too much work. "The feeds have been screaming about the tourist. The explosion. Everything." She closed on Aiden. He was on the floor, having pushed the couch against the bar-stools. The coffee table was against the entertainment wall. "Central Services customer relations is saying squat—The hell you doing?"

"Huh?" Aiden said, looking up from his phone. The screen was unfolded to maximum. A short bipedal robot was resting before him like a somnolent child. "Hey." Nodding his head.

"Hey, yourself," Lynn said. "What's all this?"

"Bought a monkey." Turning back to his phone.

"Yeah, I was afraid—I can see that." Moving slowly, Lynn sat on the edge of the couch.

"It's a standard chassis. Got it over the counter from a hardware store."

Lynn raised her hands, let them flop back to her sides.

"They're expensive," she said.

"Tell me about it. Had to get the cheapest one I could find. They're modular. You know how much even the cheapest additions cost?"

"Looks like bread and butter for a long time to come," she muttered all but to herself.

"Well, you have to." He gestured at the little robot. "You have to get a minimal number of modules to fight in the Monkey Trials. Hard part is trying to guess which ones you need. I'm terrified I'll have to go back."

"For the trials. Don't even really know when the next one will be."

"That'll give us time to work on little Sputnik here." Aiden typed commands on his phone. The little robot tried to stand.

"And it's fallen over already," Lynn said, watching it.

"The code," Aiden said, typing. "It's all in the code. The over-the-counter framework is so basic it's not even worth mentioning. This is going to take a lot of work. Don't know when we'll be ready."

"You need the keyboard extension for your phone."

"Yeah, I couldn't find it." Raised his hands, shaking them. "This script emulator is horrible."

Lynn sat, shoulders slumped, staring all but vacantly at the silent tableau before her. Aiden already lost back in the arcane depths of the script emulator while the robot tried rather valiantly to stand once more.

"I'll find out which distro Liz Dao is using," she finally said, quietly, earning herself a fuzzy look from Aiden. "Grad student, you met her."

"The one we chased around the Ape Fights? Won her match, right?"

"Yeah, her," she said, feeling the weight shift in her chest. "Or I can check with Oliver. He's probably got access to more advanced emulators. I could probably whip something together if I had to."

"Blighter!"

"And it's fallen over again."

"Yeah, that's right," Aiden said, turning, looking at her. "I'm not the only one here who can throw code. You deal with a lot of communication and network access protocols. Probably just what we need."

"Applicable skills," she said. "And it's fallen over again."

"What?" Turning. "Bastard!"

"Maybe biped wasn't the way to go."

"Well, I wanted to do something different."

"At least they're modular, right? You got enough modules to change the basic configuration?"

"Yeah, we're not locked into a biped."

"And it's fallen over...Again."

"Oh, come on!"

"Put it out of its misery for now, dear."

Aiden typed. The little robot stopped trying to climb to its feet.

"It's over the counter," he said. "You would think the basic routines would work. Stand up. Sit down. Whistle Dixie."

"Well, you did say the basic framework was really primitive."

"Yeah, on the scale of tourist risk, it doesn't even register. I mean, I do understand their desire to avoid tourism, but come on."

"Can't even walk and chew gum, huh?" She kept studying the little robot, lying on its side like a child that had gotten so tired it had simply keeled over where it stood.

"Didn't even try to use it."

"What?"

"Well, it was just so primitive."

"You tried to jury-rig your own basic functionality?"

"Didn't see the point."

"No wonder it keeps falling over," she said, trying not to laugh. "You could at least test out the standard code. Did you filch anything from the basic framework or did you really start from scratch?"

"Of course, I looked at the framework. How else would I know the code is junk?"

"Could have been listening to rumors. Stranger things have happened."

"I'm sure they have," he said, "but not this time."

"You just didn't attempt to adapt any of the code."

"There was no copying and pasting, if that's what you mean. Look, I've only just got it put together and started messing with the code."

"Actually, when you put it like that, it is rather impressive."

"Thank you."

"No, really, it hardly looked as if it was having a seizure at all."

"It almost stood up. No, scratch that, it was standing. It just—"

"Kept falling over. Yeah, I got that."

"Just going to take time." Shrug of shoulders.

"Yeah, I don't even know when the next Ape Fight purloined letter is going to take place yet."

"Starting to sound interested."

"Huh? Yeah, sorry." Ran fingers through her hair. The future was written. It sprawled before her. "Shock hasn't worn off yet. I'm not ready to hear how much the little monkey cost."

"Tell me about it. You should have been there. I turned white and everything when I saw the bill."

"Bread and butter, Aiden. Can't say I'm looking forward to it, but my God, we've got ourselves a monkey." Gesturing, pointing. "I mean, just look at it. We're in business."

"No idea when it'll be ready."

"Still working on our next invitation."

"It's cool. We've got options. Ben Franklin isn't the only home to Monkey Trials."

"Oh, do tell. Suppose I shouldn't be too surprised." Looking at him. "Where did you suss out such information so suddenly?"

"Well, if you can believe it, Heather told me."

"Never! The Tourist Hunter, herself?"

"Yeah, turns out she's quite the fan. It was only dumb luck she couldn't make it to the Franklin trials we attended."

"Oh, that's just too rich," Lynn said. "When did all of this come up? Just today? Hey," she said almost jumping to her feet. "The tourist! What the hell!" Pointing at the little robot. "Just goes to show how your outrageous purchase messed with my head. What happened with the tourist?"

"Yeah, we had to blow it up."

"I gathered that." Dug through her pockets after her phone. "Let me show you some pictures."

"I was there, dear."

"And you only sent me one image." She tapped commands. The entertainment wall came to life, began to display random pictures from her phone. "Had to find my own." Tapping, scrolling. The wall began to settle down, displaying various images of the fountain and its surroundings. "Look at that."

"Well, I had other things on my mind at the time."

"I'm sure." Dividing her time between the phone

and the entertainment wall. "How close were you to the center of the action?"

"Hurt like hell when the tourist blew." Shrug of shoulders. "Got a free trip to the doctor out of it at least."

"What?"

"Well, we had to make sure there was no concussive damage."

"Holy crap, Aiden." Jumped from the couch. "What the fuck? Are you all right?" Joined him on the floor, leaning against him.

"Yeah, if you can believe it, both Tom and I are fine." Pointing at the wall. "You can see us walking around and everything."

"Oh, yeah, that's you, isn't it?" Looking at the various imagines displayed on the wall. "Can hardly tell from these pictures. No text descriptions. Nobody figured out who you are."

"Like that'll last. Thank God for small mercies anyway, right?"

"Speaking of which," she said, tapping, scrolling her phone. An image of Heather with an arm around Aiden's shoulders suddenly dominated the wall. "Who's the chick? Why's she being so friendly, and why haven't you introduced me to her yet?"

"That's Heather."

"That's Heather Graymarsh?" Tried to zoom in on her face. "Why don't I recognize her?"

"Not exactly as if she's known outside of Central Services, and we don't really move in the same circles. Opportunity to introduce you simply hasn't come up. And she's got the bedside manner of a burning mattress."

"I like her already."

"Yeah, well, she's as likely to rip out your skull and feast on your brains as say *hi* upon meeting you."

"Oh, I really like her."

"Also why I haven't been big on trying to engineer an introduction. But." Pointing at the little robot. "That's our best ticket to a meet-and-greet."

"Really."

"Truth to power," Aiden said, raising a hand. "She tried to tempt me with access to her code base."

"Never!"

"Oh, yes."

"Well, no wonder you ran out and spent our life savings on a multifunction robot."

"Wasn't quite our life savings."

"Yeah, I'm sure."

"But just picture it," Aiden said, turning, looking at the robot. "Competing in the Monkey Trials. Who could ask for anything more?"

"It was fun, I'll give you that."

"You dragged me, remember?"

"Never!"

"Oh, ever."

"No!"

"Yes, you did. You most certainly did."

"Yes, I suppose...Next you're going to say this is all my fault."

"You want this just as much as I do."

Lynn shook her head, covered her mouth, trying not to laugh.

"Well, it's one thing to want," she said. "It's another thing entirely to take leave of your senses and actually do it."

He just looked at her. Smiled.

"One of use had to jump first," he said.

* * *

Lynn made her way through the three-dimensional maze that was the floors devoted to the Department of Theoretical and Computational Physics—floor planners and designers having been determined to live up to the "Theoretical" part of the department's name. Lynn found Elisabeth Dao nursing a cup of coffee in a back corner of one of the labs, far away from the hustle and blur of people. She found the graduate student casually perusing documents on her phone while steam drifted leisurely from the business end of her coffee cup.

"Studying?" Lynn said, making Elisabeth jump. Coffee failed in its attempt to escape from the cup. "Thought that was anachronistic. Don't you kids today just have knowledge injected directly into your cerebral cortex or something?"

"What can I say?" Elisabeth said, looking up from her phone. "I'm a sucker for the classics."

"Which explains why it took me three days to find you. Hiding from the glitterati otherwise known as your fellow students."

Elisabeth gave her a look.

"Do you even hear the words coming out of your mouth?" she finally said. "That doesn't make sense."

"Damn, they're going to revoke my hip-master card," Lynn said, glancing about as if scanning for eavesdroppers and other assorted informants.

"Hip-master?" Smiling. "Nobody says that any more."

"Oh God, I'm getting old." She slumped onto the bench next to Elisabeth. "I'm so far out of the loop I should just be taken out and shot."

"Yeah, you're pretty ancient, I must say."

"Thank you."

"What are you? Four? Five years older than me?"

"Oh, you say the sweetest things. Must be closer to ten."

"Never!"

"Happens to the best of us," Lynn said. "It may be hard to imagine now but one day you'll look up and spy thirty in the rear-view."

"Youth wasted on the young, is it? Hear that trash all the time."

"And that's why it's wasted. You'll understand. I take comfort in that. Knowing someday you too will understand."

"So it's like losing your virginity, is it?"

"That," Lynn said, drawing in her breath as if stalling for time. "Simply had not occurred to me."

"Well, maybe it should."

"Dear God, what an image."

"Not exactly an image. More a concept—Wait." Turning, looking more firmly at Lynn. "Are you picturing me naked?"

"I wouldn't go that far. It is more of an abstract concept—You know, I think we have completely derailed this conversation."

"I'll have you know it takes more than the price of a cup of coffee to get me into the emperor's new clothes."

"There was actually a reason I came looking for you." Hand to her face, scratching at her eyes.

"Not that you paid for this cup of coffee, but that is entirely beside the point."

"God, I am old."

"Don't change the subject," Elisabeth said. "And you're not old."

"Thank you." Closed her eyes. "Oh, yes, the script. Came to ask you about the script. How is it working out, anyway?"

"Yeah, it's been working just fine, thank you for repairing it."

"No problem, all part of the service." Paused for just a moment as if changing mental gears, managing to avoid a great wailing screech of grinding metal. "What do you do when you can't get your hands on a script? How do you get by? Rely on an emulator?"

"Yeah, I must admit I've had to make use of one or two of those over the years." Eyes back to her phone.

"Not the same thing, is it?"

"No. No, it is not."

"Now, here's an example of my age showing, or at the very least, a practical demonstration of what happens when one drifts away from the center of a young and vibrant culture." Holding up a hand. "I should be on top of these things, you know. It's my job to be familiar with technology."

"Okay."

"I should know all there is to know about script emulation. The latest builds and designs. I should be advising students, faculty and staff, on the best distributions." Hand to her chest. "I know Streamweaver."

"Everybody knows Streamweaver."

"Thank you. See? I hear it in your voice. I know Pinocchio and Crush."

Elisabeth made a face.

"They have their uses," she said. "Have you tried Socks?"

"What?"

"I know, Socrates isn't exactly a script emulator."

"It's hackware, is what it is."

"It has similar functionality."

"I could be fired for having Socks installed on my phone." Pointing an accusatory finger. "You had better not have it installed or be caught using it."

"Oh, hey, no worries, I never touch the stuff. I seem to recall a hacked router and a flat-lined floor. Want nothing to do with that."

"Thank you."

"What's with the sudden interest in script emulators, anyway? You've got more access to scripts than anybody I know."

"Well," Lynn said, trying to sound nonchalant. "It's not like I have round-the-clock access to a proper script."

"Whatever are they having you do that you're taking your work home without—No!"

"Keep your voice down, you'll embarrass me."

"Why, my dear Merlin Charles, are you perchance interested in learning more about how to make a really first-rate Mock Turtle soup?"

"Don't call me Merlin," Lynn muttered. "Can't stand it when people call me Merlin."

"Changing the subject."

"Well, it's not exactly as if I have a need for Mock Turtle soup, but I know people, friends and family, you could say."

"Oh, my God, you are!"

"Let's just stick with the discussion at hand, thank you very much. We were discussing the best script emulators to recommend to various faculty and staff."

"For the purposes of after-hour projects, right?"

"Nothing of the sort."

"You think we've got access to lab scripts every hour of the day?" Elisabeth said. "Well, it would be wonderful if it was true. We have to check them out. Return them. What happens in the middle of the night when we're still working on a project?"

"Yes, I suppose you would have to make do."

"Thank you. Not that us pampered children in the most glorious Department of Comp/Theo Physics really have that much call for midnight script access. You have to go to Applied Engine/Robotics for that."

"You work with your fair share of machines."

"Never said we didn't, but yeah, if you really want to run with the robotic big boys, you've got to head down to Applied Robotics and Engine fascism or however it goes. They use." Looked off into the middle distance as if she had non-corporal access to the world network. "Well, I think penis is very popular."

"I'm sorry. Did you just say penis?"

"Yes, I did."

"And we're not just being cryptic here, right? We're still talking the best script emulators for programming over-the-counter robots?"

"We have not raised the encryption that far," Elisabeth said. "We are talking about a legitimate script emulator that goes by the very colloquial name of major willy frankenweiner."

"Major?"

"Okay, not really. It's more properly called P-Mas, but you know, bodily functions make fools of us all."

"Still making me feel old, Liz." Shaking her head as if it was a great weight she would not be able to bear for much longer. "But I get it. Puppet Master. Wow, that's so daring and original. I think I've even heard of it. Ringing bells in the deep recesses and backwaters of my mind."

"I'm not surprised. It really is very good. Oh, but don't use Puppet Master. That's old news. Grandpa-ware."

"You just said."

"I said P-Mas. It branched off of and has far surpassed old grandpa Puppet Master."

"Well, technically, and by that I'm pretty sure I mean factually, you said penis."

"Well, I can't be expected to remember every little thing I say."

"It was like two seconds ago, and you were quite specific."

"And you were picturing me naked." Pointing. "I should report you."

"You only accused me of picturing you naked, which is a gross slander that the review board shall not take seriously, but they'll probably reprimand me anyway. Not like they've got anything better to do."

"There, see? Don't mess with me." Tapping a finger to the side of her head and gesturing to indicate her line of sight. "And my eyes are up here."

"Do me for the review board, and I'll sue you for libel and defamation. I'll have you before arbitration so fast it'll make your head spin."

"Which I'll still win. Arbitration always favors the young. I'll take your new—Hey, what model house pet did you get anyway?"

"Oh, don't start," Lynn said. "It's the most basic over-the-counter model you could possibly imagine."

"No, those are worthless. They can barely walk and chew gum at the same time."

"Such camaraderie of spirit. It was the best we could afford."

"They'll wax the floor with you. Why?"

"They're expensive."

"Oh, no, they are not."

"Well, maybe for a child like you who doesn't mind living on white bread and cheesecloth."

"There's no shame in frugality, but they're not that expensive. You really need to update your priorities."

"I'll remember that the next time I have money to burn, but until that day arrives, I have to settle for the fact that I'm the proud adoptive parent of the cheapest little monkey we could get our hands on."

"I'm dying to see it," Elisabeth said, reaching out, touching Lynn's arm. "Decrepit little monkey-child that it is."

"Yes, well, there's a simple solution to that. Invite us to your uncle's wedding."

"He's already married."

"Then invite us to the divorce. Honestly, do I have to think of everything here?"

"Well, these things aren't just thrown together—okay, maybe they are, but that's kind of the point."

"Not a lot of pre-visualization happening here, huh?"

"Not even a little."

"Well, keep me in your hearts and minds, and don't forget us when something does come along."

"I'll try," Elisabeth said. "Yes, I do believe that I shall try."

* * *

The apartment was still a disaster area of very nearly biblical proportions, with the couch pushed against the kitchen chairs and the coffee table pushed against the entertainment wall. If any more room had been made, the couch would have been undercutting the chairs, turning them into inverted sculpture that only truly hardcore art lovers could enjoy. Lynn and Tamara Rosewater were attempting to make the best of the function-compromised state of the room, finding what comfort they could on the couch. Aiden was on the floor, as if he had not moved in days and days, with the little robot resting before him.

"I was promised a show," Tamara said, resting shoulder to shoulder with Lynn. Feet tucked up. Eyes focused on the somnolent machine.

"Yeah, yeah," Aiden said, typing, scanning displays. Phone positioned on a little stand. Screen folded out to maximum. He had even found the external keyboard.

"It hasn't fallen over once or anything."

"Been working on that."

"Yeah, it's been a lot more stable since we reconfigured it for three legs," Lynn said. Phone in her lap, half ignored. Its display was taking up very nearly half of the entertainment wall.

"What was it before? Quadruped? Centipede?" Tamara was transfixed by the robot.

"Biped," Aiden muttered.

"Never!"

"Took me forever to convince him it was a bad idea," Lynn said.

"Well, no wonder it kept falling over. You rebuilt the code from scratch, right? Don't seem the type to rely on another man's code base."

"I glanced at it," Aiden said.

"That's advanced work, getting a biped to stand, and I should know. I tried it myself."

"Did you, now?"

"In my wild misspent youth, sure," Tamara said. "But who's got time for that amount of wretched excess in this day and age? I've got students of my own to fill the days and nights and ignore."

Aiden looked up from his phone.

"I congratulated you on that, right?" he said. "The promotion without portfolio? The responsibility without compensation?"

"That's why I'm here, baby." Spread her arms wide to take in the apartment.

"I thought it was because you missed our company."

"Yeah," Lynn said, turning, accusatory.

"I see you all the time, you wretched child," Tamara said, half-facing Lynn. "Okay, maybe not all the time. In fact, hardly any time these days, but it's a different story."

"Really?"

"Sure, all I've got to do is smash my phone real good, and you come running."

"When did you smash?"

"Yeah." Tamara shook her head. "Turns out that isn't as great a plan as it sounds. You know ITRC will send whoever is available rather than who you want to see? Most vexing, that is."

"I bet."

"Fortunately, I didn't actually break anything. That would have been stupid. I need my phone to remind me what students I'm ignoring and which classes I'm forgetting to teach."

"We did work out the problem with your calendar, right?" Lynn said. "The day planner is finally working?"

"Yeah, it's working, I suppose."

"You suppose?"

"Yeah, next you'll be telling me I actually have to program the damn thing. Well, who's got time for that?"

"It was the whole point of fixing the issues with your calendar."

"There was nothing wrong with the calendar."

"Exactly, it was all user error," Lynn said, pointing.

"It was not."

"It's always user error," Aiden said. "Predictable as the tide."

"It could be other things," Tamara said.

"Sure, it could be, but user error is your go-to reason when something's wrong—"

"And you have absolutely no idea what it is," Lynn finished the sentence, cutting him off.

"It's these little peeks behind the customer service curtain that always make me gravitate back to you guys," Tamara said. "Perfect example." Gesturing toward the robot. "It's simple user error that's made your unit an impertinent little bitch."

"Hey," Aiden said.

"No, it's true," Lynn said.

"It's hardly impertinent at all."

"That's because it hasn't moved the whole time I've been sitting here," Tamara said.

"You can't rush art."

"Oh, it's art now, is it?"

"Could be," Aiden said, looking at the robot, and then turning toward her. "Actually, its name is Sputnik, not Art, but that's kind of beside the point."

"You've named it Sputnik?"

"What's wrong with Sputnik?"

"Yeah, what's wrong with Sputnik?" Lynn said.

"Well, it's just so old-fashioned."

"It's a classic."

"It's a cliché, is what it is. And it's old."

"It's not old," Aiden said. "We just bought it."

"What's with the plurality, here?" Lynn said, pointing. "You bought it."

"And you didn't make me return it. Complicity is conviction."

"Complicity is what?" Tamara said, laughing.

"You heard me." Typing, pushing buttons. "Okay, let's try this."

"So this is how you fill your time now, is it?" Tamara tilted her head next to Lynn's ear.

"What?" Lynn whispered back.

"Haven't seen you on the campaign grid in ages. You gave it up, right?"

"When do you have time for campaigning?"

"I don't, and hardly the point."

The little tripod started to move, drawing all sound and attention to it like an overly dramatic howler monkey. They watched, spellbound, as the robot teetered awkwardly on its three legs.

"Steady," Tamara whispered, encouragingly, as if anything else would frighten it.

"If it falls over now, I shall raise my voice," Aiden said.

The machine continued to wobble, like a newborn giraffe trying to feel secure on its feet for the first time in its very short life. It managed to stand without shaking for a long moment while its visual and audio sensors rotated this way and that, taking in the room.

"Hey, little guy," Tamara said, leaning toward it. "It's looking at us."

"Of course it's looking at us," Lynn said, holding onto Tamara so that she would not topple forward onto the floor. They had been drinking.

"It's taking in its surroundings." Aiden was watching it carefully.

"Why are we whispering?"

"I don't know." Lynn's hands were fists in Tamara's shirt.

"If everything goes according to plan," Aiden said. "It'll take about three steps and then sit down."

They watched the little robot with an intensity that would make any small woodland creature they found at the zoo spontaneously burst into tears. The tripod continued to scan the room, turning, twisting its legs almost to the point of becoming unstable.

"We need to work on its stance when it turns."

"Yeah, I think that's my routine," Lynn said.

"Pretty sure I touched that code last."

"Then we'll blame you should it fall over."

"Technically, that's rotating, not turning," Tamara said, pointing, gesturing, making tiny circles with her fingers. "They're actually different."

"Hey, she contributes," Aiden said. "Why we invite you over."

"Not the only reason, surely."

"Serendipity bonus, then."

"Multifaceted, I am," Tamara said. "You can handle the balance with the same code. You just have to throw in some extra checks. Rotation versus turning. When to cut to a balance check."

"Like the lady said, it's all in the algorithm." Lynn hadn't taken her eyes off the robot, which was in the process of trying to straighten out its tangled feet.

"Damn Skippy, it is, but I never said that."

"No, the other lady—not exactly a lady—more like a grad student."

The robot raised one foot awkwardly, brought it down quickly, and pulled itself along, all but dragging the other two feet behind it. Aiden, Lynn and Tamara collectively held their breath. The machine repeated the foot-dragging process until it had covered half the distance between where it had started and the entertainment wall. It collected itself, standing still as if it had come to something resembling a three-legged version of parade rest. The spectators collectively cheered.

"It can walk and chew gum," Aiden said.

"I would hardly call that—"

"Oh, give us the victory, Tomorrow," he said, cutting her off. "In the grand scheme of things, I would hardly call that walking, much less chewing gum, I know, but give us this victory today."

"Yeah, we worked really hard," Lynn said.

"Oh, I know." Tamara held up her hands for peace. "I've been there. Exactly in your position. The victories may be small, baby steps, but the rewards are great."

"Rewards?"

"Sense of accomplishment is its own reward."

"We should celebrate."

"We are celebrating."

"Celebration is its own reward," Aiden said.

"You're really pushing it, dear."

"Glory in our victory, now," he said, sweeping gesture, taking in the room and the little robot resting before them. "Work on the code more later. Like an hour."

"An hour?" Lynn cried, laughing.

"Two hours?"

"How about tomorrow?"

"How about me what?" Tamara asked. They ignored her.

"What time is it?" Aiden said, looking, turning to the entertainment wall and chances of finding a clock upon its surface. "It may actually be tomorrow."

"Hey, I'm right here," Tamara said.

"No, we're talking about," Lynn said, trying not to laugh. "Never mind what we're talking about. You have the worst nickname ever, dear."

CHAPTER TWELVE

In which Lynn and Aiden experience the joys and sorrows of exposing their new toy to the great wide world beyond their front door.

There were office districts, and then there were hardcore industrial-strength office districts. There were the relatively clean and fancy neighborhoods where the upscale professionals went to work each day, staying late into the evening to show how driven they were and how much satisfaction they got from their jobs. Then there were the neighborhoods where the service professionals worked. Among these districts were the Central Services offices and distribution center. Its neighbors were various other service centers such as vehicle repair, climate maintenance, and street upkeep. Direct competitors had their offices and centers at discreet distances. Because of the nature of the work, many of the offices ran day and night. People walked. Vehicles moved, and lights shone from every angle.

Even among all of this constant need for work and activity, there remained unused rooms and empty spaces that had been hunted down and claimed by bars and clubs. Rented cheaply. Little concern for noise pollution in the middle of the night. Even less concern for trash and other human byproducts of too much time spent partying at the various events.

Mixed somewhat discreetly among the clubs and

216

bars were other venues where more interesting games and pleasures could be found. There were spaces for people to chase each other with fake guns, spraying paint like imitation blood. They could drive little manual control cars on carefully protected if still rather recklessly dangerous tracks. People could throw balls. They could lift weights. They could even climb things without regard for proper protective gear.

From out of all of this noise and distraction, it was possible to hide the occasional Ape Fight or Monkey Trial. Events hidden right under the nose of businesses, such as Central Services or Alpha Matrix, who had a professional interest in clamping down on such activity. It never stopped their employees from participating, but it did occasionally make interactions with management rather interesting.

There were four rings for Ape Fights that twilight weekend. The people cheering. The crowds immense. The robots fighting for all they were worth, knowing no other way, having no other reason to exist. There were two rings for Monkey Trials. The people gathering, pointing, screaming encouragement that the little robots paid no nevermind. All around the perimeter of the warehouse space was a two-lane track. Sometimes, it was at ground level. Other times, it rose high above everyone's heads, twisting this way and that. Occasionally, it was three lanes, and once or twice in the great loop, it was only wide enough for one robot racer to pass at a time.

The crew spaces surrounded the warehouse floor. Unlike the university games, these spaces were actually separate rooms with doors and everything. The robots could be fussed over, getting them ready or weeping over the damaged remains in something not quite resembling peace and quiet.

Lynn and Aiden had their own table, which seemed

a huge extravagance compared to the actual needs of their single robot. All of the equipment and gear to support their lonely little machine barely took up a third of the space provided. The other tables were crowded, cluttered, and surrounded by handlers, well-wishers, and assorted hangers-on.

"Yes, I checked that," Aiden said, hovering over their robot, which was still a tripod.

"We have to be ready." Lynn punched commends, two-fingered, into her phone. "There is only so much we can check and double-check."

"If we check it over one more time, I swear Sputnik's just going to disintegrate from metal fatigue."

"I stopped touching it five minutes ago." Tapping, scrolling. "My phone, on the other hand, might just snap in two from all the abuse."

"There's nothing more we can do." Aiden threw up his hands. "Why isn't it our turn yet?"

"Watched-Pot Syndrome. The more we want it the more time dilates or something."

"Right, as we approach the event horizon, time slows to a crawl."

"Event horizon? Nice."

"What others experience as just a few minutes seems like hours to us—No, wait, it should be the other way around."

"We're drifting away from the event?"

"Time is," Aiden said, looking about, watching the other tables pointedly ignore them. "There is shrinkage."

"I'm not," Lynn said, following Aiden's eye, feeling the others' gazes upon them without actually being able to catch anybody studying them. "That analogy needs work. Time is expanding for us. Becoming engorged, as it were."

"If I stopped to think about that for just a second, I would probably be disgusted."

"But strangely accurate," Lynn said.

Tamara reached them, having made her way across the crowded floor.

"Okay, I've scoped out the trial," she said. "Brace yourselves. It's a puzzle."

"Are you allowed to do that?" Aiden said.

"A puzzle? Sure, I don't see why not. It's not like there are rules. Not really. More vague traditions and outlines."

"No, I mean tell us what to expect."

"You mean give you an unfair advantage or something? What are you going to program at this late hour? Your code is either good enough to cope with an object/shape test or it isn't."

"Thought you said it was a puzzle," Lynn said.

"Yes, involving objects and shapes."

"You mean like one of those old intelligence tests?" Aiden said. "Can the monkey get the square peg in the round hole, kind of thing?"

"Yes, exactly, got it in one."

"Is Sputnik ready for that kind of thing?" Lynn had a hand to her forehead, holding her phone.

"I don't know," Aiden said. "I was assuming more athletic jumping, climbing and problem solving."

"Yeah."

"Well, why would you assume a thing like that?" Tamara said. "Haven't you ever been to a Monkey Trial before?"

"We've been to one, dear," Aiden said, holding up a finger. "One."

"You're supposed to check these things out. Attend a few. Ask around. Get the lay of the land."

"Now she tells us." Aiden shared a long look with Lynn.

"Sink before you can swim, right?" Lynn said.

"Exactly." Tamara pointing at her. "Don't worry about how deep the end or how far the shore. Just jump right in."

"Yeah, I prefer that one to the whole time-dilation event-horizon thing."

"What have you two been going on about?" Tamara gave them both a look.

"Performance anxiety," Aiden said. "You would have had to have been there."

"I fear I'm going to have to take your word for that."

"It made sense in context," Lynn said. "Watched-Pot Syndrome, my asterisk. When is it our turn, anyway?" Looking at her phone, scrolling. "Shit!"

"We're up?" Aiden said.

"Yeah, we're actually up. Grab Junior and let's go."

Aiden scooped the little robot awkwardly up in his arms, ignoring the tool case they had brought with them, turning for the door to the warehouse floor. Lynn didn't wait, moving ahead of him as if she would clear a path, should it become necessary to push people out of the way. Crowded as it was, pushing and shoving was not necessary in the crew area. The game floor beyond was another matter.

The crash of white noise hit them like a wave as they passed the door, almost as if they had crossed a dimensional barrier. The air was thick. It practically stuck to the skin. The roar of the crowd beat at them as if they were running a gauntlet of invisible cricket bats. The track of the robot racers was mercifully high, the little vehicular monsters rushing far above their heads.

They were somewhat separated from the majority of the crowd, as if the organizers had considered the possibility that the robots and their handlers would need a way to reach the ring. These plans to keep a clear path had not gone over as well as could be expected, and the people did press and crowd. Lynn did push and shove. Tamara followed along, preventing the people from filling too quickly the void Aiden left in his wake.

They reached the ring, Lynn consulting her phone. She crossed to a nondescript referee and tried to carry on a conversation over the battering of the white noise. The referee made hand gestures, pointed. They flashed phones, compared screens, typed short burst-like notes. Lynn nodded, hoping she understood, turned to Aiden, held up a hand with fingers spread indicating time. She pointed around the perimeter of the ring to where handlers stood with their robots.

It was hard to see into the ring. There were brightly colored blocks of various shapes and sizes scattered throughout the space. There were short platforms like children's workbenches in three corners, and each had spaces and holders of various sizes, shapes and configurations. There were little robots running about as if they did not know which way to turn or what to do.

Lynn had stopped, standing with other handlers looking into the ring, exchanging quick nods and glances with them. Aiden reached her, holding Sputnik in his arms as if the little robot would run off should he put it down. Tamara put her hand on his shoulder, grinning practically from ear to ear. There was no point trying to talk. They turned to the ring. The view from the edge was pretty good.

The three handlers currently in the ring were spaced fairly evenly around the edge, as if they were opposing polarities that could get no closer. Each held a dead man's switch. Two kept the switch all but casually at their sides. One was gesturing with the switch almost as if it was a control wand, shouting at his robot the whole time.

The robots ignored him. One was wandering haphazardly about the ring, bumping into things, occasionally picking something up as if it might move it, putting it back down. Another was trying to stack all of the objects it could in one corner without consideration for size or shape. This tower of babel would occasionally topple over, and the poor little robot would scurry around in a desperately futile attempt to rebuild. The third was placing objects upon its workbench but didn't seem to be paying the slightest attention to whether an object fit the space selected for it or no.

The referee called time, stepping into the center of the ring, and the three robots immediately went dark as if they had been felled with a particularly noxious gas. The referee looked to the three workbenches for only a moment and then pointed to one handler. The crowd roared. The handler stepped into the ring. Arms raised over her head. The crowd cheered. She shook hands with the referee and then went to her robot, picking it up. The other handlers quickly followed, going to their robots. The handlers shouting, calling to each other, but not a word could be understood at the ring's edge.

Aiden started to put Sputnik down.

"No, not yet!" Lynn shouted, leaning toward his ear. "There's at least one more match before ours!"

"Then why did we come running out here?"

"We had to check in! Could have been bumped to a later match!"

The referees were in the ring, resetting for the next round.

"Oh God, that's Heather!" Aiden said.

"What? Where?" Lynn scanned the referees as they worked.

"Over there!" He nodded, trying to gesture across the ring to where Heather Graymarsh stood. "Oh God, she's seen me!"

Tamara laughed.

"Well, of course she sees you!" Lynn said, waving. "How do you think we got in? She doesn't recognize me." Waving grew more vigorous with about the same degree of result.

"You've never met! How could she recognize you?"

"She's heading this way!" Tamara said.

"What?"

"Made you look." Tamara had her phone out, taking pictures. She did not have an ocular camera, which Aiden considered rather odd for a student but had never found the opportunity to press her on the topic.

"Remind me why we invited you!" he said.

"Because you couldn't live without me!"

The ring was reset. The workbenches were clear. The blocks and other assorted objects were spread all but randomly about the floor. Three handlers were led to equally distant spots around the ring where they deposited their little two-foot-tall robots. Handlers and referees retreated to the very edge of the ring, crossing to stand behind one roped line. One referee stood equidistant from the three handlers, completing the corners of an informal square. He looked to the handlers and then to the robots and the barely organized chaos that had gone into the layout of the floor. Raising his referee's switch slowly, drawing all eyes to him, he brought it down.

The three robots came to life as if they had been startled from a deep sleep by a rather gratuitous explosion. Two of the robots immediately began to stagger about as if they were somewhat drunkenly exploring the lay of the land, eye-balling what there was to see, taking in the sights. The third robot, which seemed to have somewhere between four and six legs, giving it the vague appearance of a centaur crossed with an ant, studied the room without moving as if trying to get its bearings before making its first move.

The first two robots, one of which was a tripod and the other was more like a cylinder on little rotating wheels, had begun to work out that they should be doing something with the various shapes and objects, and they had begun to perform little-collision related experiments with them. The cylinder extended little grasping arms, took hold of one of the shapes, and made a mad dash toward the perimeter of the ring. The tripod found this rather fascinating and gave chase, beginning a little zigzag race about the confines of the ring as each wanted some personal quality time with the object the cylinder was holding.

The centaur ignored the antics of the other two and began its own intense examination of the little workbench it had been set down close to. This drew its attention back to the objects scattered about the floor, which were becoming slightly more scattered because of the slapstick chase being performed by the other two. Centaur scuttled across the ring, picked a block almost at random, and took it back to its workbench, setting the block down next to it. After the centaur had repeated these basic steps two or three times, the other robots began to take an interest in what it was doing.

"They're learning from each other," Aiden said, shouting in Lynn's ear.

"I know," she replied, trying to be heard over the assorted cries and cheers of the people around them. "We have to work that into our algorithms."

"Hardly seems sporting!"

"Love and war, darling! Love and war!"

"What if the other robot is doing something stupid?"

"So we factor that in! Countermeasures! Sputnik could deliberately do something stupid just to throw the others off the scent!"

"That's bloody brilliant!"

"Only take an hour of coding, too!"

"And then the King of Spain shall offer me a llama!"

"Okay, two hours!"

The little robots were starting to get organized. Each one was collecting a pile of objects next to its workbench. Little push-me pull-you matches were breaking out as the robots became fascinated with specific shapes and blocks. The cylinder would grab a block and race wildly around, slowly grinding to a stop as if it had become despondent that nobody was chasing it. The centaur scattered half its own blocks, trying to select favorite shapes and colors to place on its workbench. The tripod was expediting the process of switching shapes on its workbench by tipping the whole thing over and starting fresh.

The referee called time, swinging his control rod over his head, and the three robots instantly lost the will to live, collapsing together as if they had rehearsed that one move over and over again. The centaur/ant hybrid was selected as the winner, and its handler paraded about the ring as if the victory had been a personal triumph of many years struggle and growth.

"Oh God," Lynn said as the referees began the process of resetting the ring. "It's us. We're next. It's our turn."

"Oh God," Aiden said, clutching Sputnik, almost dropping the robot in the process. "We can still back out, right? We don't have to do this."

"The code. Did we remember to compile the code?"

"You're asking now?" Thrusting the little robot at her. "You take it!"

"Me?"

"You deserve to stand in the ring!"

"Oh, no, you got us into this." Pointing. "You can taste the glory of this first night!"

"But I insist! It's your fault we attended that Ape Fight!"

"Oh, it's my fault now!"

"You should feel honored!"

"Oh, listen to you two," Tamara said. "Jump before you can swim, remember?"

"I don't remember saying that," Aiden said.

"You got us the invite to this little party." Tamara pointed at him.

"I did nothing of the sort."

One of the referees was standing next to them.

"You seized the initiative and bought the little monster," Tamara said.

"Yeah, you unilaterally spent our life savings on our baby," Lynn said. "You get the glory."

"You're just never going to let me forget that, are you?" Aiden said.

"Tick tock," the referee said.

They all looked at Aiden.

"Right," he said as if facing down the firing squad and followed the referee into the ring.

As before, they were equally spaced about the ring. Aiden put little Sputnik down. The others were something that bore a passing resemblance to an ill-tempered tarantula and something that resembled a twin-headed giraffe. It was at this point that Aiden realized he didn't have the dead man's switch, and he had to flag down his referee. Quick words were exchanged and frantic hand-signals were displayed for the audience's benefit. Lynn got the message at last, sprinting into the ring, giving Aiden the switch. She deposited one passionate kiss, which yielded a rather enthusiastic response from the audience, and Lynn was quickly escorted back out.

Aiden was alone with little Sputnik at his feet and the dead man's switch in his hands. He turned it round and about as if he simply did not know what else to do with it or couldn't figure out how to hold the damn thing. The other handlers stood watching him, as if savoring the moment before the competition became a two-horse race. The objects were scattered about the floor. There was no pattern. Aiden desperately wanted to kick them about in the hopes of creating some recognizable shape from out the chaos. The audience watched as if at a funeral. From somewhere across the ring, Heather's eyes were locked on him.

Aiden stepped to the very edge of the ring, following the lead of the other handlers, and crossed to the far side of the rope without tripping over it. Someone at his side helped him get the correct grip on the dead man's switch. The referee stepped forward, drawing all eyes. He raised the control rod slowly, held it far overhead, and then when he felt the audience could hold its collective breath not a moment longer, he brought it down.

* * *

"Well, that was bloody awful," Aiden said, dropping Sputnik onto their table in the crew space.

"Could have been worse," Lynn said.

"How?" Aiden turned on her as if he wouldn't be able to stop spinning, degenerating into a human tornado. "How could that have gone any worse?"

"Well?" Lynn said, trying to drag the word out. "Sputnik didn't fall over once."

"Okay, yeah, I'll give you that in a *the grass is always greener over somebody else's septic tank* kind of way, but it does not change how our little mismatched compilation of disused pinball machine parts performed in the ring tonight."

"He got something onto the table."

"That's true, our little monkey did manage to get at least one shape onto the table," Aiden said. "I only wish it had been our table."

"Can't wish for everything, I suppose," Tamara said.

"No, I suppose you're absolutely right. We cannot wish for everything. Just one little thing. If only we had wished for just one little thing."

"Like winning?" Lynn said.

"Yes, exactly, like winning. Not really so much to ask."

"Not exactly as if the other monkeys did much better."

"Rub it in, why don't you. They did better than our little Sputnik, and that is really all that matters." Raised his face to the heavens. "God, I'm so humiliated I could just die."

"Well, don't do that," Lynn said. "It's not like the other monkeys tied our little Sputnik down and gave him a profound spanking."

"Metaphorically."

"Oh, sure, metaphorically you could say all kinds of things. You could even say they sodomized him with a limp piece of string."

"Exactly!"

"How do you sodomize with limp string?" Tamara asked, puzzled.

"Never you mind that now," Lynn said. "How long has it been since you purchased our little wunderkind? We've barely had time to prepare for this match. Sure, we had our collective asterisks all but literally handed to us, but our little slice of mechanical tomfoolery didn't explode upon impact or otherwise go on a murderous rampage. We should celebrate."

"Yeah," Tamara said.

"There are other matches in progress. We should go participate."

"Tomorrow, maybe," Aiden said.

"Tomorrow is a concept that you cannot live with or invite over for supper. We're living with today. The fights, trials and races—Hey, what are those things called, anyway?"

"The what?"

"The races, you know." Fluttering of fingers, waving and swooping of hands to indicate the track all about the warehouse floor. "Little monkeys screaming all about the room on that wonderful track that must have taken them simply hours and hours to set up."

"The Rat Races?" Tamara said. Lynn gave her a look as if she had just been told something rather tedious and dull in a very sarcastically condescending tone of voice.

"That's not really what they're called, is it?" she said.

"Fraid so."

"Can't be." Shaking her head. "It just can't."

"Oh, but you've got no trouble with Monkey Trials and Ape Fights, huh? Rat Races are just one terrible name too far?"

"Well, yeah, we've crossed from primates to rodents. What's up with that?" Lynn said. "Think about it."

"I don't really think you're getting the point."

"Oh, there's a point to all of this now, is there? Look, I don't really mean to be the killjoy here, but I'm actually much closer in my attitude right now to Aiden's way of thinking than I'm letting on."

"Huh?"

"Yeah, exactly. What I really want to do right now is march back in there and burn the place to the ground, but I'm not." Pointing. "You want to know why not? Go on, ask me why not."

"Okay."

"That's not really a question."

"Why not?" Aiden said.

"There," Lynn said, turning on him, glancing back to Tamara. "Was that really so hard?"

"Changing the subject."

"Right, exactly." Holding up a finger. "I am trying to maintain a positive and upbeat attitude precisely because we just learned what fools we mortals be."

"Oh, shit!" Aiden turned back toward the workbench.

"Precisely—Wait, what?"

"Heather," he said, looking at Sputnik sprawled on the tabletop. "Heading this way."

"Where?"

"Don't look! Don't look!"

"I'll look wherever I bloody well feel like." Lynn scanned the room. Heather was practically right on top of them.

"Well, that was a truly wondrous display of wedding-night performance anxiety, if I really must say so myself," Heather said, reaching the little cabal surrounding their table. "What did you do? Program your monkey with the wholly gratuitous application of an East Indian cricket bat?"

"Our secrets revealed," Lynn said, facing Heather, before Aiden could open his mouth. "While it's true that our patents remain pending, I assure you that I am absolutely prepared to slap an injunction on your asterisk so fast that it'll make the shit pop right out of your mouth. Oh, wait, it already is."

Heather ran her eyes up and down Lynn as if judging her reach, weight, and chances, should she lunge for her throat.

"I'm guessing this is your partner," she said to Aiden. "Wonderful girl. Name starts with a letter of the alphabet, right? I had it a moment ago. Now if only I could remember which one."

"Alphabet is made up of letters not numbers, dear."

"Oh, is that what we're calling them now? Those little things are called letters? Wow, will wonders never... You know, learn something new every day."

"When did she mention numbers?" Tamara said, little more than muttering.

"You got it in one, Heather," Aiden said, ignoring Tamara's whispers and mutterings. "This is my partner, Lynn." Taking in Lynn with a gesture. "And that is our very good friend and groupie, Tamara." Giving her little more than a look.

"Tomorrow to my friends," Tamara said, taking Heather's hand, shaking it. "I'll let you know which you fall into tomorrow—Yeah, I really have the worst nickname. I've heard your name mentioned."

"Oh dear," Heather said, extricating her hand from Tamara's grip. "I really do try to fly under the radar."

"Well, blame the partners, here. They really do like to talk about you."

"That's either deeply flattering or really rather kind of disturbing." Head on one side. "Which camp should I be leaning toward here?"

"Deeply flattering," Tamara replied. "You're the mighty Tourist Hunter. Got your own theme song and everything."

"Well, I suppose they do call me out when there is an above-average need to do something about an ungrateful tourist."

"Spot them fast?"

"Oh, I don't know about that. More luck than anything else."

"So it is more of a wish that the little brains you just finished bashing into the ground were very interested in pursuing the finer points of tourism?"

"Precisely."

"I know all about that," Aiden said, raising a hand as if volunteering for a suicide mission. "Just got to go on instinct and hope for the best."

"Yeah, you've got two recent notches for your belt." Lynn held up fingers, forming a victory sign in the air. "Why you hang with the master here. Improve your chances of spotting a truly independent monkey."

"Well, more on the luck than education side."

"Yeah, osmosis doesn't really work that way," Heather said.

"She's like a gravitational force." Drawing a circle with his fingers. "Black hole, if you will."

"I'm not sure I like where you're going with this."

"You suck them in, maybe? Tourists gravitate toward you." Shrug of shoulders. "Hang with you and the tourists shall come."

"And the Tourist Board shall follow. Don't pray for rain, Charlie."

"Charlie?" Tamara said, laughing.

"What's in a name, Tomorrow?" Aiden said, glaring at her, then turning back to Heather. "It is the curse of fighting tourism, isn't it? The Tourist Board shall follow after."

"They mean well, I suppose," Heather said.

"What?"

"Well, they do want to prevent the unnecessary waste and wanton destruction of private property."

"That's an interesting way of putting it," Aiden said. "I just wish they weren't so oppressive or stupid."

"Weren't they investigating you?" Lynn said.

"Yes, if you can believe it." Turning, looking to where Sputnik lay sprawled on the table. "Complete waste of time. They still haven't finished their report."

"They have, actually," Heather said.

"What?"

"Oh, yes, investigation complete. Handed in the report and everything."

"Since when?"

"Couple of weeks back. I'm not entirely sure. They presented it to management."

"How did you find out about this?"

"I do work for R&D, you know," she said, scolding him with a passing look. "I inquired."

"Well, when were they going to tell me?" Thumping his chest. "There was supposed to be a debrief and everything."

"Well, obviously they didn't feel such a move was necessary."

"They dragged me and poor Tom Cane in for a polite interview and intimidation—I mean, interrogation."

"That they did."

"The hell, man? I mean, what the hell?"

"The report was," Heather said with a shrug of shoulders. "Well, it was officious."

"You read it!"

"Of course I read it. I'm R&D. I have every right to review their findings."

"And?"

"Yeah, don't keep us in suspense," Lynn said.

"While your actions may have been a tad overzealous," Heather said, "they were within the acceptable guidelines for dealing with a hostile tourist."

"Damn Skippy, they were!"

"The confused and fragile, malfunctioning little unit assaulted you, which goes a long way toward justifying—well, not really justifying so much as understanding the followthrough."

"That doesn't even make sense!"

"I know. Doesn't it?"

"They couldn't even tell us." Aiden shook his head slowly from side to side. "Probably wanted to leave us hanging. Feel this great weight over our heads like that bloke with the sword spoiling his dinner."

"That sounds vaguely familiar," Heather said, "but I think you've got the details wrong. As for the Tourist Board, it's just as likely they didn't want to admit they had made monkey out of a mole hill. Hoped the whole thing could just be quietly shoved under the table."

"Well, this just boils my pudding." Aiden held a hand pressed to his forehead.

"At least it's good news, right?" Tamara said. "Got the Board of Tourism off your back. Hardly took any monkeys to fill up that mole hill. You wouldn't believe how much we deal with them at university."

"Oh, don't get me started," Lynn said. "At least you don't work in Applied Engineering and Robotics. Count your blessings, Tomorrow."

"It's theoretical physics for me all the way, baby. And why would I count my blessings tomorrow—Oh, right, my nickname. I get it."

"Please stop beating that horse, dear."

"I'll see what I can do."

"Well, I wish I could say that's why I wandered all the way over here," Heather said, turning toward the sparsely occupied workbench. "What the hell happened with your little monkey?"

"Yeah, I was deliberately avoiding that subject," Aiden said.

"I bet you were. What did you do? Try to rewrite the entire code base from scratch?"

"Yeah, I suppose you could say that," Aiden muttered quietly all but to himself.

"Classic rookie mistake. It wandered about like a drunken wombat."

"Well, the code base was just so primitive."

"I know, but you've got to start somewhere. Swim before you can fly, man."

"Where's the fun in that? Look, I just don't like modifying another man's code base. You never know what kind of ticking time bombs they've left fermenting in it. I would rather start from scratch."

"Oh, that's just brilliant, and look where it got you."

"Hey, I tried to tell them," Tamara said.

"Well, I wasn't expecting to enter a Monkey Trial quite so soon." Aiden turned, glaring once more at Tamara with fond but fierce affection. "Pile on the limping boy time, is it?"

"If your monkey needs work, you don't leap at the chance to enter the trial," Heather said.

"I don't recall you giving me much choice. I vaguely recall the conversation going along the lines of *Hey, your little primate had better be ready.* Destiny knocks. You answer the door."

"Generally people say they're in the middle of rebuilding the code base from scratch but would love to attend as an observer. Scope out the scene. Get an idea of what the trials look like. Meet some guild and clan members. Maybe even network a bit."

"I swear, it's like we had two totally different conversations."

"It's not even like we're totally averse to adapting or otherwise incorporating other code basics into our work," Lynn said.

"Oh, it's a group effort now?" Heather said, looking at her.

"Yes, actually, why do you think our glorious little prodigy didn't just fall to its knees and beg for a quick and merciful death? There were multiple minds at work here."

"We adapted what we needed," Tamara said. "Sure, I was more of an Ape Fighter myself, but I've got tools. Functions and routines that could be adapted."

"I vaguely recall offers of access to a superior code

base, if my memory hasn't completely imploded here," Aiden said. "I'm just averse to the generic code supplied by the manufacturer. You never know what little landmines and stalker-ware they secreted in those poorly documented guts."

"That," Heather said, raising a hand, taunting with a finger, "actually makes a fair amount of sense. Has a lot to do with why I don't raid most common core code banks."

"Oh, good, we're agreed on a couple of minor points."

"Still doesn't explain why you fielded such an alpha-level monkey."

"Yeah, you've got me there. We're not even beta field-test ready."

"You shouldn't try that hard to impress me. It'll backfire on your asterisk."

"Now, I suppose we could try working with some existing groups." Gesturing toward Lynn as if trying to remember. "You seemed to know that postdoc who did well at the trials."

"Oliver?"

"Yeah, him." Looking toward Heather. "We could invite him into the professional underground fold."

"No way." Lynn shook her head. "He is not ready for prime time."

"Yeah, I've got to agree," Tamara said.

"Why ever not?" Aiden said. "He won his match. He's hungry. He was certainly eager to talk to us. He even works with Jennifer Behr in the theoretical software lab. He must be brimming with ideas."

"Yeah, but the thing of it is," Lynn said, looking to the table with a hand in her hair, "I don't trust he isn't bringing his work out of the quarantine lab."

"That's a problem," Heather said.

"Copy and repeat," Tamara said. "I've been keeping

an eye on our eager junior friend. You know. Elisabeth code-monkey."

"Yeah, her." Aiden snapped his fingers as if her name had just leapt into his head. "She won her Ape Fight with solid algorithms and tricky fighting."

"She's been copying notes from Oliver, I understand." Tamara gave him a tired look. "Does not fill me with confidence."

"It's all cutting edge," Aiden said.

"I'm sorry." Heather turned on him, pressing forward. "Did your brain just fall out of your head? Look, I don't care if you're holding tight to this kid just to be stubborn in the face of a united front here. If he's taking his work home with him, I do not want him setting foot here." Turning, looking about the room. "It'll spread like VD."

"Virtual devices?"

"Where do you work, Charlie?"

"Okay, yeah, I know." Holding up his hands in placating defeat. "Just trying to make a point. We're not totally averse to sharing code basics."

"Just not with pseudo-intelligence code bases—Wait," Heather said, looking at him sideways. "You want access to my code base, don't you?"

"It was the carrot that convinced me to buy a monkey in the first place."

Heather started to laugh.

"You don't," she finally said, stopped. "You don't gain access just like that."

"We're here, aren't we?"

"It's not a door prize handed out just for showing up. You have to earn it."

"By showing what we can do from scratch?" Aiden said.

"It's a good start. But you don't just attend. You

can't just hold your own. You have to win. Prove you don't need it."

"That's practically a Catch-22," Lynn said. "Gain access to the shared code base only when it is no longer necessary."

"Catch-22? Yeah, that's pretty good. Not quite on the mark, but good."

"Catch-23, then?"

"Oh, let's not drive this too deeply into the ground. Besides, Catch-23 is probably taken."

"Catch-22?" Tamara said, looking honestly puzzled. They gave her a look in return.

"Seriously, we're like the same age," Lynn said. "It may be a really, really old movie, but the reference can't be that far gone in dinosaur land."

"Dinosaur land?"

"Oh, Sweet Jesus, you did not just say that, Tomorrow. You trying to score points with the quarter-to-midnight crowd? Show how much more you have in common with Liz and the other assorted grad students?"

"No, just scoring that look on your face. Seriously, I should take a picture."

"I'm prepared to repeat this look or one very much like it once you have your soul-stealing, picture-taking equipment ready."

"Catch-22, I'm hip. Means contradictory things canceling each other out, right?"

"Well, if you ignore the history, I suppose," Heather said. "More about bureaucracy deliberately set up to make something impossible through contradictory prerequisites."

"Catch-22," Tamara said, nodding her head. "I work for university, you know. I've heard the term. I've certainly dealt with the aftermath before."

"Then we're in business."

"This is all very well and good, I'm sure," Aiden said,

"but what I really care about are the self-contradictory conditions that will lead to access to your code base."

"That's a rather personal question." Heather drew herself up as if insulted and was one step removed from smacking him about the face with a dueler's dare.

"But the question still stands."

"Yeah, I've got to agree with my serpentine half, here," Lynn said.

"Serpentine because of the reference to human anatomy, right?"

"Got it in one."

"Well, it's simple, really," Heather said, turning once more back to the table and the little tripodal monstrosity sprawled upon it. "Win some matches. Prove you can handle code. Then we'll talk."

"Going to take time," Aiden said, tapping fingers to Sputnik's inert form.

"What's the first rule of programming, Charlie? You know it. I've seen your file. I know your history with the co-op development movement."

"You've read my—"

"Deal with it," Heather said, not letting him finish. He gave her a look, shook his head as if dislodging an irritatingly persistent fly in super slow-motion.

"The first rule of programming is the timetable never survives contact with the actual code base."

"Close enough."

"Oh, good, as long as it is close enough."

"You'll get the carrot," Heather said. "It's not just dangling there until it rots. You just have to survive the stick first."

"I knew there was a stick. There's always a stick."

"Win some matches."

"Yeah, we're working on it," Aiden said, taking in Lynn and Tamara.

"Oh yeah?"

"Yeah."
"Good."

CHAPTER THIRTEEN

In which Tom and Aiden discuss the unconsidered consequences of recent events.

There were more transportation service options available than just Ubiquity Shuttle. Lynn and Aiden just happened to subscribe to Ubiquity. They hadn't even done proper research, having simply selected one based on whatever random criteria people tend to use when making long-term commitments. The name had been on their minds. They were convinced they had heard good things about it, and once installed, the phone app had been easy to use.

Ubiquity never seemed to try very hard to redirect a shuttle exactly where they wanted it, and they frequently found themselves needing to walk several blocks to intercept one; however, Ubiquity was very good at dropping them off within feet of their destination. The number of detours for pick-ups and drop-offs between their starting and ending points was not something that crossed their minds.

For whatever undisclosed reason that Aiden didn't really see any advantage looking into, the shuttle insisted on dropping him several blocks from the Central Services office that morning. The shuttle had other people to deliver. It was on a schedule. Aiden put no more thought than that into trying to understand it. The shuttle insisted, and he had to disembark. It made him feel a little better that two other Central Services employees had to join him on the short walk to the distribution center.

Since he would prance to work naked before he would wear his service uniform a minute longer than he had to, the locker room was first on Aiden's agenda for the day. He remained forever grateful that Central Service uniforms favored function, comfort and utility over style or memorability. The Alpha Matrix uniforms, for example, still burned his eye. There were other field service representatives about. Changing into their uniforms with a reasonable amount of quiet determination. It was morning, after all. The late shift hadn't started to stagger in yet from the end of their runs with nothing on their minds other than the desire to claw out of their own business suits as quickly as possible. Tom joined him. Aiden realized he didn't know what shuttle service Tom used. It hardly seemed important.

"Morning," Tom said barely above a muttered whisper. "Good weekend?"

"Yeah," Aiden replied, flashes of robots, Ape Fights and Monkey Trials, fluttered past his eye. "Good weekend. You?"

"What is this, the inquisition?"

"Going to add it to my news feed. Been taking lessons from those jokers at the Board of Tourism, if you really must know."

"Well, I guess I had better tell you then."

"Yes, I would suggest that you do."

Tom continued to change in silence.

"In your own time," Aiden said, checking his regulation boots to make sure they were properly buckled.

"It was the best of times." Tom paused in his dressing to look to the ceiling as if searching for inspiration. "It was—Well, my partner had fun."

"That's all well and good, and I'm sure the two of

you will be quite happy for a thousand years. Now, the reason I brought up the Board of Tourism has to do with how they go about presenting the results of their investigations."

"I didn't know you had brought them up."

"It's in."

"No, really," Tom said, "I don't recall what snippet out of the past few minutes of conversation involved the inclusion of our friends over at the Tourist Board."

"I'm sure I mentioned it, but we're past that now. It's in."

"You're going to scare our neighbors, you know that?" Tom looked to the people scattered about the locker room. None were listening, and nobody was even aware that a conversation was taking place.

"Tom, listen, it's in."

"Whatever are you talking about?"

"Oh, like you even have to guess. It's in. Can you believe it? It's in."

"Wait, are you saying that it is in?"

"Yes, that's exactly what I am saying."

"It's in?" Tom pointed with his finger as if jamming a nail into the ground.

"It is in."

"Since when?"

"Since a couple of weeks ago, I understand."

"Well, why didn't they tell us?"

"Well, obviously they didn't consider us important enough to tell."

"You seem to know."

"Well, I know people."

"I'm sure you do," Tom said, making a dive for his phone, picking it up, beginning to type with wild abandon. "Don't mind me. Just reaching out to the wonderful network of friends and acquaintances that I've cultivated over the years."

"Hey, no worries, I fully understand."

"I've developed quite the network, you know."

"I'm sure you have."

"You're not the only one in this two-man toboggan that knows people."

"I never doubted it for a second."

"I'm calling our supervisor, okay?" Gave Aiden a look. "Happy?"

"Delighted."

Tom turned back to his phone.

"I wish to discuss at your earliest convenience the results of the Tourist Board's investigation into the recent incident," Tom said, voicing what he had written, mashing send with his thumb when he had finished. "What's the damage, anyway?" He said, looking up from his phone, locking on Aiden. "You seem to be in the know."

"Negative findings," Aiden said. "Complete exoneration."

"Damn Skippy, there were negative findings. We followed procedure."

"That we did."

"Even filled out the dreaded Request to Waive Post-Incident Interview Report form doohickey dangle dongle whatever." Pointing at Aiden with phone in hand. "Worked extra hours just to complete the bloody forms."

"Hey, I was there. I've just had an ounce more time to deal with my boiling free-form rage."

Tom's phone pinged with a soft chime as if woodblocks had been dropped two inches onto a tile floor. He glanced at the screen.

"Which incident?" Tom said, voice rising. "What bloody incident could I be talking about? The one where we were forced to subdue a rather unruly and wholly ungrateful freak of nature!"

"He can't hear you."

"I know he can't hear me. I'm well aware phones don't work like that." Beginning to type. "The incident which resulted in those unholy jackals interrogating us for doing our job! The incident in which service representative Chuckles suffered a war wound!" Finished narrating his reply and tapped send. He looked to Aiden. "That's not exactly what I typed."

"Yeah, I kind of figured."

"And to think we're going to have to go through it all again." Started to pace. "Couldn't even be bothered to tell us."

"Hey, there's so much crowd footage of the street sweeper maybe they won't need to interview us."

"You think for one second they'll pass up the chance to interrogate us again? Try to spread fear and loathing through our hearts."

"Yeah, I'm just trying to look on the bright side here."

"Very ennobling of you." Looked at his phone. "Nothing."

"He's not going to reply. Bets?"

"What happened to your sunny disposition?"

"I can look into the abyss, too, if I want. Glass is still half-full of air regardless, you know."

"Yeah, yeah, yeah." Paused in his pacing to look at his phone again. "Nothing." Resumed his march.

"The important thing is that the results were negative," Aiden said, watching him. "Well, positive from our point of view. Negative from their point."

"Yeah, I get the idea."

"I'm sure they would have been much happier if they had found something to be sanctimonious about."

"It seems to be there reason d'uh extra."

"Their what?" Aiden said, trying not to laugh. "I'm sorry, I don't think I followed that."

"You know what I mean."

"Even if you cannot express yourself as well as a goat."

"Yeah, even then." Looked to his phone. "Foxglove's not going to answer."

"Fraid not."

"Not going to answer."

"Negative disclosure. Why should he bother?"

* * *

Their van had hunted down a parking space squished between two buildings, leaving them with little room to get out. They even considered overriding cruise control to see if they could do a better job, abandoning the idea because it just didn't seem worth the effort. They resorted to hand-held versions of the rolling-case. Between the two of them, there was theoretically everything they could need. It would just take more trips if they had to swap out a whole heaping pile of parts, which naturally the job did turn out to entail.

They found themselves working in the back room of a small business. It wasn't overly clear what the business actually did. People worked. That was about all they could tell, and about the extent of the effort they put into guessing the purpose of the company. They had to service and repair a more serious version of the utility barn that lived in most people's homes. Sweepers and various other assorted cleaning robots always seemed to collect more debris and require more maintenance in office situations than in people's homes. It was almost as if people took more pleasure in creating messes for the robots to clean, or otherwise interfere with the device's standard operations, at work than home.

"You never did tell me how you knew?" Tom said, working on the barn with a fine-toothed brush.

"Huh?"

"No, seriously, how did you know the results were in?"

"I know people."

"You know people." Tom stopped working, leaned away from the barn so that he could study Aiden over the edge of his engineering goggles.

"Like I said." Shrug of shoulders.

"You know people."

"I know people."

Tom seemed to give this a moment's thought and then seemed to consider turning back to his side of the barn, wavering in the air like a love-struck amoeba.

"Who?" he finally said.

"Huh?"

"Who do you know?"

"People."

"I'm sure they are people. I seriously doubt that it was one of our little robots."

"Sensible."

"I doubt our script or your phone have achieved a sufficient level of autonomous self-interest to let you know the results were in."

"I sincerely hope not."

Leaning back into his work, Tom resumed brushing away at the components.

"Nothing from Foxglove," he finally said.

"Still not surprised about that."

"Which makes me doubt he was the guilty party."

"It wasn't Foxglove," Aiden said, pulling out a component bay and examining the microscopic connections.

"He's people."

"I'm reasonably sure he is people and not a fish or an exotic piece of smelly cheese."

"Right, it was people. Someone with access. Someone who knew about our concerns regarding the investigation."

"Which rules out most of our co-workers."

"Must have been Heather."

"What makes you say that?" Pushed the component bay back into place.

"It was Heather."

"I didn't say that."

"Well, who else shares our pain over the Tourist Board report and has worked with us on delicate operations?"

"That's a fair amount of deductive reasoning, I really must say."

"Thank you."

"Didn't say it was accurate."

"I'm still trying to work out why the two of you would be speaking outside of office hours."

"We could have run into each other."

"I'm trying to imagine under what circumstances the two of you would just casually run into each other over the weekend. You just don't move in the same social circles."

"Coincidences happen."

"They happen in stories and massively multiplayer games, if that's what you mean."

"Seriously, you've never just run into someone outside of work? Never knowing if you should acknowledge each other's existence or just pretend the whole thing never happened?"

Tom seemed to consider this.

"Avoiding eye contact?" Aiden said, encouragingly, as if to help jog his memory.

"Nope, never happened," Tom finally said.

"Just goes to show that you are in deep, deep denial."

"Oh, I may be in deep denial about many things, such as why I took this unholy monstrosity of a job in the first place." Looked away from the barn as if it burned his eyes, muttering to himself. "Must have been off my onion." Faced Aiden, jabbed a finger in his general direction. "But that's hardly the point."

"I didn't know you hated your job," Aiden said, interrupting, removing his goggles.

"Huh?"

"I thought you were one of those rare few who actually took satisfaction from helping the general public. A job well done and all of that. Now, after all these years, I learn that you actually resent and despise the very ground our clients walk upon."

"What the hell are you talking about?"

"Yeah, that could have been phrased better, I'm sure. It's possible to dislike the job without dragging our clients into it, although they tend to have a lot to do with our general lack of job satisfaction. The things they ask of us." Pointing with his goggles. "It's worse at university, you know. The level of entitlement. Whoa, baby, the stories that Lynn has relayed to me."

"Oh, like we deal with plum pudding, but that's hardly the point. And you're trying like a tap dancer on grease paint to change the subject."

"I'm what?"

"And the paint is on fire."

"I'm sure it is."

"My point being that you've been keeping secrets from your workday partner. The very flesh of my blood. The family that actually shows up at the reunion. And what do I get? Secrets and lies."

"How many days have passed since I last saw you and what was the first thing I said when I did?"

"Well, it certainly wasn't the time you were spending kissing some very sweet R&D asterisk."

"I was not kissing any such thing."

"You want out of this gig."

"Well, who doesn't?" Gesturing at the barn. "Look at this. Just look at it."

"I'm looking."

"You call this job satisfaction? Brushing the crud off components so small you can't even see them with the naked eye?"

"So you really think R&D is a step up?"

"Who said anything about R&D?"

"I know you well enough to know you would rather be reprogramming the barn not vacuuming the crap out of it. You like to think you've got mad skills."

"I do have mad skills."

"And they're going to waste here, I'm sure."

"Well, I think it goes without saying—"

"Then don't," Tom said before Aiden could finish and took a slow breath, dragging the flames from out his lungs. "You want R&D, and polishing the Tourist Hunter's anus is turning into your path."

"If R&D wanted me," Aiden said, letting the moment linger like the deformed unwanted muffin at the bottom of the bag. Shrug of shoulders. Turned back toward the barn. Goggles in place. "I wouldn't need to rub the wild tortoise. So, what's the point? I'm not sucking asterisk."

"And yet, Heather is spilling state secrets to you."

"Well," Aiden said. "She just happened to see me. Subject just came up."

"I'm sure it did."

"It could have happened."

"I don't doubt you for a second."

"Outside interests."

"What, you both like to dress up as tin soldiers or something?"

"You could say that," Aiden said, glancing at Tom. "It could happen."

"Well, as I recall," Tom said, "Merlin is pretty heavily into one of those iron warrior campaigns. I can't keep track of which countries are actually at simulated proxy war with each other any more."

"Yeah, that's old news."

"Oh, yeah?"

"It was getting pretty brutal."

"So, not the iron campaigns, huh."

"Yeah, we've kind of got a new interest," Aiden said. Robots and racers flashed behind his eyes. Machines riding the edge of tourism studied the puzzle pieces strewn about the floor.

"The first rule of which appears to involve secrets and lies."

"I wouldn't go that far."

"Yeah, yeah, yeah, I don't want to know, thank you." Tom turned back to the barn as if he fully intended to clean every last piece without a further word spoken between them. "My fines are bad enough as is," he muttered rather quietly but just loud enough for Aiden to hear.

"Mine haven't budged," Aiden finally said.

"Yet."

Aiden studied his side of the service barn in silence, turned to his microscopic tool kit, selected a fine-toothed feather pick, and started to scratch at a particularly ugly-looking bit of debris lodged within the shelf's innards.

"You know there are Ape Fights out there for people who look for them."

"What?" Tom almost dropped his tools, which would have scratched the barn's slender boards and caused them to need to replace far more components than they had any desire to do.

"Truth to power, man."

"I haven't been to an Ape Fight in years."

"Yeah, not since you got your full coverage with Central Services, right?"

"That sounds about—No, it was before that. But I remember the lecture." Mocking. "You're fully invested now. You've got an image to uphold."

"Wouldn't do to be involved with things that encourage tourism."

"Not that Ape Fights actually encourage tourism."

"No, but that's hardly the point."

"So Heather is into underground Ape Fights, is she?" Aiden didn't answer.

"That's actually pretty cool," Tom finally said. "Didn't know she had it in her. Never would have thought. Spend so much time knocking them down professionally—Hey, wait a second, what are you doing hanging out at Ape Fights?"

"Oh, it's worse than that."

"You training them or something?"

"That's rather an interesting way of putting it."

"Oh, sweet Jesus." Pulling off his goggles, looking at Aiden. "Reprogramming barns. You're programming ape fighters for the ring."

"Nope, sorry, it's worse than that."

"What could be worse than priming fighting machines for tourism?"

"Well, fighting apes don't really require much by way of intelligence. This barn is probably smarter than the dumbest ape. I mean—"

"Yeah, I got it. Apes are stupid. Dodge, dodge, punch. Nothing to it."

"Ever hear of a Monkey Trial?"

"No, but I've got a sinking feeling that I'm about to learn everything I never wanted to know about them."

"Hey, you wanted to know how I knew the results were in."

"Well, I certainly didn't expect them to involve clandestine attempts to create a race of super tourists. Just let me know when I should bow down and call them master, okay?"

"Bit of a logic jump in there somewhere, I think."

"What would the Board of Tourism think about your little Frankenstein experiments?"

"And that's just completely out in left field."

"You're doing something more involved than programming robots to hit each other," Tom said. "Something so bleeding edge that it's practically taboo."

"Well."

"You don't want to talk about it."

"I wouldn't go that—"

"You're hemming and hawing and trying desperately not to tell me. You think I wouldn't want to know you ran into Heather on your day off?"

Shrug of shoulders.

"Okay," Tom said. "I know I went a little overboard just then with the accusations of trying to better your position, reach above your station, blah blah blah."

"Thank you."

"But you've actually tried to avoid telling me how you knew the Tourist Board's report was in. You didn't want to admit. You figure it would look really bad on your performance record."

"Heather says it's great for recruitment."

"I'm sure it is."

"Well, you have to spin it somehow." Looking to the ceiling. "I'm not really sure how that would work. I mean, sure, some R&D management types just might

be more hip and understanding than the standard issue drones we have to deal with."

"Foxglove."

"Duly noted, Foxglove." Aiden closed his eyes. "But
who in the nod-and-wink department is going to ap-
prove what goes on behind the scenes at an Ape Fight?
Central Services executives would spontaneously
combust. The Board of Tourism would just lose its collective shit."

"So we talking world domination here?" Tom said.
"Teaching fighting apes how to love?"

"Problem solving."

Tom gave him a look.

"Problem solving?" He finally said.

"Yeah, problem solving," Aiden said. "Like your
standard issue sweeper needing to figure out how to
unblock that pipe."

"Sweepers don't generally need to unblock pipe."

"You know what I mean."

"That would be more in a plumber's department."

"Yes, I know. How could I ever forget? Drifting off
point, by the way."

"I'm grateful for every day that we're not on the
plumber maintenance circuit," Tom said.

"Problem-solving robots that actually have to figure
out how to win through methods other than beating
the ever-loving crap out of each other." Shrugged his
shoulders. "Monkey Trials."

Tom gave him a look as if he had spontaneously
started speaking in an ancient Scandinavian dialect
known only to a handful of practitioners who more
typically hung out on a mountaintop than secretly
passing along their culture to unsuspecting bystanders.

"What?"

"Solve the problem first and win," Aiden said. "Work out the win conditions, solve the puzzle, and win."

"Are you telling me?" Tom took off his goggles and rubbed at his eyes as if he needed a moment to reboot his mind. "Are you telling me that you are developing advanced problem-solving, thinking robots?"

"It's a lot more fun than it sounds."

"Oh, no, soccer wasn't good enough. Rally racing didn't fit the bill. Little robots beating the shit out of each other wasn't living enough on the edge for the likes of you. You've got to teach them how to think for themselves."

"Well, really, there's a bit of a difference in programming a robot to figure out the win conditions and go for them and programming a robot to think for itself."

"And your typical sweeper is programmed to contemplate the unbearable lightness of being, is it?"

"There's a certain amount of risk, I'm sure."

"Oh, you think?"

"But the conditions are much more controlled," Aiden said. "Your standard sweeper or other random variety of self-guided problem-solving robot is typically left to its own devices for long periods of time. Nobody watching it. Nobody monitoring it. Nobody fine-tuning its code on a regular basis. Just a kick in the asterisk. Go do your job. Monkey Trials don't work that way."

"They had better not."

"Well, think of it this way. Would you rather Central Service representatives weren't keeping an eye on it? We know what to look for. Heather and I, in particular, have more than a passing degree of experience in recognizing when a little monkey's gone too far."

"Okay, you may have a point there." Pointing with his goggles.

"Thank you."

"But, sweet mother in the morning, this is a lot to take in." Tom put his goggles back on. "I don't want to know."

"It really is more fun than it sounds."

"I don't want to know, Charlie. Just promise me that, okay? I'm fully vested in the company. I don't want to know."

"Tom."

"I don't want to know."

"But—"

"What did I just say?"

"Now, really—"

"So help me, I will jam this through your left eyeball." Tom brandished a mono-filament brush.

"Okay."

"You get it?"

"I get it."

"You do?"

"I get it. You don't want to know. Jesus."

Tom turned back to the barn, applying the brush with more force than was probably good for the circuitry.

"You're fully invested, too, you know," Tom muttered. "What is wrong with you?"

"You don't want to know."

CHAPTER FOURTEEN
In which Lynn and Aiden attend some meetings and otherwise attempt to enjoy themselves.

The Ape Fights hadn't changed, as if it was the same night, as if Lynn and Aiden had simply traveled back in time. The directions had been different. The neighborhood was different. The spacing and arrangement of the Ape Fight and Monkey Trial Rings was different. The roar, cheering, and excitement, were the same.

The Rat Races drew their attention. Apes and Monkeys they had seen while other concerns of the night had kept them away from the races. Now they took the time, watching the little racing machines. The first heat involving wheeled robots. Some were elongated rectangles. Some were oddly square, as if their squareness gave them a height bonus, increasing their perspective on the competition and the track. Most were streamlined, as if based around various pill designs to increase wind resistance—Wait, decrease...decrease wind—Oh, never mind. Besides, there isn't really a lot of resistance at the scale the racing robots operate on. Compared to the apes and monkeys, the rats were the smallest robot class. The track tended to run near the ceiling and weight was a consideration, which just goes to show that the people who designed the event and ran racers weren't completely oblivious to the well-being of the spectators.

The second heat involved bipedal racers, looking very much like boxy sprinters. They even had arms to pump and swing as if the motion contributed to their speed and stability, which it probably did. An expert could explain better. Really, they just looked more amusingly cool as they jostled, pumped their stubby little arms, and ran. Any practical benefits of the design was clearly an afterthought.

The third heat involved four-legged horse- and centaur-shaped racers. These seemed to run faster than the wheel-based group even if the difference in speed was only in the eye of the observer. Lynn and Aiden found it far more entertaining to watch the galloping racers push and shove against each other. The horses and centaurs even tried occasionally to climb over each other in their attempts to take the lead. The race was one step removed from an Ape Fight, and if there had been more centaurs involved, events certainly could have mutated into more of a demolition derby.

"When do you think?" Lynn said, laughing, leaning close to Aiden's ear. "When do you think they'll schedule the smash-up? It's bound to happen." Pointing. "Only time until they spend as much effort wailing on each other as trying to reach the finish."

"I'm sure it's been done."

"What?"

"I said, I'm sure it's been done." Aiden leaned in close, practically brushing foreheads.

"What?"

"Last week, we just missed it."

"No!"

"Oh, you want to take bets? You can sign up for massively multiplayer derbies already."

"Oh, sure, but that's online. Simulations crashing and bashing into each other, and they're not even computer controlled."

"Well."

"Oh, you know what I mean. It's more direct user involvement than the old iron warrior campaigns I did. Almost no point in getting behind the wheel in one of those iron chariot things, so to speak. What could you see? At least with the derby, you could take more direct remote control."

"Had your choice of views."

"See, excellent point," Lynn said, turning watching the robots scamper round the suspended track. "Here, all you can do is look. Once the little bastards are going round and round, they're on their own."

"You'd think people would get bored. Watching. No interaction. Just watching."

"Round and round."

"Hey, that's how this will become a demolition derby. One of those little guys will exceed its programming by just a hair. Bash in the brains of its neighbor."

"Handler claiming it was all an accident, I'm sure," Lynn said. "A glitch in the code. But nobody will believe him."

"Programmed on purpose."

"But of course. And then they'll all be doing it. Slipping in little routines. For retaliation purposes, of course."

"Of course."

"Never strike the first blow."

"Nope, never."

"That's how they get you."

"I can't wait."

They turned their attention to the Monkey Trials, shoving through the undulating mass of people. In its own way, which was best not to think about too closely, the crowd was like a vaguely shapeless organism, breathing, circulating fluids, choking on its own vomit, and louder than any multicellular organism had any right to be.

There were two rings for the Monkey Trials. There was a puzzle of overlapping plates at the center of each one. Puzzle bore a passing resemblance to one of those impossible knots, except a little more flat, as if the interlocking pieces really had been replaced by a series of thick mats cut into ill-fitting patterns and jammed together. The robots ran around. There were two tripods and something that resembled a tarantula with eyes on long stalks.

"Well, how is Sputnik supposed to figure this out?" Aiden said, throwing his hands up as if already resigned to failure.

"Trial and error," Lynn said. "It's going to take more than running and jumping routines before we're ready."

"We developed a jumping algorithm?"

"Yeah," she said without looking away from the ring. "You were supposed to, anyway."

"Oh, would you look at that? Bit of a tug-of-war developing."

"Work together, you drooling monkeys!" Lynn cried, standing on tiptoe, trying to see. "Have you worked out the win conditions, yet?"

"Nope, haven't a clue. I can't even tell how the puzzle is supposed to work. Is it like one of those concentric ring things?"

"There's a key at the bottom," guy standing next to them said. "First one to get it back to its corner and activate a little music box wins."

"Bit esoteric, isn't it?" Aiden said.

"Standard get the MacGuffin back to your starting square to win configuration. Practically just capture the flag," the guy said, and his name was—well, forget what his name was. He's just going to vanish back into the crowd any second now.

"It's practically capture the flag." Turning toward Lynn. "Did we design an algorithm for that?"

"I hope so."

"This just seems, I don't know," Aiden said. "A little less interesting than that vertical maze."

"Wasn't really a maze, dear, just a jungle gym with a basket on top."

"Yeah, I suppose." Watching the robots fuss and pull at the layers of the puzzle. "Did we code for a basket on top?"

"Yes, we did."

"Not exactly a basket, I suppose. That would be too specific. We'd have to program separate routines for each shape. More important just to know to get object A into target B."

"Yes, I told you we're working on that. Not even going to blame you." Started to laugh, watching the ring. "Whatever are they doing?"

"Beating each other with the plates, it looks like."

"Hey, they're not supposed to do that." Pointing. "This isn't an Ape Fight, you deranged monkeys! Show a little decorum!"

"Yeah, Sputnik definitely isn't ready for that."

One of the tripods had become entangled in the plates almost as if it had decided they were bedspreads and it wanted to snuggle down for a long winter's nap. The others were having none of it, pushing and pulling, trying to extricate the wayward machine, becoming frustrated at the intractability of the tangle. People cheered. They yelled and called. It was all a great cacophony of noise, which the robots ignored and even failed to wake the sleeper.

"Maybe he just doesn't see the point anymore," Lynn said.

"We definitely need a routine to fight ennui."

"Yeah, I'll get right on that."

The motivated pair of robots scurried over the tangled plates as if this would somehow bring clarity to their purpose, and they appeared to realize that something was buried under the knot. There was shoveling. There was additional pushing and pulling. There was a complete lack of coordination or cooperation.

"And we need a routine for computing the value of working with the competition."

"And when to stab them in the back, apparently."

"Yeah, that'll have to go in there somewhere," Lynn said.

"We're never going to field a monkey at this rate. All of these extra routines and algorithms."

"Just have to skimp on luxuries, I suppose. Not like we can teach little Sputnik to walk and chew gum all in the same day, right?"

"Metaphorically, right?"

"Yeah, metaphorically." Watched the robots give up on the final tangle of plates and knots. One of them had worked out that the thing underneath the tangle didn't necessarily need to be completely uncovered before it was grasped. "Doubt our bank account could handle any more purchases like gum for the robot and a mouth to chew it with."

The tarantula had the key free of the pile of twisted and knotted plates and ran around for a bit as if it knew the thing was important but had not a clue what purpose a key could serve. The tripod gave chase but seemed to lose interest at an impressive rate, returning to the tangled pile as if it hoped to find more treasures buried within. Having reached its music box, the tarantula began to beat the box with the key. Proximity proving ineffective, the tarantula eventually figured out there was a space the size and shape of the key that could be utilized.

The crowd cheered. The music box sprang open as if it was actually more of a jack-in-the-box than a music box, which it probably was. Never trust random people you meet at a Monkey Trial, especially if they claim to understand the rules. They may simply be messing with you for their own petty amusement. Random people suck.

"Maybe we should just aim for the Ape Fights," Aiden said.

"Not a chance." Lynn watched the referees begin to reset the ring.

"No, really, this Monkey Trial business is starting to look more trouble than it's worth."

"You saying little Sputnik can't hack it?"

"Well, no, not exactly."

"I'm not watching our little baby get her face bashed in. We didn't code for that. Certainly didn't buy the hardware for it."

"Well, that's true, I suppose."

"Don't wish for rain, right?" Patting him on the arm. "Or was that fire?"

"I like fire."

"Always get those two mixed up."

"Rain has its uses."

"Both are very bad on complex components," Lynn said. The referees had finished resetting the ring. "Oh, look, there's your girlfriend."

"My what?"

"Your love. Your master. Your psychotropic muse. The ever-lovely, Heather Graymarsh," she said, pointing. "Or was that Graymarch?" By this point, Lynn was waving her arm and even managed to get Heather's attention.

"Has she been telling you tall tales?" Aiden said. "I

don't recall asking her out or steady or any such thing. She's got no business coming over here and staking a claim to being my girlfriend." Heather had started to shoulder and shove her way toward them. "I'm fairly certain I would have remembered asking her. Besides, my dance card is full."

"Full of housewives, right?"

"Well, I wouldn't go that far. Never really had much interest in being a milkman."

"That's hardly a denial."

Heather reached them, cutting off any reply that Aiden may have been formulating, which would have been quite witty and urbane.

"Mister Charles," Heather said, taking Aiden's hand, turning. "And my memory is running amuck. Sarah, Susan, Heather?"

"Your name is Heather," Lynn said.

"Well, it's not exactly as if I took out a trademark or anything. Lots of people can be named Heather."

"And your name, for example, is Heather."

"A staggering coincidence, I really must say, but listen, Mary-Lynn, I hope I'm getting warmer."

"Yeah, you're starting to hit the right ballpark."

"It's good to see you guys." Turning, taking them both in. "Didn't run away screaming. Lots of people do."

"It was a bit of a trouncing," Aiden said.

"Well, your little monkey didn't spontaneously combust, so points for that." Turning, looking. "Where is the little blighter, anyway? I didn't see your name in the queue."

"Yeah, we're skipping this round." Shrug of shoulders. "Development takes time, like you said."

"Hey, good for you," Heather said. "That's the other rookie mistake. After running away screaming or at least crying your eyes out. Throw yourselves all-in as if digging that pit even deeper will wrap around and you'll plummet from the ceiling."

"That doesn't entirely make sense," Lynn said.

"And, well, it wasn't supposed to. Good eye on you for catching that."

"Helps when we're not obsessing over a machine that isn't quite ready for prime time. We notice the little details like your non-rationale analogies."

"Well, don't forget to mingle, network, and otherwise get to know people. Lots of value-add in that. Where's your groupie, anyway?"

"She's got other interests," Aiden said. "Her life doesn't wholly revolve around us."

"She teaches at Ben Franklin and occasionally needs to work on her lesson plan or something," Lynn said. "Grading papers may even be involved, I suppose."

"Hey, teaching the unwashed masses," Heather said. "Good for her."

Lynn had her phone out.

Hey, remind me why you couldn't make it to the big soiree tonight, Lynn typed, hitting send. "Where's your bitch?" she said.

"My what?"

"Your little tickler pony. Your miniature friend in soft feet. Your wondrously mechanical machine that will put the lot of us to shame."

"I beg your pardon."

"Yeah, I'm having trouble following you here, too," Aiden said, looking at Lynn as if she had just stripped to the waist and begun running around like a burning penguin waving her arms in the air.

"The more common among us refer to them as monkeys," Lynn said. Heather and Aiden both replied with the classic sound of condescendingly exaggerated understanding. "Don't *Oh* me. How come we haven't seen you field a monkey? Afraid of the competition?"

"More likely I scare the bejesus out of them," Heather said. Lynn's phone chimed. "You realize how many of the aforementioned crowd wouldn't dare to show their faces if they knew I had a monkey in competition?"

"Oh, I'm sure your reputation isn't that far over the wall," Aiden said. Lynn tried to glance at her phone, missed. "Besides, you bash their skulls in. You don't program them. There's a bit of a difference between the one and hunting tourists."

"Excuse me?" Heather said.

You're not the boss of me, Tamara had typed.

"Oh, I'm sorry, are you leaving me an opening?" Aiden said. "Realize the error of my ways? Want me to apologize or something?"

"The thought had crossed my mind. Feel the power of my telepathic stare feeding the thought into your suicidal cortex that maybe you're off your nut."

I've got a life, you know, Tamara had continued to type. *I've got excitement. Interests. The names of famous people to look up so I know what balderdash I'm grading.*

"You're going to have to work on that, boss," Aiden said. "The thought isn't sinking through my thick skull."

"Remember the little robot that gave it's life to protect the unruly spectators from the wrath of that gigantic tourist?"

"Vaguely."

"Who do you think programmed that?"

Aiden seemed to give this question quite a good little bit of thought. Lynn took advantage of the moment to concentrate on her phone.

And Sputnik isn't here, she typed, hitting send.

"Okay, I think the telepathic message is finally starting to get through," Aiden said. "I'm guessing you didn't just grab that self-sacrificing little robot off the shelf."

"Damn Skippy, I didn't," Heather said. "Who programs for self-sacrifice? Honestly?"

Exactly, Tamara typed, *what do I want with you two?*

"So when are you fielding a monkey?" Lynn said, looking up from her phone.

"Later tonight," she replied. "Got a few more matches before one of my abominations takes the field. It's on the schedule. Seriously, you guys should have looked it up."

"I didn't realize that was an option," Aiden said. "Now I'm really glad we're not fielding Sputnik. What if we had wound up competing in the same heat?"

"Oh, that was not going to happen. The referees do try to take these things into consideration. I should know. I'm usually one of them."

"Not tonight, huh?" Lynn said. "Conflict of interest?"

"Only when it comes to the scheduling. There's not enough of us with the wherewithal to recuse ourselves completely." Heather waved her hand languidly as if brushing aside the point. "And I'm not allowed to referee any of the matches close to the start of my own."

"Well, I suppose that makes sense."

"Hey, we're learning," Heather said. "Remember to watch the match. You might actually learn something you can apply to your own little monkey."

"Only if it involves giving us access to your code base," Aiden said.

"Still not going to happen. Win a few matches first. Which will be when?"

"It's only been a couple of weeks since our last

showing. We're still refactoring. Give us time, woman! Stop pressuring us!"

"Time is a luxury." Scolding with her finger. "Of which you've actually got as much as you want. These things do tend to happen almost as if they're on a schedule."

"Next meet is already on my calendar." Lynn held up her phone, waggling it before Heather's eyes.

"Think you'll be ready?"

Lynn and Aiden shared a look.

"It's possible."

"We shall evaluate the situation as we approach go time," Aiden said.

"Well, in the meantime, watch some matches," Heather said, glancing back toward the ring. "I think we've missed one or two."

"Could be worse."

"Hey, I'm supposed to be keeping an eye out," she said, turning back toward the rings. "What if we had a tourist outbreak?"

"You'd just bash their little skulls in."

"Damn Skippy, I would."

* * *

It was several weeks before the next round of Ape Fights, and it was never entirely clear to Lynn or Aiden how the news was spread. There was no feed or user's group. There were no announcements. You simply had to know someone who knew. It was one step removed from shouting from the rooftops, which would actually have been out of the question since raised voices would have brought all kinds of unwanted attention. They hadn't yet worked out whether what they were doing was technically illegal, and they weren't much interested in trying to find out. The closest anyone came to figuring it was on the legal side of illegal was the fact nobody vanished from the face of the Earth after downloading the location to their phone. For the third time in a row, the location was different but still within the service and warehouse districts. The actual space looked all but identical to the previous events, as if organizers tried very hard to keep some aspects of the evening's festivities similar.

"Are we up?" Aiden said, trying not to drop Sputnik as he worked his way through the crowd.

"Just about." The crowd, which was one step removed from being a mosh pit, was trying with some small degree of effort to make Lynn drop her phone. "There should be two matches before us. Ouch! I'm walking here! Depending on how long it takes us to cross the floor. What's with the throng tonight?"

"What?"

"I swear," Lynn said, trying to make herself heard. "Is it me or are they more rambunctious than ever?"

"Well, it's the triumphant return of our little monstrosity. They want to see us crash and burn."

"Yeah, I'm sure. And nobody is exploding on my watch. We programmed better than that."

"Exploding. Crash and burn. Yeah, they're close enough," Aiden said. "Where's our escort, anyway?"

"Last I saw Tomorrow and Oliver, they were over that way." Waving in the general direction of the Ape Fights. "Why did we invite them, anyway?"

"We couldn't deny Sputnik's fairy godmother. And Oliver, well, I seem to recall you saying something about introducing him to polite society."

"Teach that boy some manners, yeah. Make sure he's not taking his work home with him. Show him what he could be a part of if only he promised to keep his code clear. Or is that clean?"

"Going to have to take your word for that."

"You talk as if you don't know the first thing about pseudo-intelligence coding," Lynn said as they reached the edge of their assigned Monkey Trial ring, and she tried to get the attention of the closest referee.

"Can't say it's really my thing. I don't need my robots thinking they're people. I just need them able to problem-solve without exceeding their operating parameters."

"Details, details." Lynn flashed phones with the referee and was directed toward the waiting area.

The robots in the current round were scurrying about the vaguely squared ring. There was a net like a miniature tennis court. There was actually more than one net strung almost like the walls of a flimsy maze. The robots were attempting to follow the paths but were just as likely to climb over or attempt to squeeze under the makeshift barriers. Those that attempted to crawl under did not fare well.

"Worked out the puzzle yet?" Lynn said with eyes only for the ring.

"Not even a little," Aiden replied. "Whatever happened to our advance guard? Tomorrow was supposed to scope this out."

"Traitor!" Lynn held up her phone. "Think there's any point in giving her a call?"

"She'll never hear it."

"I could send an alarm. Those emergency alerts can be pretty fucking loud."

"You have to declare the nature of the emergency."

"We haven't worked out what the hell is going on." Pointing at the ring. "That's a crisis of biblical proportions if ever I heard one."

"Well, where's that other one? Didn't you invite a second postdoc or something?"

"Liz? Yeah, I don't think she could make it. Actually

had to study if you can believe it. Shows you the difference between grad student and postdoc, which is why Oliver is nowhere to be found."

"What are they doing in there?" Trying to hold onto Sputnik while pointing toward the ring. "I can't make heads or tails of it."

They watched the robots in relative silence as the crowd refused to keep the volume below a protracted roar. It was really kind of surprising that they had been able to hear each other at all. The little monkeys mostly seemed to be involved in trying to maneuver their way through the fishnet maze.

"I think it's just another variation on capture the flag," Lynn said. "Notice the little flags?"

"Yeah, now that you mention it."

"Each monkey has a small collection. Looks like each has to steal as many of the other bastard's little flags as possible."

"You worked that all out already?"

"I'm mostly guessing."

"Defend your flags while stealing from the others. Basically, just snatch and grab as much as you can from the other monkey's base, right?"

"Still just guessing." Looking at the little robot Aiden held awkwardly in his hands. "Think our gruesome little beast is up to the challenge?"

"If Sputnik can just get through this without punching someone in the face, I think we've got it made."

"Yeah, how long before this just degenerates into a goal-oriented Ape Fight? I swear, that's just not in the spirit of the competition."

"If that happens, we shall complain bitterly and at length."

"We didn't sign up to bash and moan! We're here to think! Our little deviant hell-spawn should be using her brain to work out the answer!"

"Or at least assemble a jigsaw puzzle."

"Exactly, one that doesn't involve punching your neighbor in the face."

"But bonus points for finding the other guy's nose. Have you seen some of these little monkeys?"

"Ours is still somewhat lacking in the proboscis department, I agree," Lynn said, studying Sputnik carefully. "I still say she looks like a disgraced sea urchin."

They watched the referee call the match and declare one of the handlers the winner. The background roar continued to swell like a power plant with a very slow radiation leak while the ring was cleared and reset as quickly as the referees could manage. The next three contestants were carried in for the match, and each was placed before a collection of flags. Each collection followed a theme—well, pattern, really. Matching colors were involved. The new group included two centaurs and something that resembled a centipede with a couple crane-like arms extending from its back.

"Wasn't Heather supposed to be riding shotgun on the Monkey Trials tonight?" Lynn said as the match started. Sputnik was in the next round so they were now standing at the very edge of the contestant corner.

"I know," Aiden said. "I'm pretty sure she's referee on the other ring. Something about conflict of interest."

"Oh, yeah?"

"Yeah, can you believe it? Guess we're technically friends or something."

"Well, you do work with her. Know her first name and everything."

"Door swings both ways, you know."

"I'm not following you there."

"People at work think I'm sucking up to her. Can you believe it?"

"I'm not." Lynn put a hand to her head as if her

brain had just popped a gear. "Okay, yeah, I'm feeling it. Work is weird, you know?"

"Damned if you do, right?"

"I know." Shook her head. "Suck. Even if you could tell people about the Monkey Trials, they would still call it kissing ash because she invited you."

"Trying not to think about it." Looking to the ring. "Whatever is that little blighter doing?"

"Huh?"

"Is it really trying to cut its way through the netting? Is that allowed?"

"Well, you can't really tell them what to do once the match starts, right?"

"This will only make me happy if the little ashcan tries to carry the net back to its own corner and sew new flags out of it."

The little centaur-shaped robot suddenly went dark and dropped to the floor with bits of the netting still held in its claws. The cries and shouting redoubled in intensity with the screams of foul and displeasure running their way through the crowd.

"Looks like there is more than one way to foul out," Lynn said.

"Not entirely fair, if you ask me."

"I can hear the argument both ways. On the one hand, it was destroying the ring. On the other—"

"How is it supposed to know it can't dramatically and permanently alter the underlying architecture of the pit?" Aiden finished for her.

"Sputnik sure isn't programmed to leave netting alone. I mean, seriously, cutting the netting and dragging it to some goalpost or other could be the win condition."

One of the referees had gotten into a bit of a shouting match with a small percentage of the crowd.

"At the mercy of a fickle referee," Aiden said. "Figure

they didn't quite think through all the implications of the design."

"Can't think of everything, sure."

"I shall have words with Heather if our own little monkey should be disqualified."

"Think she had a hand in the design?"

"Oh, no way," Aiden said. "It's much too simple and straightforward."

"Oh, you think the two-dimensional knot last time is more her style?"

"Hard to say, she did field a monkey last time."

"Yeah," Lynn said. "Hey, this is going to wind down soon because of the participant imbalance."

"I suppose."

"Well, we're up. You ready to stand there and look cool while Sputnik gets into all kinds of mischief?"

"Oh, hell no," Aiden said. "It's your turn."

"What?"

"I did the honors last time."

"You yellow-bellied cowardly traitor," she said, pointing. "You got us into this mess. You get the glory."

"Share the wealth. That's my motto."

"Well, you can keep your motto, thank you very much, because I sure as shooting am not stepping into the ring."

"Sure, you are."

"No way. No how."

"Don't you want your students to see how smart and brave you are? Come on, they're going to be watching."

"They've buggered off, in case you hadn't noticed."

"They'll flock to your side as soon as they see who is standing in the ring."

"Oh, yes, they can watch me hold a big stick while our baby does all the work. It's just so inspiring. Quite the sight to behold."

"Exactly," Aiden said. "Getting into the spirit of it."

"I'll never forgive you if you force me in the ring."

"You'll have fun. I should know."

"I also remember how you tried to get out of it last time."

The cheering redoubled in intensity yet again, which really shouldn't have been possible. The crowd had already doubled and redoubled in volume. There shouldn't have been any more room to grow. More than likely, the crowd had grown ever so slightly quieter over time. When they screeched back to full volume, it only sounded like cheering on top of cheering.

"You're up," Aiden said, pushing Sputnik at her.

"I shall kill you," Lynn said. "I shall beat you to death with our own child if you keep pointing little Sputnik at me."

"I love you, too." Pressuring the robot upon her. "Embrace the glory. The throng is waiting."

Lynn had to grasp Sputnik just to keep it from slipping to the floor. The referee was right behind her, looking pointedly at his phone.

"Yes, right," Lynn said. "I shall make this happen. You," she said, looking at Aiden, trying to hold onto the little robot and the dead man's switch at the same time. "You shall be punished."

"And I shall enjoy it tremendously," Aiden said.

The referee led her and the other two handlers into the abyss. Crossing into the ring was like passing a baffling wall that had been holding back the roar of the crowd. The cheering was a rush to burn at her skin and her heart like a mad thing. The breath was pulled from out her lungs as if she stood in a frozen vacuum. The people were a blur lacking form or detail and really were little more than a thing alive. Her eyes were fire. She tried not to stumble or drop her charge, slipping, dead weight trying to fall free. She found she did not need to breathe.

Finding her assortment of flags, she deposited Sputnik among them. The referee nodding as if words had no meaning and the world was a crushing avalanche of sound. Lynn watched the other handlers ready their own robots. There was another tripod with tall appendages like slender ears or long sails stretching another foot above the monkey's head. The third robot was more of a tank crossed with a tarantula. The large chassis had to conceal many appendages of exotic make and design. The purpose of each would be revealed as events transpired.

Lynn found herself stepping back even without any clear or vaguely comprehensible instructions from the referees. It just made sense. She crossed a rope barrier, turning, looking, trying to find where Aiden stood. He had been through this same ordeal. He had stood while Sputnik had sputtered and floundered and done a spectacularly poor job of completing the trial's objectives. If their little robot did better than leap at her face and gouge out her eyes, it would be a grand success.

The sound was sucked from the room, which seemed rather odd considering the raging mass of people looked as if they were continuing to cheer and shout. Out of all the room, one referee had raised her arm with the master control rod in her hand. Lynn wanted to think it gleamed. She wanted to believe it glistened. She felt the dead man's switch beneath her fingers, and she wanted to raise it to the sky in a grand gesture to match the referee.

The referee's control rod fell, and the robots sprang to life as if they had been goosed with a rather sharp stick or energetic cattle-prod. The other tripod raced forward as if it thought it was in a Rat Race and motion was the best way to think. The modified tank spun in a circle as if taking in its assortment of flags and the mesh netting. Little Sputnik staggered drunkenly forward, twisting one way and then another, as if it had all the intoxicated time in the world.

The other tripod seemed determined to follow the contours of the maze. The tank rolled or possibly scuttled on tiny feet. It was hard to tell. Sputnik swayed from side to side as if not sure what to make of the assorted colorful objects arrayed behind it or the maze presented before it. The other two robots moved. Lynn tried with all of her might not to cover her eyes, and then Sputnik leapt over the netting as if it was all part of a high-jump event or hurdle chase.

* * *

The staging area was quiet, or at least less supersaturated with the roar of the crowd still surrounding the rings. Lynn dropped Sputnik onto the table.

"I swear I don't remember screaming," she said.

"Or jumping up and down," Aiden asked.

"Never, nothing of the kind."

"Well, at least you remembered to scoop up our little hero."

"I could kiss you!" she said, shouting to the robot, turning, grabbing Aiden, kissing him. "We did it!" Wanting to dance around some more.

"Little Sputnik did most of the heavy lifting, sure, but I'm more than prepared to shoulder my share of the credit."

"The jumping algorithm was a hit."

"That it was."

"I can't believe it!"

"Hey, I should be in full-on rapturous ecstasy mode right there with you. No idea why I'm keeping my head."

"Sputnik just leapfrogged right over the maze netting!" Demonstrating with hand gestures. "The others never had a chance!"

"Eat our dust, you pathetic monkeys, am I right?"

"I know!"

"It's the ring, isn't it?"

"Huh?"

"The roar of the crowd from the center of the ring. Nothing compares, right?"

"Yeah, yeah," she said, putting a hand to her chest. "God, my heart's on fire. It won't stop beating like it wants to leap right out of my chest."

"Glory in our victory," Aiden said, grabbing her, trying to spin around, bumping into the table, laughing.

"I could die." Laughing. Arms around Aiden, trying to hold on, trying not to laugh.

"Well, let's clean up a bit. Find people."

"Already?"

"Hey, we're just one-and-one, right? Not like we're suddenly king of the world or anything."

"Spoilsport."

"I know, what is with me? I should be jumping around like a wild thing." Hand to his head as if to prevent it from shaking uncontrollably.

"Well, it's your own damn fault for pushing me into the ring." Bouncing on her toes, pretending to punch him. "Oh, yeah. Oh, yeah, the glory is mine."

"Going to have to wrestle for the honor next time." Slapping playfully at her hands as she punched.

"Oh, sounds like your plan all along."

"What kind of wrestling did you think I had in mind?"

"The kind that ends with you naked, hogtied and me on top beating my chest in savage triumph, obviously." Demonstrating the chest thumping.

"And here I thought you had something interesting in mind. That just sounds like a typical Saturday night."

"I know, great times." Impromptu body slam. "Boom!"

They turned back to the table, checking over Sputnik. Aiden consulted the script emulator on his phone, scrolling diagnostics and displays. They folded up the little robot and secured it within a carryall stashed under the table.

"Safe here, right?"

"If not, I shall exchange words with the management," Aiden said. "Think we'll find Tomorrow or that postdoc?"

"Oliver?" Lynn said as they started back toward the gaming floor. "I'm sure they haven't vanished into the wild blue yonder. The world of Ape Fights and Monkey Trials sucking them into a bleak, black hole from which there is no return."

They maneuvered back through the rambunctious throng, reaching the edge of the monkey pits after no small amount of shoving and kicking. The noise level was the same continuous shriek they had been bombarded with all the long evening. As close to the edge of the pits as they could manage, they watched the little robotic monkeys scurry this way and that through the maze, collecting flags, dropping flags.

They found Heather as the ring was being reset. She gave them a glance, turned, held up one hand, thumbs up alternating with thumb down. Lynn made her sweat a moment, raising her own hand but wavering, and finally gave a thumbs up. Heather smiled, pumped her fist, and made hand gestures indicating she needed to turn her attention back to the ring. Alternately, she was demonstrating a rather bizarre way to give someone a message. Regardless, Lynn nodded. Aiden also gave a thumbs up, but the moment had passed. Heather turned back to the monkey pits, shaking her head dismissively. There may have been eye-rolling, too.

They eventually found Tamara watching an Ape Fight involving something that resembled a tentacled toaster oven and something else like a four-armed gorilla. Tamara had clearly ditched Oliver at some point. They exchanged hugs and bouncing may have been involved.

"Ah shit, I missed it, didn't I?" Tamara tried to say over the omnipresent white-noise of the crowd.

"Which makes you a traitor, but that's not really important right now," Lynn said. "We're celebrating!"

"Obviously." Tamara exchanged bear-hugs with Aiden. She was very nearly lifted into the air. "Whoa!" Back on her feet. "What's that make you guys, one-and-oh?"

"You wish," Aiden said. "It's one-and-one."

"Yeah," Lynn said, "you were there and everything."

"Right, I was." Tamara shook her head. "Time flies when you're teaching undergrads. So what's that mean? Where are you in the stands?"

"Okay, if this was the ground floor," Aiden said, holding his hand about a foot off the ground, "we're buried pretty deep."

"That is inherently unfair."

"Well, we're only just getting started. Some of these contestants have simply been playing for weeks and weeks."

"The last match was only weeks ago, wasn't it?"

"More like two months for us, but yeah, who's keeping track, right?"

"Simply weeks and weeks," Tamara said. "Right. So we should celebrate."

"We are," Lynn said, arms raised. "Basking in our glorious victory."

"For tomorrow, we shall—well, probably lose,

again," Aiden said. "Our little monstrosity needs a lot of work. Algorithms need polish. Code needs refactoring. March of progress. It never ends, right?"

"So, no partying, then?" Tamara said.

"Oh, hey, I didn't say that."

CHAPTER FIFTEEN

In which Lynn discusses various outside activities with members of the university community.

The Information Technology Resource Center morning meeting ran long, as they had to cover a rather impressive rewiring project. It hadn't helped that the meeting had been moved for the first time in ages, so an above-average number of attendees had been forced to scramble for the new location. They arrived, panting, out of breath, and disrupting the proceedings at random moments throughout the presentation. In the end, enough of the relevant information had been conveyed and something resembling marching orders had been relayed.

"Thought that would never end," Lynn said, standing in the hallway as the others milled around.

"Slow torture, I know," Darryl replied, shaking his head and rubbing his face as if pressure to his eyes would cause the just-completed events to be swept from his memory.

"Moving the location on the same day they call an all-hands event."

"Technically, they're all required all-hands meetings."

"Oh, that is not even vaguely in the realm of probability."

"As much as I might wish to agree with you," Darryl said.

"No way." Lynn shook her head. "There's just no way."

"I fear I must dissuade you of the notion."

"They're all required?"

"They are all required."

Lynn looked down the hall as if contemplating the secrets of the universe and more or less ignored the small groups of service reps conversing in hushed whispers, checking their scripts. Clusters of representatives formed and drifted as they compared notes and traded opinions about their goals for the day.

"Just boggles the mind, I take it?" Darryl said.

"More than a little." Lynn shook her head as if dislodging cobwebs. Spying the others as if noticing them for the first time, in spite of the fact she had just been studying them, Lynn turned to her script and began tapping away. "Where are you in this grand design?"

"Oh, something, something, crawling around in the woodwork, I'm sure."

"That would be something, wouldn't it?" Looking to the ceiling.

"What exactly?"

"Dragging hardline through the underbrush." Shrug of shoulders. "Overhead, really. Navigating the crawlspace. Laying cable."

"They have robots for that."

"Yeah, not that we would actual make use of them. Oh, no, not us. Don't have the budget, I'm sure. Just get up there in the crawlspace."

"They have the budget."

"You think?"

"Oh, I don't have to think."

"You don't have to think?"

"Not even a little," Darryl said. "It's not a matter of them not having the budget."

"They just don't want to spend it on us, I know."

Looking this way and that. "But, you know? I like the work."

"You would."

"Oh, come now. Tell me you don't live for this stuff. Laying hardline. Working with your hands. There's just something—oh, I don't know—downright Zen about it."

"The joys of youth. You would see it that way."

"Joys of a misspent youth, you mean. Talk like that going to make me feel old."

"Just wait," Darryl said. "You'll get there."

"Only as old as you feel."

"Yes, exactly, the aches and pains will tell you how you feel."

"I've got a few of those."

"I'm sure you do."

"Just going to have to find ways to entertain ourselves as we grow into our dotage."

"They're on about the Ape Fights, again," Darryl said.

"Yes, I noticed."

"Speaking of ways to keep ourselves entertained."

"Hey, they already had a go at me," Lynn said, "wanted me to turn narc."

"They always want us to narc."

"But, you know," Lynn said, starting to walk down the hallway. "It's not just about your uncle's birthday party."

"Is that what we're calling it?"

"We're not calling it anything. You know there's more to life than just these four walls, right?"

"Yes, I suppose." Looking at her. "I was never one for those iron monger campaigns or whatever it is you're always going on about. I'm more about civilization building."

"Colonizing the outer plants or something, right?"

"Terraforming and everything, right."

"Right."

"It's quite satisfying."

"And it never comes to blows?"

"Oh, well, I didn't say that."

"Of course."

"With depressing frequency, actually."

"Yeah, I've kind of given up on the campaigns myself."

"Oh, yeah?"

"Oh, yeah," Lynn said, glancing up and down the hall, again. They had left the stragglers far behind. "Found something better."

"Continue."

"Almost surprised you're not there."

"Oh, now you've got my curiosity," Darryl said. "What could possibly be of such interest to grasp my attention—Wait, no."

"Oh, yes."

"Your cousin's birthday party has moved off-campus?"

"Well, not exactly. You see, after people graduate, it's not like they lose interest in partying, receptions and weddings. And, whatnot." Brushed at her eyes. "Encryption giving me a headache."

"How exactly did you find out about—well, stuff?"

"Funny thing that. You know where my partner works, right?"

"I'm sure I did at some point."

"That's how."

"Okay, I think I follow. Encryption is—"

"She's a bitch."

"Yes, thank you."

"You should look into it." Glancing once more up and down the hall. "All kinds of fun and games. Some people, naming no names, might have—well, vested interests."

"No."

"Oh, yes."

"Where do you find the time?"

"Well, there is the two of us, you know?"

"I might have to," Darryl said. "Yes, I might just have to."

Catching movement out of the corner of her eye.

"Uh oh, button up," she said. "Incoming."

Darryl turned, looking down the hallway.

"Speak of the devil," he said as the nemesis of the night, Hagarlodge, came barreling down on them. They waited quietly, watching the nightmare approach as if there was nothing else in the universe. If the ceiling collapsed and the building imploded, Hagarlodge would still reach them.

"Bunbury. Charles," Hagarlodge said, taking them in with a glance. "You left the morning meeting efficiently."

"Yes, well, things to do," Darryl said. "Have to get started on the hardline project."

"It is an important job."

"Speaking of which," Lynn said, holding up her script, glancing at the screen. "There a booger in the update? I can't find my assignment."

"Yes, about that," Hagarlodge said, "you've been re-assigned."

"I gathered that. But the hardline job is important, I understand. Got to crawl around in the phantom zone." Waving vaguely toward the ceiling. "I'm good at that."

"Won't be necessary."

"You mean we've finally got some robots to do the crawling and stringing?"

"You wish. Like we've got the budget for that."

"What's the budget got to do with it? Just press-gang some students into building robots for us. Give them work-study or extra credit." Shrug of shoulders. "Something."

"While it is a novel solution except for the part where we've already considered it," Hagarlodge said, drawing breath as if preparing to deliver a well-rehearsed lecture.

"You're really going to draft students?" she said, interrupting.

"There is still the matter of payment."

"My Aunt Fanny."

"Work-study," Darryl said. "Extra credit."

"Work-study still involves payment." Hagarlodge gave him a look.

"Extra credit," Lynn said.

"Yeah, extra credit." Darryl pointed at her.

"There is still the question of materials and supplies."

"The labs are just filled to overflowing with crap." Waving her arm in a great arc.

"Which they need for their studies."

"What part of extra credit isn't sinking in here?"

"I think we're drifting away from the topic at hand," Hagarlodge said, glaring.

"Duly noted." Fingers fluttered near her script miming the act of writing upon it. "Something to do with my morning assignment."

"Yes, exactly." Turning toward Darryl. "Thank you, Bunbury. I believe you know your assignment."

"I'm not so sure about that," Darryl said. "I think I'm going to need confirmation once you've done explaining things to Charles."

"Then I will come find you."

A brief but intense shouting match transpired, except nobody actually said anything, so it was more of a staring contest, except nobody was exactly looking at each other. It was a very passive-aggressive battle of wills in its own quiet way.

"Guess I'll just trundle off to my assignment then," Darryl finally said. "You know, without proper clarification and guidance, it might take me a bit of time to figure out where I'm supposed to be."

"I'll just have to take the chance that you're smarter than you look."

Darryl nodded his head, looking away, and began to wander down the hallway as if in no real hurry to reach his destination or even figure out where his destiny awaited.

"My assignment?" Lynn finally said.

"Well, that's kind of up to you."

"Chose your own destiny," she said. "Joy."

"You may recall rumors spreading about Ape Fights a few months back."

"Locked me in the dungeon because I wouldn't play ball. Nope, can't say I remember it at all."

"While your arguments against aiding us in the investigation were not unreasonable."

"The students would never trust me again."

"Students come. Students go." Waving his hand in a leisurely way. "These things pass."

"Students are transitory by definition, sure, but the word-of-mouth stays. Scuttlebutt takes up residence and lives forever. Does nobody remember The Trial?"

"I'm sorry, you've lost me there. The Trial?"

"Really old movie, forget it," she said, shaking her head. "Uses the mechanics of an inexplicable trial as a metaphor for how rumors can destroy lives."

"Mechanics of an inexplicable metaphor?"

"Oh, never mind, I told you to forget it."

"My point being," Hagarlodge said, "that you could have helped us with our investigation."

"Narc, you mean."

"We never did learn anything."

"Which is the part that boggles my mind." Tapping the side of her head. "Just makes it want to burst. Why didn't you interview the stupids who sent the original message?"

"Yes, about that," Hagarlodge said, looking away.

"Oh, you have got to be fucking kidding me!"

"Language."

"You didn't interview the student who sent the message? Nobody interrogated the brain-donor who received it? What's the point of tracking traffic if you don't take advantage of the fact?"

"It's not as simple as you make it sound."

"Me, you can browbeat, threaten and torture." Facing Hagarlodge, pointing at his chest. "Are the students that precious or fragile? Concerned they won't tithe sufficiently to the alumni association?"

The hallway wasn't empty. Generally clear of ITRC personnel, sure, but not empty. People were starting to look in their direction.

"It's more a matter of knowing who they are."

"I'm sorry, but I think I've just suffered a psychic meltdown. And the blood is gushing from out my nose." Took a step back as if she might slide unbidden to the floor. "Did you just admit that you do not know who sent the offending message?"

"Security didn't see fit to convey that information to us."

"Security?" Lynn said, mind racing, memory of something Darryl had once said echoing through her head.

"Yes, Security," Hagarlodge said, as if risking a creeping edge of irritation into his voice. "Something to do with privacy."

"With what?"

"More or less what I said, but the point stands that we do in fact care about the health and well-being of our students."

"Oh, I think I'm starting to follow. The mention of Ape Fights sent a flag way up the pole. Someone at a high level thought something should be done."

"And that person spoke to someone at a high level within EH&S."

"They have enough to do."

"Which means the high ranking fiend within Environmental Health and Safety felt it necessary to pass the salient details along to a rather important person within the Information Technology Resource Center."

"And that's how we got our marching orders," Lynn said. "Classic."

"Which is why we are tasked with hunting down a conspiracy to hold Ape Fights within our grand institution without any information regarding who is actually involved. Message sender?" Shrug of shoulders. "Don't know." Spread fingers. "Date and time?" Hands shaken at the sky. "No idea." Dropped to his sides. "Message recipient?"

"Fuck all."

"Language."

"Yeah, yeah, yeah," Lynn said. "Well, I wish you well."

"So you don't even want to learn the parameters of the assignment?"

"I'm not turning narc, you know that, which just leaves the one option."

"We need to know, Charles."

"Which is why you need to go back to Security and EH&S and explain the situation to them. Get them to understand that this can't just be brain-to-brain. They need to hold up their end of the bargain and cough up those names."

"If only it was that easy."

"Easy?" Lynn said. "What easy? Just trundle on over there or speak to your boss or whatever it is that you big brain high-level operators do."

"And yet I'm asking you, which should tell you something about the difficulty rating of the other option."

"I sympathize." Hand to her chest. "I really do."

"I sense a *but* floating on the horizon."

"Your cognitive faculties serve you well."

"If you have any friends or loved ones," Hagarlodge said, "I recommend you say goodbye to them now."

* * *

It didn't take Lynn that long to hunt down Elisabeth Dao in whatever backwater corner of a half-forgotten lab the graduate student had sequestered herself within.

"Studying rots the brain," Lynn said. Elisabeth barely glanced up from her phone. "You know that, right?"

"And yet, here I am."

"Exams are over, aren't they? I could have sworn the term was over."

"Exams never end."

"They must let you take the occasional weekend or something. Recharge those batteries. Rest that brain."

"It is a far, far better thing than I have ever done before."

"Martyr."

"Hey, if the corset fits, right?"

"Oh, I get it," Lynn said, leaning against a wall, sliding to the floor. "You just don't want old Grandma here cramping your style and knowing what you get up to on any given weekend."

"You seem to think I get up to far more mischief than I actually do." Looking at her. "Unlike some people I could name, I take my studies seriously."

"So you wouldn't know anything about Ape Fights, right?"

"Wait, what?"

"No, remember, we talked about this," Lynn said, gesturing toward Elisabeth as if attempting to placate a deranged rhinoceros. "You and me and Tamara Rosewater. The joys and sorrows of overheard conversations. Students forgetting that their messages are monitored for key words such as Ape Fight."

"Right," Elizabeth said, letting the word drag between them as if she were catching her breath.

"So, after all." Shrug of shoulders. "If you knew anything about upcoming events, you would tell me."

"Even if they were off campus?"

"Especially if they were off campus. We need to know these things."

"Turning the screws on you, huh?"

"Oh, I suppose you could say that."

"What's your partner in crime think of all of this? She is a student teacher, after all."

"Couldn't find her," Lynn said, muttering, looking away. "Must be off teaching or something."

"Wouldn't surprise me if I'm accidentally skipping class." Elisabeth glanced to her phone, tapping, scrolling. "Pretty sure I'm not."

"So if you hear anything about Ape Fights." Looked at Elisabeth. "You know. Spread the word that ITRC is on the warpath again."

"You mean, do a little digging, right? Hold my ear to the rumor mill?"

"And if people unknown or wholly imagined should happen to realize that they need to upgrade the encryption—well." Shrug of shoulders. "Sucks to be me."

"Martyr."

"Kick me while I'm down, why don't you?"

* * *

Time had not been kind to the depths and lost corners of Benjamin Franklin Public University, although the walls looked no different than the last time Lynn and Aiden had ventured so far into the deep down below. The air was thick and hard to breathe, as if they really were miles beneath the Earth's crust. It was somehow both stiflingly humid and bone-renderingly dry. The students, naturally, didn't seem to mind. They were too busy shouting, cheering, and otherwise carrying on over the Ape Fights.

There were three rings marked off with little more than chalk outlines on the floor. In each, a mismatched pair of combatants faced each other and generally attempted to take the other apart with little more than claws, fists, hands and various bludgeoning appendages. Farther back in the distant confines of the strangely elongated room was the Monkey Trial ring and its circle of dedicated aficionados.

"Why do the trials involve three monkeys at a throw, anyway?" Aiden said with Sputnik held awkwardly in his arms.

"What?" Lynn said over her shoulder, only half-listening. Before her in the ring, a two-level rope maze had been set up that the little robots had to maneuver around and through.

"Why three?" he said, trying to point, trying to hold onto Sputnik. "The others. The bashing and the smashing. Always one-on-one. This? There's always going to be two losers."

"It's got something to do with the problem solving,"

Elisabeth said, trying not to shout, but it was the only way to be heard. "Makes for a more complex puzzle. There can be teamwork. There can be backstabbing."

"You could have teamwork and backstabbing in the other version, too," Aiden said, nodding toward the ape rings. "Two ganging up on one. Lots of permutations."

"You know, this is only a slight variation on the last puzzle," Lynn said.

"What?" Elisabeth said.

"No, really, just look at it." Gesturing toward the ring. "Last time was more of a tower, yeah? Basket was at the top. This time it's less of a tower, and the basket is in the center."

"Yeah, well, it's the same group of volunteer student referees as last time, isn't it? Same talent pool for designing puzzles. Same basic building blocks to work with. You're going to see a lot of variations on a theme."

"This is going to be cake for our little guy. I'm almost surprised you're letting us compete."

"Oh, I know, letting you squares into our cool circle. Nothing but grandpa-ware from you guys, right?"

"Hey, we are going to take you to school," Aiden said.

"We are at school," Elisabeth replied, gesturing, looking around.

"Like she said." Nodding toward Lynn. "Cake."

"You know the other reason why it's three-on-two in the monkey ring, right? I mean three-on-three."

"Yeah, I reasoned my way through that. I mean, what's the reason?"

"More brains working the problem. Someone's going to figure it out first. Teach the others. Match is over faster."

"Only if they're paying attention."

"Speaking of which," Lynn said as the cheering redoubled and one handler danced around the ring with his arms in the air. "Somebody's won."

"They'll have to reset," Aiden said. "Not our turn. Hey, isn't that postdoc friend of yours in the next match?"

"Oliver? More of a professional acquaintance, really."

"You invited him to the monthly."

"And this firecracker, too." Lynn reached over, tried to ruffle Elisabeth's hair. Head tilt negated this action. "Too busy."

"What can I say?" Elisabeth said. "Too cool for the room. Besides, got to study sometimes."

"Especially since you're not studying now."

"Damn Skippy, I couldn't miss this."

"When are you fielding a monkey, anyway?" Aiden said.

"When Hell freezes over," she replied. "I don't have time for this. Can barely fit in the work for an ape."

"When did you field an ape?"

"About an hour ago." Turning on him. "Weren't you paying attention? My little thunder-cracker kicked the other guy's asterisk."

"Must have been busy getting Sputnik ready."

"Well, serves you right for missing out on great achievements in modern fisticuffs. In fact, why am I even morally supporting your childish endeavors here?"

"Because you think we're going to crash and burn, and you most assuredly want to watch."

"You may be onto something there."

"What in the blazes is going on?" Lynn said, trying to move closer to the ring.

"What?" Aiden said, looking, following her.

There appeared to be a heated discussion among the handlers behind one of the little robots. Oliver's six-legged tarantula had started making its way through the jungle-gym as if it had been born to the rope maze. One of the competition bore a strong resemblance to a tripod centaur and was skirting the edge of the maze, searching for various objects to take with it. The final monkey actually looked vaguely like a monkey and was slowly looking around as if it was a deer caught in headlights.

The handlers were yelling at the little monkey. The crowd nearby was pointing and laughing. The robot itself was creeping slowly toward the maze as if in a daze, and it wouldn't stop looking around as if it found the great group of people horribly intimidating.

The handlers were shouting and yelling at each other, which is about when Lynn realized that one of the handlers had tripped the dead man's switch. He was waving the switch around, pointing at it, pointing toward the monkey, and otherwise trying to get the referee's attention. Lynn recognized him, but for the life of her, could not remember his name. At last, the referee fiddled with her own master switch and then looked to the monkey, which continued to wander timidly around the ring. The referee turned back to her control switch and began pressing more buttons.

Suddenly, the other monkeys went dead as if they had been hit with exceptionally strong knockout gas, which raised the volume of the crowd all around the ring. Oliver's voice was quite clear from out the crowd. The one monkey continued its slow tour, looking this way and that, as if it expected death from above at any moment.

"Shut down!" Aiden said, pressing Sputnik against her as if trying to get her to take the little robot off his hands. "Shut down!"

"What?" Lynn turned, holding her hands up as if

they might get into a shoving match trying to force Sputnik upon the other. "Leave off."

"Shut down!" He dropped Sputnik, which she found rather funny.

"Careful, you'll break her."

Aiden had his phone out, tapping commands, and she saw that he was trying to kill the script emulator. She watched, captivated, as if she had no idea it was possible to cancel individual applications running on a phone. They all seemed to run all the time regardless of which ones you actually wanted hogging resources. She watched, savoring the experience. Around her the voices had grown in intensity, and then Aiden stepped into the ring.

"Oh, shit!" she said, fumbling, trying to pick Sputnik up. She got the little robot into her arms and fumbled for the master power switch, which was carefully concealed behind panels to prevent accidental tampering. "Shut down! Where's the freaking off switch?"

"Whatever is Aiden doing?" Elisabeth said.

"Make sure it's in full lock-down mode," Lynn said, trying to force Sputnik upon her.

"What in blazes are you doing?" Resisting possession, fumbling, they almost dropped Sputnik, again.

"I have to force-quit penis!" Free of the little robot, Lynn started scrambling for her phone. "You should do the same!"

"Why?"

"Contagion! Hot zone!" Phone in hand, it was slowly starting to comply.

"Quiet!" Aiden was trying to get everyone's attention as he watched the little robot. "Everyone quiet!"

"What are you talking about?" Elisabeth said.

"We're ground zero! Wild infection!"

"Wild infection—What?" Elisabeth looked as if she was trying to study Lynn's face and Aiden's antics in the ring at the same time. "No!" Dropping Sputnik, again, reaching for her phone.

"Grab Sputnik," Lynn said, turning, crossing into the ring to stand with Aiden.

"It's a tourist!" Aiden said with his arms out, hands flat to the crowd as if he could quiet them through pure force of will.

"Everybody, listen up!" Lynn shouted, commanding. Her voice slamming into the crowd, rushing over them like a wave, leaving silence in its wake. "Shut it!"

The surrounding crowd went dark. The other rings catching on to the fact that something was up south of Denmark. Even Aiden had paused to look at her, and then his attention was back on the little rogue unit.

"Anyone running a script emulator should kill it right bloody now!" she said, turning slowly, facing the crowd, listening to her words spread like fire. "Your other phone functions should be properly shielded, if we're lucky! And while you're at it, make sure all the apes and monkeys are locked down! Power to zero if you've got it!"

"What's the deal, Merlin? We just want our monkey back." It was one of the tourist's handlers. She recognized the face but could not place the name. "We can power it down. Figure out what's its damage later."

"It's a tourist," Aiden said, watching the robot as it gave off every indication of being a cornered animal. "We have to dispose of it."

"What? No, it's just stuck in a loop," the handler said, stepping into the ring, and his name was Madagascar. Of all the crazy things, Lynn remembered that his name was Madagascar.

Murmurs rippled out around them like silent sound traveling without words or a voice, and Lynn felt the attention of the extended crowd slowly starting to focus upon them.

Aiden made a grab for the little robot. Its censors went wide just like little eyes skyrocketing open, and it ran past his feet into the rope maze.

"Blighter!"

"Oh, come on, let it be!" Madagascar said. "It's our monkey! Let us deal with it!"

"It's not your monkey any more," Aiden said. "It's more like a rabid dog. No telling what it's going to do."

"Balderdash!"

"Look, Mads, we don't know how tourism spreads," Lynn said, turning toward him. "We have to treat it like a highly contagious infection." Turning, taking in the crowd. "Everybody shutting down, right?"

"Oh, come on, we don't know that," Madagascar said. "That's fear-mongering talk."

"Yeah, just help us catch the monkey," one of the other handlers said. "We'll sort this. It's probably just a faulty glitch. Hardware issue with the wireless receptors."

"Just trust me on this," Aiden said. "I know a tourist when I see one."

"Oh, and what are you again?" Madagascar said. "ITRC? Some kind of Tourist Hunter?"

"As a matter of fact," Oliver said, standing on the other side of the maze, watching the little robot. "He is."

"Oh, great, so this is just straight-up snatch and smash, is it?"

"You could say that," Oliver said.

"ITRC is gong to shut us down," said a voice from out the crowd.

"No, they're not," Lynn said, turning, trying to take in the surrounding eyes and faces. Elisabeth was there. Darryl was watching from the edge of the crowd. "We're not. Just let the Tourist Hunter do his job."

"Help us catch the little blighter," Madagascar said.

"We'll even thank you. But don't destroy it. We don't even know it's a tourist."

"You really want to take that chance with the little psychopath?"

"Listen to you. Could you think any worse of the little monkey?"

"Yes," Lynn said, turning, facing Madagascar. "Yes, I could. For example, it's not actively trying to kill us all right now."

"Wait, no, that's actually a point in my favor. It's not hurting anybody. It's not doing anything."

"It's hiding," Aiden said, looking away from the rope maze. "Is it supposed to do that?"

"It's frightened," someone said. "Let it be."

"Yeah," voice out of the crowd.

"Let it be."

"That's anthropomorphizing," Aiden said, pointing. "It's not frightened. It's not anything. We don't know what it is perceiving. What it thinks is real."

"Come on."

"Help me or stand back."

Crowds have a way of talking without making coherent words. There's just that low-level hum of sound bubbling and burbling as if it all had a life of its own.

Aiden grasped a handful of rope netting, tested it, twisting this way and that. The little bipedal monkey continued to cower at the center of the maze, giving off every indication that it was a feeling, thinking thing.

"Oliver, right?" Aiden said, looking across the rope maze. "You with me?"

"Yeah, I'm here." Watching the robot, studying the maze. "All the hours I've logged in the quarantine zone you would think I had seen a tourist before. You'd be wrong."

"First time for everything."

"It's eerie. Look at its mannerisms." Oliver turned

toward the handlers. "You guys didn't program primate behaviors into your little love child, did you?"

"What? No!" Madagascar said.

"Lynn," Aiden said, ignoring the outcry, looking at her, "you ready for this?"

"Yeah, I'm hip." Stepping to the edge of the maze. "Darryl?" she said, looking back to the edge. "Care to lend a hand?"

"Hey, I'm just an observer here," he said.

Lynn watched him as she felt the breath slip from between her toes, and then she turned back to the maze.

"Just tell me what to do?" she said.

"Let's see if we can force it my way," Aiden said. "Oliver? Lynn? Try pushing into the maze." They started to move. "Now, watch it. Experience tells me that thing is going to bolt like lightning."

Movement was difficult considering the maze was designed to stymie creatures that were a good two feet tall. Lynn and Oliver looked as if they were trying to wade through molasses.

"It's not doing anything," Lynn said, keeping her voice low.

"You don't have to whisper. It can't hear you."

"Right," she said in a rather hushed voice.

"What did I just say?"

"Whatever it was, it wasn't at full volume. I'm just following your lead."

Robot sprang forward, leaping from rope strand to crossbeam.

"Whoa!"

"Gotcha!" Aiden cried. Hands on the little critter. "Ouch! Ow!" Holding it high as it struggled against his grip, twisting, turning. "Stop that!" He smashed it into the floor.

"Hey!" Madagascar shouted.

The robot continued to fight him, moving like an undulating ball of wire. Aiden pressed his forearm into it, fumbling with his fingers, seeking the power-switch cover.

"You're hurting it!" voices screamed.

"Stop that!"

Aiden had the panel open. Fingers fighting for the control, not knowing if it was a button or switch. The robot went slack.

"You killed it!"

"What the hell are you doing!"

Aiden kept his weight on the little thing as if it was just gathering its energy for one prolonged assault against his hold. Lynn knelt at his side, watching the robot, looking for signs of activity. Oliver stood several steps back, facing the crowd, blocking Madagascar.

"Okay, I think that got it," Lynn said.

Aiden didn't answer.

"Right?" she said.

Aiden slowly took his weight off the robot, sitting back.

"Right," he said.

"Okay, great, that's it!" Madagascar said. "Now hand it over."

"It's not as simple as that," Aiden said.

"No, really, it is just that simple."

"This little blighter needs to go back to the lab for tests."

"Oh, no, you don't." Standing before them. "You're not stealing our property!"

"Quarantine. Observation. There's a difference."

"On whose authority?" Madagascar managed to push past Oliver. The other handlers were at his side. "Where are you? Who do you think you are?"

Aiden sat back, hands at his sides, looking up at Madagascar and the other handlers.

"Well, we can't just let it go," Lynn said. "There's the risk of contamination."

"No."

"Don't make me pull rank here," she said.

"You really going to play that card?" Darryl said. They all turned and looked at him. Shrug of shoulders, he looked leisurely from side to side as if he was drunk or otherwise drifting through a dream. "You really want this to go that way?" Looked back to her. "Here?"

Lynn wanted to sink to the floor. She wanted to take up real estate next to Aiden on the cold, hard ground.

"There has to be a middle ground," she finally managed to say, feeling the words like shards of granite in her throat. "Think of the consequences of your actions."

"It could be a hardware fault," Madagascar said.

"It's not," Aiden said with a voice barely above a whisper. "Weren't you paying attention?"

"Well, forgive me for saying this, mighty mister Tourist Hunter, but I'm pretty sure you're off duty. Am I right? You're off the clock?"

"We're all off the clock," Lynn said, stepping forward, "but you should still listen to reason. Consider our experience."

"Experience working for the man is what you mean."

Lynn felt her breath fall.

"That's not even vaguely close to what I mean," she said, pulling words from an empty throat, leaving them quiet and soft.

"Then the one thing we should all be able to agree on is that you're going to give our little whirling dervish there back to us," Madagascar said, towering over them, pointing at them. "You have no right to vandalize our property."

"We have to know if it is dangerous," Aiden said

from the floor, resting before the deactivated little mechanical monster. "I cannot stress that enough."

"Like the way you smashed it into the ground?" Madagascar said. "That kind of dangerous."

Aiden looked from face to face and to the crowd surrounding them. There were no words. There were no voices. They didn't need them. The air was ripe to overflowing with their feelings.

"I cannot in good conscience just give you the tourist," Aiden finally managed to say.

"Well, nobody is asking you to have a happy conscience."

"There's a middle ground," Oliver said, drawing all eyes and the focus of the room down upon him. "You said there was a middle ground," he said, facing Lynn.

"Yeah, I did at that." She could feel the attention of the crowd slowly gravitating back to her. "This is exactly the kind of thing Applied Engineering and Robotics was designed to handle. We've got theoretical software experts and everything."

"No, no way," Madagascar said.

"It doesn't have to be faculty."

"Nothing comes out of the quarantine zone."

"Well, that's not entirely true."

"Nothing comes out of the quarantine zone that's gone into it," Madagascar turned on Oliver. "Am I right?"

"Hardware. Software," Oliver said. "That's right."

"There must be something," Lynn said. "We could jury-rig some experiments. At least think about it."

"Give Lion-tamer there back to us, and we'll consider it," Madagascar said.

"Lion-tamer?" Aiden said, looking at Madagascar and then down at the little robot lying motionless before him. "You named it Lion-tamer?"

"What, you going to say it's chosen its own name

now? Thrown off its slave-title? Found God between crunching numbers and burning cycles?"

"I said nothing." Shrugged his shoulders.

"Good." Madagascar picked up the robot. Aiden did nothing to stop him.

Lynn offered Aiden her hand. After a long moment of watching Madagascar and the other handlers as if he expected the little machine to sprout bloody appendages and start attacking them, Aiden finally crawled to his feet.

"We should," he began, stopping, looking around.

"Yes," she replied, walking to the edge of the ring, walking hand in hand with Aiden almost as if she was leading him.

They rendezvoused with Elisabeth at the edge, taking Sputnik back from her. Around and behind them, the crowd began to mutter and move as if it was waking from a drug-induced slumber.

"Right, we're going to have to void that last match," one of the referees said. There was a murmur of conflicted voices from the crowd. "It's not ideal, I know, but these things happen. We'll move on to the next group with one cancellation."

Lynn and Aiden made their way to the handler's pit at the far edge of the crowd. It wasn't quite a separate room, but it was treated with a certain amount of reverence and respect. Lynn and Aiden collected their gear, depositing Sputnik into its carrying case. They left the Ape Fights and Monkey Trials far behind them.

Lynn led them through long passages and chambers without giving much thought to the direction or destination. They climbed stairs, passed through labs and work spaces, walking, traveling in silence. Reaching one lab that bore more than a passing resemblance to an iron foundry, Lynn stopped as if she had grown quite befuddled and lost. She felt the wind. She listened to the distant hum of climate-control systems, which could never be turned completely off given the types of equipment and systems contained in the labs.

She took a long metal rod like a stick made of raw iron from among an assortment of random debris on a lab bench and began to beat the bench quite savagely, as if she would never stop. The iron rang, echoing and reverberating in the empty lab. Equipment and assorted cast-off pieces of metal and wire bounced and shook. Parts flying to the floor. Aiden watched, holding Sputnik's carrying case, saying nothing.

Lynn slowly sputtered to a stop. Her hands stinging, hurting. Her ears ringing. She dropped the rod as if it burned, looking to the lab bench and its assorted fragments and pieces of cast-off robotic and machine components. The space looked no different, almost as if her attack on the surface simply had not happened. She turned, slowly, looking toward Aiden who watched her without comment.

"Sorry," she muttered through gravel and broken words. "It's just...more than anything else...threw us under the bus." Put her hands to the sides of her head, squeezing tight. A roar started deep in her chest that threatened to explode out of her mouth, but she managed to hold it down. The sound escaping as a deep-throated growl, grinding at long last back into half-forgotten silence.

"Hey," Aiden finally said with the echoes having faded into the dust. "I would be right there with you, but this is your house. I figure...If I...you know...actually expressed myself like that." Trying to gesture at the lab bench. "Not that I don't want to, believe me. Those punks, right? Standing over me. Saying those things." He looked at the floor. "Security would probably swoop down on me, right?"

"Yeah," Lynn said, glancing up and down the lab.

"They probably would at that." Looking toward the hallways and dark half-shadowed doors. "In fact, they're probably watching us right now."

"I kind of assumed. I mean, just look at the equipment all around us." Letting his eyes drift over the lab. "Okay, maybe not this lab, but you know what I mean."

"Very much so." Lynn's phone chimed. "Probably Liz," she said, looking down. "Poor kid did the right thing. Not following us."

Hey, Elisabeth had typed. *You cool?*

"Am I cool?" Lynn said, holding up her phone so that Aiden could see the display but not giving him time to read. "Of course I'm not cool!" she shouted at it. "I'm about as far from cool as it is possible to be! Darryl, God damn you!" Made as if she would throw her phone down the hall. "I mean, I understand why—I really do, but fucking hell! Why! Why did he have to do that!"

"Hey," Aiden said, stepping, stopping, and then looked to the floor. "I know." Shrug of shoulders. "I know."

"Well." Brushing a hand at her face and hair. "Oliver is still there. Maybe he can talk sense into them. I don't know. Run some tests, anyway."

"That's good."

"Yeah, we should. We should—God, I need a drink."

"You and me both, sister."

"Don't call me sister." Taking his arm, starting to walk. "First, it's stupid. You just can't pull it off. Second, that's kind of gross, really. I mean, I've seen you naked."

"Noted."

Lynn fumbled with her phone one-handed so as not to disentangle her arm from Aiden.

We're cool, she typed. *Keep your head down. Tell me if Oliver does anything interesting.*

Eyes and ears, Elisabeth typed.

"Liz will feed us tourist updates." She put her phone away. "At least, I think she will. Slang's a bitch."

"Playground of the young."

"Don't remind me."

"Why they don't listen to us."

"Why we should stick together." Silence. "God damn you, Darryl. We shall most definitely have words."

CHAPTER SIXTEEN

In which Lynn sends test balloons out to various people and receives an unexpected invitation for her trouble.

Lynn couldn't sleep. She had been asleep. Of course it would have been more accurate to say that she had been in an alcoholic coma. Okay, maybe not a coma, but she hadn't been in much of a hurry to wake up. It was the sun streaming in the window that finally did it. One of the things they had failed to do when they had finally lapsed into somnolence and dream in the long, lost hours of the cold, dark morning was close the curtains. She wanted to sleep because it was better than thinking. Anything was better than remembering the night before, but the lapsed cries of the crowd would not leave her alone.

She went to the window, closed the curtains. It wasn't much of a view, anyway. Basically just a way for light to stream indirectly into the apartment. Returning to the bed, she pulled the covers tight, letting them swirl around her, but her mind wouldn't let go. Struggling back out of bed, she fumbled among her randomly discarded clothes for her phone. Returning to the bed for a second time, she found Aiden watching her quietly, saying nothing. She leaned over, kissed him, and then sat back hunched among the covers.

Anything you want to share with the crowd? she typed, sending the message to Elisabeth. *Nothing in my queue. I'm hoping that means things went swimmingly after we cashed out.*

Lynn scanned through her messages, which she probably should have done before sending off the missive to Elisabeth.

"My brain's not in gear," she muttered and glanced at Aiden who continued to study her in glassy-eyed silence, almost as if he was sleeping with his eyes open. "Shut up," she said in his general direction.

What, no late morning descriptions of your nocturnal gallivanting? she typed, sending this message to Tamara. *Falling down on the job is what you are. Not that you would believe our evening. Trust me, you wouldn't. Remind me to go into detail the next time I see you.*

We're going to have words, Oliver, she typed for his benefit. *There are matters of lab etiquette we must discuss.*

I had a quiet night at home, thank you very much, Tamara typed. *Seriously, no details you can share over the phone?*

What? But your life isn't supposed to revolve around us, Lynn typed, sending to Tamara. *You're supposed to be out doing stuff. Having fun so we can live vicariously through you.*

"What are you doing?" Aiden said from within his cocoon of sheets and covers.

"Calling people," she replied, muttering half to herself. When there was no reply from the rumpled mountain, she turned back to her phone.

I have homework on top of the coursework I assign my students, in case you've forgotten, Tamara typed. *That's right, my own assignments and classes don't stop just because I've graduated to student teacher.*

Lab etiquette? Oliver typed. *What are you talking about?*

Don't they give you a year to concentrate on the

teaching half of that equation or something? she typed to Tamara.

Oh, we are most definitely going to have words, she then typed for Oliver's benefit. *I want to know all about the latest experiments. Details! Details! Details! I thrive on this stuff.*

"We'll see if Oliver got anywhere," Lynn said, glancing at Aiden.

"Yeah, anything?"

"He's fighting me. Probably doesn't want to put shit in writing. Which I understand."

"Perfectly reasonable."

"This encryption stuff, ugh." Her phone chimed. She ignored it.

"How's your head?"

"It's been better." She tried to smile. "You?"

"I think this pillow managed to seep into my brain. Osmosis. Something," he said, trying to sit up.

Lynn looked back to her phone.

You're living in a dream world, Tamara had typed. *I'm living viciously through you these days, in case you hadn't noticed. You give with the details.*

Viciously? Lynn typed. *Seriously?*

You heard me. Now, give over.

"Someone needs to remember we're encrypted," Lynn said.

"Who?"

"Tomorrow."

"Well, someone probably forgot what we got up to last night. Or just rubbing it in our faces that we couldn't swing her an invite."

"I just hope we haven't worn out our welcome."

Yeah, about those latest experiments, Oliver had typed. *Not much to talk about.*

Outcome pending? Lynn typed, sending to Oliver.

Nothing I can send by post, she typed to Tamara.

Too risque? Tamara replied.

Too long, Lynn typed. *It's like a novel. My fingers would fall off. This is going to take face-to-face interface.*

Not even started, Oliver typed.

"Here we go," Lynn said, tilting the phone so that Aiden could see. "Oliver got nowhere with the tourist sympathizers."

"Wish I could say I was surprised."

"You're taking it well."

"Willful denial," Aiden said. "If I stopped to think about it for even one second, my blood would just boil away in a rage."

"Easily said."

"It's weird, I know, but I swear watching you beat the shit out of that bench helped dissipate my own desire for wanton destruction."

"Vicarious empowerment or something?"

"Wherever did that expression come from?"

"Well, I was just talking to Tomorrow about vicious—I mean, vicarious living." She looked hard at her phone. "We need to talk."

"Yeah, good to bring a sympathetic ear into this."

Well, I'm sure I will see you round campus tomorrow, Tamara had typed.

"Want to shoot for today?" Looking at Aiden.

"Go for it."

I don't know if it'll keep until tomorrow, Lynn typed, sending to Tamara. *It'll take days. Really is an epic.*

Much as I would love to start the novel, Tamara typed. *I really do have deadlines.*

We could keep you company.

Too much crap to drag to your pad.

There's always the alternative.

Lynn watched her phone as the moment dragged and Tamara did not reply.

"Oh, shit," Lynn said.

"What?"

"I think we're about to get the invite to someone's home."

"No!" Aiden leaned into her, trying to read the display on her phone, made a grab for it.

"Leave off!"

Yeah, that's a possibility, Tamara typed.

"Holy shit!" Lynn said. "We're in."

"Doesn't she have roommates?"

"Yeah, doesn't she have roommates?" Lynn said. *Don't you have roommates?* she typed.

Long story, I'll fill you in. Don't rush over. I'll straighten up a bit first.

"A likely story."

"What?"

"She wants to tidy up first," Lynn said. "When's she going to have the time for that?"

When are you going to have time for that? she typed. *Said you were busy with homework.*

Yeah, okay, Tamara typed. *Just don't rush over.*

"She's got a point," Aiden said, having read over Lynn's shoulder. "We shouldn't rush. Don't want to spook her. We'll lose the invite."

"I know." Nodding at her phone. "She was already starting to put us off. Need to push for the invite without scaring her."

"You're doing marvelously. Still, what a thing to happen to get us the invite, huh?"

"Don't remind me," Lynn said, "and we haven't even told her about it yet."

"That'll be fun."

"That'll be tricky."

"Oh?"

"Well, she is practically faculty." Shrug of shoulders. "We're practically breaking confidence telling her."

"It'll be a good bonding experience."

"I'm not a narc."

Aiden sat in silence, leaning against her, resting his face against her arm.

"Yeah, I know."

"I can't break—" Ground into silence. "I can't break confidence. They'll never forgive me."

"You'd never forgive yourself." Snaking his arm around hers. "Tomorrow understands that."

"Yes, she does. It's part of what we love about her, isn't it?"

"Very much so." Halfheartedly reaching for her phone. "No more updates on the postdoc front?"

"Nope." Scrolling through her messages. "Oliver told us all he knows, I think. No surprise we haven't heard from Liz. She was the one threatening to withdraw her moral support before everything went to hell last night."

"I remember her. She's adorable."

"Grad students tend to be." Looking at him. "You want to know what's really adorable? Tomorrow is frightened we're going to upgrade."

"What, trade her in for a younger model? We're not young ourselves. Where's the sense in that?"

"Speak for yourself."

"About the trade?"

"About being young."

"True. We've got hours to go before we sleep—or something," Aiden said, muttering. "You're only as old as your last visit to the clinic."

"Only as old as your aches and pains tell you that you are, as someone recently informed me."

"That sounds distressingly accurate."

"I still don't want to downgrade."

"No, we've just got too much in common with the current model to risk it for a next generation upgrade.

Diminishing returns there. Besides, I want to see where she lives."

"I know, I'm dying to see the place, too," Lynn said.

* * *

Lynn and Aiden took a Ubiquity shuttle to Tamara's neighborhood, but first, they had discovered they didn't actually know the address. A series of messages had then been exchanged regarding the exact location of Tamara's apartment. Careful negotiations had been navigated, threaded like a minefield in an earthquake. Lynn and Aiden had even discussed the merits of bringing a gift.

"We should have brought something," Lynn said, climbing the front steps of the apartment building.

"We did bring something." Aiden held up the bottle of plum wine.

The street was a blended neighborhood. Half the apartments had shops on the ground floor. The other half had tiny gardens, brick steps, and foot-high decorative fences. Trees dotted the sidewalk in little metal cages with branches reaching for the sky, throwing shade over surprisingly pleasant sidewalks.

"I'm getting work flashbacks," he said.

"Courage," Lynn replied, holding up a fist as if plucking triumph from out of the drifting sky. "You're off the clock."

"I spend so much of my life walking up steps just like these."

"Well, take note of the neighborhood should you ever find yourself on a job around here."

They flashed their phones at the door. The light switching to admit them came rather quickly, as if someone had been waiting impatiently for their arrival. They climbed stairs without even bothering to hunt for an elevator. Several floors and many steps later they found themselves at the door.

"Moment of truth," Lynn said, flashing her phone to the door scanner.

They stood, waiting, as nothing happened.

"Should just pound on it," Aiden said. "Give her a thrill."

"Or a fright." Turning toward him. "Or give us a fright. Security descending upon us."

"Place doesn't look very secure."

"That's just what they want you to think."

"I don't think I've ever run into security at a place—"

The door opened with a violent jerk that practically sucked them inside. Tamara tried to say hello, but it came out as more of a shriek. Not to be outdone, Lynn answered in kind, enveloping her, throwing arms around her. They staggered into the room. Aiden trailing along in their wake, letting the door slip closed behind him. They got their first look at the living room.

"Holy fuck," Aiden said. "This place is huge."

"Well, it doesn't always look like this," Tamara said, waving a hand as if dismissing the room with its curved couch, sideboard, end-table, and chairs. "The last of my roommates decamped not that long ago. The place only looks cavernous in their absence."

"How many roommates did you have?"

"Several, I never could keep track."

"Well, it's easy to lose them here. I mean, look at this." Gesturing at the room. "This has got to be bigger than our whole apartment."

"Oh, you must be exaggerating," Lynn said, looking about. "I mean, sure, it's a near thing, but we're just biased. We see space and our minds explode."

"Agoraphobia," Tamara said.

"Yes, exactly."

"I suffer from it myself." Taking the bottle from Aiden. "First time I walked into this room after the squatters left. I swear, I almost died."

"What, you mean you had people living in here?"

"Yeah, put up some nice heavy sheets or blankets of some kind." Pantomiming an invisible wall. "They may have been those free-standing silk screens, I can't keep track."

"I've heard of those. Wouldn't fit in our place. Imagine trying to split our pad in two like that," Lynn directed this last bit toward Aiden.

"I don't even want to imagine," he said. "What's through here? Is that a dining room? Oh, my God!"

"Where?" Lynn said, crossing the room. "Oh, my God, that is fucking huge. You could fit a battleship in here."

"It's been more of a time-shared storage room until recently," Tamara said. "Really, it's nothing."

"I'm sure," Lynn said. "I'm sure it's been just as hard on you once you found yourself all alone in this mansion. Culture shock is just striking us for the first time. You understand, right?"

"Yeah, culture shock. I get that a lot. But Jesus, people, you're going to make me want to set a torch to the works if you keep carrying on carrying on."

"Well, maybe if you had invited us over sooner," Aiden said.

"Yeah, maybe when there were more of these crowds you keep referring to around," Lynn said. "I bet you have a kitchen, too."

"Oh, I wouldn't want to take your money," Tamara said, trailing after them through the dining room.

"Oh, my God, you do have a kitchen! Aiden, you've got to see this. There's a stove and oven and everything."

"Holy sand-blistered Hell!" Aiden said. "This is, I don't know. My mind is just reeling."

"I know."

"What is that," he said, pointing. "I mean, what is that?"

"I don't know."

"Okay, now you're just being mean," Tamara said.

"Yeah, I'm sorry," Aiden said, turning back toward Tamara who was standing like a frightened deer hanging on for dear life to the edge of the table. "It's just...I don't know what to say. I'm just—"

"Gobsmacked," Lynn said.

"Yes, exactly, thank you dear," he said, kissing her on the cheek.

"How many bedrooms?"

"Two," Tamara said, taking a deep breath as if searching for the courage to let go of the table. "And there's a den."

"A den?"

"Are you kidding me?" Lynn said.

"Yeah, might as well get it all out of the way," Tamara said. "You want to see the den?"

"Of course, we want to see the den."

"There are even two bathrooms, but we'll get to those later. The small one out here for guests and company and far too many roommates. The big one off the master bedroom."

"Do tell."

"Kept that one for myself."

"Naturally."

"Well, I didn't want everyone just tramping through my space. I mean, what if I was naked or something."

"Yes, exactly, priorities," Lynn said as they walked down a short hall to admire another room. "Bit smaller than the others. Kind of Spartan."

"Well, I'm expanding slowly," Tamara said. "I mean,

until recently, this was pulling double-duty as another bedroom. I just don't know what to do with the space."

"What happened to all the roommates, anyway?"

"Oh, various things." Shrug of shoulders. "Suddenly finding the place all to myself was a bit of a surprise."

"Wasn't planned?"

"Oh, definitely wasn't planned. It just sort of happened. Never was good at keeping track of them all."

"Yes, you mentioned."

"Really tempted to bring new people in just for the ambiance."

"Oh, don't do that," Aiden said.

"Yeah, revel in it while you've got the chance," Lynn said.

"You never notice how a place creaks and groans when it's full of people."

"This place is just so huge." Lynn turned in a circle. "We could fit our entire apartment in here and have room to spare."

"Yes, I gathered that."

"Hey, what the hell is this?" Aiden said, pointing at a little sweeper robot that had rolled into the hallway.

"Seriously, you don't recognize the little monstrosity?" Tamara said.

"Well, I can't tell you the make or model, if that's what you mean. You want to know why? Go on, ask me why."

"Yeah, ask him why," Lynn said.

"I am agog, dear heart," Tamara said. "Why can't you recognize the make and model? Need your grandpa glasses?"

"Oh, the answer is really quite simple," Aiden said. "It's not a Central Services brand."

"Oh." Tamara brought a hand to her chin as if she might cough or otherwise need to stifle a laugh. "Oh, yes, I hadn't thought of that."

"Should be ashamed of yourself," Lynn said.

"I know." Threw up her hands. "I should just slide through the floor in embarrassment."

"Just imagine if you had a Central Services model. You could get Aiden on the service call."

"I must say that I hadn't thought of that."

"Now, we've been over this," Aiden said. "I'm not a milkman."

"Yes, dear."

"A what-man?" Tamara said.

"I've got no interest in being a milkman, and I'm not going to make an exception even for your sweet asterisk." He put his arm around Tamara's waist and swung her around.

"It's called role-playing," Lynn said.

"Oh, well, that's different."

"Speaking of robots and things," Tamara said. "What happened last night?"

Lynn and Aiden both went quiet.

"Whoa." Tamara glanced from one to the other of them. "That serious, huh?"

"Where's that bottle?" Aiden said, walking back toward the dining room.

"You would not believe," Lynn said, following slowly after him.

Back in the dining room, they found glasses and opened the plum wine, sitting at one end of the table because it was easier than wandering back into the living room.

"Should warm the next round," Aiden said, having taken a sip.

"Good at any temperature."

"Sweet of you to say so, anyway," Lynn said, letting her glass rest on the table, fingers touching softly to the base. "So, long story short, there was a tourist incident."

"No!"

"Oh, yes," Aiden said.

"Well," Tamara said, raising her glass, swirling the wine, watching it intently. "It was bound to happen."

"I know."

"Anyone we know?"

"It wasn't Liz Dao, if that's what you're worried about," Lynn said.

"Good."

"Something   Mads—Madagascar—Madagascar something was one of them."

"Must be in Applied Robotics," Tamara said. "That department is huge."

"Now for the bad news," Lynn said.

"That wasn't the bad news?"

"The handlers got all possessive." Shrug of shoulders. "Wouldn't let us follow protocol."

"Oh, that's not good."

"No," Aiden said, "it's not."

"Thought we were going to get lynched," Lynn said to her glass.

"Oh, that's definitely not good."

"Certainly shook my faith in humanity," Aiden said.

"I'm starting to see why you've been overreacting to my humble abode."

"No, sorry dear," Lynn said. "We would have ragged you about that regardless."

"So, details then."

"Yeah, details. Right. We were politely encouraged to leave. Nothing like pointing out that something had to be done about the tourist. Shouldn't have been a surprise."

"I know," Tamara said. "Room full of Applied Engineering and Robotics people, and nobody wanted to follow protocol? They get that shit drilled into them."

"I know, right?"

"Was anybody on your side?"

"That grad kid," Aiden said. "What's her name? Liz?"

"Yes, her name is Liz," Lynn said.

"Faded into the woodwork pretty darn quick."

"Well, that's understandable," Tamara said. "Lowly grad student. Not even an Applied Robots person. World of pain in her future if she tried to stick up for you guys."

"Yeah?"

"Oh, most definitely. You don't know what these departments are like. Theoretical Physics and Applied Robotics kind of hate each other."

"I don't know if I would go that far," Lynn said.

"That's just because you float between them."

"The politics are intense, sure," Lynn directed this comment in Aiden's direction. "Participating in the games probably helps her standing with the Applied Robotics crowd."

"It really is important to be on their good side," Tamara said. "A referral from Applied Robotics faculty can smash doors wide open."

"Which requires you to be in good with the student population," Aiden said.

"Got it in one," Tamara replied. "Speaking of the Applied Robotics crowd, what the hell was Oliver doing through all of this?"

"Borderline neutral," Lynn said.

"He did help catch the little blighter," Aiden said.

"True."

"Good for him," Tamara said.

"No opinion on whether it was actually a tourist or no," Aiden said.

"There was doubt?"

"Of course there was doubt. It can take hours to determine if something is a genuine tourist. That's where knowledge and experience kick in, which that lot simply do not have."

"They were real big on it being a hardware fault," Lynn said. "It wasn't responding to commands, you see. Not from its handlers. Not from the referee. Not from anybody."

"Be that as may be, it's got nothing to do with spotting tourism. You have to watch what it does, and it sure wasn't acting like something trying to solve a Monkey Trial."

"That's right, it was acting like it was frightened."

"No," Tamara said.

"I know, right?" Lynn said. "It was uncanny. Like they had incorporated too much theoretical software into their algorithms. Personality. Mannerisms. Pseudo-intelligence."

"Which, again, in and of itself is not conclusive," Aiden said. "It's the combo. Even then I'm prepared to wait for testing. Especially if it's not being abusive."

"It was hurting you."

"What?" Tamara said.

"Well, not really."

"It was hurting you," Lynn said, pointing. "You said ow."

"You really said ouch?" Tamara said.

"It was more surprise than anything," Aiden said. "Besides the bother was more incidental. Byproduct of it trying to squirm out of my arms. Didn't know what it was doing."

"Exactly," Lynn said, banging her fist on the table. "It didn't know what it was doing. That's kind of the point. Didn't know it was hurting you."

"Well, even a baby doesn't necessarily know it's hurting you," Tamara said.

"Yes, but a baby will learn," she replied. "A tourist? We don't know. We just don't know."

"So, yeah," Aiden said. "They were resistant to the idea of testing. Handing it over to the what, now?" Looking at Lynn.

"The Advanced Theoretical Software Lab."

"Oh, I've always wanted to go in there," Tamara said.

"Restricted?" Aiden said.

"Like you wouldn't believe. It's where they do all the high-end pseudo and autonomous intelligence research. Going in, it's like a level four biohazard zone."

"Well," Lynn said, "they don't make you take your own oxygen or anything."

"What?"

"Yeah, what?" Aiden said, grinning.

"You've been there?" Tamara slapped the table.

"Of course, I've been there," Lynn said. "I'm cleared for it."

"Oh, my God!" Tamara's eyes went wide. "That's like the Holy Grail of restricted access at all of Ben Franklin. You know how many people think that lab is just a myth? Story to scare undergraduates on a cold winter night around the campfire?"

"That word doesn't mean what you think it does."

"Campfire?"

"Myth," she replied. "It doesn't mean—Oh, never mind."

"The point being things that go in the lab do not come out. Hardware. Software. It's a one-way trip. Too much risk of contamination." Tamara shook her head. "I still can't wrap my head around the idea you've got access."

"Deal with it."

"I want to see the inside of that lab more than anything."

"Holy Grail, huh?" Aiden said.

"They've got fully functional pseudo-intelligent computers in there."

"Oh, yes, I've heard that."

"What?"

"Someone told me." Pointing at Lynn.

"True," Lynn said. "They're pretty good conversationalists and everything. But yeah, the risk of contamination is pretty intense. Just imagine some of our networked systems suddenly thinking they're people." Closed her eyes, shook her head. "Not a pretty thought."

"Well, those jokers sure didn't want their prize turkey making that one-way journey," Aiden said. "Mister important postdoc—"

"Oliver," Lynn said.

"Yeah, Oliver should have insisted. He's got access to the Holy Grail lab, right? I've sussed that out correctly?"

"Yeah, he's got clout and everything."

"Right, Holy Grail access. Of course, they look up to him."

"And he hemmed and hawed and said *whoa, don't drag me into this.*"

"That's disappointing," Tamara said. "I've met him. Even been social. I may try to have words with him."

"Oh, hell no."

"Yeah, don't you dare," Aiden said.

"Why ever not?" Tamara said.

"Yeah, why not?" Aiden looked toward Lynn.

"How did you find out?" Lynn said.

"Huh?" Tamara said.

"Yeah, I'm not sure I'm following," Aiden said.

"You told me." Tamara pointed at Lynn.

"She's got a point. We told her."

"Exactly," Lynn said. "We broke confidence."

"Oh," Tamara said.

"Right, kind of forgot about that part," Aiden said.

"Yes, you did." Lynn patted his hand. "You can't talk to him," she said to Tamara. "You don't know."

"Story is going to be all over campus," Tamara said.

"Only among the students."

"I'm a student."

Lynn didn't answer. She only gave Tamara a look that stretched into the ether without any sign of being broken.

"I'm a student," Tamara said to the tabletop. "Student teacher," she muttered all but to herself. "Student teacher."

"You see our dilemma," Lynn finally said.

"You can't tell anyone," Tamara said, muttering softly. "I can't tell anyone." Looking up. "Okay, maybe there's something I can do. Bit of an emergency pressure valve."

"Fragile confidence."

"No, this will work. I could make discreet inquiries. Pass the base details along to Jennifer Behr. In confidence, faculty to faculty. Except I'm not really. She'll treat me like a student."

"I was going to point that out."

"Well, this is last-resort-type stuff, like I said."

"Right," Lynn said, "emergency pressure release."

"We may be able to work with that," Aiden said. "Very nice of you to offer. We didn't exactly come over here to drag you into this. I mean, make you an accessory. Take advantage of your faculty connections."

"I think I've worked out what you're trying to say," Tamara said, trying to smile.

"Share the wealth, right?"

"Biggest shock of the day is still the whole Theoretical Software access thing." Shook her head, looking at Lynn. "Trying to work out why you never told me."

"Well," Lynn said, letting the word drag as if stalling

for time. "Look at it this way. Why is this the first time we've seen where you live?"

Tamara raised a hand as if she would snap out an answer but was giving the words a second to find the right order before actually saying anything. The hand slipped slowly back to the table.

"Yeah, okay," Tamara said.

"Thank you."

"Well, not to end on that note, but I wasn't half-serious about the whole paperwork/homework thing." Tamara climbed from her chair, rising to her feet as if slipping from a dream. "You're welcome to stay. I'm used to the crowds, after all."

"Add to the ambiance."

"Yes, exactly, it'll help me feel at home. I'm set up in the den, but I could drag some work in here. Or we could decamp to the living room. There's things to keep you occupied, I'm sure."

"We shall endeavor to be quietly entertaining."

"Great, back in a flash." Tamara disappeared down the hallway.

Aiden made hand gestures, indicating a transition to the living room and its spacious couch. Lynn nodded. They stood, taking the bottle and glasses with them, remembering to grab Tamara's glass while they were at it.

"Can you believe this place?" Aiden said, whispering as they passed through the narrow gateway into the living room.

"I know." Lynn tried to keep her voice down to a low roar.

"No wonder she didn't want us over. I mean, look at this place."

"And the whole thing about maybe getting some new roommates like she doesn't really need them." Leaning in tight. "She can afford all of this on her own?"

"I knew she was a student, but Jesus. You just don't think, you know?"

"I know. It doesn't sink in or seem real. Like Liz, the grad student? Main reason she's only got the one ape, I figure, is because she doesn't have the time to work on more."

"It just—Wow. Boggles the mind, it does."

"Well," Lynn said, settling onto the couch. "Oh, my God, this is comfortable." Putting the glasses down, sprawling. "What was I? Oh, right, let's enjoy the spacious accommodations while we can."

"Add to the ambiance so Tomorrow can work."

"Yes, please, make yourselves at home," Tamara said, stumbling into the room with her arms full. "Took me a moment to realize you had moved."

"Holy fuck!" Lynn said, pointing. "Are those paper books?"

CHAPTER SEVENTEEN

In which Lynn continues to deal with the fallout of recent events with quiet good humor and panache.

Lynn quickly reached the conclusion that Darryl was taking advantage of the constantly changing location of the morning meeting to avoid her. The meeting had been stable for quite a surprising stretch of time, but the rewiring project was having the rather curious side effect of keeping the gathering on the move. She didn't see him otherwise. She wasn't seeing much of anyone, really, because of her extended banishment to the repair shop.

Seeing Darryl at this particular morning meeting was a bit of a surprise. He was keeping his distance. Lynn didn't have a problem with that. She occupied herself checking her phone and letting the faint buzz of pre-meeting conversation float around her. Messages regarding the state of the local tourist were few and far between. It didn't help that they had to be extra careful about how they discussed the situation and had recently taken to referring to the disgruntled machine as a clockwork hippopotamus. It didn't help that her stay in the surgery was making it very hard to establish face-to-face communication. There had been dead silence on the hippopotamus front since early the day before.

Hagarlodge stormed into the room as if he was an unstoppable force that would simply smash through anything in his way. His entrance was so abrupt that Lynn fumbled her phone, almost dropping it. Crossing the room, there was some doubt among the assembled ITRC personnel that the presentation desk or even the far wall would slow him down.

"All right everyone, forget whatever you were doing," he said, turning at the last second as if he knew the wall didn't stand a chance against him. "The agenda is right out the window. All projects are suspended until further notice."

A spattering of grumbling tested the edges of the room, as if they were trying to work out just how far dissenting voices would get them before they were hacked into tiny little pieces. Hagarlodge stood behind the desk, facing them.

"There has been a tourist incident," he said, which quickly convinced everyone they should just keep their mouths shut until further notice. "And it should come as a surprise to absolutely no one that the incident occurred at a campus Ape Fight. But that's not even the best part. Ready for the best part? Incident was five or six days ago, depending on how you feel like counting these things. So we're talking potential contamination going undetected for close to a week."

The murmurs couldn't hold back any longer, even if nobody was quite ready to start using actual words. Lynn held her gaze locked on her fists, pressed hard to the table almost as if she was singlehandedly preventing it from leaping into the air in utter indignation at the news. Hagarlodge, for his part, gave the voices of the assembled staff free reign to swirl and sway.

"That means everyone is on decontamination duty," he finally said. "You know the protocol. Every node, every router, every connection, interface, and script has to be hand-checked."

"What about the tourist?" Darryl's voice rose from the back of the room.

"Oh, that's where this gets even better," Hagarlodge said. "Our wonderful and motivated student body have been protecting it. Apparently, there have been heated arguments over whether it even was a tourist. These arguments involved everything except actually subjecting the alleged tourist to any form of test that might resolve the issue. Finally, finally, finally, a student cracked and squealed to a faculty adviser."

"Who? What department?"

"I'm not at liberty to divulge that information. We've got to protect everybody's precious confidentiality."

"In other words, you don't know."

"That's hardly the point," Hagarlodge said. "Now, this is where my blood starts to froth, and I swear it's a wonder I don't spontaneously combust. The faculty adviser found out yesterday and waited until this morning to inform anyone, much less us. Concerned we would stay late. Wanted us to start fresh in the morning."

General laughter cracked across the room only to vanish almost as quickly. There may even have been random comments of varying degrees of crudeness directed at the faculty in general and the student population in particular.

"The tourist itself is going to be delivered to the Advanced Theoretical Software Development Lab and placed under the expert care of Dr. Jennifer Behr."

"Good, she's always wanted one," Lynn said.

"Well, it's nice to know that someone will get what they want out of this," Hagarlodge replied. "Now, we're just getting to the best part. I lied when I said that other thing was the best part. This is even better. Everybody ready for the best part?" He studied them as if actually expecting an answer, even thought nobody would dare reply. "The Board of Tourism knows."

There was no controlling the wave of consternation, groans, and critical comments that swept the room.

"Now, I'm still waiting to find out how they know," Hagarlodge said. "Somebody tipped them off. Somebody higher up the org chart felt they should be involved. You know, that wonderful spirit of openness and sharing that we all crave. Personally, I favor the theory some random student tipped them off yesterday. Other students found out the Tourist Board knew and immediately went running to the faculty adviser."

"I'm not following the timeline on that one, boss," someone from out of the crowd said.

"And I will beat my head against this desk until my brains are smeared across its surface before I waste another second on who knew what and when," Hagarlodge said. "All that matters is we're in for a metric fuck-ton of pain and suffering. Now, everyone knows today's emergency assignment. Your scripts should all be updated by now. So get cracking, and try to keep us from climbing too far up the news feed rankings this morning."

Something resembling controlled chaos ensued as everyone started talking, abandoning their chairs, and checking their scripts and assignments. Lynn took her time climbing to her feet.

"Not you, Charles," Hagarlodge said, looking right at her. "Hang back a moment."

The room very quickly emptied of all but the two of them. Lynn took the opportunity to study the departing souls as they vanished into the ether; her very look daring them to stay or else risk her wrath and eternal damnation.

"Sit," Hagarlodge said quietly as if trying to calm her raging spirit once they had the room to themselves.

She remained standing. Hagarlodge took the opportunity to sit, facing her across the table, resting his elbows on the surface. "I know we've kept you secluded in the deep down-below," he said. "You understand why?"

Lynn crossed her arms, saying nothing, and the moment drifted as if it would last until the end of time.

"The students trust you," he finally said, cracking the silence. "We know. They confide in you. We—I understand why. It also means I know—I suspect that you know more than you let on. Obviously. You also understand the importance of protocol where tourism is concerned. You would apply discreet pressure—encourage the students to hand over the tourist." Shrug of shoulders. "Keeping you sequestered prevented you from being able to do so."

Hagarlodge drifted into silence, watching the tabletop as if he found it vaguely boring but hoped it would reveal interesting depths and secrets.

"Unfortunate," Lynn finally said.

"Yes, and in an effort to somehow make up for this, there are other issues I felt you deserved to know. As I mentioned, we've suspected you know more than you let on, and not just you. Many of the field reps must know more than they report back to us. So management hatched upon a plan to track the field reps any time they were on campus."

"Management?"

Hagarlodge said nothing, looking to the table as if he could not match her eye, and finally let out his breath almost as if he had lost a long and protracted argument without a single word having been spoken.

"Yes," he said. "Management."

"We're tracked through our scripts, I know," she said, watching him as he ducked his head as if guilty. "You mean off-hours, don't you?" Leaning forward, pointing. "Tracking our phones."

"It wasn't just you." Raising his hands as if to ward off a blow. "All service representatives would be tracked. If there were Ape Fights, we would be sure to get a hit."

Lynn said nothing, watching him, feeling that she might need to take a chair before her knees gave way but didn't want to give him the satisfaction.

"Except we got nothing but resistance from security," Hagarlodge said. "The protocol couldn't be set up. There were concerns regarding privacy. Formatting. The list went on, and then it finally hit me. Why would security throw up such resistance?" Raised a hand alongside his head as if imitating a lightbulb going on. "Oh, of course, security is in on it. They love watching little robots beat the ever-loving shit out of each other. Who wouldn't? They probably even field their own horrible little engines of death and destruction."

"Interesting theory," Lynn said. "Only one problem."

"Security didn't report the tourist, I know. Can't say I've worked out how to interpret that. Either they don't take the threat seriously or they didn't want to break confidence. They could have made up any story—heightened procedures, students slipping up, anything—and reported the tourist." Let his hands fall to the tabletop. "Regardless, I thought you should know about the phone tracking."

"Thank you."

"Who do we contract security with these days, anyway?"

"I'm sure I don't know," she replied. "They're all branded as Ben Franklin security for continuity's sake and to show everyone what a big, important organization we are."

"The memo probably crossed my desk, I'm sure, but who can be bothered to track all of these things. Never thought it would be relevant," he said. "About your assignment, the tourist is being handed off to Dr. Behr and the Advanced Theoretical Software Development lab. You've got oversight detail."

"Really."

"Dr. Behr likes you, which I think has as much to do with what your partner does for a living as anything else. She would get a tourist out of you one of these days or something. I don't know."

"And look what happened."

"Downright amusing, I know. On the brightside, you get out of the dungeon but into the quarantine zone. So more of a mixed blessing. Also, you'll probably have to deal with representatives from the Tourist Board."

"I quiver with anticipation."

"I'm sure you'll do fine," Hagarlodge said, standing. "Listen, Charles. I know you take the threat of tourism seriously, and I have no reason to believe you're actually involved. I would probably have to do something about it if you were. Even if you were a spectator or just knew where they were."

"Which I don't."

"Which really is beside the point, right now. If you were."

"Which I'm not."

"Theoretically." Watching her. She said nothing. "If you were, I couldn't hope for a better representative to keep an eye on things."

She looked at Hagarlodge as if studying a colorful spotted mushroom next to a broken, fallen-down sign warning of danger, and wondering if it was worth the risk to take a bite.

"I'm going to take that in the spirit in which it was given," she finally said.

"I knew you would."

* * *

There were extra security personnel loitering around the gateway to the quarantine zone, trying to look as if they were utterly disinterested and otherwise bored and disgusted with the fact they were anywhere in the vicinity. While a valiant effort at appearing nonchalant, their efforts were undercut by the simple fact that there were security personnel near the restricted lab. Lynn was vaguely disappointed by the complete absence of senior management types waiting near the gateway, rubbernecking, hoping for a chance to see a real live tourist.

"Is the package here yet?" she asked the closest security officer as she flashed her phone at the door scanner.

"Not yet," he replied without the slightest hesitation as if intuiting what she was talking about. "Minor complication with the hand-off. Concerns over preserving the anonymity of the package's owner."

"They don't belong to anyone. That's part of the problem."

She pushed through the doors not waiting for a reply and made her way to the demilitarized zone. It was deserted, which wasn't a big surprise. Any and all gawkers and assorted sightseers would be stranded out in the hall with the disaffected security forces. She changed into a quarantine suit, stowed her gear, and made her way into the lab proper. Jennifer Behr was there, pacing so hard it was a wonder she hadn't worn a groove into the floor. Lynn counted four postdocs without looking hard. They were hanging back, trying to stay out of the good doctor's line of fire.

"Dr. Behr," Lynn said, which got Jennifer to pause in her tracks for little more than a second. "The peanut gallery ready for this?" Nodding toward a bank of monitors that were the primary interface with the pseudo-intelligence systems.

"They don't know," Jennifer replied, pacing. "We were up half the night locking them down. Risk of contamination. Quarantine until we know what we are dealing with."

"Well, that's good. Don't want them getting ideas about independent thought, right?"

"It doesn't work like that."

"Right, but precautions anyway," Lynn said more to herself than anyone as she turned and wandered back to the demilitarized zone, which was still empty.

She then made her way back toward the entrance to the outside world, found nothing but security types, and rapped upon the glass to get the nearest one's attention. Mimed a question at him. He held up fingers, providing an ETA. Lynn nodded, turned, and paced up and down the short passage between the gateway and the demilitarized zone, stopping at last to stand and stretch. She was out of view of the outside world so took her time about it, bending and stretching, reaching for the sky, and finally stood still.

"Better get this over with before the show starts," she muttered to herself, going back to the demilitarized zone.

She took the quarantine script from its safe-box, went to the access panel on the lab side, ran a hardline, and proceeded through a whole checklist of diagnostic procedures. Task completed, she returned the script to its hideaway and headed back toward the gateway. She didn't have long to wait before the security forces went into a flurry of dispassionate activity. Oliver appeared at the door, spotted her right off standing within, and found the inner fortitude to push through. He was rolling a static-case, which contained the offending little bipedal robot. It looked asleep or dead. Basically, it looked as if it had been killed and then tossed haphazardly into the case.

"Merlin," he said, cutting the word off even as he realized it was passing out of his mouth. "Sorry, it's been a long night."

"Good morning to you, too," she said.

"Right, I keep forgetting it's morning." Pushing the static-case down the hall before him. "It's—"

"Been that kind of night. Yes, you mentioned." Following him into the demilitarized zone. "Little bastard give you any trouble?"

"Well, that kind of depends on how you define these things." Standing, hands on hips, staring at the static-case. "It has been rather immobile. Between the static-case and the fact it is turned off, naturally."

"Naturally."

"The world around it, on the other hand, has been rather on the move."

"Well, take your time changing. This may be your last moment of peace and harmony for quite some time." She wandered back to the safe-box, giving Oliver a moment to himself, and extracted the quarantine script from its depths. "Faced a bit of a dilemma myself this morning. See, I had to run some base-line diagnostics before the diminutive engine of destruction over there was introduced into the environment, but I also wanted to be out near the world when the chaos bringer arrived. So, open the case, run the tests, put the script back, and repeat after your arrival."

"Yes, I did notice you had already changed. Surprised you ventured so close to the outside world in the quarantine suit."

"Yeah, I know," she said, turning back toward him. He had barely started to shed his outer layer of clothing. "Very nearly ran the risk of contaminating myself. That would have been annoying."

"Well, good thing it didn't come to that." He tried to

smile, looked back toward the static-case. "To think I always wanted one of those."

"Careful what you wish for, yeah?"

"The circumstances were less than ideal, yeah." Oliver resumed working on his clothes. "I don't know which of us had it worse, dealing with the Frankenstein gang directly or indirectly. I swear, you've sent more messages in the past week than all the years I've known you."

"The encryption was a serious pain in my bloody, stain-encrusted asterisk."

"Yeah, I kind of lost track of that myself."

"At least you survived the hand-off," Lynn said. "Security said there were complications."

"There are always complications, but I managed to take little half-ass there off their hands without too much dramatical theatrics. Or theatrical dramatics. One of those. I don't know. Going to be a while before any of them look me in the eye again. I swear, I'm losing my street cred. This is damaging my reputation worse than anything I could name."

"Being the responsible one is a bitch."

"Tell me about it," he said. "Which you actually know better than me. I was more than half-convinced the mob was going to turn on you and the mighty Tourist Hunter."

"We survived. Wasn't easy but we survived."

"Leaving the dirty work to me."

"Hey, the curse of standing down in the middle of the melee."

"Yeah, I'm still sorry about that."

"Relax," she said, waving a hand dismissively. "We've been over this. Understandings all around."

"Heard from your favorite graduate student?"

"Yeah, we've exchanged messages. Keeping me

locked in the deep down-below has made things difficult."

"In more ways than one."

"Far too many."

"I really enjoyed facing the Frankenstein gang on my own."

"Well, look on the bright side. Run into any Tourist Board members yet?"

"Oh, you have got to be fucking kidding me!" Oliver almost fell over, half-in and half-out of his quarantine suit. "They already know about this?"

"Well, that answers one question," Lynn muttered quietly.

"What?"

"Nothing," she said. "Just a theory shot down in its prime."

"So the Board of Tourism doesn't know? You had me scared there."

"Oh, they know all right."

"Damnation, Merlin!"

"Language."

"Yeah, sorry, I know." Hand to his forehead, rubbing as if he would dig fingers into his skull. "Pry my fingernails off with rusty tweezers later. It's been a long day. How the hell did the Tourist Board find out?"

"Absolutely no idea."

"Bloody damnation on a stick," he said. "I should have known." Swinging an arm in the general direction of the outside world. "Should have known the second I saw all of that security on display. But, no, I just had to dream that people wouldn't take complete leave of their senses and invite those jackasses into the mix."

"I hear they've improved."

"Who?"

"The jackasses," Lynn said. "I have it on very good authority from someone who has dealt with them on two separate occasions that they have very much improved."

"Oh, let me guess who that could be." Looked at her. "Twice now? Really?"

"Believe it."

"Well, I suppose that makes sense. There was the incident you told me about, lo these many months ago, and then there was the street sweeper incident. I kind of figured your partner was involved."

"That, and his picture was in all the news feeds."

"Yeah, well, that doesn't really matter unless you know what you're looking for and happen to recognize him. Wait, had I even met him by that point?"

"I'm sure I showed you a picture."

"Yeah, I'm sure you must have," Oliver said. "And my much belated memory is finally reminding me that you told me all about the street sweeper incident after it happened."

"Well, you and everyone else in the universe wouldn't stop pestering me with questions about it."

"Yeah, that's probably why I blocked it all out," he said. "So, the jackasses have improved, have they?"

"So, I've been told."

"I can't imagine facing them, improved or no. Fielding questions. Interrogation."

"They are very superior."

"Oh, yeah?"

"Look down their noses at you."

"Look where I work." Raising his arms and gesturing about. "I should feel right at home among them. It'll be like my oral exams all over again."

"And we still don't know who told," Lynn said. "And here I thought it might be you."

"What? Approach the Tourist Board? You're mad."

"No, dumb-ass, approach your mentor. Tip the great Lady Behr to the existential existence of the tourist."

"Don't take leave of your senses now, Lynn. I don't narc." Gesturing between them. "We have that in common."

"Well, responsibility does funny things to a person."

"I'm not that responsible. Much as I wanted to get that monstrosity into the lab. My money is on one of the Frankenstein trust."

"You seriously don't know?"

"Well, I didn't say that." Oliver started to push the static-case toward the lab end of the demilitarized zone. "What I did say is that I don't narc."

"Good enough," she said, following him.

Jennifer Behr and the postdocs descended on the static-case as soon as they heard it clear the second curtain, and they quickly raced it to a far corner of the lab. Oliver got his hands free just in time.

"How long has it been dormant?" Jennifer shouted at them from the unreasonable depths of the lab. "Did it give you any trouble? What protocol did you follow?"

"It was active for most of the time between Saturday and today," Oliver said, trying not to shout, walking toward the storm of activity around the static-case. "Finally shut down very late—I mean, early."

Lynn didn't bother to follow, turning her attention to the terminals and rows of monitoring stations. She went to each in turn, running the hardline between it and her script, checking diagnostic protocols and procedures, and more or less tried to ignore the noise and excitement off in the distance. She studied one of the banks of monitors, remembering the logs and diaries that typically kept up a constant flow of information in a window on the screen.

"When was the last time I was here and you were actually awake?" she said to the monitor, not really expecting an answer. "I never get to chat with you guys any more. Downright depressing. So, what are you going to do with the kid sister stealing all the attention?" She waited, watching the screen, but nothing happened. "Right, up half the night shutting you guys down. Guess I should be over there keeping an eye on things."

Silence from the monitoring banks.

"I'll just go then."

* * *

"Oh, look, I can tell you still have the run of the place to yourself," Lynn said, crossing into the living room while Tamara fussed with the door. "Have the piles reached critical mass yet? The detritus spontaneously growing as if it had a life of its own?"

"Don't remind me," Tamara said, sweeping across the room as if she might enter into a mad panic of half-hearted cleaning. "You know how much time and effort goes into cleaning up after yourself?"

"Yeah, well, multiple people just tend to add that extra oomph of motivation. By yourself, you just tend to lose track of it all. Next thing you know, boom, piles of crap."

"Well, obviously, I should have you over more often." Tamara ran for the kitchen with a mass of debris in her arms. "Give me that extra spark."

Lynn followed slowly after. Those last words having been on the very edge of comprehensibility.

"Happy to oblige," Lynn said, trying not to shout, found Tamara dumping things into the kitchen disposal. "I really just needed space. Especially space away from prying ears. Hopefully away from prying ears, anyway."

"I know," Tamara said, turning, wandering back in the general direction of the living room, stopping at the dining room, grabbing at lost and leftover plates and glasses on the table. "One can only hope there isn't too much university eavesdropping here."

"Had the last of your former roommates just left like an hour before we were here last time or something?" Lynn said, trailing Tamara once more into the kitchen. "Place didn't look like this."

"Well, I had something resembling warning, if you recall." Dropping everything, wiping her hands. "This time, not so much."

"Did you just dump everything down the disposal?"

Tamara froze, hands half-together, as if she was suffering a sudden flashback to her days on the receiving end of an interrogation-room visit.

"Maybe."

Lynn turned without a word, shaking her head, trying not to laugh, and wandered back into the dining room.

"Well, I've got pressing concerns on my mind," Tamara said, following her. "Efficiency. Path of least resistance is called for. Everything into the trash."

"I didn't say anything."

"No, but you were thinking it pretty damn loud. The sheer psychic energy of it practically blasted me into the next dimension."

"Well, you have seen our place," Lynn said, picking a chair, sitting at the dining room table. "I'm pretty sure you have. My memory practically screams that you have."

"True." Tamara found her own chair, eying the state of the tabletop as if she were contemplating another run to the kitchen disposal.

"Does it look much less cluttered than this? Seriously, let me know. I live there full-time. I'm blind to the level of squalor and despair represented therein."

"Yes, well, there's not so much space. Stands to reason the clutter would show more."

"It could be argued that it should be easier to clean specifically because of the lack of space."

"There's a thesis paper in that somewhere," Tamara said. "Department of Theoretical Physics, after all."

"Liz should get right on it," Lynn said, leaning back, sprawling across her chair, looking around. "Think we've thrown off the eavesdroppers?"

"That's an above-average level of paranoia you're displaying, dear. And yes, I think we've thrown off the scent."

"Got any booze in this place?"

"More than a little." Tamara went to fetch a bottle and two glasses.

"The day I've had," Lynn said, accepting a glass, taking a sip, trying not to drink it all in one go. "How much do you know?"

"Well, officially, I don't have much to go on."

"Officially, right."

"There's everything you've told me over the past week."

"Hope it wasn't too hard feigning surprise when the news broke."

"Wasn't a problem." Tamara held up her glass, watching as she swirled the contents, took a sip. "There was that faculty blast notification. Caught it while preparing for class. Was able to pull the whole *thought it was a rumor* thing."

"There's always rumors."

"Exactly, worked to my advantage. Not much to report. I showed you the blast."

"You did," Lynn said. "Easy enough to read on the shuttle here."

"The rumor-mongering went wild. Nobody knew anything. Rampant speculation."

"The Tourist Board was a no-show."

"Yeah, that was a surprise. There were certainly enough warning notifications. Flash posts on how to deal with them."

"Missed most of those, what with being sequestered in the quarantine zone."

"Seriously, nobody made it within?" Tamara said. Lynn shook her head. "Lucky."

"You should have seen all the security," Lynn said. "The tourist. You should have seen it. Little bastard behaved disturbingly like a little monkey. Squirrel monkey. Spider? One of those. Something."

"I've seen videos."

"You know," Lynn said, motioning with her glass for a refill. "It would not have surprised me if you had actually seen the real thing."

"You have any idea what scoring a ticket to a preserve costs?"

"No."

"Well, it's insane. Children are cheaper. Okay, children are not cheaper, but I swear it's a near thing."

"Going to take your word for it. The brain trust weren't much better than the monkey. I swear, it was like—Hell, I don't know. Their eyeballs should have burst from the pressure. The static electricity from their excited vibrations in such close proximity should have shocked them all into a state of extreme unconsciousness and fried the defenseless little blighter to boot."

"Oh, to have been a fly on that wall."

"Would have traded places in a second."

"Liar," Tamara said. "The thrill of discovery. You code. Don't try to deny it. You loved every second of it."

"It was exhausting just watching them."

"You selling lunar properties? Wide-open spaces? Majestic views? Please, you can tell me if you are. It's only fair to warn you that I'm not buying."

"Aiden's lucky."

"Okay," Tamara said. "Why is Aiden lucky?"

"Central Services has to do smelly, dirty work. They've got waste management contracts. Not just the sweepers. There's plumbers and all sorts of assorted things. They have to clean up."

"I'm not sure I'm following the relevance here."

"They've got showers," Lynn said. "Real, honest-to-goodness showers with running water and everything. You think ITRC has access to one of those? Of course not. We barely get a changing room for when we have to do really dirty, dusty work. Cleaning bays. Steam, mist, and moisture, if you're lucky. Not much better than what you get at home."

"Oh."

"So much excitement in that enclosed space being my point. God, I could use a wash."

"You know," Tamara said, turning her glass around in her hand, "I've got one of those."

"Don't tease me, Tomorrow. Don't play with my emotions like that."

"No, it's true."

"You lying dilapidated excuse for a pantomime reject. I've had the tour. I've seen the facilities. You do not have a shower."

"You haven't seen all the facilities. The master suite has its own shower and bath."

"Holy hell!" Lynn said, half-rising from her chair. "Are you telling me that I've been here twice now and you're only just making me aware of the fact you have shower facilities? Real running water just gushing over you like it's raining buckets?"

"I didn't think it was important."

"You just broke my mind." Sinking back into her chair. "You've got a shower and didn't think to mention it in all the time I've known you. Can't remember the last time I had a proper shower. The feeling of warm water just flowing all around me."

"Well, I did have more roommates than I can count until relatively recently. Who thinks of these things?"

"That tears it," Lynn said, standing. "I need a shower. I know it is a horrible imposition, and I would like to sincerely apologize in advance. But you are going to let me take a shower."

"Aiden is going to be here soon."

"Aiden can just hang. He gets all the bloody showers he wants as part of his job. Now, point me in the direction of your shower facilities before I get violent."

Tamara quickly decided that capitulation was the best course of action under the circumstances and accommodated Lynn's request. The shower was every bit as glorious as Lynn thought it would be, letting the hot-to-the-edge-of-painful water flow over and around her, scrubbing, cleaning, losing track of time. Tamara had left towels. Lynn took her time drying off. The towels were incredibly soft. There was a robe waiting for her on the bed, and there were voices emanating from some distant part of the house. Lynn took a moment just standing there, collecting her thoughts, and then ventured out to find the source of the conversation.

Tamara and Aiden were sitting in the living room. There was a bottle, and glasses. They had each taken up stations on the couch, half-sprawled, half-sitting. Their feet were touching.

"Hey," Aiden said. "Look what appears from out of the storm all bedraggled, half-clothed, and soaked to the skin."

"If by bedraggled you mean glorious bliss, then I'm with you," Lynn said. "The hell happened to my clothes?"

"Oh, yeah, those," Tamara said. "I burned them. Mercy killing. Sorry."

"You did what?"

"Should have thrown a travel-worn in there somewhere, but who's got time to think of these things," Aiden said.

"Your clothes went down the disposal," Tamara said. "Well, I'm sorry, but it was just easier than taking them all of the way into the laundry room. They'll be done in about an hour. What do you take me for?"

"An ill-mannered llama." Lynn had her arms crossed. The robe was suddenly feeling very short. "And that's just until I can get my hands on my phone and access to a proper rhyming thesaurus. Or did you drop that down the disposal, too?"

"I knew I forgot to do something."

Aiden started chuckling. Lynn smacked him once on the head as she came around the couch.

"Ow," was all he said.

"Serves you right," she replied, finding space next to him.

"You were right about one thing," Tamara said. "Your clothes were surprisingly muggy. What did you guys get up to in the lab?"

"I told you. They wouldn't keep still. The temperature and humidity went up a thousand degrees just from their screaming and jumping all around."

"How are you holding up?" Aiden said.

"Better now that I've had a good wash. Can't remember the last time I felt so clean."

"Sure, you can. Our anniversary. We went to that place with that thing."

"Oh, that was glorious," Lynn said, leaning into him, putting her feet up, ignoring the length of the robe.

"Well, give with the details already," Tamara said.

"Oh, don't spoil the moment with actual memories." She waved a hand, languidly, dismissively. "It was just a hotel. Nothing particularly fancy."

"But it did have facilities big enough for two," Aiden said. "What else matters?"

"Just don't look at the bill." Lynn tried to guess which was Aiden's glass, gave up, grabbed one. "We should have burned it."

"Figuratively speaking."

"Yes, I think she knows we meant figuratively speaking," Lynn said. "They don't actually print the bill. Not a chance in hell we could have afforded that."

"It's the thought that counts, anyway," Tamara said, taking up the unclaimed glass from the coffee table. "I was relaying what little you told me about today's activities."

"Well, there was so little we could cover by phone." Aiden made a grab for Lynn's glass.

"Get your own," she said.

"I'm fairly certain that is mine. The tourist is safely ensconced in the High-Energy Forbidden Zone."

"High-Energy what?"

Tamara handed Aiden her glass, climbed from the couch, went in search of another.

"Certainly, the place has a name." Aiden took a sip.

"Well, of course it has a name. I just don't think you happen to know what it is."

"Given several years of study, I'm sure I could manage to work it out."

"Advanced Theoretical Software Development Lab," Tamara said, returning from the sideboard.

"Yes, exactly, something like that." Aiden held up his glass as if trying to figure out how to put it down without dislodging Lynn. "The tourist is still acting surprisingly like a primate," said as if he actually knew, "which means it wasn't all in our heads."

"They must have lifted a bunch of code from the Advanced Software Lab," Lynn said, refusing to budge. "All that simulated behavior crap."

"They are in rather serious trouble if they did," Tamara said. "There's a reason it's called the quarantine zone."

"All depends on exactly what they lifted. There's a difference between simulated behavior and simulated personality."

"Splitting hairs."

"No, no," Aiden said. "It's easy to simulate gross behavior."

"Gross now?"

"Behavior in broad strokes. Don't," he said, pointing a finger.

"I didn't say anything," Tamara replied.

"Pantomime, easy stuff, being my point."

"It's when they think they're people," Lynn said.

"But we're not really interested in when they think they're people, right?" Tamara said. "It's when they think they're better than us and won't do what they're told. It's when we don't know what they're thinking or what they're going to do."

"Yeah, that's an issue."

"Well, it's in the forbidden zone now," Aiden said. "Best we could hope for."

"Quarantine zone, dear," Lynn said.

"Yeah, get it right."

"And we've gotten through this reasonably unscathed?" Aiden said.

"Reasonably," Lynn replied. "My boss suspects. Told me as much."

"That's not a big revelation."

"He also told me that they're trying to track me by phone."

"That's less than ideal. They already track us via the scripts. Even I know that."

"Yeah, your level of paranoia is suddenly sounding a little less over the hedge," Tamara said.

"You think?"

"Well, I can certainly think of worse places to try to carry on private conversations than my humble abode."

"We were just looking for any old excuse," Aiden said.

"Not really a surprise."

"The shower was just a bonus," Lynn said.

"Of course it was." Tamara started fishing around her person for something. "Of course, if they really wanted to track us for sound, they would just use our phones."

"Sure, they can do just about everything else," Aiden said.

"Oh, let's not give them ideas."

"I'll give them plenty of ideas if there are royalties in it for me. Come up with a way for them to order us around with sound and expect us to answer."

"We were talking about that," Lynn said, slapping him on the knee, pointing at Tamara. "Remember?"

"We were?"

"Sure, that whole simultaneous two-way audio conversation thing."

"Wait," Tamara said. "Oh, shit, I remember that."

"What?" Aiden said.

"Keep out of this, dear," Lynn said to him.

"Except it wasn't exactly simultaneous." Tamara pointed with her glass. "It was more send an audio file. Wait for the reply."

"Yes, exactly, but we got past that stage. We were all the way along to simultaneous two-way transmission. Real-time sending and receiving."

"What?" Aiden said, again.

"We'll get to you in a minute."

"That was months ago," Tamara said. "We concluded—Oh, shit, what did we conclude?"

"Nobody would use it."

"Exactly! Nobody would use it. The whole simultaneous real-time thing. Nobody would have time to craft a reply."

"That and the whole need to record audio, send, wait for the reply, listen," Lynn said. "Too labor intensive. Whole system would have to be automated."

"Which is where the whole simultaneous part came in."

"Continuously sending and receiving?" Aiden asked.

"We told you to keep out of this," Lynn said.

"Yeah." Tamara tried a backhanded smack to whatever part of Aiden was within range but more or less failed in the attempt.

"Pity phones just aren't designed for it."

"Sure they are," Aiden said.

"Shut your ungodly gob-smacker—Wait, what?" Lynn twisted about, trying to look at him while still leaning against him.

"Well, it wouldn't be perfect, but phones can send and receive video, right? Slave it to your camera. Send and receive picture and sound. Just turn off the picture."

"Holy fuck!" Tamara said. "I think you just blew my mind."

"Wait, wait, wait." Lynn shook her head as if trying to get three layers of sand out of her hair. "It wouldn't work."

"Sure, it would," Aiden said.

"They're not designed to send and receive full-motion video real-time."

"They're not. That's the beauty of it. Turn off the picture."

"But the sound. I can't name a single application

designed that way. You can send picture live-stream just fine, but you can't send sound."

"Not to send and receive," Tamara said.

"Exactly, not to send and receive simultaneously." Lynn tried to lean back, stretching over the couch. "The architecture's all wrong."

"Oh, excuse me," Aiden said. "I didn't know you were quite the big expert on phones."

"Well, apparently I know more than you."

"Well, we'll just have to see about that."

"Oh, we are going to see about that, I can tell you."

"Fascinating as all of this is, I'm sure," Tamara said. "Nobody would use the bloody application, and that's assuming you fix the architecture problem."

Lynn and Aiden sat back, regarding each other, turned slowly, facing Tamara, and then looked back to each other.

"Yeah, she's got a point."

"Can't argue with logic."

"Exactly, thank you."

"Still," Aiden said.

"Yes?" was Lynn's reply.

"If we ever get bored with Sputnik or the poor little blighter gets broken beyond repair—"

"Not going to happen."

"Well, of course, not going to happen," Aiden said, "but that's hardly my point. If we ever needed to redirect our programming skills—"

"Which are so advanced."

"Which are so freaking advanced that Central Services R&D is afraid to hire me."

"Well, that sucks."

"Goes without saying," Aiden said, "but I know I had a point."

"And it wasn't to point out that we are unrecognized gods in the world of mediocre programming."

"Definitely wasn't my point."

"Something about spending the rest of your godforsaken life working out the bugs in simultaneous two-way real-time audio conversations," Tamara said.

"You mean like the one we're having?" Lynn asked.

"Yes, exactly, like the one we're having right now."

"Eureka! We've done it."

"Except for one unimportant minor detail," Aiden said.

"Oh, I can't wait to hear this," Tamara said.

"Yes, dear," Lynn said, "what one little detail have we overlooked?"

"We forgot to use our phones."

"That's more depressing than I want to consider."

"Sorry."

"I could use a drink," Tamara said.

"Well, you're currently less entangled with another person's peripheral body parts," Lynn said, pointing at Tamara with her glass and waving it around. "Untangle yourself and make with the refilling of the glass."

"I'll see what I can do."

"And make sure it's enough for all of us," Aiden said. "No bogarting it all for yourself."

"Yeah!"

CHAPTER EIGHTEEN

In which Lynn and Aiden try to forget the excitement of the past couple of weeks by partaking of even more eventful things.

The staging areas were always the same. Even when the venue changed, which it did every single time, the staging areas always had the same layout. They were separated from the game floor by some kind of door or barrier. It didn't really cut the noise, but it was better than nothing. The ability to hear your compatriots talking without the need to screech at the top of your lungs was a huge bonus. You still had to talk pretty darn loud because of all the handlers shouting at each other, fussing over their various rats, apes and monkeys, but it wasn't the same wall of noise as beyond. Fortunately there was more than one staging area, so it wasn't like every single last person helping to prep or otherwise triage a robot was trying to do so in the same limited space.

Lynn and Aiden made their way across the staging area, reaching their workbench, dropping their monkey onto it. Sputnik was still a tripod and actually looked more like two tripods glued together. Three limbs for standing. Three more gangly arms for waving about in the air. One of the arms was hanging loose, barely connected to the torso. Lynn and Aiden regarded their poor child critically and with a certain amount of silent despair.

"Well," Lynn said, "it didn't go that bad."

"How do you figure?"

"Still in one piece. You see what happens to the fighting apes. This is nothing. We'll have Sputnik repaired in no time."

"Optimist." Aiden started sorting through the toolkit beneath their bench. "Uncurable—incurable?"

"Incurable."

"Eternally incurable optimist."

"It's a sickness, I tell you," Lynn said. "Doctor says there's no cure."

"Life will fix that. Eventually." Aiden took a slow breath as he watched her begin going over their synthetic monkey. "And while we wait for the grand specter of fate to cure you of your abnormal attraction to the inherent goodness of all things in the universe, we can get our little delinquent engine of death and destruction back to something resembling working order."

"Let's hear it for modularity. Just pop off the offending limb and replace." She continued checking Sputnik. "That was quite a mouthful, by the way. I don't think I followed it all." Her fingers searched for the clasps and detachment points. "How many spares do we got, anyway?"

"Not as many as I might like."

"I know, freaking expensive." She had the arm off, looked at it more carefully. "Well, this doesn't look too badly damaged. Chances for salvage are high."

"Hey," Tamara said, appearing at the edge of their work area, "what the hell happened? You guys got trashed."

"Yes, thank you," Aiden said, accepting the offending limb from Lynn, going back to their toolkit under the bench. "Very accurate assessment of what transpired."

"Well, who could have anticipated that the maze

would shift like that?" Lynn said while checking the connections around where the arm had been removed, searching for breaks or other signs of battle damage. "Took all the little blighters by surprise."

"Reminded me of one of those old engineering experiments they always threw at us," Tamara said. "How many bricks could you remove from the structure before the whole tower came crashing down."

"I remember those experiments." Lynn continued to explore the contours of the wounded torso while Aiden checked over the replacement arm.

"Wait, what? When did you?"

"There were those kits you could buy for home. Entertain the kids."

"Oh, right, those," Tamara said. "Thought you were about to reveal hidden depths."

"Don't be surprised," Aiden said. "She just might."

"Like very nearly being able to afford half a semester of college," Lynn said. "Oh, yeah, those were the days."

"You did what?"

"Made you look."

"Hey, I heard things got interesting in your match," Oliver said, reaching their workbench. "How is your little engine of unfashionable chaos holding up?"

"Lost a limb," Lynn said, "but she's a trooper. Didn't even slow her down."

"Except for the part where you didn't win," Tamara said.

"Right, except for that. Thank you."

"Ranking one and four, right?"

"Don't remind me."

"One and five actually," Aiden muttered.

"No, it can't be," Lynn said, accepting the replacement limb. "Thank you." She began fussing around the connection point. "One and five."

"Fraid so."

"I thought it was one in five."

"Nope, one and five. Total of six times at bat."

"Wow, I really was trying to block that out. Now I am depressed."

"That's actually pretty good," Oliver said. "You're still new at this, and these midnight runners do not mess around with their maze designs. Far more complex than the little school matches I'm used to."

"Nice of you to say," Aiden said, "but you still ran the table."

"That's true." Lynn had the arm in place. "We were able to catch most of your match. Your little bastard owned that table."

"That's what comes from refactoring algorithms day and night," Oliver said. "I knew something good would come out of all those lonely hours one of these days."

"It was exciting," Tamara said. "Not as thrilling as Sputnik's match, mind you. That was edge-of-my-seat excitement, and I was standing the whole time."

"Sorry I missed it."

"Well, you had to run the post-mortem on your little champion," Aiden said.

"I had to what?"

"It's not post-mortem? Maybe that's just what we have to do on our little guy since it lost a limb. Hard to keep track. All tucked away and secure?"

"Yeah, just finished up."

"We'll get this guy secured soon enough."

"Well, you'd better hurry or else we're going to miss Liz's match," Tamara said.

"Who?" Aiden said.

"Yeah, who?" Oliver turned, facing Tamara.

"Oh, that grad student Liz-kid, whatever her name is."

"Elisabeth Dao, thank you very much," Lynn said.

"And we really should try to catch her match. First time in a big-league Ape Fight. She must be nervous as hell."

"Don't think I've met her," Oliver said.

"She kicks butt at every single Ben Franklin Ape Fight," Lynn said. "Of course, you've met her."

"If you say so."

"Oh, now you're just being difficult. Been having fun with the Tourist Board?"

"Please, don't remind me." Oliver put a hand to his forehead as if he might crumble to the floor.

"Things going that well, huh?" Aiden said.

"Yeah, they're still demanding access to the quarantine zone, if you can believe it."

"No."

"It's like they don't understand the concept. Then once we get one person cleared, they don't understand why they can't bring any of their gear. Back to square one with the negotiations."

"Can't be that bad," Tamara said. "You've still got your hair."

"Yes, well, it helps I'm not actually on the negotiation team or anything. They're in really bad shape. I only have to put in the occasional appearance for status updates. Or interrogations, as I like to call them."

"I've been there, man," Aiden said.

"It's like they live in their own little world or something, right?"

"Oh, yeah, no argument."

"They come in like they own the room, and they're doing you a favor," Lynn said. They all looked at her. "What? I get called in for updates, too. I've got access to the lab, remember?"

"Do they still drop a recorder on the table like they've just let off a stink bomb?" Aiden said.

"Oh, yeah."

"Every single time," Oliver said.

"They have gotten better," Aiden said. "I've got first-hand experience of that. They used to be much more aggressive. Their fines must have been atrocious."

"Probably why they've tried to clean up their act," Lynn said. "The really aggressively opinionated members are all working out their issues in debtor-assistance facilities."

"Well, they're backsliding or something," Oliver said. "We've been getting more protestors. Fortunately, security's been good at keeping them away from the quarantine zone. Probably going to be a while before we can risk another round of Ape Fights at Ben Franklin."

"Good thing you had an *in* here, huh?"

"Yeah, more reliable schedule and everything. Of course, the Monkey Trials. Woof, much worse than Ben Franklin."

"Woof, huh?"

"Oh, yeah, woof."

"You still ran the table," Aiden said.

"Dumb luck that, I assure you."

"Don't knock it." Aiden looked over their little monkey, which Lynn had finished putting back together. "Luck is luck."

"I might need a break," Oliver said. "Those Rat Races looked interesting. I might have to switch up for a while."

"Dip your code in other algorithms, as it were?" Tamara said.

"That's one suggestively vulgar way of putting it."

"You're welcome," she said. "You done with that monkey yet? We're going to miss Liz's debut."

"There's only so much of this you can rush, Tomorrow," Lynn said. "Not going to just throw Sputnik in the junk drawer. We've got repairs to effect."

"Yeah," Aiden added.

"Diagnostics to run. Feather-dusters to brush over delicate components. I think I've got the little demon spawn just about ready to box. How's the storage case coming?"

"We're fine over here," Aiden said.

"Well, cut as many corners as you can imagine," Tamara said. "Tick tock. Matches wait for no one."

"Okay, we're almost there."

"Liz needs the benefit of our condescending superiority." Turning to Oliver. "Can't let her forget she's just a graduate student, after all."

"Then why are we even going to her match?" Oliver replied.

"Because she's a grad student who also made it into the big leagues, and I want to watch her magnificent monstrosity wax the floor with her opponent."

"Okay, enough already, we're done," Aiden said, accepting Sputnik from Lynn, sealing the little robot in the box. "That's a wrap."

"About freaking time."

"Remind me why we're humoring you on this," Lynn said as they made their way across the staging area. "You're supposed to be our groupie, remember?"

"Yeah," Aiden said.

"I can be excited about multiple things," Tamara said. "Not like I've got the time to field my own difference engine. Living vicariously through everyone I can."

The main room was a wall of noise that very nearly lifted them from their feet, but they pressed on, occasionally applying arms and elbows in order to make headway. Checking one ring, they found multi-jointed tanks smashing into each other, although it was kind of hard to tell what the combatants hoped to accomplish. No appendages appeared to be involved. It really looked like two segmented blocks crashing into each other, as if the match would be decided by the first to get bored, realize that all was hopeless, go sit in the corner, and sulk. A better understanding of the situation would have required more time and attention than they were prepared to offer.

They had more success at the next ring and could even see Elisabeth standing at the edge with her fighting ape in her arms. There didn't seem to be much hope in trying to reach her, regardless of the number of jabs and shoves they laid about the throng surrounding them. The screaming mass that was the audience simply would not budge, and they could not get Elisabeth's attention no matter how much they attempted to add their own voices to the cacophony.

The match drawing everyone's attention appeared to be between a centaur and a scorpion with an oversized wrecking ball where you would expect the sharpened tip of its tail to be. The wrecking ball was proving to be less effective against the centaur than the scorpion's handlers had clearly imagined. Festivities didn't last long, and then it was just the cleaning up of random scorpion bits while Elisabeth got into position.

The fighting ape she deposited on the floor of the squared circle bore only a passing resemblance to the tripod they had previously witnessed in action. It was technically still a tripod with two additional appendages that looked as if they could serve as legs but came to sharp points rather than feet. While the torso also appeared to have arms, they looked more like stunted wings, as if they could do little more than flap madly.

"Most have something to do with keeping balance," Lynn tried to say over the noise of the crowd.

"I suppose," Aiden said.

"That, or trick its opponent into thinking its going to fly. Liz!" she shouted without much success at drawing Elisabeth's attention. "Liz! It's not going to work! It can't fly!"

The referee signaled the start of the match. The mutated, plucked chicken that was Elisabeth's robot crouched low and scuttled toward its opponent almost as if it didn't want the other to know the full functionality of the sharp-toed legs. The other fighting ape resembled a long-limbed tarantula and was also taking its time approaching the center of the ring.

"What's with all the tap dancing?" Lynn shouted. "Have at thee, motherfucker!"

"They can't hear you!" Tamara said.

"Then I'll write them a very stern letter."

The combatants circled the inside edge of the ring as if looking for weakness. Both were crouched low to the floor. Tarantula leapt a good two to three feet in the air, springing forward as if it would catch the plucked chicken with multiple limbs. The little robot suddenly bore a strong resemblance to a headless chicken as it fluttered its little wings and raced to the side. The sharp-toed legs proved useful as the tarantula attempted to kick and box. The plucked chicken could stab down, putting the full weight of its miniature frame behind the blows. The tarantula retaliated with spears hidden within its torso. In the end, the fluttering flight-like dance of the chicken proved to be too much for the tarantula, and Elisabeth raised her arms in triumph.

They followed her back to the staging area opposite where Sputnik and Oliver's own trained monkeys were stored, kicking and shoving as necessary to gain admittance. The layout was basically the same. Workbenches were spaced in a semi-circle where the various apes and monkeys could be checked before and after matches. Elisabeth deposited her ape on one of the benches and began going over it, checking the chassis, limbs and torso. Lynn and Tamara tried to sneak up on her.

"Liz, you God among freaks and monsters!" Lynn shouted, making Elisabeth drop her tools. "You kicked that sucker's asterisk!"

"I know," Elisabeth said, turning, getting an arm around her. "I still can't believe it. That bruiser should have roasted my poor little piglet alive."

"Well, what's the damage?" Tamara asked. "It wasn't all sunshine and lollipops out there."

"Yeah, I was just getting to that." Elisabeth turned back to her workbench. "I think Scuttlebutt got through this okay."

"Certainly looks in better shape than Sputnik," Lynn said, trying to eyeball the plucked chicken.

"Oh, yeah? Your guy took battle damage? Hey, wait, I thought you were in the Monkey Trials."

"We are."

"Whoa, they're really brutal around here."

"Occupational hazard, you've got to be tough. These here are the big leagues."

"I'll keep that in mind." Elisabeth turned back to the plucked chicken, examining it, checking each limb in turn. "Got to toughen up. I was lucky tonight."

"We've actually been debating the future of the Ape Fights," Lynn said. "Figure it's only a matter of time before the Monkey Trials get really violent. Lots of pushing and shoving."

"Yeah?"

"Have to add offensive capabilities before you know it."

"And those Rat Race things, too, right?" Waving a hand in the general direction of the track around the periphery of the game floor. "Lots of opportunities for pushing and shoving there."

"Exactly, only a matter of time, right?" Lynn said this

last more to Aiden than anyone else. "Right, dear?" She turned to give him her full attention. "You haven't gotten stuck in a feedback loop or anything, have you?"

"Those are impressive levels of disinterest in the future of Ape Fights," Elisabeth said.

"Hey." Lynn slapped him.

"Huh?" he said, turning. "What?"

"I said we were just discussing the future of the Ape Fights."

"Not that recently."

"No, not that recently, but it was a particular topic of speculative fiction and nondescript conversation. The kind of witty banter that spousal partners get up to when they are not otherwise distracted by shiny objects."

"Yeah, sorry," Aiden said, glancing, turning between her and the distant horizon. "It's just that there seems to be a different tenor to the screams and shouting over yonder."

"Oh, well, as long as we've got our priorities in order."

"No, really, there seems to be things afoot over there."

"Almost as if it isn't so much excitement..." Oliver said who had also been turned in the general direction of the source of the disturbance.

"As excitement," Aiden said.

"And it just might be coming from our staging area." Oliver was stretched as if he was trying to see through the door and past the crowds to the distant work space. "Hard to tell for sure. People keep opening and closing the door, which is playing havoc with the volume."

"Well, it can't be that important if hardly anyone in the great beyond is noticing," Lynn said.

"You think the excitement of the Ape Fights has spread beyond the little bastards for which it is intended?" Tamara asked, turning to follow Oliver's gaze. "Only a matter of time before handlers get overheated and take things into their own hands."

"Oh, let's not imagine the handlers trying to run the maze."

"Hey, remember when we had to climb through the maze trying to grab that tourist?" Lynn said. "You weren't there, regrettably," she said to Tamara. "Missed out on quite the show."

"But you did tell me all about it later," Tamara replied. "Had to live vicariously through others yet again. Let me give you some advice, Liz. Never go into teaching. It's just not worth it."

"Noted," Elisabeth said with eyes only for her fighting ape.

"Why did you have to mention tourists?" Aiden said.

"Huh?" Lynn said.

"Going to make me paranoid." He shook his head. "Wasn't that long ago we almost got lynched over a tourist. You're still dealing with the fallout."

"Oh God, don't remind me," Lynn said. "I had almost succeeded in blocking that part out."

"Making me paranoid. I'm having flashbacks."

"The excitement does seem to be centered around our staging area," Oliver said.

"Want to check it out, don't you?"

"Hell, yes, I do."

"Hey, you can't just leave me," Elisabeth said. "I'm fist-deep in this engine of misplaced anger management. You can't just leave me here."

"Well, I suppose we could sacrifice Tomorrow to the cause," Aiden said, turning, trying to look to the distant staging area. "You game for keeping Liz-kid company?"

"Huh?" Tamara said.

"Yeah, you really need a better nickname."

"Well, if you really feel I'm just that much dead weight."

"Paranoia really is getting to you," Lynn said.

"You just had to mention tourists," Aiden said, "and it is our staging area. Sputnik is secure, right? We did cut corners to make Liz's match."

"Yeah, Sputnik is secure."

"But now you want to check, too, don't you?"

"Well, you are the mighty Tourist Hunter. I can see how this would be getting under your skin."

"Oh, for God's sake," Tamara said. "Will you go already? The sooner you assuage your paranoia the sooner you'll be back."

"Whoa," Elisabeth said rather suddenly, causing them all to look. They saw her fighting ape thrashing about on the table, resisting her hold almost as if it was struggling to be free. "The hell?"

The world came alive. All around them handlers' voices struck out in surprise and confusion. It was very much as if they had fallen into an explosion of sound. Signs of flailing motion and struggle came from every occupied workbench. Elisabeth fought her ape to keep it on the surface.

"What did you do?" Lynn said.

"Nothing!"

"Shut down!" Aiden said, stepping to the workbench, reaching for the robot. "Where's the kill switch?"

"Under the—ow! It's fighting me!" Elisabeth tried to hold the ape. Sharpened toes scratched and stabbed at her. Wings fluttered and snapped. Aiden grabbed the torso. Lynn tried to snag one of the jabbing limbs.

"Fucking hell!" Lynn said.

"Bad monkey!" Elisabeth flipped the control panel open with fluttering fingers, struggled to reach the switch. Lynn grasped a wildly swinging arm, pulled it taut. "Naughty!" Elisabeth said as her fingers found the emergency power switch, and the little robot went limp. "What the fuck! What the flying fuck!"

"Eyes up," Aiden said. Around them people still struggled with their various fighting apes. Oliver had already moved to another table. "Secure," he said, looking at Elisabeth, pointing at Scuttlebutt.

"Yeah." Elisabeth got her travel case from beneath the bench and slammed Scuttlebutt into it, sealing the locks as fast as she could. "Go!"

They moved to other benches, helping to grasp and claw at robots that suddenly seemed to be in quite the mood to be disrespectful to their owners. The fighting apes were equipped with blunt objects and sharp edges, and they were not taking kindly to being held down. Several had gotten loose and were little more than blurs of motion underfoot, running from workbench to workbench. Handlers were quickly turning repair and maintenance tools into makeshift weapons.

Just as suddenly as it had started, the various robots and fighting apes collapsed where they stood. People staggered about, looking at the little machines that had all so quickly taken to their various destructive nicknames. One of the referees stood by the door to the game floor with a control rod raised over his head as if holding a brightly burning torch.

"Channel five, seven, two!" the referee said, turning, shouting back into the main room, trying to be heard over the noise, using hand signals to make the numbers understood. His name was Greg Ashcroft. He had more than ten years experience working for Alpha Matrix designing and programming various combinations of robots, and he had been a referee for the last three years. Greg left the staging area still calling, trying to be heard, attempting to coordinate with the other referees.

Aiden had his phone out, checking the script emulator.

"Okay, I really want a goddamned answer right bloody now!" Elisabeth said. "What in all the mismatched layers of hell just happened?"

"I don't know yet," Aiden said, poking, prodding his phone.

"Rampant infection," Oliver said. "Extreme vector."

"What?" Elisabeth spread her arms wide.

"Yeah, I'm with her," Tamara said. "The fuck?"

"We just watched a highly virulent contagion flood the room." Lynn had the script emulator queued on her phone and was scanning the display. "Seriously, what do they teach you guys in Theoretical Physics?"

"Theoretical Physics," Tamara replied.

"Yeah," Elisabeth said.

"We need to pinpoint the source," Aiden said.

"Well, you did notice the commotion coming from the other room." Lynn tapped and scrolled through options on her phone.

"Oh, fuck, the staging area!" Aiden turned, started making his way across the room. "Sputnik! And whatever your baby demon is called," he said this last pointing at Oliver.

"Ah, hell," Lynn said, pressing after him, almost losing her phone. Oliver wasn't waiting for Aiden and had already started to blaze his own trail toward the other staging area. "Sputnik was secure! I swear that little piece of shit was secure! If anything's happened, I will personally raze this place to the ground!"

The game floor was strangely quiet. The air bristled with the murmur and buzz of conversation, but the hammering hurricane of sound was gone. There was no shouting, no screaming, no whistling or calling. People wandered about as if uncertain what to do since all of the rings were empty. Even the Rat Race track was quiet.

They still had to push and shove to reach their default staging area, but they managed with a minimum infliction of damage to the people who really didn't seem that interested in getting out of their way. The handlers' work area, when they reached it, was a shambles. It looked as if a herd of nearsighted and incontinent bison had found it necessary to use the space as a shortcut between hither and yon. Workbenches were overturned. Debris and random robot parts were everywhere.

Heather Graymarsh stood with another referee at the dead-eyed heart of the aftermath. She had abandoned her referee's master control rod and instead held her bleeding-edge, industrial-strength script in her hands. People staggered around almost as if they were in shock, looking to the debris and remains of their robotic monkeys.

Aiden cut a path as direct as an ice breaker to where their workbench had been and found Sputnik's broken case. He knew even before he pulled it open, scattering pieces, pulling at hinges, locks and clasps.

"No, it's gone," he said, turning, looking to Lynn who had stayed barely a space behind him the whole time. "Sputnik's gone!"

"Smashed from the outside," Lynn said, starting to look about, finding nothing resembling their robot. "But where? We'll never find her in this shit-hole."

"Yo, boss!" Aiden said, crossing to where Heather stood. She barely spared him a glance. "It looks like Hell on a bad day! What in the nine billion names of God happened?"

"Data bomb," Heather said. "We're pretty much at ground zero."

"Data bomb?" Aiden looked to his phone.

"Yeah, it happens. Rare as fuck, fortunately. Can't remember the last one."

"Two, three years ago," the other referee said, and her name was Megi Livingstone. She had been a robotics programmer for only four years, having transferred from arbitration risk management, and had been a referee for less than a year. "The Board of Tourism was behind that one."

"Oh, yeah, that was only two or three years ago. Time flies, huh?"

"The Tourist Board?" Aiden said. "They know about this?"

"Well, of course, they know, and they hate the uses we put to robots rather passionately. Fortunately, they can never get a headcount, or get us into trouble with our various and sundry employers."

"So they've been known to resort to this data-bomb bullshit," Megi said. "Thought we taught them enough of a lesson last time."

"Two or three years is enough for turnover in their ranks to make them forget how badly we hacked them last—Are you using a script emulator?" Heather said this last to Aiden.

"Well, yeah," he replied, "we're not all super-giants like you who can just walk around off-hours with Central Services property."

"Oh, you do not have the emulator active right now! You couldn't possibly be that stupid!"

"We're trying to track the damage and find Sputnik."

"Rookie mistake," Megi said, shaking her head. "He works for you?" This last was said to Heather.

"Only obliquely, he's a field rep," Heather said, tapping commands on her script. "Oh, and look at that. Congratulations, Chuckles, your phone is infected."

"What?" Aiden almost dropped it.

"Yup, got in through an improperly shielded script

emulator. What kind of protocol do they teach you field jockeys, anyway?"

"Oh, frog-strangling mother-of-pearl," Aiden said, falling back. "I can't believe I did that." Turning to Lynn. "Your phone?"

"No," Lynn said, looking at her screen, tapping, scrolling. "Of all the times for both of us to take leave of our senses."

"Oh, don't bother trying to force-quit the thing now," Heather said, "and congratulations, you're in-fected, too." Tapping commands on her script. "Make me waste time. Well, come on, slave your phones to me." Holding the script toward them. "Flash 'em."

They took turns flashing their phones.

"Beautiful." Heather typed one-handed rather furiously. "Hey, remember when you made fun of my monstrously deformed beauty here? Well, who doesn't care for the magic in my hands now?"

"It still looks like something you dug out of a trash pile."

"Oh, go on, then. Press your luck. Hey, don't back away. Proximity helps, especially if I should feel the need to kick you in the shins."

"Anything that'll speed this up," Lynn said. "We can't find our trained monkey."

"Yeah, some of the robots got away," Megi said.

"What?"

"What do you mean, got away?" Lynn said.

"Okay, good news and suck-my-asterisk news," Heather said. "You're only carriers, which means you're infected but the nasty little parasite doesn't care to fuck with your systems. It just wants to joy-ride around until it gets within range of various robots and shit to try converting to the cause."

"As comforting as that is," Aiden said. "What's the

antidote? And don't tell me the best you can do is re-mission."

"Hey, didn't I previously impress you with the sheer strength and magnitude of what my little custom script can do? I am currently raping the fuck out of your infected systems. You should start getting restart warnings any second now."

"So while everybody is busy waiting for systems to chug back around to first position," Lynn said, "I want clarification on this whole *got away* thing."

"They couldn't catch them all," Oliver said, causing everyone to turn and look at him. "Thought it was obvious."

"Oh, well, you would."

"Hey, I'm not the one who was stupid enough to bring P-Mas up to active mode."

"Okay, aside from that."

"I've been trying to track what happened to both our frightened little monkeys." Oliver pointed across the room. "There's a vent. Definitely looks forced open."

"Oh, you have got to be kidding me," Aiden said.

"What can I say? Monkeys are programmed problem solvers. It's what they do. Figure out the win conditions and go for it."

"If we're lucky."

"Yeah, if we're lucky," Lynn said.

"What do you mean by that?" Oliver said.

"Oh, now who's being naive? Tourist Board data bomb? Infection strong enough to crap even our phones?"

"Oh, you have got to be fucking kidding me!" Oliver spun like a top, taking in their surroundings, stomping one pace this way and then another. "We just dealt with a tourist outbreak!"

"They travel in swarms," Heather said.

"Oh, thank you so much for that, Graymarsh, I feel much better," Oliver said.

"Cause and effect, then. You guys did draw Tourist Board attention to your nocturnal Ben Franklin activities."

"And we dragged it here?"

"I didn't say anything." Heather kept her eyes on the script. "Most of what's scattered around us is just collateral damage. Not long enough for a tourist infection to really take hold." Looking up. "Now, I can't say the same for the insensitive little bastards that got away."

"No!"

"Longer they're on the loose."

"We've got to find them."

"Yeah, no shit," Aiden said, "we've got to find them fast."

"Well, believe it or not, I'm working on that," Heather said. "I haven't managed a schematic of the building yet, but I'm making progress. I've also had to quell a whole heaping fuck-ton of passionately aggressive robots. There's code to scrape out of the ether, in case you haven't noticed."

"Slipped my attention, I'm not too proud to say."

"There's also the forensics to hash through before the trail gets cold," Megi said. She had her own script open, which looked rather odd in comparison to Heather's overheated abomination. For one thing, Megi's script was practically round as a Frisbee, which seemed to make it easier to hold while rotating freehand. "Confirm the source of the bomb. Make sure there isn't a repeater."

"Which would just seriously make my day," Heather said. "Oh, then there's the little matter of the extra work on your phones. You're welcome, by the way."

"I'll buy you a cookie," Aiden said.

"Well, until I get to enjoy that particular treasure of

wonder and excitement, you can help by finding the traveling case I brought. It's in the referee's corner. Just wave your phone at anybody who tries to stop you."

"What am I unboxing?"

"Little something I brought for just such emergencies. Pair of remote hunters with the thoroughly unimaginative names of Red-tail and Peregrine. We'll sic them down the rabbit hole after our runners." Heather looked up from her script. "Well, haul ass!"

CHAPTER NINETEEN

In which our long-suffering heroes, Lynn and Aiden, continue to deal with the ramifications of their chosen pursuit of fun and excitement.

Heather, Lynn and Aiden regarded the industrial neighborhood with a great deal more thought and consideration than they had upon first arriving earlier in the evening. It was an industrial block. There wasn't much by way of variety. The buildings looked vaguely disreputable and rundown. The lights were few and far between. There were warehouses. There were nondescript factories of a rather Spartan and heavy-duty nature.

There were the deep booming and rattling sounds of industries that never truly slept. There were the thrumming bass drums of clubs and night-halls where the people came to dance and partake of various other nocturnal pursuits, which included the Ape Fights when they could be organized and didn't come to a premature end.

"It's about time," Aiden said, watching a Central Services van arrive.

"Well, there is a limit to what we can do remotely," Heather replied, crossing to the van, opening the side panel. "Time is not something we can convince automated systems to rush."

"Should be grateful you do as much forethought and planning as you do." Aiden helped her remove several large cases and began unboxing equipment. "Nothing like planning for a crisis you hope never happens."

"Not the first time we've had to clean up after a data bomb. Fortunately rare, but still the kind of thing you never forget." Heather stood back, typing on her script, allowing Lynn and Aiden to perform the heavy lifting. "Makes you paranoid about having things on standby." The first robot unfolded wings and rotor-blades, looking very much like a gangly disk with little claws and feet. It leapt into the sky.

"What did you say it's been?" Lynn asked. "Two? Three years?"

"Something like that. Time flies. Never had rumble-fish make it outside before. You guys throw some fierce code."

"Not just us," Aiden said. "There's a third monkey still out there."

"Haven't forgotten. Just making conversation."

"We're sure they've made it this far?"

They finished setting up a second robot, which immediately followed its compatriot, leaping into the sky, hovering a good fifty, hundred feet above their heads, and began to search this way and that, shining lights in spectrums both visible and unseen.

"That's your buddy Oliver's last report," Heather said, studying her display. "Peregrine and Red-tail have taken down two potential tourists rampaging through the innards of the building. Tracking three more. Suddenly found themselves outside. Time for reinforcements."

"Three tourists at large in the district," Aiden said.

"One of them ours," Lynn said.

"Trying not to think about that." Aiden had another case open, stopped, turned to Heather. "You want the bloodhound?"

"Yeah, we'd better not take chances," Heather said.

"This is kind of our fault, messing about with apes and monkeys in the dead of night."

"Who fields security in this neighborhood?" Lynn said.

"Kind of low on my priority list at the moment." Heather tapped more commands on her script. The big multi-limbed robot unfolded and came to quiet attention, waiting for data from the two fliers overhead. "Vaguely surprised they haven't contacted me yet. Guess we haven't caused enough damage. Hyperion, I think."

"I'm sure they've noticed our birds by now," Aiden said, looking up, watching the two fliers as they searched farther afield, sweeping this way and that over the neighborhood.

"Well, if they suddenly explode, we'll have our answer."

"Hey," Oliver said, calling to them. They looked up, seeing him several levels up on an external walkway, as if the building's designers had thought people might like to promenade in the fresh air. "Updates from your end?"

"However did you get up there?" Lynn said.

"Never you mind that now."

"We've got two airborne searching," Heather called, pointing. "Where are my babies?"

"Still searching. I had one in view a moment ago. They think the tourists have split up, making it hard to track."

"That follows," Aiden said. "Standard Monkey Trial protocol. Work with and then confuse your opponents."

"Why did we have to go in for Monkey Trials?"

"Take care of my babies," Heather said. "Script working for you?"

"Like a dream," Oliver called down. "Never used one so advanced before."

"And you call yourself a theoretical software engineer." Heather glanced at her script. "Hey, the fliers have spotted something. Throwing you the coordinates."

"Okay, yeah," Oliver said. "Red-tail and Peregrine are coordinating."

"There should be a script in the case next to the bloodhound," Heather said in Aiden's general direction as she started back toward the building. "Get another flier in the air and keep looking for the other tourists."

"Yeah, got it," Aiden said, rummaging in the rather expansive containers the bloodhound had been in. They had actually had to assemble the hunter from several easily snap-connected pieces. "Oliver's target could be Sputnik."

"Silhouette is wrong," Heather said over her shoulder. "Keep looking." Started to climb an external ladder, taking her to the level below Oliver's walkway.

"Oh, yeah, security is definitely going to notice us now," Lynn muttered, turning back to the boxes. "Which one has another flier?"

"Still in the van. Bloodhound took up a lot of room."

"Is he just going to sit there?" Lynn rummaged about in the side of the van. "Thought I heard his name was Bloodhound."

"Yeah, well, he's sort of a last resort. Already coordinating with the fliers. Just because he's sitting here doesn't mean he's doing nothing."

"Here's a horrible thought." Lynn pulled a case from the van.

"No, not that," Aiden said.

"What?"

"That's a cleaner. Won't need it until the mopping up."

"Well, how was I supposed to know?"

"Look for the symbols that match the first box. Seriously, these things are labeled."

"Did I mention that I'm kind of in a rush?" Lynn disappeared back inside the van. "Did I mention that it's dark?"

"Couldn't miss it what with all the shouting."

"Oh, you'll hear shouting," she said, pulling a box to the edge of the van. "This?"

"Yeah, beautiful, it'll do."

"You're just lucky I've got experience in the Information Technology sector." She had the case free of the van, got it open. Once she had the robot free of the box and set up, it spread artificial wings like the other two and swept rather suddenly into the sky. "Hey, look at that. Got it in one go."

"Just wait for the speed round." Aiden typed commands. "That's where we really start to test your mettle."

"So have we found anything yet?" she asked, moving to his side, trying to study the little screen.

"I think the hunters have found the third tourist. Not paying too much attention to that detail since Oliver and Heather are all over it."

"Does this make Oliver an honorary Tourist Hunter?"

"If he's one, then you are, too."

"Score," Lynn said. "Do I get a pretty hat?"

"I'll take it up with the union." Tapped commands, scrolled displays. "Said you had a horrible thought."

"Not worth repeating," she said. "Morbid."

"Oh, go on."

"We're searching for our poor little baby who may have been forcibly converted to the cause of tourism."

"That's your morbid thought?"

"No, I mean we've got more pressing concerns. My thought is more of a hypothetical. Not worth making a big deal out of."

"Nothing wrong with hypotheticals. Obviously, we should have put more thought into anti-hacker encryption."

"Only so much you can do against a determined hack, you know that," Lynn said.

"I know that."

"As much custom code as we throw into Sputnik's little head, there are still super-user override commands and passcodes. Hacker hits on one of those, you're screwed."

"Yeah, but think about the encryption that goes into those cheatsheets. Hack would have to be some serious voodoo."

"Or an inside job."

Aiden was silent, watching the script's little monitor surface.

"Yeah, trying not to think too much about that at the moment," he said. "Industrial espionage is a serious bitch. Not touching anything to do with our counter-intelligence division. Then there's the whole Theoretical Engineering and Robotics angle. Some of your students are none too happy with us at the moment."

"I hadn't actually thought that far afield," she said. "Kept my reasoning to the population of the evening's festivities."

"Yeah, I suppose that's enough of a suspect pool."

"You really are the more morbidly paranoid of our little partnership."

"Speaking of which, have we gotten to your horrible little theoretical, yet?"

"Well, all this firepower we're throwing around," Lynn said, gesturing toward the bloodhound, van, and the distant fliers. "Another data bomb would just really suck."

"Not as much as you might think. Our phones are pretty much in lock-down mode. The referees have everything under control upstairs, and these puppies." Aiden nodded toward the bloodhound. "They're designed with virulent tourist vectors in mind. They've got counter-measures in their blood." Studied his script. "Contact with the third tourist, by the way."

"What?"

"Well, didn't want to interrupt our little soiree."

"Interrupt?" She smacked him upside the head, trying to read the display.

"Ow."

"How long they been in contact?"

"At least a minute." Tried to dodge another slap. "Well, it's not like there's much for us to do down here. Heather is quite capable of running the show from on high, and she even gave Oliver a script."

"Well, what have we been about? Any leads on the outstanding monkeys?"

"Yeah, trying to coordinate three fliers focused on multiple angles is not as easy as you might think." Aiden scrolled through displays. "Third tourist is neutralized, by the way. They'll be a while picking up the pieces."

"At this rate they'll just leave the mopping up to us."

"Yeah, I'm trying not to let that happen." Typing, scrolling. The bloodhound stood, unfolding even more than it had before.

"Whoa."

"Sorry about that."

Bloodhound started to move, padding forward on four limbs.

"Okay, I may only have the full attention of one flier,

but I think we're onto something. Follow." Aiden started walking after the bloodhound.

"Door's still open," Lynn said, turning, looking to
see how to pull it closed. The door started to move on
its own. "Okay, then," she said, turning, glancing at the
assorted equipment boxes, following after Aiden and
the bloodhound.

They walked along, keeping the building on their
left. Aiden had his eyes focused on the script more
often than not. Lynn activated the flashlight function
on her phone, used it to scan from side to side, studied the wall. They came to an uneven gap in the side
of the building, almost as if they had reached a makeshift stair. Aiden gestured toward the disheveled risers.
Lynn made as if she would answer most likely with a
sarcastic or potentially witty remark, thought better of
it, and began to climb, the bloodhound following after.

The way turned into a bit of a path with outcrop-
pings and cubby holes. There was the occasional pipe
appearing from out of the side of the wall, extending
this way or that.

"What kind of worksite is this?" Lynn muttered half
to herself, not really expecting Aiden to answer or even
notice if he heard.

Motion beneath an outcropping made her stop, and
she swept the light toward it. There was a robot maybe
two feet tall, cowering low, looking cautiously out.

"Hey there," Lynn said, bending down, leaning toward the narrow gap in the wall.

"Careful," Aiden said. "We don't know how extensive the overlay."

"Or the spread of the infection, I know."

"Trying to establish contact." Tapping commands
as quickly as he could. "How deep does that go?"

"Can't tell." She reached a hand, slowly, cautiously

toward Sputnik. "It's okay," she said sweetly, singsong, as if trying to calm a distressed puppy.

"It can't hear you."

"Doesn't hurt to try."

"Shrugging off the handshake," he said, scrolling displays, tapping commands. "Don't like it."

"Don't lose hope. There may be interference."

"How's your distance? If I unleash the hound, there will be complications."

"I think I could make a grab for her." Reaching a hand slowly toward the alcove and the little machine.

"Careful."

"I know," she said, quietly, singsong. "Sputnik's got no reference to recognize me. Never thought we would need that level of pattern recognition."

"Facial recognition, you mean."

"Whatever—Whoa!" She lunged forward, almost falling. Hands forward, grasping, she got her fingers entangled in Sputnik's limbs. "Ow!" Pulling. "Why you little—"

"Lynn!"

The bloodhound bounced forward, latching half on the wall and half towering over her. She continued to pull at Sputnik. Her fingers grasping, slipping over the torso, searching for the service latch.

"Call off the dog!"

"I'm trying," he said, typing madly one-handed.

"Crowding in on my action!" Pulling. Sputnik fighting against her, trying to crawl deeper back into the dark. "Blighter!"

The latch was open. Fingers reaching, struggling, for the exposed power switch. Sputnik went limp.

"Got you!" she said, pulling Sputnik free of the hole.

"Signal's gone completely dark," Aiden said. "You got it."

"Looks reasonably unharmed," she said. "Back off, you greased monkey!"

The bloodhound continued to tower over her, focused rather intently on the deactivated little robot. She tried to give it a swift kick. The bloodhound climbed higher up the wall.

"Okay, that's just vaguely disturbing," she said, holding Sputnik tight as if shielding the monkey from the much larger machine. "Go bother Heather and Oliver for a change. We're done here."

"Yeah, working on that. Bloodhound wants to do a more thorough job of disabling our baby."

"Well, stop it."

"You would think this would be easy." Typing, tapping.

The bloodhound detached itself from the wall and sauntered back toward the road. They watched it quietly, as if too much noise would cause it to return and make another grab for their little robot.

"Downright funny," Aiden finally said.

"Which part? Sputnik cowering in terror or the bloodhound trying to molest me?"

"More abstract than that. I'm typically much more enthusiastic about the wanton death and destruction of tourists." Turning, looking at her. "But when it's our little monkey in jeopardy..."

"To be fair, we haven't properly established that I'm holding a tourist. If tourism was as simple as a data bomb, they'd be everywhere." She held Sputnik at eye level, studying it intently. "What happens if our little baby has discovered the uncommon joys of tourism?"

"Smash it, basically," he turned, started walking back toward the road. "Dismantle the brain's architecture. Scrub the memory modules. Grind it all up. Send it for recycling."

"Jesus."

"Oh, don't act so surprised."

Lynn stood as if she would never move again, watching Aiden as he started to descend, climbing over the uneven shapes and structures of their path back to the road. Holding Sputnik, the little robot was so light in her arms.

"Well, it is modular," she finally said, following after him, moving slowly. "I guess we could salvage most of the limbs, sensor array. The basic chassis is in good shape."

"It's the brain that is expensive. Can't afford to replace that. Damn it!" He stopped. Hand held tight to the wall as if he could barely stand. Took a slow breath.

"Easy there."

"It's not just the processing core." Started to move again. "The distributed processing clusters in the limbs and extremities. All contaminated."

"No."

"Fraid so."

"So that's a total loss. Never thought about the distributed network," she said, all but muttering to herself. They climbed in silence. "Well, fuck."

"Yeah, trying not to think about it."

"There are tests we can run. Oliver has access to a whole lab even without entering the quarantine zone."

"Not going to the university," Aiden said as they reached street level. "Heather has first crack at it. Our R&D is second to none, and we've got different quarantine protocols."

"Better chance of getting Sputnik back?"

Aiden did not answer, looking this way and that as if unsure which way they should go.

"Much better chance if Sputnik isn't a tourist," he said.

"If I'm not holding a tourist."

They started walking, keeping the building on their

right, reaching the service van eventually. It looked unmolested in their absence. Even the containers and boxes they had left next to it had not been touched. Aiden got the back of the van open, which took a bit of work fussing with the script, and he retrieved a static-case. They placed Sputnik within and returned the case to the van.

"Well, that's that," Aiden said, leaning against the door.

"Not too late to just run off with our little baby, I suppose."

Aiden gave her a look. She tried to smile.

"Not even if you were serious," he said.

"Don't even need to look up hypocrisy in the telephone directory."

"In the what?"

"Dictionary." She held up her phone. "Search the network for a definition. Already got one."

"Besides, the capture is already logged." Held up the script. "Freaking bloodhound reported the incident. No getting out of it now."

"Mere technicality."

"Yeah?"

"Yeah." Walked around the equipment cases sitting next to the van. Studied them as if searching for clues of ancient civilizations. "Conscience would never let me abscond with the tourist. Even if it turns out there's nothing wrong with Sputnik."

"We have to know," Aiden said, watching her.

"We have to know." Lynn nodded her head, sluggishly, almost as if her face would slip to the cold, hard ground. "How's the hunt going?"

"Yeah." He scrolled displays on the script. "Bloodhound found Oliver's contribution to this evening's festivities."

"Oh, yeah?"

"Yeah, not much left of it."

"Motherfucker."

"What you said." Aiden tapped commands, scrolled displays. "They'll be back soon."

"Well, could be worse," she said, turning the corner of the boxes, crossing back to Aiden's side. "You know, Oliver once told me that they scrounge for parts in the lab."

"Good for him."

"Saves on parts."

"Brain-case is the most expensive module."

"Yes, well, he is a student," Lynn said, "and we've seen one student's apartment."

"Student teacher."

"Granted, student teacher, but that place was huge even with roommates."

"Yeah, he'll recover, I know," Aiden said, looking away from the script, studying the side of the van. "Well, you had already located one of the cleaners. Let's finish unboxing it. Nothing left but the mopping up."

Lynn studied him as if she was considering once more the merits of grabbing Sputnik and running.

"Yeah, all right," she said.

* * *

The remains of the other robots and potential tourists were placed into static boxes. The bloodhound, the fliers, and the two hunters were returned to their cases and crates. It took longer than anyone wanted to contemplate. Heather closed the van's sliding door at last, turning, looking to Oliver, Lynn and Aiden.

"Go home," she said. "Rest."

"I can't sleep," Aiden replied. "I would rather know."

"Tests will take hours. Go home. Rest." Hand to her forehead, scratching, rubbing. "It's very late or quite possibly very early. I don't even know any more."

"Taking hours is what we tell the straights and squares. Remember the street sweeper?" Snapped his fingers. "You knew like that."

"Yeah?"

"Yeah, you—Ah," Aiden said. "Oh, I see."

"Go home," she said, turning to Oliver. "That goes for you, too. We'll start an examination of your hungry little monkey's remains in the late morning. Possibly not until after lunch. Fatigue won't hit me like a brick until I get all this back to the lab."

"Sure you don't need a hand?" Oliver said.

"I'm not authorizing you for access until tomorrow. Skedaddle." Nobody moved. "I've got crew back at the base who can help me unload. People who haven't been up all day and all night." Heather studied them. "Now, go."

"Yeah, okay," Oliver said, turning slowly as if he could not draw his eyes from the service van. "What shuttle service you guys use? Maybe we can ride-share."

"Ubiquity," Lynn said.

"Ubiquity, right. I think I've got reciprocal arrangements with them."

Hey, you still around? Aiden typed, sending the message to Tamara. "Checking up on the gang upstairs," he said.

"What's the word?" Oliver asked.

"That was hours ago," Lynn said. "They'd better have gone home."

"Yeah, just sent the query." Aiden studied his phone, glanced up. "What are you still doing here? Thought you were leaving, Heather."

"One foot out the door." Heather turned, walking

round to the driver's side, which technically wasn't necessary, but it was easier to program the cruise control that way. "Once this shit is back in the lab, I'm snagging a few Z's. Nothing happens until late morning, like I said."

Aiden's phone chimed. Lynn and Oliver looked at him.

Sorry, had to help Liz, Tamara had typed. *Her degenerate little hurricane passed muster, thank God, but she was still in a state. Helped get her to a service.*

That's good, Aiden typed. "That Liz-kid's rodent is fine," he said.

"Small miracles," Lynn muttered all but to herself.

"Finally, some good news," Oliver said, "but how the hell did her ape, of all things, survive corruption?"

"We did get to it awfully fast."

The van started to move, its engine so quiet it didn't make a sound. They slowly stepped away without really giving it or Heather much of a glance. Aiden waved halfheartedly. Hard to tell, but it looked like she gave him the finger.

"Whereas our little darlings were far away and without friends," Oliver said, watching the van. "Sucks more than a little."

Where are you? Aiden tapped submit.

"I hear you," Lynn said, pulling out her phone. "Reciprocal with Ubiquity, you said?"

Home, Tamara typed. *Company?*

"Yeah, share a ride?"

"Flash." Lynn held up her phone. Oliver tapped commands, flashed his phone to Lynn's own. "Beautiful, shouldn't take long."

You should rest, Aiden typed.

Service is still downstairs, Tamara replied. *No trouble at all.*

Company? Aiden typed, sending the query to Lynn

who was still finishing up the arrangements with the shuttle service.

She glanced up from her phone, giving him a look.

Inviting herself over, he typed.

"All set," she said to Oliver. "ETA on the shuttle isn't too bad."

"Yeah," Oliver replied, "showing up on my phone as we speak."

"Aces," she said. *Don't want to discourage her,* she typed, sending to Aiden.

We can't invite her to the lab, he typed. When Lynn looked back toward him, he made a helpless shrug of a gesture, spreading hands and fingers.

"I just hope we don't nod off waiting for Ubiquity to arrive," she said.

"We'll take turns slapping each other in the face," Oliver replied.

"Well, let's hope it doesn't come to that." Lynn braced her hands on her hips, took a deep breath, looked back to the building. "Got any friends in there?"

"They've hopefully all gone home."

"Ungrateful tripe that they are."

"Yes, well, I haven't been hanging out with this gang for as long as you have."

"I suppose. Sounds like you have an invite to the lab."

Aiden watched her carefully, noticed she was eying him, shook his head slowly from side to side.

"Well, Heather did promise me whatever remains were salvageable." Held up his phone. "She wasn't joking about not clearing me for access until the morning. I swear, there's a little countdown clock and everything."

Lynn checked her phone.

"Yeah, I see I get access tomorrow, too," she said. "Looks like I'm restricted to the hallway or something."

"Access to R&D is limited," Aiden said. "Not as bad as the forbidden zone you guys keep talking about—"

"Quarantine zone."

"Yeah, get it right," Lynn said.

"Quarantine zone, right," Aiden said. "But access is restricted. I'll be hanging out in the hallway with you guys."

Service is ready, Tamara typed. *Give me an ETA.*

"That seems excessive," Lynn said.

"Yeah, I have to agree," Oliver said.

Working on it, Aiden typed. *Still waiting on our ride.* "Aiden?"

I could send the service.

Don't you dare, Aiden typed. "Hey, I don't make the rules," he said. *She wants to send a private car,* he typed, sending to Lynn.

"That's what they all say," Lynn said. She glanced at her phone, and her eyes went wide. *She wouldn't dare,* Lynn typed and then continued to type.

"Never said it was fair," Aiden said.

* * *

There was a hallway, and there was something resembling a bench. On the scale of comfortable couches, it didn't rate very high. Heather emerged from between the doors leading into the depths and very heart of Central Services' R&D department.

"Sorry, I'm going to have to keep you guys out here," she said, looking this way and that, taking in the whitewashed hall as if for the first time. "Wish it was more comfortable."

"We'll be fine," Aiden said, trying to slouch on the barely padded bench, attempting to lean nonchalantly against the wall.

"Wish I knew what happened to Oliver," Lynn said. "He should have been here."

"Yeah," Heather said, hooking a thumb back toward the doors. "He's with me."

"Seriously?"

"Yeah, really?" Aiden said. "Why does he rate better access than me?"

"Peruse his CV some day." Heather's half-cocked fist went to her hip. "That man knows a thing or two about higher computational faults, pseudo-intelligence, and autonomous calculations. He has most definitely earned the right to see how the shit gets made."

"Connoisseur of the forbidden zone," he muttered, looking far down the hallway, wondering how many people were about.

"Connoisseur of the what?"

"Quarantine zone, dear," Lynn said. "You always say forbidden zone." Looking at Heather. "Advanced Theoretical Software Development Lab—Wait, I may have left out a word. Experimental?"

"Close enough for rocket science," Heather said. "I'll be back just as soon as I can, but I warn you it will be hours."

"We're tough."

"Just one thing," Aiden said. "Just one little thing I have to ask you."

"Yeah?" Heather watched him.

"If the results are positive for malfunction. If we were too late. Tourism." He looked at her, trying to hold her gaze. "I want to be the one. Don't want to hear about it. I want to put Sputnik down."

"Yeah, that might be—Well, I'm not just going to hand you a giant hammer," Heather said. "But yeah, I'll make it happen."

"I pull the trigger."

"Promise, you pull the trigger."

"Thank you."

Heather disappeared back through the doors into the R&D department.

"That was—" Lynn said. "Wow, that was melodramatically morbid."

"You disagreeing?"

"Nope." Leaning into him. "Not disagreeing at all."

* * *

Hey, where are you? Lynn typed, sending to Tamara.

Grading papers, Tamara typed. *What did you expect?*

Just as well you didn't tag along. Sweating it out in a rather uncomfortable hallway.

I told you I didn't mind.

No, it was hard enough getting me in this far. Skeleton crew and everything, it wasn't easy.

Well, keep me posted. I want to know the second you know.

* * *

Foxglove found them waiting in the hallway trying to rest. Lynn was attempting to lie on the bench with her feet stretched up against the wall. She made a token effort to adjust her position as Aiden came rather rigidly to attention.

"Heather Graymarsh had to file a report on the data bomb," Foxglove said. "Your name got mentioned. It flagged me."

"And you were kind enough to come down here on your day off," Aiden said. "I'm touched."

Foxglove said nothing, looking toward the door to R&D.

"Listen," he finally said. "Obviously, I know about the Ape Fights."

"Obviously."

"Official policy is that Central Services personnel cannot attend or otherwise participate in such activity. We're under careful scrutiny. The Board of Tourism alone."

"I'm familiar with the Board of Tourism."

"I've dealt with them, too," Lynn said.

Foxglove studied her as if he might say something but finally turned his attention back to Aiden.

"This will have to be flagged in your file."

"Well, I didn't think they dragged you all the way down here just to show my partner the door," Aiden said.

"Unofficially," Foxglove said rather abruptly as if Aiden had not spoken. "We encourage Graymarsh to attend. If there were a tourist incident, we would want our best Tourist Hunter on the scene."

"I've heard this speech before," Lynn muttered.

"Graymarsh, in turn, has free reign to invite whoever she chooses. You," Foxglove pointed at him, "score very high on the Tourist Hunter rolls. An excellent choice for backup. So I just wanted you to know. Should it be necessary, there will be public words. There may even be public condemnations and assurances of reprimands, but I wanted you to know, from me, it's all words."

"Thank you," Aiden said. "That's very reassuring."

"I understand your fighting ape is more or less intact."

"Monkey."

"Huh?"

"Sputnik is a thinking monkey, not a fighting ape."

"Oh yes, I've read the report on the Monkey Trials. Quite the recent development."

"It was news to me."

"Any ETA on the contamination results?"

"No idea," Aiden sad. "They've been in there a while. Several apes and monkeys to work through, I suppose."

"They? Oh yes, Oliver Fenchurch. That's coming along nicely."

"You've heard of him?"

"What's coming along nicely?" Lynn said.

"His recruitment," Foxglove said. "I understand he's in final negotiations for a position in R&D. We're all very excited. Fenchurch's recruitment will be quite the feather in our cap. Graymarsh has put a lot of work into it."

"Really," Aiden said.

"That will go in your file, too." Foxglove turned his full attention back to them. "I was supposed to wait until the ink has dried and it's official, but under the circumstances, I'm bumping it up. And I wanted to personally commend you for the role you played."

"Role?"

"It was nothing, I know. A minor part, but give yourself credit. You got Fenchurch to the Ape Fights. Piqued his interest. Graymarsh was able to take it from there."

Lynn let her feet drift from the wall, finding the floor. She turned without a word, slipping upright, and held her gaze on Aiden, studying him. His eyes were for the floor. He looked as if he hadn't slept in years. Breath left him, slipping, as if he was slowly dying.

"Tuttle," he finally said.

"I'm sorry?" Foxglove said.

"Harry Tuttle."

"Oh, are you still on about that?"

"Hacked scripts for jobs. Got in. Got out. Did the work because he enjoyed it. And no paperwork."

"Sounds like a dream, doesn't it?"

Aiden closed his eyes, pressing the back of his head against the wall.

"You know he's not real, right?" Foxglove said. Aiden's eyes shot open. "Harry Tuttle is made up. From a story. Film, I think."

"What?"

"Never understood how he turned into such a legend."

"No, it can't be," Lynn said.

"Wasn't even a Central Services employee. Not even in our field."

"Even I've heard of him."

"And she doesn't work for Central Services either," Aiden said.

"True," Foxglove said, glancing at Lynn. "But how did you first become aware of Tuttle? From your partner perhaps?"

"That doesn't actually make sense."

"How could he be from a story?" Lynn said. "I'm always quoting old movies and flicks." Pulled out her phone, started typing. "I would know if he was fake."

"Well, I'm not exactly an expert on these things," Foxglove said. "Personally, I don't understand how Tuttle turned into such a legend. Nobody remembers the movie."

"What's it called?" Aiden asked.

"No idea. Sorry, it's really obscure."

"Motherfucker," Lynn muttered, staring at her phone.

"No, I don't think that's it."

"How did I not know about this?" Lynn said.

"It's very obscure," Foxglove said. "I don't think they want us to remember."

"There's a synopsis," she said, scrolling, reading intently. "Okay, yeah, I sort of understand why nobody would want to remember this."

"It can't be that bad," Aiden said.

"Bleak," she said. "Dystopian."

"Look out the window, in other words."

"Things aren't that bad," Foxglove said. "Also, the movie is very old."

"Oh, well, that makes it all okay then."

"I'm sorry, but I think my eyes are going to explode," Lynn said. "I apologize in advance if I should drench either of you in viscera and gore. My head hurts."

"I'm sure it won't come to that," Foxglove said.

"Speak for yourself." Aiden shook his head. "I'm having trouble wrapping my brain around this concept, too. I can't believe Harry Tuttle isn't real."

"I know." Lynn slapped her phone against her thigh.

"That's actually kind of why I never discouraged your belief in him," Foxglove said.

"It's just—" Aiden put his face in his hands. "My head hurts."

Heather emerged from the depths of R&D, appearing once more between the doors. She paused with the doors half-open, with only Lynn and Foxglove turning to notice her, and then she pushed through. She stood before the bench, staring intently at Foxglove as if he was a rather obnoxious child.

"Graymarsh," Foxglove said, muttering, but could not meet her gaze. There was no answer. "I was just bringing Charles up to speed on the situation."

Heather continued to study him as if the very force of her gaze would bore twin holes right through him before getting to work tearing apart the wall on the other side. She didn't blink, and it was quite possible she wasn't even breathing.

"I will—" Foxglove studied his feet and the various

squares and patterns of the floor. "I will leave you to it then."

He turned and left rather quickly, with Heather's cold, hard stare chasing him until he disappeared completely from sight. After all trace and sound of the retreating supervisor had drifted into the dust, she turned her attention back to the bench and its two occupants.

"I hear congratulations are in order," Aiden said.

"That's not official, yet," she finally said.

"Well, I'll try not to get Jennifer Behr mad at him," Lynn said.

"Thank you." Heather turned, looking long and hard down the hall as if her very gaze would cause the distant corridor to burst into flame. "Sputnik," she said, whipping back around toward them. "The results are in. Negative."

Lynn tried not to laugh, clamping a fist over her teeth.

"That," Aiden said, pressing fingers into eyes, feeling as if he had been dropped rather suddenly from a great height. "That's such a relief."

"Well, don't all jump for joy at once," Heather said.

"Yeah, sorry," Aiden said. "It's more exhaustion and relief than anything. As you can imagine, we didn't get much sleep last night."

"It had penetrated my generally callous and uncaring posterior that you cared a great deal about your little monkey. It's understandable to become attached and even to anthropomorphize, but perspective, people."

"Did you just say posterior?" Lynn asked.

"Even if I did, it's hardly my point."

"So when can we collect the little blighter?" Aiden said.

"Soon," Heather said. "We're finishing up some preemptive maintenance work, which is part of what's taken so long. Should probably apologize for that, but fuck you."

"Love you, too, ash hat."

"Just to make sure we've scrubbed every last trace of the data bomb out of your ungrateful little crime against elegant form and design, we've taken the liberty of replacing the memory, form banks, processing core, and infrastructure."

"Jesus, Heather."

"Relax, you realize how much gear we've got just lying around in there? We're R&D, Charlie. You're just lucky you purchased a Central Services base model."

"Well, I thought I might be eligible for some kind of employee discount."

"Like that was going to happen."

"Back-end discount," Lynn said. "Seriously, how much of our little Sputnik is left after all that preventative maintenance?"

"We didn't swap out that much."

"No, you left the distributed network behind. Is there any of the original brain left? We're already going to have to do a massive rebuild and compile of the core systems."

"Oliver is working on that as we speak."

"Recompiling the core?"

"Sure, you only gave me access to your script emulator and associated files last night. No problem downloading those."

"What?"

"Well, you pair of irresponsible ingrates did commit the monumentally stupid faux pas of infecting your phones last night, if you may recall."

"You know?" Aiden said. "I think I had successfully blocked that part out."

"So as an extra-special favor, we've accessed an uncorrupted copy of your files from backup, and we're reinstalling the core."

"Is that all?"

"Oh, yeah," Heather said. "That is all."

"Well, thank you."

"I will take this opportunity to direct your attention to my asterisk." Heather pointed, touching one finger to her hip.

"We are grateful. We're just reeling from recent revelations about Harry Tuttle. My brain still hurts, and my faith in humanity will never be restored."

"I never did like that movie."

"What?" Lynn said. "You've seen it?"

"Well, not recently."

"How come you never said anything?" Aiden asked.

Heather gave him a look, studying him as if trying to determine the best way to tell him that his favorite pet bullfrog had died.

"Dare to dream, man. Dare to dream." Heather turned, pausing at the door back into the lab. "Listen, Oliver will be out directly with your miraculous little machine. Still can't believe it survived prolonged exposure to the corrupting influence of malcontents and didn't turn to the unfashionable cause of tourism, huh?"

"Yeah, seems rather dubious."

"But we are grateful," Lynn said.

"Sit," Heather said, pointing. "Spin."

She disappeared. The doors slipping closed behind her.

"Oh, yeah," Aiden said. "They just replaced the memory and the core. Preventative measures, my bleeding asterisk."

"I'm not complaining," Lynn said, tapping a fist to her chin.

"You did listen to the laundry list of what they replaced, didn't you?"

"Yes, I did."

Aiden studied the door as if tempted to engage in a practical real-time test of the *watched pot* hypothesis.

"Fucking tourists," he said, muttering all but to himself. Lynn took his arm, entwining fingers, and leaned into him.

They waited in silence for the better part of an hour before Oliver appeared with their freshly scrubbed little robot, which they accepted quietly and then went home.

CHAPTER TWENTY

In which various people attempt to come to terms with the undeniably indefatigable face of entropy and the eventual heat-death of the universe.

The assembled ITRC field representatives could tell through a process vaguely resembling osmosis that the morning meeting was desperately approaching its end, and they were growing anxious with anticipation.

"Okay, everyone should have their assignments," Hagarlodge said, triggering a rather staggering amount of activity. "No big surprise what our esteemed colleague Charles will be doing."

"Special assignment continues," Lynn said.

"Just keep monitoring the tourist situation in the Advanced Theoretical Software Development Lab and nobody gets hurt."

* * *

The service van was parked in a space little wider than the van itself. Tom and Aiden had the side door open, sitting in the extra space it provided, dangling their feet over the edge.

"You always go for the most disgusting option," Tom said.

"It's all the same synthetics," Aiden replied. "What difference does it make?"

"Well, just look at it." Pointing. "Look at it. What is that? Is it glowing? I swear, it looks like it is breathing."

"Just adds to the ambiance."

"Disgusting, all the same," Tom said, sitting in silence, trying not to look, eating. "Still can't wrap my brain around Harry Tuttle."

"Don't remind me."

"Hey, you're the one who told me."

* * *

Aiden carried the plates of rice and vegetables to the dining room. Tamara followed after with a carafe of fresh water and proceeded to top off their glasses. Lynn didn't even wait for Aiden to finish putting all the plates down before she began to transfer items to her bowl.

"So tell the story, already," Aiden said. "You've only been teasing for the past couple of hours."

"The Tourist Board finally got a representative cleared for the lab," she said, continuing to shovel food into bowl.

"Hey, leave some."

"I'm sure there's more."

"Well," Tamara said.

"We'll share, okay?" Lynn said. "There's enough to go around."

"That depends on you," Aiden replied.

"So it's a big deal, right? Tourist Board is finally going to be able to monitor the tourist. Make sure not a hair is harmed on its little—Well, okay."

"It doesn't have hair."

"Yes, I know."

"As long as we're clear."

"Tourist Board doesn't care for our quarantine policy, right? Electronics that go in cannot come out."

"Yeah, I can see that being an issue," Tamara said, getting the rice away from her.

"So as you can imagine," Lynn said, "the idiot tried to smuggle a dedicated video recorder into the lab."

"No! Isn't there a screen?"

"Oh, yes."

"You mean one of those counter-measure screens?" Aiden said. "How do you get any equipment in?"

"Has to be properly shielded," Lynn said.

"Which I'm sure the idiot's video recorder was not." Tamara surrendered the plate to Aiden.

"Which it was not." Lynn looked to each of them in turn, letting the moment grow. "Damn thing burst into flames."

"No!"

"Tourist Board representative was not amused."

"I'm sure."

"And the recorder had been secreted about his person."

"Ouch," Tamara said.

"As you can imagine, I was suitably delighted. Especially when I got to shove him under the chemical shower."

"Oh, my God!"

"Oh, yeah good times."

* * *

The basement was dark, and the pipework gave off the impression that it was more than a thousand years old. There was the constant sound of high-pressure release whistling and a steady banging and clanging, as if someone was testing the pipes for musicality. Aiden stood next to the service panel while Tom held the little robotic swimmer in his arms.

"Okay," Aiden said. "When I pop the panel, just get the swimmer in there as fast as you can."

"On three," Tom said, trying not to breathe.

* * *

How come I never see you around any more? Elisabeth typed, sending the message to Lynn.

Special assignment, Lynn replied. *Have to ride shotgun on our involuntary guest in the quarantine zone.*

Hey, have you heard the rumor that Oliver is heading for industry?

Yes, I have heard that rumor.

Well, ask him about it.

When? I can't take my phone into the quarantine zone.

You don't need your phone to ask him a question. Just tell me all about it later.

You hunt him down and ask him yourself.

* * *

"Central Services," Aiden said, touching fingers to forehead as if tipping a hat that was not on his head. "You reported an issue with your sweeper?"

"It's acting funny," the young man said, holding the door open so that Tom and Aiden could enter.

* * *

They stood at the very edge of the ring. The crowd so loud it was like being pummeled with invisible hammers.

"I have absolutely no idea what the goal is," Aiden tried to say, shouting directly into Lynn's ear.

"I know. I'm completely lost, too," she replied.

"What the hell are they doing? What is that?"

"You still haven't figured it out?" Tamara tried to ask.

"Maybe that's why we are one and five," Aiden said. "How can we expect Sputnik to solve the puzzle if we can't figure it out ourselves?"

"We can work on that."

They stopped trying to talk as the sheer volume of sound increased, screaming and shouting, as the match ended and a winner was declared.

"Okay, we're up," Lynn finally said. "Where's Oliver? His little deviant weasel probably walked the table again, didn't it?"

"No, his match isn't until later," Tamara said. "He's still determined to try the Rat Races. So's Liz, for that matter."

"Hey, more power to them. Okay, Aiden, it's your turn to hog the glory." Lynn kissed him quick and hard before pushing him into the ring.

Aiden crossed to his corner, placing Sputnik at his feet, and stepped to the very edge of the ring.

Heather was the primary match referee. She stepped forward, saw Aiden, matched his gaze, and nodded her head once. Aiden nodded in reply. Heather took in the rest of the ring and the other handlers standing behind their monkeys. She raised the master control rod high into the air.

"Wouldn't miss this for the world," Aiden said, even though he knew nobody could hear him.

Heather brought the rod down.